Praise for Keri Arthur

"Keri Arthur's imagination and energy infuse everything she writes with zest." —Charlaine Harris

Praise for Full Moon Rising

"Keri Arthur skillfully mixes her suspenseful plot with heady romance in her thoroughly enjoyable alternate reality Melbourne. Sexy vampires, randy werewolves, and unabashed, unapologetic, joyful sex—you've gotta love it. Smart, sexy, and well-conceived, *Full Moon Rising* left me wishing I was a dhampire." —Kim Harrison

"A deliciously sexy adventure through a supernatural underworld that pulls you in and won't let go. Keri Arthur knows how to thrill! Buckle up and get ready for a wild, cool ride!" —Shana Abé

"Unabashedly and joyfully sexual... Arthur never fails to deliver, keeping the fires stoked, the cliffs high, and the emotions dancing on a razor's edge in this edgy, hormone-filled mystery." —TheCelebrityCafé.com

"Keri Arthur is one of the best supernatural romance writers in the world." —Harriet Klausner

"Strong, smart and capable, Riley will remind many of Anita Blake, Laurell K. Hamilton's k~~~~ ~~~~~~~ hunter....Fans of Anit~~~~ ~~~~~~~~ ~~~~~~~ Sookie Stackhouse vamp~~~~ ~~~~~~~~~~~
—*Publishers Weekly*

"Fun and feisty...[An] effective crossbreeding of romance and urban fantasy that should please fans of either genre." —*Kirkus Reviews*

"Well-done and entertaining." —*Sunday Oklahoman*

"A sexy and fast-paced novel aimed at the mature reader...The author excels at showing not just characters, but how they interact as a society....There are consequences and drawbacks to being a member of a race that simply can't deny sexual urges at certain times of the month. It may sound like great fun, but Arthur doesn't shy from the logical result of such behavior." —DavisEnterprise.com

"Sexy and exhilarating. Provocative and edgy with enough heat to scorch the paper it's written on. It's a pleasure to see that within a genre that is getting crowded with uninspired and repetitive stories it is still possible for this author to create a unique and very strong heroine. For those who like Anita and Elena the kick-ass and sensual Riley is worth a loud and satisfied howl." —ARomanceReview.com

"Arthur creates a shadowy and believable world where werewolves, vampires and other supernatural creatures co-exist with humans, and where Riley and her kind are held hostage by the monthly lunar cycles....Arthur also cooks up a nicely paced cloning plot that Riley has barely begun to unravel by story's end—leaving the door wide open for all kinds of possibilities. *Full Moon Rising* definitely grabs the attention and Keri Arthur is an author to watch." —BookLoons.com

"Unbridled lust and kick-ass action are the hallmarks of this first novel in a brand-new paranormal series.... 'Sizzling' is the only word to describe this heated, action-filled, suspenseful romantic drama....Keeps readers on their toes in constant suspense...breathtakingly scorching. *Full Moon Rising* sets a high bar for what is now a much-anticipated new series." —CurledUp.com

"Keri Arthur has done a wonderful job with *Full Moon Rising*. It's a great story that's suspenseful, has hot werewolves, sexy vampires, a huge amount of butt kickin', and no-holds-barred sex. If you like a twist to your paranormal romance, you'll love this book."
—FreshFiction.com

"An enjoyable paranormal with romantic elements and an exciting, action-packed plot, *Full Moon Rising* is a gripping tale, which grabbed my attention from the very beginning and didn't let up until the very end....I highly recommend *Full Moon Rising* to paranormal readers."
—ParaNormalRomanceReviews.com

"Grade A, desert island keeper...I wanted to read this book in one sitting, and was terribly offended that the real world intruded on my reading time!...Inevitable comparisons can be made to the Anita Blake, Kim Harrison, and Kelley Armstrong books, but I think Ms. Arthur has a clear voice of her own and her characters speak for themselves....I am hooked!"
—AllAboutRomance.com

ALSO BY KERI ARTHUR

THE RILEY JENSON GUARDIAN SERIES

Full Moon Rising

Tempting Evil

Dangerous Games

Embraced by Darkness

The Darkest Kiss

Deadly Desire

Bound to Shadows

Moon Sworn

THE MYTH AND MAGIC SERIES

Destiny Kills

Kissing Sin

A Riley Jenson Guardian Novel

KERI ARTHUR

A DELL BOOK | NEW YORK

2010 Dell Mass Market Edition

Copyright © 2007 by Keri Arthur

Published in the United States by Dell, an imprint of The Random House Publishing Group, a division of Random House, Inc., New York.

DELL is a registered trademark of Random House, Inc., and the colophon is a trademark of Random House, Inc.

Originally published in paperback in the United States by Dell, a division of Random House, Inc., in 2007.

ISBN 978-0-440-24639-8

Cover design: Jae Song

Printed in the United States of America

www.bantamdell.com

2 4 6 8 9 7 5 3 1

I'd like to thank the following people:

My wonderful agent, Miriam; editor extraordinaire,
Anne; and everyone at Bantam who helped
make this book possible.

This book is dedicated to the two people in my life
who matter the most—Pete and Kasey.

Kissing Sin

Chapter 1

All I could smell was blood.

Blood that was thick and ripe.

Blood that plastered my body, itching at my skin.

I stirred, groaning softly as I rolled onto my back. Other sensations began to creep through the fog encasing my mind. The chill of the stones that pressed against my spine. The gentle patter of moisture against bare skin. The stench of rubbish left sitting too long in the sun. And underneath it all, the aroma of raw meat.

It was a scent that filled me with foreboding, though why I had no idea.

I forced my eyes open. A concrete wall loomed ominously above me, seeming to lean inward, as if ready to fall. There were no windows in that wall, and no lights anywhere near it. For a moment I thought I was in a prison of some kind, until I remembered the rain and saw that the concrete bled into the cloud-covered night sky.

Though there was no moon visible, I didn't need to see it to know where we were in the lunar cycle. While it might be true that just as many vampire genes flowed through my bloodstream as werewolf, I was still very sensitive to the moon's presence. The full moon had passed three days ago.

Last I remembered, the full moon phase had only just begun. Somewhere along the line, I'd lost eight days.

I frowned, staring up at the wall, trying to get my bearings, trying to remember how I'd gotten here. How I'd managed to become naked and unconscious in the cold night.

No memories rose from the fog. The only thing I was certain of was the fact that something bad had happened. Something that had stolen my memory and covered me in blood.

I wiped the rain from my face with a hand that was trembling, and looked left. The wall formed one side of a lane filled with shadows and overflowing rubbish bins. Down at the far end, a streetlight twinkled, a forlorn star in the surrounding darkness. There were no sounds to be heard beyond the rasp of my own breathing. No cars. No music. Not even a dog barking at an imaginary foe. Nothing that suggested life of any kind nearby.

Swallowing heavily, trying to ignore the bitter taste of confusion and fear, I looked to the right.

And saw the body.

A body covered in blood.

Oh God...

I couldn't have. Surely to God, I couldn't have.

Mouth dry, stomach heaving, I climbed unsteadily to my feet and staggered over.

Saw what remained of his throat and face.

Bile rose thick and fast. I spun away, not wanting to lose my dinner over the man I'd just killed. Not that he'd care anymore...

When there was nothing but dry heaves left, I wiped a hand across my mouth, then took a deep breath and turned to face what I'd done.

He was a big man, at least six four, with dark skin and darker hair. His eyes were brown, and if the expression frozen on what was left of his face was anything to go by, I'd caught him by surprise. He was also fully clothed, which meant I hadn't been in a blood lust when I'd ripped out his throat. That in itself provided no comfort, especially considering *I* was naked, and obviously *had* made love to someone sometime in the last hour.

My gaze went back to his face and my stomach rose threateningly again. Swallowing heavily, I forced my eyes away from that mangled mess and studied the rest of him. He wore what looked like brown coveralls, with shiny gold buttons and the letters D.S.E. printed on the left breast pocket. There was a taser clipped to the belt at his waist and a two-way attached to his lapel. What looked like a dart gun lay inches from his reaching right hand. His fingers had suckers, more gecko-like than human.

A chill ran across my skin. I'd seen hands like that before—just over two months ago, in a Melbourne casino car park, when I'd been attacked by a vampire and a tall, blue thing that had smelled like death.

The need to get out of this road hit like a punch to the stomach, leaving me winded and trembling. But I couldn't run, not yet. Not until I knew everything this man might be able to tell me. There were too many gaps in my memory that needed to be filled.

Not the least of which was why I'd ripped out his throat.

After taking another deep breath that did little to calm my churning stomach, I knelt next to my victim. The cobblestones were cold and hard against my shins, but the chill that crept across my flesh had nothing to do with the icy night. The urge to run was increasing, but if my senses had any idea what I should be running from, they weren't telling me. One thing was certain—this dead man was no longer a threat. Not unless he'd performed the ritual to become a vampire, anyway, and even then, it could be days before he actually turned.

I bit my lip and cautiously patted him down. There was nothing else on him. No wallet, no ID, not even the usual assortment of fluff that seemed to accumulate and thrive in pockets. His boots were leather—nondescript brown things that had no name brand. His socks provided the only surprise—they were pink. Fluorescent pink.

I blinked. My twin brother would love them, but I couldn't imagine anyone else doing so. And they seemed an odd choice for a man who was so colorless in every other way.

Something scraped the cobblestones behind me. I froze, listening. Sweat skittered across my skin and my heart raced nine to the dozen—a beat that seemed to echo through the stillness. After a few minutes, it came again—a soft click I'd never have noticed if the night wasn't so quiet.

I reached for the dart gun, then turned and studied the night-encased alley. The surrounding buildings seemed to disappear into that black well, and I could sense nothing or no one approaching.

Yet something was there, I was sure of it.

I blinked, switching to the infrared of my vampire vision. The entire lane leapt into focus—tall walls, wooden fences, and overflowing bins. Right down the far end, a hunched shape that wasn't quite human, not quite dog.

My mouth went dry.

They were hunting me.

Why I was so certain of this I couldn't say, but I wasn't about to waste time examining it. I rose, and slowly backed away from the body.

The creature raised its nose, sniffing the night air. Then it howled—a high, almost keening sound that was as grating as nails down a blackboard.

The thing down the far end was joined by another, and together they began to walk toward me.

I risked a quick glance over my shoulder. The street and the light weren't that far away, but I had a feeling the two creatures weren't going to be scared away by the presence of either.

The click of their nails against the cobblestones was sharper, a tattoo of sound that spoke of patience and controlled violence. They were taking one step for every three of mine, and yet they seemed to be going far faster.

I pressed a finger around the trigger of the dart gun, and wished I'd grabbed the taser as well.

The creatures stopped at the body, sniffing briefly before stepping over it and continuing on. This close, their shaggy, powerful forms looked more like misshapen bears than wolves or dogs, and they must have stood at least four feet at the shoulder. Their eyes were red—a luminous, scary red.

They snarled softly, revealing long, yellow teeth. The urge to run was so strong every muscle trembled. I bit my lip, fighting instinct as I raised the dart gun and pressed the trigger twice. The darts hit the creatures square in the chest, but only seemed to infuriate them. Their soft snarls became a rumble of fury as they launched into the air. I turned and ran, heading left at the end of the alley simply because it was downhill.

The road's surface was slick with moisture, the streetlights few and far between. Had it been humans chasing me, I could have used the cloak of night to disappear from sight. But the scenting actions these creatures made when they first appeared suggested the vampire ability to fade into shadow wouldn't help me here.

Nor would shifting into wolf form, because my only real weapon in my alternate shape was teeth. Not a good option when there was more than one foe.

I raced down the middle of the wet street, passing silent shops and terraced houses. No one seemed to be home in any of them, and none of them looked familiar. In fact, all the buildings looked rather strange, almost as if they were one-dimensional.

The air behind me stirred and the sense of evil sharpened. I swore softly and dropped to the ground. A dark shape leapt over me, its sharp howl becoming a sound of frustration. I sighted the dart and fired again, then rolled onto my back, kicking with all my might at the second creature. The blow caught it in the jaw and deflected its leap. It crashed to the left of me, shaking its head, a low rumble coming from deep within its chest.

I scrambled to my feet, and fired the last of the darts at it. Movement caught my eye. The first creature had climbed to its feet and was scrambling toward me.

I threw the empty gun at its face, then jumped out of its way. It slid past, claws scrabbling against the wet road as it tried to stop. I grabbed a fistful of shaggy brown hair and swung onto its back, wrapping an arm around its throat and squeezing tight. I had the power of wolf *and* vampire behind me, which meant I was more than capable of crushing the larynx of any normal creature in an instant. Trouble was, this creature *wasn't* normal.

It roared—a harsh, strangled sound—then began to buck and twist violently. I wrapped my legs around its body, hanging on tight as I continued my attempts to strangle it.

The other creature came out of nowhere and hit me side-on, knocking me off its companion. I hit the road with enough force to see stars, but the scrape of approaching claws got me moving. I rolled upright, and scrambled away on all fours.

Claws raked my side, drawing blood. I twisted, grabbed the creature's paw, and pulled it forward hard. The creature sailed past and landed with a crash on its back, hard up against a shop wall. A wall that shook under the impact.

I frowned, but the second creature gave me no time to wonder why the wall had moved. I spun around, sweeping with my foot, battering the hairy beastie off its feet. It roared in frustration and lashed out. Sharp claws caught my thigh, tearing flesh even as the blow sent me staggering. The creature was up almost instantly, nasty sharp teeth gleaming yellow in the cold, dark night.

I faked a blow to its head, then spun and kicked at its chest, embedding the darts even farther. The ends of the darts hurt my bare foot, but the blow obviously hurt the creature more, because it howled in fury and leapt. I dropped and spun. Then, as the creature's leap took it high above me, I kicked it as hard as I could in the goolies. It grunted, dropped to the road, and didn't move.

For a moment, I simply remained where I was, the wet road cold against my shins as I battled to get some air into my lungs. When the world finally stopped threatening to go black, I called to the wolf that prowled within.

Power swept around me, through me, blurring my vision, blurring the pain. Limbs shortened, shifted, rearranged, until what was sitting on the road was wolf not woman. I had no desire to stay too long in my alternate form. There might be more of those things prowling the night, and meeting two or more in *this* shape could be deadly.

But in shifting, I'd helped accelerate the healing process. The cells in a werewolf's body retained data on body makeup, which was why wolves were so long-lived. In changing, damaged cells were repaired. Wounds were healed. And while it generally took more than one shift to heal deep wounds, one would at least stem the bleeding and begin the healing process.

I shifted back to human form and climbed slowly to my feet. The first creature still lay in a heap at the base of the shopfront. Obviously, whatever had been in those two darts had finally taken effect. I walked over to the second creature, grabbed it by the scruff of the neck, and dragged it off the road. Then I went to the window and peered inside.

It wasn't a shop, just a front. Beyond the window there was only framework and rubbish. The next shop was much the same, as was the house next to that. Only there were wooden people inside it as well.

It looked an awful lot like one of those police or military weapons training grounds, only *this* training ground had warped-looking creatures patrolling its perimeter.

That bad feeling I'd woken with began to get a whole lot worse. I had to get out of here, before anything or anyone else discovered I was free.

The thought made me pause.

Free?

Did that mean I'd been a prisoner in this place? If so, why?

No answers emerged from the fog encasing the part of my brain that held my memories. Frowning, I continued down the street. The road banked sharply to the left, then fell away, revealing the lower half of the complex. Partially built houses and shops lined the rest of this road, but this time they were interspersed between lush gum trees. At the end of the street stood a formidable-looking gate, and to one side of this, a guard's box. Warm light seeped out of a small window at the side of the box, suggesting someone was home.

To the left, beyond the partial buildings, there were concrete structures lit by harsh spotlights. To the right, a long building that looked like stables, and beyond that, several blocky concrete structures and lots more trees.

And surrounding the whole complex, a six-foot wire fence.

"Any sign of Max or the two orsini?"

The sharp voice came out of nowhere. I jumped a mile, my heart racing so hard I swear it was going to tear out of my chest. Wrapping the cloak of night around myself, I melted back into the shadows of the shopfront and waited.

Footsteps approached, their leisurely manner suggesting the missing Max and orsini weren't yet causing concern. Though considering I'd probably just killed Max and seriously damaged the missing orsini, that lack of concern would very quickly disappear.

A figure appeared out of a small lane just ahead. He was human—had to be, because anything else I would have sensed. He was dressed in brown, and like the man I'd killed, had brown hair and eyes. He stopped, his gaze sweeping the street. The spicy scent of his aftershave stung the night air, mingling uneasily with the reek of garlic on his breath.

He pressed a button on his lapel, then said, "No sign of them yet. I'll head up to the breeding labs and see if Max is there."

"He was supposed to have reported in half an hour ago."

"Won't be the first time he's slacked off."

"Might be his last, though. The boss ain't gonna like this."

The guard grunted. "I'll give you a call in ten."

Ten minutes wasn't much time, but it was better than the two it would take him to walk up the road and discover the knocked-out beasties.

"Do that."

I waited until the guard came close, then clenched my fist and let rip with a blow to his chin. The force of it sent a shockwave up my arm, but he was out long before he hit the ground. I rolled him into the shadows of the fake shop's doorway, then scanned the road ahead.

With the main gate guarded, I'd have to try and climb the wire fence. The best place to do that was in the shadows created by the stable.

I ran down a side road into a slightly larger street. More mock shopfronts and houses met me, but the night air carried a hint of hay and horse. It *was* a stable. What in hell would a testing ground want with horses?

As I raced down the road, a strident alarm cut through the silence. I slithered to a halt, my heart back to sitting somewhere in my throat and my stomach battling to join it.

Either they'd discovered the bodies, or someone had finally realized I wasn't where I was supposed to be. Either way, that alarm meant I was in deep shit.

With the alarm came lights, the sudden brightness stinging my eyes. I swore and ran off the road, keeping to what little shadows the shopfronts offered. The perimeter fence was lit up like a Christmas tree. There wasn't a hope of getting over it unseen.

Footsteps pounded through the night. I stopped, pressing back into a doorway. Five half-dressed guards went past, running as if the hounds of hell were after them.

When they'd gone, I edged out of my hidey-hole and ran down the lane they'd come out of. The stable loomed above me, the smell of horse and hay and shit so strong I wrinkled my nose in disgust. The many snorts and stomps indicated more than one animal was housed inside. If I released them, they might just provide enough confusion to help me escape.

The stable doors loomed. From the night behind me came the sound of more footsteps. I quickly pushed through the smaller of the two doors, then closed it behind me and looked around.

There were ten stalls in all, nine of them occupied. A single globe hung off a wire halfway down the center walkway, its pale light sparking off the hay bales lining the edge of the floor above.

Heads swung my way, dark eyes gleaming intently in the muted light. They were all tall and strong-looking, most of them chestnut, gray, or bay. The stallion closest to me was a truly stunning mahogany bay, though with his ears pinned back and teeth bared, he looked anything but friendly.

No surprise there. Horses and wolves were rarely the best of buddies.

"Hey," I muttered, swatting his nose as he lunged at me. "I'm just as pissed off at being here as you, buddy boy, but if you promise to behave, I'll let you and your friends go."

The horse snorted, glaring at me for a moment before nodding its head, as if in agreement. Chain clinked as he moved. I frowned and stepped closer. I wasn't hearing things. And it wasn't ordinary chains that held the stallion. Having been shot with silver a couple of times, my skin was now oversensitive to its presence.

And there could only be one reason to use such restraints on a horse.

I looked up sharply. "You're a shifter?" And if so, why hadn't I sensed it? Shifters might not be weres, and they certainly weren't forced through the change every full moon like we were, but they were from the same family tree as us rather than the human side of things. I couldn't sense humans, but I *should* have known what he was straightaway. Should have smelled it in his scent.

The stallion nodded again.

"And them?" I waved a hand at the other horses.

A third nod.

Fuck. Looks like I wasn't the only one caught in this web. Whatever this goddamn web was.

"You promise not to stomp on me if I come into the stall?"

The stallion snorted again, and somehow it sounded disdainful. I opened the door carefully. I might not have had a whole lot to do with shifters in the past, but the few I had dealt with tended to treat us weres with as little respect as humans did. Why, I had no idea, especially considering our "animal" tendencies were the same as theirs.

Well, except for the moon heat—and they could hardly look down their nose at us for that when a good percentage of them enjoyed the week of the moon heat just as much as any were.

The stallion didn't move, just continued to stare down at me. At five seven, I wasn't exactly small, but this horse somehow made me feel it.

The sharp snap of a latch being pulled back made my blood freeze. I swung around and saw the main stable doors opening. Swearing under my breath, I relocked the stallion's door and scrambled into the corner.

The stallion snorted, his dancing hooves inches from

my toes. This close, his rich coat was dull, and he reeked of dried sweat and blood. Barely healed welts marred his rump.

Obviously, he had not been a model prisoner.

Footsteps entered the walkway, and stopped.

"Told you she wasn't in here," a harsh voice said.

"And I'm telling you we'd better check all the stalls or the boss will have our hides."

Light pierced the stallion's box. My breath caught somewhere in my throat and I clenched my hands. If they wanted me, they were going to have to fight me. I'd be damned if I'd go anywhere willingly.

But in this case, I had an ally. The stallion lunged forward, his chest hitting the door before the chains around his neck snapped tight. One of the men swore, the other laughed.

"Yeah, she's really going to be hiding in that bastard's stall. We have to drug him just to get the specimens we want."

"Could have mentioned that," the second man muttered.

The two of them walked away. The rattle of latches indicated they were checking the rest of the stalls, then their footsteps receded and the door down the far end opened and closed. I waited several seconds, then rose and peered over the stall door. Nothing but horses.

Letting go of the breath I'd been holding, I turned and studied the chains. They were padlocked to rings concreted into the walls on either side of the stall.

I looked up and met the stallion's keen gaze. "So, where's the key?"

He snorted and pointed with his nose toward the

main doors. I scanned the wall and, after a moment, saw a small cabinet. I undid the latch and walked over. The cabinet held a single key. I grabbed it and went back, swiftly undoing the padlocks then carefully pulling the chains over the stallion's head. Though I was barely even touching them, the silver burned my fingers. I cursed and threw them into a corner.

A golden shimmer appeared on the stallion's nose, quickly dancing across the rest of his body. I stepped back, watching him change. He was just as magnificent in human form as he was in horse, his mahogany skin, black hair, and velvet brown eyes a truly striking combination.

"Thank you," he said, his voice deep, and somewhat husky. His gaze swept down me, lingering a little on my breasts before sweeping down to the cuts that decorated my side and thigh. "I gather you, too, are a prisoner here?"

"Wherever here is."

"Then we'll help each other escape and worry the whys and hows later. But first, the others."

I tossed him the key. "You unlock them. I'll keep watch on the doors."

"Bolt this end closed. They often do, as they tend to enter mainly from the other end."

I did as he suggested, then ran down the far end and cracked open the smaller door. The boundary fence wasn't that far away, but lights still swept it, and the wail of the siren was almost lost to the grating howl of those bearlike creatures. The hunt was well and truly on. If we didn't get out of here soon, we wouldn't get out at all.

I looked behind me. Men gathered in the shadows.

When the stranger had freed the last of them, he joined me by the door. He still smelled of hay and horse and excrement, but this time it was entwined in the musky, enticing scent of man.

"Not good," he muttered, peering out over my head.

"The main gate is barred and guarded. I think the only way out is over that fence."

He glanced down at me. "Can a wolf jump that high when she's wounded?"

"I'd jump the moon if that's what it took to get out of this place."

His sudden grin was warm, crinkling the corners of his velvet eyes. "That I believe. But for safety's sake, you'd better mount me. I'd hate to see my savior left behind."

I frowned. "You sure you can leap that high with a rider?"

"No probs, sweetheart. Trust me."

I glanced at the fence and nodded. He was right. While the wounds on my side and leg weren't particularly painful, they were still weeping, and the strength in my leg might give way at a vital moment. And there was no way in hell I was going to risk being left behind. "Let's get those doors open."

We did. When the stranger had shifted back into horse form, I grabbed a handful of mane and pulled myself aboard. Once settled on his back, I twisted around. "Good luck, everyone."

Horses snorted softly in response. I took a deep breath, clenched my legs against the stallion's belly, then said, "Ready."

He sprang forward, all raw muscle and power. We

sped down the road, arrowing toward the brightly lit fence, the wind a howl that snapped at my hair and stung my skin with ice.

The clatter of hooves on stone sang through the night. A shout went up from the left of us. Pain flicked my ear, and I jerked away, catching sight of sparks as something hit the road. Warmth began to trickle down my neck.

"They're shooting at us," I yelled. "Faster."

He surged forward. Behind us, a horse screamed. I looked over my shoulder, saw a bay go down, half his head missing. Fear knotted my stomach. They'd rather see us dead than have us escape.

The fence loomed. I closed my eyes and held on tight as the stallion gathered himself, then rose. The sensation of flying seemed to go on and on, then we hit the ground with enough force to jar every bone in my body and almost dislodge me.

But we were over the damn fence.

Now all we had to do was shake any pursuers, and find out where the hell we were.

Chapter 2

The stallion ran until the howls of the pursuit were lost to silence and all that surrounded us were trees and mountain.

Eventually, we hit a stream, and he slid to a stop. I fell more than jumped off his back, but my legs were like jelly and collapsed underneath me. Flopping onto my back, I watched the golden haze sweep across the stallion's body. In human form, he fell beside the river, sucking in water as greedily as I sucked air.

"Not too much," I said, my voice little more than a pant of air. "Cramps."

He grunted, but stopped drinking and rolled into the water instead. His mahogany skin gleamed with heat, and his breath was little more than a wheeze.

It was amazing he'd run as long as he had, especially if he'd been locked up for any length of time.

I turned my gaze to the night sky. The moon I couldn't see was beginning to wane, suggesting it was around three in the morning. Though we'd run for a good two hours, we had to be a hell of a lot farther away by dawn if we wanted to remain free.

The trembling in my legs finally eased enough that I could push onto all fours. I crawled to the river and scooped up handfuls of icy water, sipping it until the fire in my throat had eased. I splashed some over my face, then more over my neck and ear to wash away the blood, but I felt no better. What I needed was a hot bath, a big fat steak sandwich, and a large cup of coffee. And not particularly in that order.

"You'd better wash those body wounds down, too," he commented, husky tones so soft his words barely carried.

I glanced at him, but his eyes were closed. "I intend to." I shifted shape first, just to help the healing process along a little more, then changed back and pushed up into a sitting position and began to clean not only the blood and dirt from the wounds, but the horse hair and sweat from my legs and nether regions.

I don't know what Lady Godiva's caper was about, but she obviously *hadn't* been riding that horse bareback for the sheer pleasure of it. Horse sweat against bare skin was *not* nice.

"Do you think they'll still be giving chase?" he asked, after a few moments.

"Oh yeah. Those things hunt by scent, and we weren't exactly careful about not leaving a trail."

He grunted. "I just wanted to get away from the bastards."

Didn't we both. "How long were you there?"

"Months. Some of the others had been there over a year."

"And they were...ummm...milking you all?"

He opened an eye and gave me a measuring sort of look. "How did you guess?"

I shrugged. "The guard said they were taking specimens."

"Even so, that wouldn't have been my first guess."

"Two months ago, it wouldn't have been mine, either." But I'd learned a lot since then. Been through a lot.

"Meaning you have some idea as to what was going on in there?"

"Vague suspicions, nothing more."

"Like what?"

I grimaced. "Gene research. Crossbreeding."

His face was expressionless, his eyes slightly narrowed. He obviously suspected I knew more than what I was saying, but all he said was, "How long were you in there?"

"Around eight days, but tonight is the first night I can really remember."

He grunted. "It was like that for me, too. Though I was apparently there for two months before I came to my senses."

Then obviously, we'd all been drugged. But why did it take two months for the effects to wear off the stallions, and just over a week for me? Was the simple fact that I *shouldn't* have woken yet the only reason I'd been able to escape?

I scrubbed a hand across my eyes and wished the fog would clear so I could remember what had gone on. "Did you ever try to escape?"

"No, because it was impossible. The chains were never off us, and the stables were fitted with psi-deadeners, just in case any of us tried to get cute that way."

At least that explained why I hadn't sensed what they were—though *he'd* known what I was, which was interesting. Or maybe it was simply a matter of a horse being sensitive to the odor of a wolf.

"Did they do any more than milk you?"

"No, thank God."

"Did you ever see any other type of shifter?"

"We were never out of the damn stable."

Then he had to have been superbly fit before he'd been captured to still carry any sort of strength and endurance months down the track. He crawled out of the stream on all fours, and stretched out on the grass.

My gaze traveled down the length of him. It wasn't only his coloring that was magnificent. He was built like a thoroughbred—broad shoulders, powerful chest, slim hips, and long, strong legs. His rump and back still bore the barely healed whip scars, but he had the best ass I'd seen on a man since Quinn had walked in, and then out, of my life.

I'd never met a horse-shifter before, and had to wonder where they'd been hiding all my life. If this man was a sample of what they had to offer, I might be tempted to seek one or two out the next full moon. If they could get over their instinctive hate of wolves, fun could definitely be had.

"There's no vibration of steps through the earth," he said.

"They could be *way* behind, but they will be following us."

He shifted, his expression intent as his gaze met mine. "You seem very certain of that."

"They tried to kill us rather than capture us. That suggests they value secrecy more than they value us."

"Then we'd better get moving again."

Moving was the *last* thing I wanted when every bone ached with weariness. I needed to sleep even more than I needed coffee—a big statement considering how hooked I was on caffeine. But staying put, even for a few hours, wasn't an option when we were still so close to that complex.

He climbed to his feet with effortless grace, then offered me a hand. His fingers were warm despite the time he'd spent in the water, and his palm was rough against mine. He pulled me upright then let go, but made no immediate attempt to move away.

My gaze rose to his. Awareness burned in his brown eyes, and suddenly I remembered that this was a man who hadn't been with a woman for many months. The icy water had washed the stable smells from his skin, and his musky odor, rich with the scent of desire, swam around me. Lust stirred, warming the chill from my flesh.

He raised a hand and brushed wet strands of hair from my cheek. "May I know your name?"

His fingers trailed heat where they touched. It felt nice, and the stirring lust sharpened. Though nowhere near enough to wipe out the fear of recapture and the need to get moving. I quickly said, "Riley Jenson. You?"

"Kade Williams."

"We need to get moving, Kade."

"Yes, we do."

But he didn't budge and the smile that tugged his lips went beyond sexy. My hormones did an excited little jig. Of course, my hormones never needed much of an excuse to get excited about a fine-looking man, and if we'd been anywhere else but in the middle of the forest with hairy monsters and psychos with guns chasing after us, I might just have given my hormones free rein.

"But first," he continued softly, "a kiss to thank my savior."

"This is hardly the time or place—"

"I know," he interrupted, "and I don't care."

As his lips claimed mine, his hand slid around my waist, his fingers pressing heat into my spine as he pulled me close to his warm, hard body. For half a second, I resisted, but he felt so good, tasted so good, that I just gave in to the moment. And as my resistance melted, the initial tentativeness gave way to passion, and the kiss became fierce and explorative.

After what seemed like hours we came up for air. The rapid pounding of my heart was a cadence that filled the silence, and it was accompanied by the heated rush of blood through my system.

The full moon might have passed, but the fever still burned in my veins. An indicator, perhaps, that while sex had been on the menu during the eight days I couldn't remember, satisfaction had been absent.

But I was not ruled by my hormones—at least not until the moon was full. I might want this big, strong shifter, but not enough to take what was being offered right here and now.

That could come later, when we were out of the woods—literally and figuratively.

I pulled out of his arms and stepped back. "We'd best walk in the water for a while, to throw them off our scent."

The smile that tugged his lips was decidedly sensual. "Upstream, not down."

I raised an eyebrow. "Why?"

"Because most people would take the easy way and go downstream, and that's probably what they'd expect of us."

"I guess that's a good enough reason."

He nodded. "When the water gets too cold for your feet, climb onto my back."

"I'm shifting to my wolf shape."

He shrugged. "The offer's there when you need it."

"Thanks."

His eyes twinkled. "Never had a naked woman ride my alternate shape before. It's rather...erotic."

I grinned. "So Lady Godiva wasn't as stupid as I thought?"

"Not if that horse of hers was a shifter."

My gaze drifted downward, coming to rest on the tent pole he had going. *That* would certainly explain the silly woman's satisfied smile. I waved a hand toward the river. "After you."

He shifted shape, waited until I'd done the same, then led the way upstream. We walked through the remainder of the night. When the icy water became too much for my paws, I shifted shape and climbed onto Kade's back, moving in rhythm with him as he picked his way through the rock-strewn stream.

Dawn was beginning to taint the sky with flags of rose and gold when we finally left the stream. Kade walked to the edge of an outcropping of rock. Before us stretched a tree-filled valley, and nestled in its heart was a small town. The drop down to that town had my stomach flip-flopping, and I slid off his back, barely keeping my legs from buckling as I staggered away from the edge.

Kade shifted to human form. "You okay?"

I took several deep breaths, then nodded. "I hate heights." And cliff tops, thanks to the fact I was thrown off one when I was a pup.

He motioned down to the town I could no longer see. "Recognize it?"

"Not in the least. You?"

He didn't answer directly, just frowned. "Are those specks soaring above the town eagles?"

I watched the two brown shapes, sensing nothing more than ordinary eagles. But, given the distance, that wasn't surprising. We couldn't afford to presume *any*-thing was as it appeared when we were still so close to that complex. "They may be shifters. They may be watching all the towns near the complex."

His gaze narrowed a little, but again, he didn't voice his suspicions. "So we go around it and keep walking?"

"No. I really can't walk much farther. Not until I get some coffee, anyway." I edged closer, until I could see the town but not the actual drop. There was an iron-roofed house barely visible through the trees that had distinct possibilities.

"What about that one?" I said, pointing. "We should be able to make it down there without being seen."

"That's a good two hour walk, at least." His gaze rolled languidly down my body—a touch that wasn't a touch and yet one that made my toes curl. "You up to that?"

I'd already said I wasn't, but I couldn't exactly stay here, either. Or ask him to carry me—a horse would be too easily seen in the thinning trees. "I'm a wolf, and stronger than I look."

"I know." He grimaced and rubbed a hand across his ribs, though it was amusement rather than pain that shone in his brown eyes. "And I have the bruises to prove it."

A smile teased my lips. "Sorry, but I haven't had much experience riding stallions."

"Then that's something we'll definitely have to remedy."

Warmth fled like quicksilver through my veins. I raised an eyebrow and said, "And what if it takes more than one lesson?"

"Then I shall have to stay until you are proficient."

Couldn't be sad about that. If nothing else, having Kade around for a while would have the added benefit of driving my brother crazy with lust. And after the teasing he'd been giving me about my love life—or lack thereof—he certainly deserved having mahogany perfection slapped in his face.

Kade led the way down the mountain, and I kept my gaze centered on his broad and muscular back. The sharp descent had my stomach wavering more than a few times, especially when I inadvertently glanced at the drop to the side of us. But I made it down without puking, and the sheer relief had me trembling.

Or maybe that was exhaustion settling in.

The sun had well and truly risen by the time we

reached the house, and by then, my feet felt like lead and every step was an effort.

Kade wasn't in much better shape. He leaned a brawny arm against a fence post, sweat gleaming on his forehead and cheeks as he eyed the weatherboard house. "I can't hear anyone. Can you smell anyone?"

All *I* could smell was eucalyptus and sweat—his *and* mine. "No."

"I'll check the garage, you check the house."

I glanced up to ensure none of those circling eagles were in sight, then unlatched the gate and stumbled to the nearest window. The room was pale yellow in color and dominated by a luxurious—and empty—bed. I almost wept at the sight. God, I needed to rest. *Sleep.*

I pushed away from the window and walked around to the back of the house. The door was locked. I felt around the frame, looked under the mat, and finally found the spare key under the blood-colored geraniums filling the window box.

The door creaked as I opened it. I winced, and didn't move. The old house was still, but not entirely quiet. A clock ticked steadily in one of the rooms, and the aroma of mothballs and lavender vied for attention on the air.

Kade came up behind me, pressing warmth into my spine as he stopped. "Anything?"

His breath caressed my ear, sending little shivers of delight lapping across my skin. My body might be exhausted, but my hormones certainly weren't. I shook my head and pulled away from him again. "You?"

"No car, and the garage doors don't look as if they've been opened for a few days."

"Then we might have found a refuge for a few hours."

"Hopefully." He took the key from me, then locked the door and hung the key on a handy nearby hook. "I don't think I could have walked much farther."

The first doorway off the small hall led into the kitchen. Kade went inside while I continued to explore. The house was small, little more than the kitchen, a living room, bathroom, and two bedrooms. All the walls were either pastel or covered in flowery wallpaper, and there was lace everywhere. Combined with the overwhelming scent of mothballs, it was pretty evident older people lived here—a fact backed up by the clothes I discovered hanging in the closet.

Still, thieves couldn't afford to be choosy.

I retraced my steps to the bathroom. After running the water to ensure it was hot, I jumped in the shower and cleaned myself up, feeling a hundred percent better once I had. I dried myself, then wrapped the towel around me, and returned to the kitchen.

"How do you like your coffee?" Kade said as I walked in.

"Hot, preferably."

His gaze skated down me, and a luscious smile teased his lips. "You smell almost edible." He poured hot water into two mugs, then slid one across to me.

"So does that." I plonked down on the nearest stool and sniffed the coffee appreciably. "It looks like our unwitting hosts have been gone for a few days."

He nodded. "A fact backed up by the lack of perishables in the fridge."

I sipped at the coffee, then asked, "Is there a phone here?" It was the only thing I hadn't seen on my search.

"On the wall behind you." He studied me for a second, then added, "There's someone in your life you need to ring urgently?"

I raised an eyebrow. "Would it make a difference if there is?"

His expression tightened a little. "Of course it would."

"I thought stallions were into collecting harems?"

"Yeah, but unlike our animal counterparts, we draw the line at stealing other stallion's mares."

"Ah." I drank some coffee, letting him wonder for a little while. "So how many women have you got in your herd?"

"Four before I was captured."

"A nice even number."

He raised an eyebrow. "You don't seemed shocked."

"Wolves tend to have several mates at any one time— at least until we find our soul mate."

"So at the moment?"

"I'm playing the field. But I've had up to five mates." Though not at the same time. Male wolves tended to get a little testy about sharing *that* way.

"And when you find your soul mate?"

"We're monogamous."

"Unlike us stallions."

It was a warning—a gentle one, but a warning all the same. A smile touched my lips. "When I take on a permanent mate, it'll be a man from my own race. I want to have babies one day." Though my vampire half might already have snatched that desire away from my grasp. Rhoan, my twin, had discovered two weeks ago he was infertile. I'd been undergoing similar tests, but whether I'd gotten the test results was anyone's guess, as I could remember going there, but not leaving.

"So, the people you must ring are . . . ?"

"The pack-mate I live with, and my boss."

"Meaning you're sleeping with your boss?"

I choked on my coffee. "No," I said, when I could. "I work for the Directorate of Other Races. They tend to get a little concerned when one of their people disappears—even if it is a lowly paper pusher like myself."

"Then I'll go have a shower while you ring them."

He walked out. I enjoyed the sight, then grabbed the phone and dialed Jack's work number. All I got was a computer voice telling me the number did not exist. His home number got the same result, as did my home number, so I tried their mobile phone numbers. Both were either turned off or out of range.

That bad feeling reappeared, sitting like a lump in the pit of my stomach.

Kade came back a few minutes later, as deliciously naked as before, but looking and smelling fresher.

"Nothing," I muttered, throwing the phone on the bench.

He frowned. "The phone's not working?"

"It's working, but the calls aren't going through."

"Then try again later. It's still very early."

Not for Jack. And not for Rhoan. He'd probably be in a state of panic by now, and I seriously doubted whether sleep would be on his agenda.

"Why don't you try?"

Kade reached for the phone and dialed a number. He

listened for several minutes then pressed the end button. "Recorded message telling me it's the wrong number."

I nodded. "So who did you try ringing? One of your mares?"

"No. After all this time, they'd be with someone else."

"So who?"

"Are all wolves this nosy?"

I shrugged. "I like to know a little about the man I eventually intend to fuck."

Heat flared in the depths of his velvet eyes. "Eventually?"

I nodded. "Escape first, fun later."

"A plan I could live with."

"Good." Because as much as I was attracted, I wanted safety more. We might have found ourselves somewhere to have a bit of a breather, but I very much doubted we could stay here for long. The orsini looked like hunters, and I had a bad feeling they wouldn't be fooled by our little walk through the river. "So, who were you calling?"

He grinned. "My business partner."

"And your business is . . . ?"

He studied me for a moment, his dark gaze somewhat assessing, then said, "I'm a building contractor."

"Houses or offices?"

"Houses. Ever heard of J. K. Constructions?"

"Not a whisper."

"Not surprising, really. We're one of the smaller building contractors in South Australia."

The cold lump in my stomach got larger. "You're from Adelaide?"

"Yeah. Why?"

"I'm from Victoria."

He stared at me for a moment, then closed his eyes. "Fuck."

"Yeah. And maybe *that's* the reason the phone wouldn't work." Because we were no longer in the same state, which meant I'd have to use the proper state code to get through to either Jack's phone or Rhoan's cell. Unlike many cell phone systems the world over, Australia's didn't automatically get shunted to voice mail if the caller was out of range.

I picked up the phone and dialed Jack's work number, this time adding Victoria's STD code. It barely rang once before it was answered.

"Parnell here."

I closed my eyes, never in my life more relieved to hear my boss's gruff tones. "Jack, it's Riley."

"Jesus, girl, where are you? We found your car—"

I cut him off. "I have no idea where I am, but I need you to come and get us."

"Us?" His voice was sharp.

"Yeah. Long story, but I'm here with a shifter by the name of Kade Williams. He helped me escape what I think was another gene research lab."

Jack's next few sentences were long, loud, and inventive.

Kade chuckled softly. "The man has a fine line in swearing."

"Where are you?" Jack eventually asked.

"That's the problem—I don't know. But we're not in Victoria or South Australia."

"I'll do a tr—"

"Riley? Are you all right?" Rhoan's warm tones

replaced Jack's, and I closed my eyes at the hoarse tiredness in my brother's voice.

"Yeah, I'm fine."

"So what happened? We found your car crashed into a tree. Blood was everywhere, and we'd thought the worst."

I couldn't remember the crash. Couldn't remember getting hurt. And I was mighty pissed that I'd crashed my car—I'd only had the damn thing a week.

"I'm fine," I repeated. "But I can't remember anything about the last eight days."

"Got it," Jack said in the background. "They're in New South Wales."

"New South is a mighty big state," Rhoan grumbled. "Care to define it a bit more?"

"I'm working on it."

"So," Rhoan said to me, "did I hear you say you were there with a shifter?"

My gaze went to Kade's and I grinned. "You certainly did."

"And he's being good to you?"

"Oh, I intend to be very good to you," Kade murmured wickedly.

Oh lordy... Were all stallions this damn hot?

"He made me coffee," I said, "and that's a fine start."

"Uh-huh," Rhoan said. "Just remind him you've got a ferocious pack-mate who will stomp all over him if he so much as bends a fingernail."

Kade snorted softly, and I grinned. "He's quaking in his boots as we speak."

"Good." Rhoan hesitated. "So, did this place do anything to you?"

"I don't know. They were milking Kade and the other stallions, though."

Silence met this remark, and my smile grew.

"He's a horse-shifter?"

"Yes."

"Damn. You get all the luck."

I laughed softly—and knew that's exactly what Rhoan had intended. "This from the man who currently has how many mates?"

"Only three."

Which was two too many in Liander's view, but both he and I knew my brother wasn't ready to settle down yet.

"Trace is in," Jack said. "They're in Bullaburra."

"Which is where?" Rhoan asked, before I could.

"In the Blue Mountains. Tell them to stay put. It may take a few hours to get things moving, but we'll be there as soon as we can."

"Leave your mobiles on," I said, "so we can contact you if we have to move."

"Will do. You be careful."

"Natch. See you soon." I hung up and met Kade's gaze.

"You're close to your pack-mate," he said.

"Very. We're wolves, and pack is all to a wolf." Especially when there was only him and me in the pack, thanks to the fact our mother's pack had thrown us out when we'd reached maturity. "But we're not physically close, if that's what you're getting at."

"Why not?"

"Because he prefers men." And because he was my brother. I mean, that was illegal, not to mention icky.

Kade drained his coffee, and put it in the sink. "So, how long have we got before we're rescued?"

"Four hours, at least."

He raised an eyebrow. "So what do we do in the meantime?"

The look in his eyes set my pulse racing yet again. But I meant what I'd said earlier, and no matter how much my hormones might be pleading to be set loose, I just didn't dare do it. No matter how good having sex with Kade promised to be—and I had no doubt that it *would* be good—it wasn't worth the risk of recapture. "I think we should sleep. Or rather, take turns sleeping and keeping watch."

"That's boring." He reached across the bench and untucked the end of the towel, his fingertips brushing heat across my skin. "Especially when there's other things we could be doing."

"Down boy." I slapped his hand away and re-tucked the towel. "The last thing we need is to be attacked by big bad hairy things because we were too busy having sex to notice they were near."

"It's a risk I'm willing to take. Especially for such a delightful piece of tail."

I smiled. "Well, the piece of tail would prefer to wait until the danger is over."

"Such a shame."

"You could at least say that with a little more sincerity."

His soft laugh sent goose bumps rippling. He leaned across the bench, and slowly, languorously, kissed me. "How much more sincere do you want me to be?" he said, after a while.

"I think"—the words came out all husky, and I quickly cleared my throat—"that *that's* more than enough sincerity for the moment."

"You sure I can't change your mind?"

I was sure that he could, actually. Thankfully, he didn't try. "Yes. So, who rests first?"

"Well, given I'm not going to be able to sleep until certain parts of my body relax, it's probably better if you take the first shift."

I raised an eyebrow. "And just how badly do these parts need relaxing?"

"This badly." He stepped back, and that's when I saw the stallion in all his proud glory. My mouth went dry. Obviously, the tent pole I'd viewed earlier had only been half-mast. Lord, he was *big*.

"You're right," I said. "There's not going to be much sleep happening with that hanging about."

"If it was hanging about, it wouldn't be such a problem." His chocolate eyes twinkled lightly with the mirth tugging at his lips. "Go, before the temptation gets too much."

I went. A few hours' sleep was never going to be enough, but it was better than nothing. I did a changeover with Kade, and spent the next hour and a half alternating between drinking coffee and prowling the premises. There was nothing and no one around.

Maybe I was wrong about the orsini. Maybe they couldn't track us as well as I thought they'd be able to.

I made myself yet another cup of coffee and leaned on the bench, warming my hands on either side of the cup as I stared out the main kitchen window.

Dappled light played across the yellowing grass, and

in the shade along the fence line, daffodils bobbed. The forest beyond was filled with shadows, though sunlight danced amongst the leaves and cast occasional sprays of green and gold waltzing across the tree trunks.

There was nothing or no one moving out there. Nothing or no one moving in the house. And yet...

Unease stirred. And I had no idea why.

"Why the pensive face?"

I jumped slightly, and looked around as Kade came into the room. "I just realized I've used up all the instant coffee," I said. "A very sad thing when you're as addicted as I am."

He stopped behind me, one brawny arm going around my waist, pressing his body against mine as he leaned forward and kissed my ear. "That's very sad indeed," he whispered, his breath so warm against my skin. "You want me to make you feel better?"

A smile twitched my lips. "You're as insatiable as a wolf in moon heat."

"Hey, I'm a randy stallion who hasn't had sex for over two months, and I'm standing behind a woman who is both luscious and naked. What do you expect?"

"A little restraint until we're safe, perhaps?"

"I *have* been restrained, sweetheart. Trust me on that." His lips touched my spine, a butterfly kiss that was powerfully arousing. "So, who were you thinking about when I came in? A lover?"

"No."

"But there is a lover who is causing some grief?"

"Yes." I twisted around to look at him. "How did you guess that? Are you a telepath?" And if he was, how was

he reading me? Quinn—the lover I'd mentioned before—couldn't, and yet he was not only one of the most
powerful vampires I'd met, but also one of the most powerful telepaths.

"No. Telekinetic. But I'm very good at reading women."

I raised an eyebrow. "Just women? Not men?"

His smile was devilish. "I have no interest in men."

And wouldn't my brother be pissed at that. "So, what
do you think you saw in my expression?"

"Regret."

He *was* good. While I hadn't actively been thinking
about Quinn, those thoughts were always present, sitting
at the back of my mind, waiting to pounce the minute I
relaxed my guard.

"Tell me," he added.

"Why?"

He shrugged. "Wolves aren't the only ones who can
be nosy."

I looked away, studying the shadows beyond the fence
line again. "He doesn't like what I am."

He brushed another kiss across my spine, but higher
this time, closer to my shoulder. Goose bumps fled excitedly across my skin.

"A paper pusher?"

I smiled. "No, a werewolf. He thinks us little more
than whores."

"I'm betting he doesn't think the same of your pack-
mate."

"According to him, it's okay for men to sleep around."

"Has to be a human." Disgust edged Kade's voice.
"Because only they would say something dumb like that
to a werewolf."

I smiled. "He's a vampire."

He shrugged, something I felt rather than saw. "Same thing, as most vamps were once human and have all the old prejudices." He paused. "You loved him?"

"I barely knew him."

His touch trailed up my stomach until he'd reached my breasts. Lightly, teasingly, he began to pinch the engorged points. My breath caught somewhere in my throat, and my heart began to race. I knew I should move, should put an end to it now, before it went too much further, but somehow, I just couldn't force the thoughts into action. Part of me—most of me—hungered.

"That's not what I asked," he said.

"No." I hesitated. "And no, I didn't. It's just that there was something between us, something I wanted to explore. He refused, simply because I am wolf."

"You don't look the type to give up."

"I'm not." I *had* tried. I'd rung. I'd even met him for dinner a couple of times. But Quinn had made it patently clear he didn't want anything more than what he'd already had. In the end, I'd walked away. As Rhoan had noted, it was Quinn who was the loser, not me.

"So why have you given up?"

"Because I'm far from desperate, and he's not a wolf."

"And you want children eventually?"

I nodded. "As I tried to tell him, I wasn't after anything deep or everlasting. I just wanted to explore."

"You know, I've found that jealousy works a whole lot better than trying to talk sense to people like that. Flaunt your conquests under his nose, and watch his pulse rate go up."

His teeth grazed my shoulder, nipping lightly. *My* pulse skipped into race mode.

"Hard to make him jealous when he doesn't even live in the same state."

"Then forget him. He's obviously a man who doesn't know a true prize when he finds it."

Amusement ran through me. "And you are?"

"Sweetheart, when I find a prize worth having, I grip on tight and ride it until it's mine." As if to demonstrate, he slid a hand down to my leg, his grip bruising. I barely had time to register it when his grip shifted and his thumb began to caress my inner thigh, sending little shivers of desire scooting across my body.

"This from a man who warned me, ever so gently, not to expect anything more serious than a good time?"

"If you were a horse-shifter, I'd pursue you until I won you, and you wouldn't have a hope of ever leaving my herd." His touch and his voice left me in no doubt as to his sincerity, and suddenly I felt a whole lot better about myself. After Talon's betrayal, Misha's probable involvement with the people behind my kidnappings, and Quinn basically dumping me, I'd been beginning to wonder if I'd had a sign on my back saying, "Stomp all over me, I love it."

"Of course, you're not a mare, so I'm just going to have to settle for a little fun."

Amusement bubbled through me. "So the planned riding lessons will still be going ahead?"

"As soon as possible."

Which would be *real* soon if I didn't get my act together and move. Not that I did. His touch had finally moved up my leg and it just felt too good to end it all so soon. "So, how many offspring have you got in your herd?"

"None. The government shoves the same hormonal chip in us stallions as they do you wolves." He hesitated. "Of course, the chip was taken out in that place, which means I'm more than likely fertile right now."

"Then it's just as well it's extremely rare for interspecies breeding to happen."

Of course, it *did* happen—I was living proof of that—so it was probably just as well I couldn't get pregnant without medical help. In fact, I might not be able to get pregnant at all, if my latest tests came back like Rhoan's.

He raised an eyebrow. "Then you're not chipped either?"

"No." It had been taken out over a year ago by Talon, and I'd never bothered getting it replaced. Couldn't really see the point of it, when most of the docs considered me the werewolf version of a mule and felt it was unlikely I'd *ever* fall pregnant. "But it won't matter. I have medical problems that prevent conception."

"So we can play without worrying about consequences?"

It was becoming extremely hard to concentrate on what he was saying when his clever fingers were doing all sorts of wonderful things. "We most certainly...ohhh!"

He laughed and placed his large, warm hands on either side of my butt and lightly kicked apart my legs. "Sweetheart, you ain't felt nothing yet."

He thrust into me, sliding deep and hard, and I groaned in pleasure. He stilled, and I closed my eyes, enjoying the connection of flesh, the pulse of warmth deep inside. I knew, like he knew, that this wasn't entirely wise. That it was dangerous to give in to pleasure when we were far from home, and far from safe. But danger is something of an aphrodisiac to a wolf, and I was a wolf who couldn't remember feeling *any* sort of pleasure in over a week. I needed this as badly as a vampire might have needed blood.

He began to move, stroking long and deep, and any lingering reluctance dissolved into intense pleasure. The rich, low-down ache grew, becoming a kaleidoscope of sensations that washed through every corner of my mind, the intensity of which increased sharply as Kade's tempo increased. All too soon the shuddering took hold as pleasure ripped through my body, my mind. I gasped, grabbing the bench for support, my cries of pleasure joining Kade's as his own orgasm hit.

When the tremors finally eased, he laughed softly and rested his forehead against my back. "I think we both needed that."

I smiled. "I think we did."

He dropped a kiss on my shoulder, then wrapped his arms around my waist and pulled my back against his warm body. "Next time I promise to take more time."

I opened my mouth to reply, but in that moment, I heard it.

The faint scrape of nail against concrete.

We were no longer alone.

Chapter 3

I froze.

"What?" Kade asked immediately, his voice barely a whisper.

"Something's outside." I scrambled to the window, carefully peering out. Nothing moved in the yard. Nothing but sunlight danced in the shadows of the trees.

Yet something was out there. I was growing more and more certain of it.

I ducked past the window. "Check the back. I'll check the living room and side."

He left the room. I crept into the living room and peered out the windows. No creature crept across the lawn or hid in the nearby trees. I retreated to the bathroom.

And heard a familiar rumble.

It was one of the orsini. Against all the odds, it had

tracked us here. I wondered how far behind human pursuit was.

I went to the bedroom and grabbed some clothes, but left the shoes. Not only because they didn't look as if they'd fit, but because I didn't really need them. My feet had thick soles thanks to the fact I only wore shoes when I had to, and I suspected Kade, as a horse-shifter, would be the same.

He was standing to the side of the window when I got to the kitchen, but looked around as I entered. "Nothing here."

I tossed some clothes at him, noting with amusement that his cock was still ready to play. Obviously, not a man easily deterred. "Did you ever see any of the creatures they had patrolling that place?"

He frowned. "I saw a hairy thing once. Looked like a warped bear."

"That's what's outside."

He put on the black pants and shirt I'd given him. They were tight—not indecently tight, but not that far from it. Rhoan was going to blow a fuse—especially if Kade remained in his current state.

"How many?" he asked.

"It seems to be by itself, but more will surely be on their way."

I put on the revolting floral shirt and black skirt I'd chosen for myself, but skipped the undies. Granny clothes I could handle, but granny knickers? No way.

I wrapped an old tie around my waist to keep the skirt up, then grabbed the phone and quickly dialed Jack's mobile number.

"Riley?" he said immediately. "Is there a problem?"

"Yeah. They've discovered us and we have to run. How far away are you?"

"Half an hour, at least."

Not close enough to help us, then. "Give us directions and a place to meet. We'll get there when we can."

Rhoan was swearing in the background.

"There's a town called Leura about nine kilometers away from Bullaburra." Jack hesitated, and I could hear my brother muttering instructions. "According to the com-unit, there's a cabin resort there called Blue Haven. Rhoan's booking us a cabin. We'll be there in twenty."

"We'll be there when we can."

I hung up and met Kade's intense gaze. "We have to leave."

"That thing will track us."

"Not if we stop it."

He raised an eyebrow. "You mean kill it?"

He didn't seem too fazed about it, but then, maybe horse-shifters had an entirely different set of sensibilities to wolves and other shifters. After all, the male of the breed collected and kept a herd. Maybe they saw killing as a necessary part of protecting that herd.

"I mean stop it. Any way we can."

He nodded. "There's twine in the drawer to your right. I'll get a knife, just in case it does come down to killing."

I got the rope and the rolling pin that happened to be in the same drawer, and he got the knife. The scrape of nail came again, this time near the kitchen window.

Kade moved to my side, and leaned close, his lips brushing my ear as he said, "How do you want to play this?"

"You hold it kinetically, and I'll bop it over the head and tie it up."

"Where?"

I pointed to the window. He nodded and moved away. I took up my position, and raised an eyebrow in question. He nodded again.

I said, "Hey," as loud as I could, and that's all it took. The window exploded inward, the deadly shards of glass flying through the air as a mass of hair and snarls leapt into the room. Kade froze it in midair, and I hit it across the head with the rolling pin, knocking it out. Then I grabbed the twine and tied all four legs together as well as its snout.

"Okay, you can let it—"

The rest of my words were cut off as a second mass of hair and teeth and claws leapt through the smashed window. It hit me chest-on, knocking me down and back. I slid across the glass-covered floor, hissing in pain as I thrust out my hands, grabbing the thing by the throat and barely keeping the snarling, snapping teeth away from my face.

As suddenly as it had hit, it was torn away. There was a crash, then chair parts flew. I scrambled to my feet, saw the flash of metal in Kade's hand a second before he buried the blade in the creature's side.

The creature made an odd coughing sort of sound, and was still. Kade swung around and came to me.

"You all right?"

He didn't wait for my reply, but turned me around and studied my back. Pain flared as he lifted the shirt and began to pluck shards of glass out of my back.

"We have to get moving," I said, twitching under his touch.

"Two more pieces to go." He plucked them out, then added, "I doubt whether we'll get out of here without being seen."

"Our only chance might be to run for the trees and edge our way around the town."

"Once we're a safe distance away from this house, how about we steal a car?"

I turned. "I thought you were a respectable builder?"

"Now, yes. As a youth?" He grinned, velvet eyes twinkling mischievously. "Let's just say that stallions tend to be wilder than most teenagers. I've done things that would make your hair curl." He caught several strands of my hair and tugged on them lightly. "Which would actually look quite pretty."

I smiled, rose up on my toes, and brushed a kiss across his lips. "Thank you."

His arm slipped around my waist, holding me carefully but close. "What for?"

His breath teased my lips, and had me trembling. "I'll explain when we have more time."

"Good." He kissed my nose then released me. "You might have to shift shape. Some of these cuts are fairly deep."

I did. "How come you're not fazed by me being a wolf?"

"Because it wasn't the wolf I first saw but a naked, luscious woman. Instinctive prejudices haven't a hope over raging lust."

My smile became a grin. "So how come you were trying to bite me when I first walked in?"

"I thought you might be another of the women they use to tease us into bloom before they milked us."

"What made you realize I wasn't?"

"The blood on your leg and side. And that punch you landed on my nose."

"That was a swat, not a punch."

"Then you must pack quite a punch." He raised a hand and brushed his fingers across my cheek.

"Perhaps." I stepped away, even though it was the last thing I wanted to do. "Let's get out of here."

"What about the mess?"

"The Directorate will send a cleanup crew. Our hosts will be none the wiser."

He followed me as far as the bedroom, then ducked inside, reappearing two minutes later with a wire coat hanger.

I raised an eyebrow. "Are there still cars out there without either central-locking or thumbprint locking?"

"Plenty of them, believe me."

I unlocked the door and walked out onto the small patio. Highlighted sharply against the stormy clouds, a solitary brown shape soared.

I motioned Kade to be still, watching the eagle until it wheeled out of sight. "Now."

We ran across the yard, leapt the small fence, and raced into the trees. The shadows soon enveloped us, and we slowed to a walk. Hurried movement would be more noticeable from above—and though Kade's red-brown skin and black clothing would make him difficult to spot, my red hair would stand out like a beacon if we got careless and hit sunlight.

There was no sound of pursuit, though it couldn't be

that far behind. Who knew how long those creatures had been out there, listening and waiting?

It took just over an hour to make our way around the outskirts of the small town. Eventually, we stopped between several gum trees. I wiped the sweat from my eyes with a slightly trembling hand. Two hours' sleep just wasn't enough.

There was a small parking lot on the other side of the road, with five cars sitting in the bays. There weren't any people to be seen. Hopefully, they'd all followed the path to the lookout point and wouldn't be back for a while.

I looked up at Kade. "You sure you want to take a car?"

"I can't see any other way of getting out of here quickly." He flicked sweat away from his forehead with a finger, then added, "Your hair is going to glow out in that sun. I'd offer to give you my shirt, but my skin is likely to draw as much attention as your hair."

I gave him a wry look. "That is such a poor excuse."

He grinned, not bothering to deny it. I pulled off my T-shirt. "You tie it back. I might not catch it all."

His gaze skated down my body and his grin grew. "Gotta love werewolves and their lack of inhibitions."

"That lack of inhibitions has landed me in court often enough already. Let's get this over with before a cop turns up and arrests me."

"Sweetheart, not even the holiest of men would be hurrying at this particular moment."

I rolled my eyes, and he chuckled softly. After covering my hair, he slid his hands around my waist, and pulled me back against his warm, hard body. As his big hands slid up to cover my breasts, he brushed a kiss across my shoulder. "When we are safe, I intend to love you senseless."

I tilted my head back against his shoulder, and his lips met mine. Our kiss was slow and tender and so very, very thorough. Neither of us were breathing very steadily by the time we'd finished.

"A vow I shall hold you to," I found the breath to say. I pulled away and twined his fingers through mine. "Now, shall we go car shopping?"

He tugged me out of the shadows. The breeze that played amongst the trees was warmer out in the open, and the road surface hot against my toes. We made our way casually across, walking along the strip of grass between the road and the car park until we came to an old blue Ford.

"And naturally, he picks the oldest, most battered of all five."

"This is what they call a classic—over fifty years old and worth a sheer fortune."

I frowned dubiously. "If it's that old, and this ratty, will it run?"

"It got here, didn't it?"

"Yeah, but maybe it's still here because it won't go any farther."

"Trust me, it'll go." He raised my fingers to his lips and kissed them before letting go. "Keep watch."

I crossed my arms, checked the skies for spies, then watched him untwine the coat hanger. After making the hook at the end tighter, he moved to the driver's door and wriggled the hook between the door and the frame. Within a minute or two there came a soft click.

Followed very closely by the rumble of an approaching car.

"Kade," I warned, and glanced over my shoulder. "A cop car. Wouldn't you know it."

"The way our luck has been running, I'm not surprised." He slipped the hanger under the car, then held out a hand, a roguish glint in his eyes. "Come here, wench."

"Planning to hide in plain sight, are we?"

"We retreat now and they'll think it suspicious."

Especially if they happened to notice I wasn't wearing a shirt. I leaned back against the door, and he pressed against me, his hands on either side of me, neatly corralling even as he hid my near nakedness.

I wrapped my arms loosely around his neck, felt the tension in his muscular shoulders. The hardness of his erection pressing against my groin. The wolf within stirred swiftly to life, and I just didn't have the strength or desire to restrain her.

I kissed his chin, and slid my hand between us. "Is the car slowing?"

"Yes." Amusement twitched his mouth. "You wouldn't dare."

Obviously, no one had ever told him it was a bad idea to dare a werewolf.

"How many cops?" I asked, sliding a hand down his back to grasp the back of his pants even as I undid his button and pulled down the zip.

"Two." He bent, groaning into my shoulder as I freed him. "Dammit, woman, they'll arrest us."

"Not if they don't see anything." I guided him past the

skirt, and into where it was warm and wet and ready. "Press closer."

He did, his body almost crushing mine, making it hard to breathe, and even harder not to respond to his closeness, to the hard and ready feel of him. Especially when he slid deep inside. Horse-shifters really did take after their animal counterparts when it came to the shape and size of their cock, and having him fill me so completely was a truly amazing sensation. Pleasure rippled through me, sharpened by the awareness of danger, the prospect of being caught.

He groaned, his lips brushing my shoulder. "They're almost on us."

"Then you had better not start making any suspicious moves," I said, even as I shifted onto my tippy-toes, sliding up and down his shaft a couple of times.

He was quivering, pulsing, with heat and desire. I raised my head, capturing his lips, kissing him as fiercely as I wanted to fuck him. This was no slow burn of desire. It was all about the heady high of risk-taking combined with combustible, unquenchable lust.

The cop car crawled past and kept on moving. I broke off the kiss.

"Now?" he asked, sweat glistening on his gloriously rich skin.

I didn't answer, delaying the moment, heightening the sense of danger, as the cop car slowly disappeared around the corner.

"Now, Kade. *Now*."

I'd barely spoken and he was there, ramming himself hard and deep. I groaned, and wrapped my legs around his hips, urging him deeper still, using the car to support my back as he thrust and thrust, until it felt as if the rigid heat of him was trying to spear right through my spine.

There was nothing gentle about this mating. The prospect of discovery meant it had to be fast and furious, and that's exactly what I wanted, exactly what I needed. Pleasure spiraled quickly and my climax hit, the convulsions stealing my breath and tearing a strangled sound from my throat. He came a heartbeat later, his body slamming into mine, the force of it rocking the car behind us.

When the tremors eased, he leaned his sweaty forehead against mine, his breathing harsh, velvet eyes alive with amusement and surprise.

"Good God, that was fantastic."

I grinned. "There's something to be said for lovemaking under the threat of discovery."

"There certainly is." He cupped my cheek with a heated palm, and brushed a kiss across my lips. "I'm so very glad I met you."

"Well, if you hadn't, you'd still be a frustrated old stallion stuck in a stable." I shifted my legs, and let him redress. "Shall we get—" I stopped, looking upward at the brown shape soaring high in the sky. "We're being watched."

He squinted up. "Could be just a bird. Not every winged creature is going to be theirs."

"Do you care to take that chance?"

"No. Get in."

He opened the driver's door, then leaned across the seat and opened the other one. While I climbed in, he did something to the ignition switch. The old car roared to life.

"Which way?" he asked, as he reversed out of the parking spot.

I pointed in the direction the cops had gone.

He raised his eyebrows, amusement crinkling the corners of his eyes. "Care for a secondary bout of danger, do you?"

"Wouldn't mind, but the truth is, that way lies help."

"Ah." He pulled out onto the highway, and the old car began to pick up some speed. He glanced in the rearview mirror, then at me. "So, what happens after we meet your boss and your pack-mate?"

"They'll want a debriefing."

He nodded.

"And they'll undoubtedly want to try and find the place again."

"Meaning we might have to lead them back there?"

I studied him for a minute. "I don't know about the 'we' part."

His brief look was hard, determined. It was totally different from anything I'd glimpsed of him so far, and was a quick reminder that I really did know nothing about this man. Not even if I could trust him.

"Sweetheart, those bastards stole months of my life. I'm not walking away from the investigation until I'm sure whoever's behind that place is made to pay."

"You may not have that choice."

His expression was grim. "No one can force me to do anything I don't want to."

"Jack, my boss, can. He's a vampire, and a strong telepath."

"It won't matter. Horse-shifters can't be mind-read—not by *any* race."

"Really?" I dropped my own shields and reached out telepathically. I hit a wall as solid as the one that protected my brother's mind. Surprise rippled through me. "How come?"

He shrugged. "It's similar to the mind-blindness often found in humans."

"So how can you be mind-blind, and yet have a psychic talent?"

"You tell me and we'll both know."

I considered him for a moment, then said, "This will be a Directorate investigation, and you're not Directorate personnel."

He shot me a look. "I thought you were just a paper pusher?"

"I am. Mostly."

"Meaning?"

"Meaning this is part of an ongoing investigation that I was forcibly placed upon." I hesitated, not wanting to tell him too much. "They kidnapped Rhoan a few months ago, and that got me involved."

"Then you'll understand when I say this is personal."

I did understand. I just didn't think Jack would. But then again, he'd let Quinn in, and he'd all but roped Liander in. He might surprise me again. After all, he *was* trying to build a new daytime unit—one that he wanted me to play a serious part in.

One that I had no intention of being hijacked into unless there was absolutely no other choice.

And *that* was looking more and more likely.

I rubbed a hand across my eyes and said, "Let's just concentrate on one problem at a time."

"Agreed. What hotel are we looking for?"

"A place called Blue Haven in Leura." I unwound the shirt and put it back on. "Let's hope we find the town before the owners of this car discover it's been nicked."

"Let's hope we find it before our hunters find us," he corrected grimly.

His words had me looking out the window, up at the skies. I couldn't see any soaring shapes, but that didn't mean they weren't there. Didn't mean we weren't being followed.

We drove on in silence. When we finally reached Leura, Kade slowed to a respectable speed and the old car stopped shaking. We drove along the pretty, tree-lined main street, and I couldn't help admiring all the quaint but beautiful buildings. It reminded me somewhat of a postcard, and made me regret meeting here. A place like this didn't deserve an encounter with the sort of darkness that was following us.

I frowned at the thought, and pushed it away. We drove on, eventually finding the cabin resort on the far side of town.

A black van with tinted windows was parked down the end. I pointed toward it, and Kade drove up and parked beside it. We'd barely stopped the engine when the door of the cabin in front of us thrust open and Rhoan spilled out, red hair gleaming like fire in the sunlight.

Grinning like an idiot, my vision blurred with tears, I somehow climbed out of the car and fell into my brother's arms.

"God," he said, his voice as hoarse as his hug was fierce. "I thought I'd lost you."

Tears crept down my cheeks. "I'm sorry."

He laughed softly. "Try it again, and I'm going to chain you up and never let you out of the apartment."

Kade came up behind us. I kissed Rhoan's cheek then pulled away. "Rhoan, meet Kade. I wouldn't have escaped if Kade hadn't helped me."

"A situation that was mutual," Kade said dryly, and offered Rhoan his hand. "Pleasure to meet you."

Rhoan gave me a look that said, "bitch," and shook Kade's hand. "Thank you for keeping her safe."

Kade laughed, a warm, rich sound. "Another situation that was entirely mutual. Your pack-mate is an amazing woman."

"Isn't she just." He threw an arm around my shoulder. "Let's get inside before any patrolling bugaboos spot us."

Rhoan motioned Kade forward, but his grip on my shoulder tightened a little, holding me back. "There's something I need to tell—"

I didn't hear the rest of his words. Didn't need to.

Because a second figure had moved into the doorway.

It wasn't Jack.

It was Quinn.

My heart did an odd little flip-flop, and for several seconds all I could do was stare. He hadn't changed any—though given it had only been a month or so since I'd last seen him, that was hardly surprising.

But oh, he looked good.

His body was athletic, lean but powerful. His burgundy sweater emphasized the width of his shoulders, while the tight fit of his jeans drew the eye to the long, strong length of his legs. His hair was night dark, longer now than it had been when I'd last seen him, and so thick, so lush. It was also unkempt, as if he'd thrust his hands through it many times. Those hands were currently in his pockets, and looked clenched. His skin was not the white of most vampires, but a soft, warm gold, simply because unlike most vampires, he could actually stand a lot of sunlight. His face...

I swallowed. He was beautiful, truly beautiful, in a way that was anything but effeminate.

His gaze touched mine, eyes obsidian stone, and his expression shuttered. Yet something passed between us, an awareness that made my heart stutter and caused goose bumps to tremble warmly across my skin. It was an awareness that had been present from the very first time we'd met, and it was stronger now than it had ever been.

Kade suddenly stopped, his gaze swinging from me to Quinn and back again. Understanding dawned in his velvet eyes, followed swiftly by bedevilment. He took a step back, and twined his fingers through mine.

His obvious intention was to provoke a reaction, and he certainly got it. But it wasn't anything dramatic, just an almost imperceptible tightening of expression.

In some ways, Quinn's reaction amused as much as it annoyed. The slight shift in expression told me *exactly* what he was thinking, and it was annoying to realize he was continuing to judge me by human standards. Which was crazy, because no one here was human in *any* way, shape, or form. But I couldn't help seeing the funny side of a vampire with over twelve hundred years of living under his belt getting ticked off by such an obviously fake challenge.

But it *was* an interesting reaction, no matter what emotion it evoked. It suggested that no matter how many statements he made about never getting involved with another werewolf, he wasn't entirely ready to walk away. I mean, if someone like Kade, someone who was just a bit of friendly fun, could draw a response from Mr. Emotionless-face himself, then no matter what Quinn said, part of him still wanted to be in my life.

And I wasn't entirely sure how I felt about that little revelation—if it was indeed true. I mean, I'd *tried*.

Maybe it was time for him to put in a little effort. Do a little chasing.

"It's nice to see you again, Quinn."

Surprise flickered through his dark eyes. Maybe he'd figured politeness would be beyond my capacity given all the brush-offs he'd accorded me over recent months.

"And it's nice to see you whole and in one piece." His voice was rich with the lilt of Ireland, and far sexier in life than it had been in my dreams. Just listening to it again made me want to sigh in pleasure. "We'd all feared the worst."

The comment warmed places deep inside. Which just proved that no matter what I'd said to Kade earlier about finally walking away from Quinn, there was a part of me that hungered for the relationship to continue. Still, he didn't deserve to get me easily. Not this time.

I raised an eyebrow. "Why were *you* worried about me?"

It was a somewhat snarky thing to say, but hey, he deserved at least that given all the rejections. And if that was *all* the attitude he caught, then he could count himself lucky.

"Guys, can we take this mushy little meet and greet inside?" Rhoan said, voice dry. "Just in case there's spies in the air?"

Quinn glanced at Rhoan, then turned around and disappeared inside. I disentangled my fingers from Kade's and looked at my brother. "Gee, thanks for the advance warning."

Rhoan grimaced. "I *did* try. But even if I had warned you, would it have made the shock of seeing him again any easier?"

No, and he knew it.

"Play the game," Kade said softly. "Trust me. It'll work."

I looked at him, amusement twitching my lips. "And *that* suggestion isn't more than a little self-serving now, is it?"

He held up his hands, merriment dancing in his dark eyes. "Hey, I am a randy old stallion who has been locked up for months, remember."

"And has the randy old stallion forgotten we've got bad guys to round up?"

"No. But there's no rule saying you can't combine business with pleasure."

"People," Rhoan said. "We really need to move this inside."

I leaned sideways, and dropped a kiss on my brother's cheek. "If you'd stop gripping my arm so tight, I'd be able to move."

He squeezed a final time then released me. We walked inside. The cabin was small and, with all of us in here, crowded. Jack was sitting at the table down at the far end, the bright glow of the com-screen in front of him casting a bluish light across his weatherworn features and bald head. As bosses went, he was so damn easygoing it was often hard to remember that not only was he the Vice President in charge of the whole guardian division—one of the four main departments in the Directorate—but he was also one of the most powerful vampires I knew.

The other just happened to be Quinn. He'd parked his butt in a nearby armchair, cross-legged and elegant. The only other seats were the two sofas near the TV. Kade and I took one, Rhoan the other.

Jack glanced up, and gave me a toothy grin. "Good to see you alive and well, darlin'."

I smiled. "It's good to be alive and well. Jack, Quinn, this is Kade."

"I know who Kade is," Jack said. "I have his files."

Kade raised his eyebrows. "Really?"

Amusement touched Jack's green eyes. "There's no place the Directorate can't go if we so desire."

"Well, that's a little tidbit kept well away from the general population, isn't it?"

"And with good reason. Why were you in that place?"

"He's one of the shifters they were milking," I said, and added, just a touch impatiently, "I don't suppose you want to share Kade's background with the rest of us?"

"Right now? No. There's more important matters to discuss." Jack's gaze narrowed a little. "What do you mean by 'one of'?"

Kade shrugged. "There were nine of us in there.

I'm not sure what happened to the others after our breakout."

"And they were collecting specimens from you all?"

"Yes."

Jack grunted and glanced at me. "And were they collecting samples from you?"

I shrugged. "It's all very hazy at the moment. All I can really remember is waking up in a small lane beside a dead man."

"The lack of memory coming from the drugs or the accident?"

I shrugged again.

"Probably the accident," Rhoan commented, looking at me critically. "The scar on her head looks as if the wound might have been bad enough to cause memory loss."

"What scar?"

My confusion was evident in my voice. I hadn't noticed a scar when I'd showered in the old house, but then, I'd been in a hurry to get to the kitchen and find some coffee. And I certainly wasn't prone to spending hours in front of a mirror. A quick glance was all that was usually needed unless I was going somewhere special and had to apply makeup.

Kade ran a finger from my temple to the back of my head and said, "That scar, sweetheart."

I frowned. "Is it nasty?" God, the last thing I needed was another scar to worry about. I had enough as it was, thanks to childhood mishaps.

"Your hair covers it, no probs."

"So this place is in a nearby town?" Jack said, in a

voice that suggested little tolerance for slight deviances from the topic at hand.

I grinned, more than a little used to his impatience. "This place *is* a town. And a testing ground. They have mock buildings as well as concrete ones."

"Can you lead us back there?" he asked.

"I can," Kade said, before I could. "Riley was unconscious for some of the journey."

Which was so totally fudging the truth. Jack glanced at me, eyebrow raised imperceptibly. He knew the lie, but for whatever reason, wasn't going to argue it. Maybe he figured he needed a horse-shifter in his new task force. He glanced at the com-screen, said, "Area map," then looked at Kade. "You want to give us a rough location? We'll get some of our people to do a flyover."

Kade strode over and pointed at an area on the screen. "I don't think we can afford to wait for reinforcements. They'd have to realize our escape will put their position in jeopardy. I wouldn't mind betting they're pulling out even as we speak."

Jack glanced up at Kade, then at me. And I saw the question in his eyes, even though the words he said next were completely different.

"Do you think five of us is enough muscle to tackle that place?"

"No," Kade said. "But if you want to catch any of these bastards, then we have to take the risk."

And it *was* a risk. A huge risk, and everyone in the room knew that, including me. But it was one Jack was contemplating. *Had* to contemplate, if we were to have any hope of finally getting a proper lead on these maniacs.

I continued to meet his gaze, and mulled over the implications of his unasked question. Of giving him what he wanted—me on this raid, taking yet another step on the road to becoming a guardian—juxtaposed against the promise I'd made on the knoll outside Genoveve. A promise to see this through, to see it finished.

"Riley's not a guardian," Rhoan said. And though he didn't add it, the word "yet" seemed to hang in the air as he continued. "You can't expect to include her on a raid like this. It's too dangerous."

Jack glanced his way briefly. "She has senses and reflexes as sharp as yours. That alone gives her an advantage over most other races."

"A good olfactory sense and sharp reflexes aren't going to mean squat if she gets attacked again."

"I'm not stupid enough to send her in alone."

And still he continued to look at me, waiting for my answer. An answer he knew I had no choice but to give, because I wanted to see this finished as much as he did. After all, these bastards were continually coming after *me,* not him. That alone would have been reason enough to do this.

Even if it was one more step away from freedom, and the life I'd always dreamed of having.

"I'm in," I said, even as my stomach squirmed at the thought of going back to that place. "And I agree with Kade—we had better hurry."

A pleased smile touched the corners of Jack's mouth, but all he said was, "Rhoan, get Riley kitted out, then take her into the other room to catch some rest. Kade, you can stay here and give me an idea of the layout." He glanced at his watch. "We'll move at five—"

"But that's still two hours away," Kade interrupted. "We need to move ASAP."

"Unfortunately, we're restricted by the fact I'm a vampire. Some daylight I can stand, but not a whole lot."

Kade muttered something under his breath, then nodded. Rhoan cast a somewhat dark look Jack's way, then motioned me to follow him.

My gaze went to Quinn. His face was still very expressionless, and yet I had some sense of what he was feeling. Whether that was due to the link we'd formed between us—a link that was closed, and yet not—or whether it was simply wishful thinking, I have no idea. But Quinn was no happier than Rhoan about my inclusion on this raid.

Well, tough. He'd lost any right to comment on the direction of my life when he'd turned his back on me that final time.

I followed Rhoan out the door and over to the black van. Overhead, the afternoon sky was clear and blue, and free of any soaring shapes. But the day was unnaturally still, free of the busy chatter of bird life usually found in the thick bush that surrounded the hotel. My gaze skimmed the trees circling the cabins, a prickle of unease running across my skin.

"Do you hear that?" I said, as Rhoan pulled open the van's side door.

"Hear what?" he said, looking at me.

"Exactly what I mean. It's unnaturally quiet."

"We are in the mountains, not the city." Even so, he had a look around and his gaze narrowed a little. "Maybe you'd better get inside while I look about."

"Given the things that have been tracking Kade and me, I think we're better off sticking together."

"Riley—"

"Don't 'Riley' me. You haven't seen the orsini. I have. Trust me, you do not want to come upon those beasties by yourself."

"What the hell are orsini?" He reached inside the van and handed me several small laser guns and a knife. My "kit," presumably.

"Weird-looking bearlike creatures with nasty claws and big teeth."

"Ah. Well, if you survived them, I think I might be able to."

"They wanted me alive, Rhoan." Or at least they had, before I'd actually managed to escape the main compound. "It's probably the only reason the orsini didn't actually kill me when I first escaped the cage."

Though their attempts at recapture, if that's what they'd been, had felt bloody deadly.

"And you think those things are the reason for the sudden silence?"

"No. But it just doesn't feel right."

He strapped on his weapons, and slung a laser rifle over his shoulder. "Then let's go a-hunting."

I hesitated, ever so briefly. Rhoan smiled grimly. "Are you sure you're ready to do this?"

He didn't mean hunting orsini or whatever the hell else was out there. I looked down and began strapping on the weapons. "I have no choice."

"There's always a choice, no matter what the situation."

I snorted softly. "Like I had the choice of getting the

unapproved fertility treatment? Like I have the choice of how it's going to affect me? Like I have a choice of becoming a guardian if it does affect me?"

"That's different."

"No, it's not." I finished strapping on the knife and one of the lasers. The second laser was a small palm model, and that I held. I had to admit, the press of cold metal against my skin felt oddly comforting. I straightened and met my brother's gaze. "I have to go back to that place and uncover what they were doing. For my own piece of mind, if nothing else."

His gaze searched mine, then he sighed softly. "You are such a stubborn bitch."

"Learned from the best," I said, with a smile.

He shook his head, then closed the van door and padded quietly over to the trees at the end of the cabin. I followed at his back, listening to the wind, to the sounds underneath it—or rather, the lack thereof—as I scanned the trees and the dappled shadows for any sound or sight of the orsini.

Nothing.

No sound, no movement, no misshapen bear things or any other creature, nasty or not. The bush was a strange and silent place, and the sensation that something was wrong continued to scratch at my nerves.

We circled right around the property and all its building, and came to a stop near our starting point. "You'd better go get some rest."

"Rhoan—"

"Riley, you look dead on your feet. Just let me do what I'm paid to do, without arguing for a change."

I blew out a breath, then nodded. Truth was, I *did* need to sleep, though I very much doubted I'd be able to when in two hours' time I'd be heading back to a place that had snatched eight days of my life away. But that wasn't the reason I couldn't force my feet toward the cabin. It was the silence. The creeping sensation that something was near.

"Why do you think Kade is being allowed on this mission?" I asked instead, my gaze on the nearby trees.

"Because Jack knows his history and has every confidence he can handle it." Rhoan shrugged. "And we need the extra manpower."

"So you haven't seen his file?"

"No. And no, I'm not going to steal it for you. If you want to uncover his history, ask the man."

"I did. He said he was a builder."

"The horse-shifter is as much a builder as I am straight." Amusement twinkled in his gray eyes. "Now, stop delaying. Get inside and rest."

I scanned the trees a final time, finding no hint of danger or anything out of place. There was nothing around, nothing to explain the apprehension crawling across my skin.

It was probably just the fear of returning to the testing grounds—or whatever the hell that place was—that was making me so jumpy. After another hesitation, I turned and headed for the room.

I opened the door of the second cabin and stepped inside. The afternoon light swept in behind me, breaking some of the shadows holding the cabin's interior captive and highlighting the big old bed. From the other room came the sound of voices—Quinn's lilting tones and Kade's deeper resonance. Nice sounds to go to sleep by.

I closed the door and walked over to the bed, stripping off weapons and clothes as I did so.

It wasn't until I tugged back the bed covers and began to climb inside that I realized I wasn't alone in the room.

Chapter 4

The moment I paused, the shadows attacked.

Only it wasn't shadows but a creature—as black as night, as invisible as a vampire, and just as fast.

Luckily, so was I.

I rolled off the bed and twisted around, lashing out with a bare foot. The blow connected with solid darkness and the creature grunted, but didn't waver. It flowed over the bed and leapt at me, a flash of deeper black that slashed with wicked-looking barbed claws.

I ducked the blow then dove sideways, over the bed, grabbing at the weapons lying casually on the bedside table. My fingers scraped across metal, sending the lasers flying even as I grasped the knife.

"Rhoan!"

My shout rang across the silence. The creature hissed, a hushed sound that nevertheless irritated my ears. It came at me, a blur of arms and legs and claws. I backed away fast, ducking and weaving and slashing as hard as I could with the knife. One blow hit flesh, slicing deep and hard, until the shock of slicing through bone reverberated up my arm. There was a plop, followed by a gush of stinking blood, then the door was flung open and the room flooded by sunlight, revealing the creature to be humanoid in shape but not proportion.

"Drop," Rhoan said.

I did, hitting the carpet hard. My breath whooshed out as darkness ran past me, chased by a thin beam of red. Glass shattered and footsteps retreated. Rhoan ran past.

I scrambled to my feet and ran after my brother. He shifted shape mid-stride and leapt through the broken window in wolf form. I remained in human form and followed, hitting the glass-covered ground beyond and cutting my back as I rolled to my feet and ran on.

The shadowy creature flicked through the trees, fast and elusive. The still air carried no scent—if it had one at all, it was being smothered by the sharp aroma of eucalyptus and earth.

But it was bleeding, and it was the blood trail that we followed.

We ran on through the trees, dodging and leaping rocks and brush and ferns and logs. Then the air grew suddenly sharper, colder, and I looked ahead. The trees ended abruptly, leaving nothing but sky. I dove forward, grabbing Rhoan by the haunches, dragging him to a halt.

He snarled and snapped at me, his teeth grazing my skin but not actually hurting. I slapped his nose. "There's a cliff ahead, idiot."

He twisted around, looking ahead, then gave a doggy sniff and rolled out of my grip, shifting shape before walking forward. I stood but didn't follow. Cliff edges and I were not compatible items.

"There's a splattered black shape at the bottom of the canyon," Rhoan said, peering over the edge at an angle that had my nerves twitching.

"It jumped rather than be caught," I said, amazed. "Why would it do that?"

"'It' being the operative term," Rhoan said grimly. "And it either jumped because it didn't see the cliff in time, or because it thought death was better than capture."

"It'd have to be the first option, wouldn't it?"

He shrugged. "Who knows. One thing is certain, though. I've never seen anything like that before."

"No. But I very much doubt it was something nature made." I shivered and rubbed my arms.

He looked at me. "You okay?"

I nodded. "I sensed it just before it attacked, and was able to keep out of its way."

He glanced down at the body one more time, then stepped back and turned me around. "Let's get you back inside before you freeze to death."

We walked back to the cabin. Quinn was squatting down and examining the ground outside the window, but looked up as we arrived.

His gaze skimmed my nakedness, and the sweet taste of lust briefly stirred the air. But all he said, in a voice as cool as the air, was, "These footprints don't belong to any creature I've ever seen before."

Rhoan squatted beside him and ran a finger over the prints. "Claws," he said, looking up at me. "Just like its fingers."

I nodded. "As I said, I don't think it was nature-made."

"I think you're right." He paused, his gaze skirting the silent trees. "Why don't you go get some sleep? I'll keep watch for any more of these beasties."

He hadn't seen or sensed the first one, and I doubted he'd see or sense any follow-ups. Which begged the question: Why? I might not have sensed the creature until it was almost too late, but I *had* felt the sense of wrongness. So why hadn't my twin?

I didn't know. And part of me didn't *want* to know, because I had a vague suspicion it might just stem back to the drugs Talon and Co. had been feeding me.

But at least the creeping sense of wrongness no longer haunted the day. Maybe we'd be free from attack for a while. "I think I'll grab a shower first. I doubt I'll be able to sleep right now."

He nodded. I made my way back inside the cabin. Thankfully, someone had removed the severed arm, and made some attempt to clean up the blood. I wasted some time checking every little corner, then finally relaxed and headed for the bathroom.

But despite my protests, I did sleep, and sleep well.

Quinn was standing near the broken window when I woke, his hands clasped casually behind his back and body relaxed, but I could taste his tension. It stung the air, as sharp as the sudden spike in my pulse rate.

"There are fresh clothes at the end of the bed." His

voice was soft, neutral. "Rhoan thought you might appreciate something warmer. There's no shoes, however. All our feet are bigger than yours."

"I don't need shoes." I crossed my arms and stared at his back, willing him to turn around and face me. "Why are you here?"

"Here in this room, or here in general?"

"Both."

"Ah." He paused a moment. "I'm here in this room as a second defense, in case another of those creatures got past Rhoan."

"I can protect myself."

"Not when you're fast asleep." He glanced briefly over his shoulder, his dark gaze skating down my blanket-covered body before looking away. "You didn't even twitch when I came in."

Possibly because I knew his scent, and felt safe in his presence, no matter how annoying he could be at times. "So why are you here on this rescue mission?"

His shrug was little more than a slight hitch of one shoulder, and yet somehow so elegant. Muscles played enticingly under the burgundy sweater, and I had to resist the temptation to reacquaint my fingers with all that lean power.

"Because someone has tried to kill me a number of times, and I'm getting a little annoyed about it."

"That doesn't exactly explain why you're here."

"My would-be assassins were not of natural origins. I brought the bodies down to Melbourne for the Directorate to examine."

"After your own labs checked them out, of course."

"Of course."

"So, you brought the bodies down. How does that connect with you being here?"

"You went missing about the same time I arrived in Melbourne. I stayed to help with the search."

"Thank you."

He shrugged. "We are friends who have been lovers. It was the least I could do."

"Last time I checked, the definition of a friend didn't include ignoring said friend and telling them to go away."

"You know why I did that."

"Yeah, because you couldn't cope with me being a werewolf." I flung off the covers and sat up. "Would you at least have the decency to turn around and look at me when you're talking?"

"If you would have the decency to dress."

"Why? As you said, we've been lovers. You know my body intimately."

"We are not lovers now, and I do not appreciate you flaunting yourself."

I snorted softly and reached for the clothes sitting on the end of the bed. "That is *so* old-fashioned."

"I *am* old-fashioned."

Yeah, and it was one of the problems that would have lain between us if we'd been in any sort of relationship. I shook my head and got dressed. The jeans were several inches too long, but otherwise a snug fit, particularly around the butt. No surprise there, because my butt was bigger than my brother's—an injustice of nature, I think. His dark green sweater was tight, the soft wool stretched to the limits around my breasts, providing little peekaboo holes of skin. If the oncoming night hadn't promised to be so cold, I would have gone without it.

"Okay, it's safe to turn around now."

My voice was tart, but it didn't seem to have any effect. His expression was cool, almost remote. But his gaze drifted down, a slow caress that was all-consuming. Heat prickled across my skin, and my nipples hardened, stretching the poor wool even further. The deep-down ache ignited, burning through me like a tidal wave.

I crossed my arms and tried to ignore desire. There was too much to sort out with this vampire to go madly jumping his bones, no matter how enticing a thought that was. Not the least being what he wanted now, when he'd stated so clearly in the recent past that he wanted nothing else to do with me. "So, was bringing the dead bodies down to the Directorate the only reason you came to Melbourne?"

"You know it's not."

"What I know," I said, voice tart, "is that you told me to leave you alone."

"I did *not* say that."

I shrugged. "Words to that effect, then. What do you want, Quinn?"

"I think we need to talk."

"I spent a whole lot of time after Genoveve trying to talk to you. I'm done with talking."

"Then there are things I need to say. Things you need to hear."

"Unless it's an 'I'm sorry for my horrible behavior, please forgive me,' I'm not sure you *could* say anything I actually want to hear."

The door opened at that moment and Rhoan walked in. "Quinn, Jack wants to see you for a moment."

Quinn looked at me, his dark gaze promising the conversation was far from over. Then he turned and walked out.

I took a deep breath and blew it out slowly. Damn the man. Just as I was starting to get over the fact that he'd walked away from all the delicious possibilities that lay unexplored between us, he walks back into my life and raises the hope that maybe, just maybe, he'd changed his mind. I had to wonder just what I'd done to piss fate off so severely, because she sure seemed intent on throwing curveballs my way lately.

I rubbed a hand across still tired eyes, then grabbed the weapons I'd scattered earlier, strapping them on quickly before walking over to the window. Dusk was settling in, thick and stormy looking.

"Riley?" Concern edged Rhoan's voice.

"What?"

"You okay?"

"Just dandy, bro."

He walked across the room and wrapped his arms under my breasts, pulling me back against him. "Quinn?"

Like *that* was hard to guess. I rested the back of my head against his shoulder. "I still want him, Rhoan. Even though he hates what I am, even though I know a relationship between us could never be anything permanent, I want him. I thought I was over him, but I'm not."

"Because he ended it, not you."

Probably. I mean, being the finisher was always the easier option. "Thing is, I think that's why he's back. I think he may have changed his mind."

He was silent for a moment, then said, "Want a brotherly bit of advice?"

I smiled slightly. "I'm going to get it whether I want it or not."

"Ain't that a fact." Amusement touched his warm tones. "Horse boy has got one hell of a hard-on for you. Enjoy that; enjoy him. Don't chase Quinn any more than you already have."

"Kade suggested much the same thing."

"He's a stallion. They're randy old bastards who will use any excuse to get into a woman's pants."

Amusement ran through me. In many respects, horse-shifters were no different from men the world over. No matter what the race, they all wanted to get their end in. Even standoffish vampires. "If I just sit back and enjoy myself, Quinn will not come running."

"And that could be a good thing."

"Why? What's wrong with a little bit of fooling around?"

"Because it may start off as a little fooling around, but it probably won't end there. And what happens later? What about kids? You want them, and while you may or may not be able to physically carry them, there are other options you can explore. The one clear certainty is that he can never impregnate you. *Never*. What lies between you may be strong, but in the end, is it right?"

"What do you mean by 'right'?"

Yet even as I asked the question, I knew. Wolves were born with the need to reproduce, and only the desire to find the right mate stopped the world from being over-run. Something governments obviously didn't understand, because they forced the fertility controls on us all.

I wanted children. I'd dreamed of having a family of my own most of my life. Whatever else there might be between Quinn and me, there could never be life.

"Getting into any sort of relationship with Quinn is dangerous because we both know it won't stop at just a bit of fun, and *that* might just destroy the two of you."

He was right. I might want to explore what was going on with Quinn, but perhaps it was better for everyone if I just let sleeping vampires lie.

I squinted up at my brother. "Two months ago you were advising me not to give up on him. Now you're telling me to be careful, that I haven't the right of anything long-term. Why?"

"When I gave you that advice, neither of us was aware that our vampire genes were finally asserting themselves. It's too late for me to have children, but it may not be for you." He reached out, carefully brushing the hair from my cheek. "You always were slower to develop than me."

I smiled, as he'd intended, but it didn't ease the chill running rampant across my skin, or the churning in my stomach. And the cause wasn't only the fact that I may be becoming irreparably infertile. It was wondering what other changes my vampire genes might be making.

"Talon was trying to get me pregnant for a year. That suggests it might already be too late."

Rhoan snorted. "Talon is sterile."

"What?" I spun around to face him.

He nodded. "Came out during the tests." He leaned forward and kissed my forehead. "Think of Quinn as a piece of chocolate. Rich and fulfilling, and in your case, totally addictive. And like chocolate, you're better off resisting it completely, because it's just not good for you."

I gave him a weak smile. "Quinn won't give me spots like chocolate does."

"Maybe not all over your face." He smiled and slid his fingers down to mine, then tugged me toward the door. "But remember, he does tend to leave nasty little spots all over your neck."

I snorted softly. I guess that *was* true. Only trouble was, a lot of fun was had getting those particular neck spots.

Jack didn't bother looking up as we entered the other cabin through the interconnecting door. "I ran a check on that arm you severed. There's no match in the database for a creature of that type."

"Not surprising."

"No." He slammed the lid of the com-unit closed. "Especially given we're dealing with genetic engineering. Did you see any of this place at all? Are you able to back up the map Kade gave us?"

"Having a casual stroll around the place wasn't exactly a priority when I woke naked in the alley." I paused. "I really only saw a couple of streets and the stable. Kade was in there longer."

He'd also said that he'd never left the stable. It'd be hard to give Jack a map if that were actually true, so it was a safe bet that it wasn't. But why lie to me about it?

Or was it simply a matter of not knowing at the time whether he could actually trust me or not?

"I want a report of everything you remember once this raid is over," Jack said, and picked up the com-unit. "Let's go."

We headed out the door. Quinn and Kade were already in the van, Quinn in the driver's seat, and Kade

checking weapons as he sat on the floor at the rear of
the van.

He looked damn proficient in handling and checking guns. More so than any "ordinary" builder should be,
anyway. Though maybe he was a builder who went
game hunting on the weekends.

And maybe I'd grow wings and fly.

Which meant his "profession" was probably another
lie. Still, I couldn't exactly get worked up over it—not
when I could understand why he might have lied. It was
just irritating that I'd trusted *him* more than I probably
should have. Given all that had happened to me over the
last few months, you'd think I'd have known better.

I climbed into the van and sat on the floor beside him.
Between the weapons, the equipment, and the five of us,
it was rather cramped.

Rhoan sat up front with Quinn. Jack slammed the
side door shut, then perched in front of the com-screens,
undoubtedly making last-minute orders and marshalling
the Directorate's forces. And though they wouldn't get
there until after we'd gone in, it was comforting to know
backup wasn't far away.

As the van moved off, Kade threw an arm around my
shoulders and gave me a hug. It wasn't sexual in any way,
just a comforting touch from someone who knew I
needed it. I smiled and leaned into him.

The click of the keyboard and the hum of road noise
were the only sounds to be heard. With every mile we
drew closer to that place, and my stomach began to
churn with renewed vigor. Obviously, whatever had
gone on in there was pretty damn bad.

I reached for a nearby water bottle, but the drink did little to ease the dryness in my throat.

Energy caressed my mind, a tingling caress of warmth that stirred the fibers of my soul, intimate in a way that went beyond touch, beyond sex. Quinn, pushing lightly at my shields, wanting to talk to me, wanting me to open the psi-door we'd developed as a means of communication. The link between us went deeper than normal telepathic contact, and was not affected by the presence of psi-deadeners. It was a link that had saved our lives the day we'd walked into Talon's lair to take him out.

I stared toward the front of the van, but there was little more than shadows to be seen. Had he felt my growing fear? Or was this merely an attempt to finish the conversation we'd started back in the motel room?

Whatever the reason, I refused to open that door. Rhoan was right. In this one case, I couldn't have my cake and eat it too. Until I knew for sure whether or not I was fertile, I dare not get involved in *any* way with Quinn. It wouldn't be fair to either of us.

So I ignored his mental knocking. He eventually gave up and concentrated on driving again. The van rolled on through the darkness, the silence stretching my nerves to breaking point.

When we finally stopped, Kade moved his arm from my shoulder and gave me a cheerful sort of smile. "It's almost over."

I didn't answer. Couldn't answer.

Because it wasn't over. Not by a long shot.

Jack rose, the bright light of the com-screen making his pale skin gleam in the darkness. "Kade, Rhoan, and I will be going in via the front entrance. Riley, you and

Quinn are heading around to secure the back. Be careful in there, and stay close to Quinn."

Thanks, but that wasn't exactly safe right now, I wanted to say, but my tongue seemed glued to the roof of my mouth.

Jack and Kade got out and slammed the door shut. Rhoan gave me a brief thumbs-up, then disappeared into the night.

Quinn's gaze touched mine through the rearview mirror. "The seat up here is free is you want to be more comfortable."

"Thanks, but no. I'd rather not see where we are going right now."

He shrugged and drove on. Ten minutes later, we stopped again, this time deep in the trees off the side of the road. I opened the side door and climbed out.

The night was still and cold, the sky cloudy through the canopy of trees. Cicadas sung in the distance, and somewhere close to my right, a stream bubbled. It would almost have been tranquil if not for the harsh sound of my breathing. I needed to get control of my nerves. If there was something out there, keeping an eye on approaching trails, I'd give the game up a mile out.

Quinn came around the van, a shadow in black that merged with the night. "We've got twenty minutes to get up the mountain."

"What?"

"Afraid so." His gaze swept down me. "You ready?"

No, I wanted to say. Never. But I forced a nod and quietly followed as he led the way across the twig-strewn ground.

Twenty minutes isn't a whole lot of time to climb a

damn mountain, so we went up it fast. Thankfully, there were no cliff edges or long drops to make my stomach go haywire, but by the time we'd reached the plateau that held the compound, my legs were jelly and my lungs burned. While I might claim to be reasonably fit, this mountain sure as hell made a mockery of it. I was really, *really* going to have to make an attempt to get to the gym more often.

When we finally reached the clearing that held the compound, my whole body was a mess of twitching, aching muscles. I stopped beside a big old gum tree, using its girth to hide behind as I desperately dragged air into my system. Quinn stopped behind me, wafting the rich scent of sandalwood my way. *His* breathing was even. He might be over a thousand years old, but he was a damn sight fitter than me.

"It's empty," he said softly.

I lifted my gaze. Beyond the expanse of empty pasture stood the wire of the compound's fence. No lights shone in the darkness beyond that fence. The shadowy shapes of the buildings seemed to hold no life or movement in or around them. Not even under infrared. Everything was still. Eerily so.

Even so, I had to check. Just because *I* wasn't seeing it didn't mean it wasn't there. And Quinn could sense the thud of life, whereas I could not. "Completely empty? As in, no life at all, human, nonhuman, or otherwise?"

His gaze met mine, dark eyes seeming to gleam in the night. "Nothing at all."

"*No* one's there? At all?"

"From where we stand, I wouldn't be able to sense

Rhoan and the others. It's too far. But it would appear that the complex has been evacuated."

"Why would they do that? From what I saw of the place, it was huge. Why suddenly abandon it?"

"I would hazard a guess that you were the cause."

I raised an eyebrow. "Because I'd escaped?"

He nodded. "They obviously know who you are. They would know you are connected to the Directorate, even if only at an assistant level. Given what happened to the Genoveve research facility, given your part in it, they would have had an evacuation plan in place."

"How would they know my part in that?"

"Talon's mind was partially burned away, remember. Whoever did that would have done a thorough search of all his memory and thought centers first, just to check what had been happening." He paused. "At least, that is what I would have done."

A shiver ran down my spine. I didn't want to contemplate the sort of telepathic strength it took to completely burn away someone's thoughts and memories. I certainly didn't want to contemplate the fact that *this* vampire could do it as easily as he breathed.

"If this place was abandoned, and no clues left behind, it might take us ages to pick up the trail again." And I had a bad feeling I couldn't afford that.

"If they left in a hurry, there's a chance they left information behind." He glanced at his watch. "We have five minutes before we have to go in."

"Then I'm using them to rest."

I sank down on a nearby log. Quinn sat beside me, close enough that I could feel the warmth of him, but not quite close enough that we touched.

I resisted the urge to move—either closer, so that we *did* touch, or farther away, so that his closeness didn't seem to infuse my soul with heat—and kept my gaze on the fence line rather than the impressive body sitting so very near. "I very much doubt they'd have left that place unguarded. Even if we can't sense anything from here."

"Possibly."

He wasn't even looking at me, yet awareness flowed between us, as strong as it had ever been. Part of me wanted to bathe in it, to lose myself deep in its warmth and never surface.

Crazy, that's what I was.

Or was it simply a matter of wanting something I knew I shouldn't have? Like the chocolate Rhoan used to hide from me when I was a pimply teenager? It was there. I knew it was there, and I wanted it, even if I knew it wasn't good for me.

I crossed my arms, as if to ward off a chill. But the cold night air never truly had a chance to get close, chased away by the heat of Quinn's nearness.

"So, what are we going to chat about while we wait out our five minutes?"

It was an invitation to chat on a more personal level, and one I wasn't entirely sure he deserved. Still, if he was going to be involved in this investigation for any length of time, then I guess we did have to start talking.

"How about we discuss mistakes?"

"Depends on whose mistakes we're going to discuss."

"I think we should start with mine." His gaze caught and held mine, his eyes dark pools I could so easily drown in. "That's what my refusal to see you again was. A mistake."

Oh, great. Like I needed *that* statement when I was torn between the desire to explore what lay between us and the realization that it would be wrong to go there, simply because there could never be anything truly lasting. I didn't want to end up being yet another werewolf who had hurt him.

"And what has brought about this sudden change of heart?" My voice was even, which surprised the hell out of me. Recent revelations aside, he'd still basically dumped me and, at the very least, deserved to have some annoyance flung his way.

"Lots of things—"

"Like what?" I interrupted. "Are you perhaps finding sex a little hard to get after destroying your fiancée's life?"

It was an extremely catty comment. The annoyance mightn't be showing in my voice, but it was sitting there regardless.

His gaze hardened. "You know why I did that."

"Yeah. She pissed you off. Well, buddy boy, you've succeeded in pissing *me* off, and now you have to live with the consequences."

He studied me for a moment, then looked away, his face expressionless but the air vibrating with barely contained annoyance. Part of me couldn't help but be pleased with that. Hey, I *was* a bitch after all.

"I refuse to believe that you can walk away so easily."

"Why not? I'm a wolf, aren't I? We flit from one partner to another, without thought or morals."

Something flickered in his eyes. Recognition of a point, perhaps. "You're not like that."

"Maybe I am, maybe I'm not." I studied him for a moment. "I'm a wolf born and raised, Quinn. My morals and ways are never going to be compatible with yours."

"That doesn't mean we can't meet somewhere in the middle."

Yes, it did. Because he was my chocolate—and one bite was never going to be enough. But he was also a vampire, and could never provide the one thing I truly hungered for.

Damn it all, when did a simple matter like sex get so damn complicated? I rubbed a hand across my eyes. "Look, we need to discuss this more, but I don't think this is the right place. Let's just get inside and find the others."

He rose and offered me a hand. I hesitated, not wanting to risk touching him, yet knowing I'd look foolish if I didn't accept his help. Knowing also that *that* was the precise reason he was offering his hand. It was a dare, of sorts.

And I was never one to back down from a dare. I placed my hand in his, and something akin to electricity surged between us. His gaze jumped to mine, leaving me drowning in those lusciously dark depths. His fingers were so warm, so gentle yet strong as he pulled me upright. And suddenly I was reliving the moments when those clever, skillful hands were on my body, teasing and caressing and pleasuring. Lust shimmered, burning the air between us, as if, just for a heartbeat, those memories hung between us.

He smiled slowly, intimately. My already erratic pulse tripped into overdrive, and air became a scarce commodity. It was the sort of smile that might be shared by two lovers after a night of incredible sex. And we'd shared that, more than once.

His gaze burned mine for several more wild heart-beats, then rolled languidly down my body, melting where it rested, however briefly. Ice would have lique-fied under such a look, and no one could ever accuse me of being ice. Pressure exploded low down, fanning through the rest of me in stormy waves. The air was so thick and hot and needy I could barely even breathe.

One step. That's all it would take to be in his arms, kissing those delicious lips, feeling his lean body on mine. In mine.

I clenched my fists, digging my nails into my palms, using the pain to battle desire. "I won't make love to you just because you've decided you can bear to fuck a were-wolf on a regular basis."

Again, something glimmered in his eyes. "Why not? You once told me great sex was a good place to start a re-lationship."

And it was. Normally. "Things have changed since then. I've had a chance to think."

"The 'then' was only a few months ago."

I stepped back and crossed my arms. I'd obviously pissed off fate right-royally, and this was her way of get-ting back at me.

"Not here, not now, Quinn," I said, and forced my feet past him. "Let's get to the compound."

I switched to infrared, scanning the clearing and the buildings immediately behind the fence line. Still no sign of life. No whisper of movement.

We reached the fence. Quinn held out a hand, running his fingers a hairbreadth away from the wire. "Can't feel electricity running through it." He touched it lightly. "Nothing. It's safe to cut."

I stepped back and drew one of the lasers. "If the power is turned off, then this place is definitely abandoned."

"We still can't afford to relax our guard in there."

"I know." As if I could, anyway.

I cut a hole big enough for the two of us to slip through. Quinn went through first, his gaze scanning the area before coming back to me. "Nothing. Come on."

I followed, even though my heart seemed lodged somewhere in my throat and breathing had suddenly become difficult. We padded along in the shadows of the buildings, listening to the silence as we constantly scanned the area.

Nothing.

Not even insects.

As we moved in deeper, my gaze drifted up the tree-lined hill. Up there waited the place I'd barely escaped.

Quinn touched my arm lightly, making me jump. "Sorry," I whispered.

"You don't have to go up there if you don't want to. We can wait at the fence for the others."

I licked my lips, and shook my head. "I have to do this."

He nodded, and his touch slipped to my back, guiding me forward. Warmth flared where his fingers rested, rolling through the rest of me in waves. Though it was comforting, it did little to erase the knot of fear forming in the pit of my stomach.

We stealthily made our way deeper into the complex, slowly working our way up the hill. The closer we got to the lane, the slower my steps became, until I ground to a halt at the lane's entrance. My gaze came to the place where a dead man had once rested. A dark stain remained as a reminder of what I'd done.

"What's wrong?" Quinn asked.

"This is where I woke." My gaze went to the end of the lane. "And down there is where the two orsini came from."

"Orsini? What are they?"

"Warped bearlike things." Goose bumps fled across my skin. I rubbed my arms, and swept my gaze along the concrete wall. "I don't like the feel of this lane."

"There doesn't seem to be anything out of place." He wasn't looking at me as he said it, but rather, studying the lane.

"Something's down there." Something designed to kill.

"I can't feel anything human or nonhuman," he said eventually. "Nor can I hear any sort of mind traffic."

That didn't mean something couldn't be there. Especially given what this place was probably breeding. "There must be some other way into the building. Let's just—"

The rest of the words never got past my throat. Up ahead, the wall moved. Large sections of concrete seemed to peel away, and form colorless human shapes. They were huge and gangly, with long arms and legs. Even as we watched, their skin changed from the gray of the concrete wall to the black of the night. I knew they were still there, but I couldn't see them. Couldn't even feel them.

"Fuck." Quinn's voice was flat, fierce. "Chameleons."

I shot him a glance. "They don't look like lizards to me."

No amusement lit the depths of his dark eyes as his gaze met mine. "They're a rare breed of nonhuman who can take on any background, and literally *become* part of that background. They're also flesh-eaters."

Oh, fantastic. "They're obviously not as rare as you thought, because there's ten of them here."

"Blind I'm not." He grabbed my hand. "Let's get the hell out of here."

"What about the lasers?"

"There's too many of them. Even if we take out a couple, the rest of them will be on us. Come on."

He didn't give me the choice, pulling me along with him. The chameleons followed, their large, flat feet slapping noisily against the cobblestones, drawing too close, too fast.

"Scream," Quinn said, and pushed me roughly to one side.

I hit the window of one of the false shops with enough force to shatter the glass, and tumbled on through the frame. Glass flew, slicing past my face. I hit the ground with a grunt, the laser flying from my hand. I cursed and then scrambled back to my feet.

The creatures were shadows deeper than the night. I blinked, and switched to the infrared of my vampire vision. Quinn became a flame surrounded by ten muted, dark red gleams. And while I could feel the buzz of Quinn's thoughts, the creatures were a dead zone. Not dead as in mind-blind, but dead as in nothing there, just empty space.

I screamed for help as loud as I could, then drew my

remaining laser, leapt over the windowsill, and ran toward the nearest creature.

Though I made little sound, the chameleon swung, swatting at me with a huge, night-dark paw. I ducked the blow, and fired the laser. The bright beam cut across flesh, and four fingers plopped to the ground, where they wriggled and squirmed like fat worms at the end of a hook. The creature screamed—a sound so high, so inhuman, that chills ran across my flesh. Those chills only increased when I realized new fingers were already beginning to grow out of the burned stumps.

Air stirred. I dropped and swung around. Two of them had crept up behind me. I dodged the blow from one, then fired at the hand trying to grab me. More fingers plopped to the pavement, twitching like live things.

More fingers regrew.

God, how were you supposed to kill things that could regenerate so quickly?

The first creature I'd de-fingered screamed in fury. The other lunged. I kicked it away, but teeth tore into my shoulder, biting deep. I hissed, and punched backward, hitting flesh as slimy and cold as a toad's. My blow skidded along and fell away, and the creature's teeth bit deeper, cracking bone. Pain became a red tide, and sweat broke out across my brow. Bile rose, and I swallowed heavily as the other two creatures came at me. Ignoring the thing trying to eat my shoulder, I kicked out at the first creature, sending him stumbling back into the other.

Red beams of light cut through the night, and suddenly neither creature had a head. The smell of burnt flesh rent the air, making me gag. The red light bit through the night again, slicing mere millimeters away from my arm, and the creature trying to devour my shoulder released me with a roar. I shifted to wolf shape and limped away. Once I'd reached the shattered shop window, I shifted back to human form, and sunk to the ground, nursing my injured arm and hand as I watched the proceedings.

The cavalry had come to the rescue. Rhoan, Jack, and Kade had joined the fray and were dealing with the chameleons with brutal efficiency. I'd never seen my brother in action before, and it was truly scary to do so now. He was fast, efficient, and utterly ruthless—everything a guardian should be, and everything I thought my brother wasn't.

And while Kade mightn't be as fast or as furious, he was every bit as efficient. Obviously, he wasn't *just* a builder.

I looked away. The bright flame of Quinn's presence had disappeared, and for a moment, fear surged. Then the rich scent of sandalwood stung the air, and a second later, he was kneeling beside me. His beautiful face was scratched, his sweater torn, the burgundy color deepened by blood.

"Are you all right?" The lilt in his voice was as fierce as I'd ever heard it, and fear gleamed in his dark eyes. "Did they bite you?"

I showed him the shoulder. He swore softly. "We'll have to get that tended to. The bastards are well-known carriers of several different viral infections."

"The Directorate team are about five minutes off arriving," Rhoan said, appearing out of the remaining mêlée. He scooped me up in his arms. "We've a med-team amongst them, just in case something like this happened."

He ran me through the night, down the hill, and into the section I'd seen but not visited, then left. The med-team was already setting up when we arrived.

The doctor took one look at my shoulder and hand, and hustled me into the nearest room. I was stripped, cleaned, and patched, then had several of the biggest needles I'd ever seen shoved into my butt. They hurt more than the damn bite did.

"Just keep an eye on that shoulder," the doctor advised as he stripped off his gloves. "You wolves haven't a history with viral infections as a rule, but even so, if you see any inflammation or start feeling off-color, just come in and see us."

I nodded.

He glanced at the com-screen on the desk. "There's a note here on your file to remind you of your appointment Friday."

I blinked. "What appointment?"

"With Dr. Harvey. At four."

I stared at him for a moment, my heart racing. Dr. Harvey was the specialist I'd been referred to—the man who would tell me whether I could have kids or not. He wasn't a Directorate doctor, but he'd been vetted and approved by them. "Does it say anything else?"

The doc glanced at me. "It's something to do with test results."

Oh God, oh God. In two days I would know, one way or another. And now that the crunch was actually near, I wasn't sure I was ready for it.

"Thanks, Doc."

He nodded and turned away. I carefully pulled my clothes back on, then walked out to the waiting area. Rhoan rose from the chair. "Verdict?"

"I'm fine." I hesitated, looking around. "Where's Quinn?"

"Waiting outside. He didn't like the feel of that place."

A smile twitched my lips. "Really?"

"He's an empath, remember. He said the rooms held too many bad memories and pain."

Quinn had some fairly tough shields to protect him, so if he'd retreated, it had to be bad. Which made me damn glad empathy wasn't one of my problems.

Rhoan cupped a hand under my good elbow, and escorted me toward the door. "You feel ready to confront what might have happened in this place, or would you rather leave it until tomorrow?"

I'd rather not confront it at all, but that wasn't an option and we both knew it. I took a deep breath and blew it out slowly. "Let's get this over with."

His gaze searched mine, his expression filled with concern. "You sure?"

"No. But I'd rather not wait."

He nodded, and we moved out into the night. Quinn was waiting one building away, and fell in step beside Rhoan. He didn't say anything and, for once, I had no sense of his emotions.

We walked back up that hill and down the alley. We turned right, and there before us stood yet another concrete building. My steps faltered, and my mouth went dry.

I didn't want to go in that building.

Didn't want to remember.

"You don't have to do this," Rhoan said softly.

I licked my lips. "I do."

Only my knees were weak, and my feet wouldn't move, and I couldn't seem to drag enough air into my lungs.

Rhoan's grip tightened. "Deep breaths," he said.

I obeyed. It didn't seem to help much.

"I'm with you. If it gets too bad, I'll get you out. I promise."

I swallowed, pulled my elbow free, and grabbed his hand. Tight. "Let's go."

Before whatever courage I had deserted me.

Quinn opened the door. He had his vampire face on, yet concern sparkled in his eyes. Or maybe that was a trick of the light flowing from the brightly lit corridor beyond the door.

Or even wishful thinking.

Our footsteps echoed in the silence, the concrete cold under my toes. Every five steps there was a door—an indication that the rooms beyond were small. We didn't stop at any of them, walking to the end of the corridor and turning left.

Jack came out of the end room as we reached the halfway point. He was carrying a clipboard and his expression was grim. "This place is nothing more than a breeding pen."

We stopped, and my gaze went past him. Saw the white walls. The neat tuck of white sheet around the mattress. The sparkle of the chains that rested atop of it.

My stomach churned. "This was my room?"

Jack glanced down at the folder he was holding.

"Yeah." He hesitated. "You were in a coma after the accident. They didn't expect you to come out of it."

"I escaped because they didn't bother to either drug me or chain me, like everyone else."

Jack nodded. "I'm no doctor, but looking at these records I have to say it's a wonder you *did* recover."

I released Rhoan's hand and took a step toward the room. A chill ran down my spine, and something sharp flickered through my head.

I swallowed heavily, and took another step.

Red needles of fire lanced through my brain, and sweat broke out across my brow. I shuddered, clenching my fists, fighting the urge to run as far and as fast as I could from this place and the memories that stirred in agony.

Rhoan touched my shoulder, and I jumped.

"Maybe you shouldn't push," he said softly.

"There's something I need to remember."

Why I was so sure, I couldn't say. If I was in a coma, then surely this place would mean nothing to me. Yet I'd become aware enough to escape. Maybe the answers we needed were locked behind that threatening wall of pain.

I licked dry lips and took another step.

The pain became a tidal wave, and I was falling, screaming, to the floor.

Chapter 5

Memories reeled through a sea of agony, fractured images of a violent movie, viewed through a broken projector. The car that had hit mine from behind; the tree I couldn't avoid. The warm flush of blood on my face and arms, then pain, and darkness, and the sensation of floating. Nothing but floating, for what seemed like forever.

Then sounds crept into the mix. A steady beeping. The click of heels against flooring. The slap of flesh against flesh, and the sense of violation.

Finally, smells. Antiseptic. Sex. Forest, pine and orange blossom.

The last three were a strange combination I'd smelled before.

Riley!

The voice was distant. Demanding. It echoed through

the agony locking my mind, nipping like a terrier. But the pain swirled, and I couldn't tell where the voice came from. Couldn't reach it.

Riley!

It was sharper this time, more urgent. The clouds of agony stirred, dissipating. Suddenly, Quinn was in my mind, standing between me and the pain, holding out a ghostly hand. I clasped it, and it felt real, and solid, and oh so warm.

This way, he said, and led me back to the light.

Awareness returned, and I gasped.

"It's all right." Rhoan's voice was soft, soothing. His arms were wrapped around me, and he was rocking me as a father would a child. "You're all right."

The air that swirled around us was cool against my fevered skin, and the air I sucked fiercely into my lungs filled with the scent of eucalyptus and night. We were outside again.

I opened my eyes. Quinn's gaze met mine, dark depths as expressionless as his face.

"The door wasn't open," I said.

"No," he agreed softly.

"Door?" Rhoan said. "Which door?"

I pulled my gaze from Quinn's and looked at my brother. "Nothing. It doesn't matter." But it did matter, because Quinn had just breached my shields and entered my mind after telling me not so long ago that he couldn't.

Rhoan touched a hand to my cheek. "Did you remember anything important?"

"Just a smell. A man, someone I've met before."

He raised an eyebrow. "Nothing else?"

I shook my head, and he sighed. "Enough is enough. We're taking you home tonight."

And I was ready to go. Ready to just sleep and forget, if only for a few hours. "Is it safe to go home?"

He grimaced. "Not really. The three of us are heading to a safe house for the time being. When Jack and Kade sort out the mess here, they'll join us."

"Why is Kade staying rather than you or Quinn?" I asked, surprised.

"Because Kade was here for over two months, and knows this place better than any of us."

Which sounded perfectly logical, but I wasn't believing it. Jack had plans for Kade, that much was obvious. "So where is this Directorate safe house? And has it got a bath big enough for a werewolf to laze in?"

He grinned. "It's a penthouse suite in a hotel right on the shores of Brighton Beach. I think it's safe to presume it has a decent-size bath."

A smile tugged my lips. "Well, I guess if we're going to be locked up, we might as well do so in style."

"Exactly. You okay to stand?"

I nodded, and he helped me to my feet. I wobbled a little, and was glad of his support those first few seconds. "I'm fine," I said, when I was.

He released me. "I'll just go see Jack, then we can leave."

I nodded and leaned back against the concrete wall. The coldness crept through my sweater, and felt so good against my overwarmed skin.

Once he'd left, I looked at Quinn. "You have some explaining to do."

He shrugged. "There's nothing sinister in what happened. You were in great pain, and your psychic shields were low. I simply slipped past them."

"That time I was shot with the silver bullet, you said you could read no more than surface thoughts. This time it was more than that."

He studied me for a second, dark eyes glinting dangerously in the night. "What did you want me to do? Stand back and watch you suffer needlessly?"

"You lied to me." Again.

"Only a little."

I crossed my arms. "I've got a feeling your version of 'little' and mine are two entirely different things."

"It's only when you're in pain that your shields are lowered enough for me to enter uninvited. In some respects, your mind is almost as untouchable as your brother's."

I didn't believe him. "So you're saying it's only when I'm sick or injured that you can rifle through my thoughts?"

He hesitated. "Yes."

"Liar. When else?"

He looked away. "In times of passion. If I chose to, I could enter then."

Anger curled through me. "And have you?"

"No."

I only had his word on that, and right now, I wasn't up to trusting his word. "Well, thanks for pulling me out of that mess of memories, but if you ever pry into my mind without invitation again, I'll—" I stopped. What could I threaten a vampire with? Especially one as old as Quinn apparently was?

"Fine." His voice was flat. Cold. "Next time, I'll let you find your own way out."

"Good."

Silence fell between us. A silence that was tense and unbreathable. But I wasn't entirely unhappy about it, because it gave me an excuse to ignore my hormones, and keep him at arm's length that much longer.

Still, I stared up at the cloud-filled night sky, and hoped like hell my brother would hurry back. Naturally, he didn't, and the silence itched at my skin until I felt ready to scream in frustration.

When he finally did get back, he hooked his arm through mine and began guiding me away from the building. "Let's get going. You look beat."

"That's because I am." I yawned hugely, then added, "How are we getting to this place?"

"There's a helicopter waiting. It'll take us to the Directorate's jet, which is being prepped as we speak."

"Good. I need sleep."

"You can once we reach the plane."

Which I most certainly did. And when we reached the hotel, I slept some more. Only I didn't *just* sleep, I dreamed. And while this dream was new, it was similar to many I'd had since Quinn had walked away from me in Talon's lair.

Well, I *think* they were just dreams, though they felt pretty damn real.

I was in a shower. Water sprayed against my skin, the needle-sharp jets soothing and yet exhilarating. Or was it the warmth of another body so close, the scent of sandalwood and man, that had my pulse racing?

Hands touched me, turned me, then lips came down

on mine, lips that were warm and familiar and oh so wonderful. We kissed, long and hard, as the water drummed our skins, skimming our bodies, tickling and teasing.

Then he turned me, so that my back was against the hard heat of his body, his erection nudging my butt as he reached for the soap and began washing my breasts and belly. The scent of lavender touched the air, filling every breath, and it seemed so *real,* as real as the hands that were washing me so lovingly.

And oh, it felt *good.*

But being caught between the heat of his body, the drum of the water, and the caress of his hands was nothing short of torturous, and I was pretty much steaming in an instant.

When I could stand it no more, I grabbed the soap from him and turned around. His beautiful body gleamed like sculptured pale-gold marble in the half-light of the bathroom, the water reverently caressing every muscle, every curve. I followed the water's lead, soaping every marvelous inch, until he was quivering as badly as I.

He took the soap and put it back in the holder, then twined his hands in mine, raising them above my head as he pressed me back against the wet, cool tiles. The heat of him flowed around me, through me, burning my skin and contrasting sharply with the coolness seeping from the tiles.

His gaze met mine, the obsidian depths gleaming with lust and determination. "You are mine, Riley," he said softly, as he nudged my legs wider with one knee. "And I have every intention of loving you so completely—in every single way possible—that you will have no desire to turn to anyone else but me."

"That won't ever happen."

But it came out little more than a pant of air as he slid into me, filling me, liquefying me. His thick groan of pleasure was a sound I echoed. Then he began to move, and there was nothing gentle about it. His body and movements were urgent, fierce, and so very wonderful. The rich ache grew, becoming a kaleidoscope of sensations that washed through every corner of my mind. Then the shuddering took hold and I gasped, grabbing his shoulders, clambering up his body to wrap my legs around his waist and push him deeper still. Pleasure exploded between us and my orgasm ripped through my body, shuddered through my soul.

I woke, still shaking in the aftermath of that orgasm, Quinn's name dying on my lips.

For several seconds I simply lay there, staring almost blindly up at the ceiling.

God, it had felt so *real*. My skin still tingled from the drumming of the water, and the scent of lavender seemed to hang in the air. Not to mention the fact I felt well and truly sated.

Where the hell had dreams like *that* been during the few brief dry spells in my love life?

I stretched like a contented cat, then looked at the clock on the bedside table. It was nearly noon. I'd barely slept six hours, which was surprising. It felt like I'd slept twenty.

I rose up on my elbows. I couldn't actually remember how I'd gotten into bed last night but given the trail of clothes from the doorway, I'd obviously walked and stripped at the same time.

The room itself was huge. Directly in front was a curved wall of glass. Sunlight flooded in, lending the sand-colored walls an extra richness. The carpet was thick, and sea blue in color, as were the two well-stuffed sofas. To the left was a door that led into a tiled area, and what looked like the biggest damn shower ever made— though it *wasn't* the shower from my dream. But this one had obviously been designed with a party in mind, and I was definitely going to try it out.

Of course, my hormones were all for trying it out with a friend, but who that friend would be was the million-dollar question. Common sense said Kade, but after the dream, my hormones were all for sampling a real bit of wet vampire loving.

Which probably meant I'd do neither. It was certainly the saner, if less fun, option right now.

I flung off the covers and padded into the oversized bathroom, enjoying the luxurious shower alone and spending a whole lot more time than necessary simply standing under the water, letting the jets massage my skin and warm my body.

When the water finally started to cool, I stepped out. Once I'd dried myself, I went to search for clothes. And discovered several dresses and skirts hanging up in the wardrobe. Rhoan had obviously gone shopping, because everything was new, even the shoes. I frowned, hoping he hadn't blown our entire savings account. Rhoan and shopping were always a dangerous combination, and he'd overspent and landed us in trouble come rent time more than once.

Seeing the day was so warm, I picked out a flowing white cotton dress that had shoestring straps, a low back, and a hem that swirled almost indecently around my thighs. After slipping my feet into a pair of cute red and white sandals—complete with a wooden stiletto heel, which had certainly come in handy a few times in the past when I'd been caught in situations that required something more persuasive than a mere fist, but less deadly than a werewolf's teeth—I headed out to find the kitchen, Quinn, and my brother.

I found Quinn sitting in the living room, reading the newspaper. His gaze was a caress that slid down my body, and one that had me hot and bothered in an instant. God, what was it about this vampire that could get to me so easily? Okay, he was gorgeous, he was rich, and any woman with half a brain would fuck him in an instant—but there was something else between us. Something deeper.

His gaze slid back up to my hair. "You've cut it."

I nodded, surprised he hadn't noticed earlier. "Yeah. Summer's coming on, and shoulder length is easier to manage."

"It suits you."

"Thanks." I walked into the kitchen, and smelled the caffeine before I found it. "You want a coffee?"

"Yes, thanks."

I poured two then headed back out, handing him a cup before moving over to the window. Ten floors up had my stomach stirring uneasily, but I was careful not to get too close to the edge. If I couldn't see the drop, I'd be okay. Port Phillip Bay stretched out before me, filled with whitecaps that moseyed toward the shore. But given the way the trees tossed, those gentle waves were no indication of the wind's strength. I watched a beach umbrella tumble along the yellow sand, then turned and asked, "Where's Rhoan?"

"He had to go into the Directorate to chase down some files for Jack."

"Then Jack and Kade aren't back yet?"

"No."

I wondered if that was a good sign or a bad sign. Wondered if they'd uncovered anything useful in that place. Somehow, I was doubting this. This whole operation just seemed too slickly run for clues to be left behind haphazardly.

"Any idea how long we're going to be cooped up here?"

He shook his head and folded the newspaper one-handed. "No. Could be a while from the sound of it." His voice was as polite as mine, but his gaze kept slipping down my body and his hunger stirred the air. Hunger that was both sexual and blood need.

"Have you eaten lately?" I asked sharply.

He hesitated. "No."

"Why not?"

He raised an eyebrow. "What does it matter to you?"

"It matters because I can feel your need to eat."

He shrugged. "There's synth blood in the fridge. That'll do for a while."

"In the long run, you can't survive on synth blood."

"No. When that happens, I shall go seduce someone."

Oh yeah. I'd forgotten he only took blood while making love. "Don't leave it to the last second."

He studied me for a moment, then said in a neutral

voice, "I have lived more years than I care to remember as a vampire. I don't need a pretty pup telling me what I should be doing."

"This pup was only showing a little concern." I turned away. "I should have known better."

He was silent for a while, but his gaze burned into my back, and slithers of awareness scattered across my skin.

"Can I ask a question?"

"What?" I kept my voice as flat as his.

"Are you wearing any knickers under that dress?"

I almost choked on my coffee. Of all the things I'd been expecting him to ask, it wasn't that. "That's for me to know, and you to wonder."

"Well, I'm certainly wondering. And in case *you're* wondering, that dress is practically see-through when lit by sunlight."

I hid my smile and walked over to the sofa. "Sorry if the view is annoying you."

He gave me his vampire face, but underneath, frustration reigned. I could feel it, even if I couldn't see it.

"Why are you determined to take everything I say the wrong way?"

"Perhaps it has something to do with being a little pissed off at you." I grabbed the newspaper as I sat down.

"When you've stopped being pissed off, are you actually going to listen to what I have to say?"

"I don't know." I unfolded the paper. "Maybe."

"And when might that be?"

I shrugged. "Let's see—I spent a good month trying to talk to you and getting rejected. So I think a month would be fair payback."

"And here I was thinking bitchiness was beyond you."

"In case you are forgetting, I was *born* a bitch."

My gaze caught the front page banner, and I almost had a heart failure when I saw the date.

"It's Friday?" I asked, looking at the time. It was nearly two-thirty.

"Yes." He frowned. "Why?"

"I slept a *whole* day?" I stared at him in disbelief.

A smile touched the corners of his dark eyes. "Yes, you did."

"Shit." I ran a hand through my hair. "I have a doctor's appointment at four."

He frowned. "Rhoan never mentioned it."

"Rhoan never knew about it. I made the appointment the day of the accident." I surged to my feet. "Wonder if he thought to retrieve my handbag and wallet from the car wreck?"

"You can't go to this appointment," Quinn said, following me into the bedroom.

"You try and stop me, and you'll regret it."

He crossed his arms, and leaned against the doorframe. And even though I was hunting around for my handbag, I was acutely aware of his presence. Of the tightness of the jade shirtsleeves against his forearms. The way his khakis defined his hips and groin.

"What is so important about it that it cannot wait until it's safe to venture out?"

"That is none of your business." I found my wallet, but no handbag. Not that it mattered. All I needed was my credit and insurance cards.

I walked back to the door, but Quinn didn't move.

"Get out of my way."

"You can't go out alone. At least let me come with you."

I didn't want Quinn there. Didn't want anyone there. Not when this might be the very worst news I'd ever hear. "I'll be all—"

"No." His voice was cold. Determined. "Not alone. I either escort you there and back, or you remain here."

"Escort, not come in."

He nodded, and moved aside. I walked into the living room and scrawled a note for Rhoan. "What time is he due back?"

"He wasn't sure. Could be late." Keys jangled behind me. "He left us a Merc in case we needed it."

When the Directorate had personnel go under safe cover, they obviously didn't do it by halves. "Fine. Let's go, then."

We took the elevator down to the basement, and walked across to the penthouse parking bay. Quinn did the gentlemanly thing and opened the door, ushering me inside before climbing into the driver's side.

For a good ten minutes, he didn't say anything. I stared out the window, thinking about the future, and hoping like hell I actually had something decent to look forward to.

"What is the appointment for?" he asked, eventually.

"As I said, that's none of your business."

"Are you ill?"

I snorted softly. Part of me wished I *was* ill. It would be better than probably being sterile. "No."

"Then why a specialist?"

Annoyance ran through me, and I glanced at him. "You have no right to ask these questions."

"And no right to care?" he bit back. "You're a fool if you think that I don't."

I wasn't a fool. His caring had always been in his touch, and occasionally, in his eyes, even when his words had denied the possibility. But I couldn't afford to dwell on it, because right now I couldn't afford to do exclusive with a vampire. And he would want exclusive, even though he hadn't actually come out and said it.

"Quinn, I'm not up to dealing with what you want right now." Not when I *had* tried. Not when I had far bigger problems.

He didn't say anything, and we continued on in silence. He asked for the address once we reached the city, and pulled to a halt outside the Collins Street building. Ignoring the "no standing" signs, he parked the car then got out, walking around to open the door.

I ignored his offer of assistance, and looked up at the thirty floors above me. Dr. Harvey was on the twentieth, which was something of a stretch for my fear of heights. And while, technically, that fear shouldn't appear when I was in a building with four walls all around, it didn't seem to matter a damn to my stomach. Last time, I'd almost puked every time I'd looked out the doctor's office windows. And the ride back down to ground level had left me shaking and sweating. Not an experience I was looking forward to reliving.

"Are you sure you're going to be all right?"

"Of course. I'm not ill, as I said."

"I guess not," he replied shortly. "Even though you've gone as white as a sheet."

"My doctor is on the twentieth floor." And he knew

about my ridiculous fear of tall, tall buildings and their awful elevators.

"You want me to accompany you in the elevator? It might be easier if you have company."

I shook my head and ignored the caring in his voice. "I have no idea how long I'll be."

"I'll be waiting in the foyer."

"Fine." Tightly gripping my wallet, I walked past him and into the building. I didn't get far.

"Riley?"

I froze, recognizing the rich tones, knowing who it was even before I turned around.

Misha.

My ex-mate, and the very last person in the world I wanted to see right now.

He rose from the chair and strolled toward me, a tall, lean figure who caught the eye as much for the gracefulness of his movements as the expensive cut of his clothes. The sunlight streaming through the glass turned his silver hair a rich, burnished gold, but nothing could warm the cold calculation from his icy eyes.

"Misha," I said, glad to hear my voice was even. "What are you doing here?"

"Waiting for you." He stopped when there were several feet between us. His familiar, musky scent swam around me, stirring memories of all the good times we'd had together. Memories that might just be a lie, like everything else from that period of my life had been a lie.

I raised an eyebrow. "And how did you know I'd be here this afternoon?"

"Easy. There aren't many doctors specializing in nonhuman fertility problems. I merely hacked into the computers of the half dozen listed here in Melbourne, and went through their files until I found you."

If Misha knew about my fertility problems, then he was involved in whatever was going on deeper than I'd thought. "And why would you be doing that?"

"Because I needed to talk to you, and I doubted whether you'd come to me willingly."

He was only half right. I wouldn't go to him willing, but I'd certainly fuck him willingly once he'd made the first approach. He—or rather, the information he could give me—was my path back to a normal life. "You and I have nothing to talk about."

His smile was warm, yet it did little to lift the calculation in his eyes. "Oh, I think we do."

I glanced past him, looking at the clock on the wall. "I have an appointment in ten minutes. You have three to say what you came here to say."

He raised an eyebrow, his expression mocking. "Then I will get straight down to business. I know Talon was giving you ARC1-23. I know why. And I know the results."

"And here I was believing when you said you had nothing to do with Moneisha or Genoveve."

"I didn't. But we both know that Talon giving you the drug had nothing to do with either of those places. Or anything else he was involved with."

Jack was right. This wolf knew a *whole* lot more about what was going on than any of us did. "He'd been trying to get me pregnant."

"As was I."

I blinked. "What?"

He shrugged. "Talon and I have been competitors for a long time. I thought it would be interesting to see what sort of child you and I could produce."

There was more behind his decision than just a competitive urge. I could see it in his eyes. "You're *both* mad."

"Maybe. It was certainly a risk on my behalf."

I frowned. "Meaning what?"

"Meaning, Talon was given no specific instructions other than to fuck you senseless in an effort to learn more about Jack. I, on the other hand, was told to keep away." Humor briefly touched his eyes, warming the chill depths. "I thought you worth the risk."

Yeah, right. I was really believing *that*. "I'm not in the least bit flattered. And why would it be risky for you to fuck or impregnate me?"

"As I said, I was ordered to stay away."

"So who gave these so-called orders?"

He gave another shark smile and sidestepped the question. "Did you know Talon was sterile?"

I nodded, and surprise flitted briefly through his eyes. "Interesting, because Talon certainly didn't."

"Talon thought himself the perfect specimen."

My voice was tart, and Misha's smile warmed, becoming genuine for the first time. "He was never one to see his faults."

"And you are?"

He shrugged. "It pays to know one's faults. That way you can work around them." He studied me for a minute, the warmth of his smile fading, sending a chill skittering across my skin. "I have a proposition for you."

"I don't want to hear it." Such a lie, but one Misha fell for hook, line, and sinker.

"Oh, I think you will once you go up and see your specialist."

My heart lodged somewhere in my throat, and refused to budge. For several seconds, I couldn't even breathe. "What do you mean?"

He raised a pale eyebrow. "My proposition has benefits for you, the Directorate, and myself. More than that I am not willing to say right now." He glanced at his watch. "My time is officially up. If you wish to discuss this matter further, ring me on this number." He handed me a card. "It's the only secure line I have left."

I glanced at the handwritten number, quickly memorizing it before tearing the card into strips. "Don't be expecting me to."

He smiled, and turned away. Then he stopped and looked over his shoulder. "One more thing you should know."

Trepidation crawled through me. "What?"

"I haven't had the hormone chip replaced. Right now, I'm the most fertile wolf you know."

With that, he turned and walked away, leaving me dry mouthed and shaking. God, what was he saying? That I *could* have kids? Why else would he say something like that?

There was only one way to find out. Spinning, I all but ran to the elevators, my stomach churning so much that the twenty-floor climb didn't really make a noticeable impression.

As usual, Dr. Harvey was running behind schedule, leaving me sitting in the waiting room, twitching and shifting and sweating.

When the nurse finally called me in, I all but ran.

Dr. Harvey looked over his black-framed glasses at me. "You're looking a little peaked this afternoon."

I sat down on the chair and crossed my legs. "I'm worried." No lie there, that was for sure. "These results may well change the direction of my life."

He nodded in understanding, his gaze flicking to the com-screen on one end of the desk. I shifted, but couldn't quite see what was on the screen.

"Would you prefer the good or the bad news first?"

I took a deep breath and let it out slowly. "Hit me with the bad." Might as well know the worst first.

"There's no easy way to put this, so I'll say it straight out. Indications are that within a year or so, your body will fully imitate a vampire's in that you will neither be fertile nor be able to carry a child."

I simply stared at him. Deep down, I guess I'd always expected something like this would happen. Rhoan might be more vampire in his makeup than wolf, but we were fraternal twins, sharing the same father if not the same seed. Yet I'd always hoped that because past tests had indicated the werewolf gene was stronger in me, I'd be able to have a child. Or would at least be able to turn to some form of IVF when all else failed. Now even that was snatched from me, and I wasn't sure whether to laugh or to cry.

Though right now, both were looking good.

"The good news," he continued, as if he hadn't noticed me sitting there in a lump of misery, "is that the experimental drug you were given has actually achieved its aim. Young woman, your cycle has finally kicked into gear, and you are actually menstruating for the first time in your life."

I stared at him for several long minutes. "No, I'm not."

He smiled. "Yes, you are. If the results we got back were any indication, you should have had your first period six days ago."

Six days ago I'd been barely alive. "I can't remember."

He raised his eyebrows at that, but didn't question. He knew I was Directorate. Knew some things just had to be accepted without question. He clasped his hands in front of him. "Of course, given that you are no longer taking the drug, I would envisage the effects will not last very long. A last burst, perhaps, before infertility."

I blinked, and suddenly his words hit me. *Ohmygod*. I could have *kids*. I was fertile, however briefly. I felt like screaming. Dancing. Running through the building shouting the news.

"Of course," he said, his voice full of a sternness that somehow kept me anchored, "we will have to keep a close eye on what is happening, and run weekly tests. If you *do* become pregnant, it might mean hospitalization, as we cannot predict how your body, with the changes it is undergoing, will react."

I didn't care if I had to be hospitalized the whole nine months. Not if it meant having a child at the end of it. I shifted in my seat, and had to resist the impulse to ring Rhoan and tell him the news. God, he'd be over the moon!

"And," the doctor continued, "because you have such a narrow margin of fertility and will need to ensure maximum opportunity for pregnancy, you will have to watch your body's chemical and physical changes, and ensure the sexual act occurs during hours of peak receptiveness."

"And the monitoring involves...?"

"These days, it involves nothing more tedious than wearing a small monitor under your skin. It'll tingle softly to warn you when a peak has been reached."

I nodded, and wondered if I was grinning like a fool.

"Remember though, that even this machine cannot guarantee conception. It may be that you will *not* fall pregnant, especially given your history. There are never any certainties when it comes to life, even in this day and age."

"I have a chance, Doc. That's all I wanted."

He nodded. "Then you wish to have the monitor implanted immediately?"

I opened my mouth to say, "Yes, of course," but the words froze somewhere in my throat as his earlier words hit me. *The experimental drug you were given has actually achieved its aim.* The same experimental drug that had changed the very cell structure of past half-breed recipients. The same drug that, even now, could be changing my body in unknown ways.

Oh, *fuck*.

I closed my eyes, and rubbed them wearily. "I need to think about all this," I said slowly. "As much as I want to rush into having a kid, there are other considerations."

He nodded. "Just remember that it *is* a small window, and time is of the essence if you wish to attempt conception."

Like I didn't know that. I stood. "I just need a little time to think about it."

He studied me for a moment, eyes full of understanding. "I'll be here until at least nine-thirty tonight. Ring me if you come to a decision or want to discuss things

further. Other than that, we'll make your next appointment for tomorrow, same time. Will twenty-four hours
be enough?"

Twenty-four hours to decide whether or not I should
risk following a long-held dream? God, *no*. But I nodded, and left, and was in such a daze that the elevator
ride back down to the ground didn't even stir my usually
fragile stomach.

The doors opened, and Quinn was standing there, expression concerned as he reached out and gently cupped
my elbow. "Are you all right?"

My laugh was shaky. "Yeah. Just got some wonderful
news."

He frowned. "Then why are you as white as a sheet
and shaking?"

"I'm scared of tall buildings, remember?"

"I remember. But I also know you're lying." He hesitated, his dark gaze boring into mine, as if trying to reach
my soul. "There was a time you trusted me."

I *still* trusted him. I just needed to think about things
first, before I told anyone. But I couldn't think here.
Couldn't decide here. I rubbed my hand across my eyes
again. They burned, as if filled with unshed tears. "Can you
drop the questions and just drive me to Mt. Macedon?"

The elevator doors tried to close. Quinn put a hand
against them and said, "Why?"

"Because I have a decision to make, and I think better
when I'm running through trees." And Mt. Macedon
was the least developed of the big parks that surrounded
metropolitan Melbourne.

He stared at me a minute longer, then his grip tightened on my elbow, and he led me out of the building.

The strength of the sun was waning into dusk, and the wind carried the chill of the storm predicted to hit later this evening. I glanced up, watching the clouds race across the pink tinted sky. The wolf within me hoped it *did* rain, because there was nothing more refreshing, more isolating, and more primordial than racing the thunder of a storm through rain-lashed trees.

We climbed into the car and headed for Mt. Macedon. Quinn didn't say anything, and for that, I was grateful. My thoughts were a mess, going fifty different ways, and right then, I didn't have a hope of coping with any sort of conversation.

The rain began to splatter across the windshield as we entered the Mt. Macedon township. Quinn glanced at me, eyebrow raised in question.

"Go on," I said. "I don't care if it rains. Besides, I'm a wolf. We don't feel the cold."

"Werewolves mightn't, but you do."

He had a good memory. I'd only mentioned that once, in passing. "Maybe. But right now, I need to run more than I need to keep warm."

He nodded, and continued on up the mountain. We entered the park, and stopped in the bays closest to the trees. There were maybe a dozen other cars here, and most of those were parked up near the Old Tea Rooms restaurant. I climbed out. The wind tore at my dress and hair, touching my skin with chill reminders of the winter just past. I shivered, and glanced across the roof of the car at Quinn. "This could take a while."

"Be careful" was all he said.

I nodded, then stripped off my clothes, placing them in the car before calling to the wildness within. In wolf form, I headed for the trees, and just kept on running through the ferny undergrowth. I wasn't really thinking, just letting the night, the cold, and the storm run over my body. Letting the electricity that danced through the thunderous skies clear the cobwebs and confusion from my mind.

I ran for hours. Ran until my limbs were beginning to shake with tiredness, and my tongue lolled so far out of my mouth I'd swear it was about to drag on the ground. Ran until the storm had swept past, and the clean scent of wet earth mingled with eucalyptus on the night air. Even then, I didn't head back immediately to the car, but rather changed to human form and headed for the huge memorial cross that was the centerpiece of the park.

Sitting on the steps, my back to the cross, I hugged my knees close to my chest, trying to keep warm as I stared at the lights that stretched like a twinkling carpet far in the distance.

Within a few minutes, the warm scent of sandalwood mingled with the fresh aromas of the night. He handed me my dress without comment. Once I'd put it on, he placed a leather jacket across my shoulders and sat on the step beside me, a shadow whose heat I could feel even though we weren't touching.

"I've booked a table in the restaurant, if you wish something to eat," he said, after a moment.

"I might." I slipped my arms inside the jacket and zipped it up. It smelled of leather and man, and stirred me in a hundred different ways. Which was scary, because I really couldn't afford to fall for this vampire any more than I already had.

"And *have* you fallen for me, Riley Jenson?"

I glanced at him sharply. "Two days ago you said you could only catch my thoughts when I was in pain or during passion. So how come you're reading them now?"

His gaze, when it met mine, was flat and uncompromising. "We've shared blood, remember. I did warn you that makes me more attuned to unguarded thoughts."

I looked away. "Then I must remember to guard my thoughts at all times."

"Perhaps you should, if you don't want me reading them."

"You could be a gentleman, and not intrude."

"I could. But given the fact our talks so far have gotten interrupted for various reasons, intruding on your thoughts is my only way of getting information."

He obviously hadn't read too much, then, or he probably wouldn't be sitting there so calmly. I chewed my lip, watching the twinkling carpet of lights, trying not to think of anything in particular.

Yet a decision had to be made. Here. Tonight. Because if I went back to Jack, he'd make it for me. Though, considering he wanted me as a guardian, I doubt he'd want me pregnant.

"Tell me what causes you such anguish," Quinn demanded softly.

I briefly contemplated the wisdom of not telling him, but in the end, he had the right to know. It did involve him—us—in some respects.

"You're not going to like it," I hedged.

He reached out, his hand twining in mine, wrapping my fingers in heat and courage. "Tell me."

So I did. About what the doctor had said. About Misha. About the decision I'd come up here to make.

He was silent for a long time. When he finally spoke, his voice was as emotionless as ever. Yet his dark eyes held echoes of pain as his gaze met mine.

"Rhoan told you about Eryn, didn't he?"

Eryn was the wolf Quinn had been engaged to six months before I'd met him. A wolf who had used a drug to snare and keep him. A wolf who had confirmed his opinion that all wolves were whores.

"Rhoan hasn't said anything about Eryn." I studied him for a moment. "How does she fit in with the decision I have to make?"

"She doesn't. But I thought she might have been the reason you were unwilling to really talk about us continuing our relationship."

"And why would you think that?"

He looked away. I touched his arm lightly, feeling the tension in his muscles, tasting the anger that still lingered in his mind.

"We weren't just engaged," he said eventually. "We swore our love to the moon."

My heart just about plummeted to my ankles. Of all the things I'd been expecting to hear, that certainly hadn't been one of them. "*What*? But that means…"

"I would not be free to fuck anyone else." His gaze met mine, dark depths smoldering. "But I am free to be with whom I wish, because the ceremony that should have bound us as one didn't work."

"Because both parties have to be in love to perform that ceremony. Eryn obviously never was."

"In truth, neither was I. It was the drug, not real emotion."

"Yes." I paused. There was more. There had to be more. "But I'm gathering that is the least of her crimes?"

He looked away. "At the time, I did believe the ceremony had locked us together for life and prevented either of us from taking other partners. I discovered her lie the hard way."

Oh dear... "You found her with another wolf?"

He nodded. "And she was pregnant by him."

"Shit." No wonder he hated the werewolf lifestyle so much.

He nodded. "Hence my suspicion that Eryn might have had something to do with your reluctance to get involved with me again."

"Well, she doesn't. But like her, I want a kid, whether now or later. And that makes getting involved with someone who can never offer me that a difficult choice."

Especially when they didn't like being one of many.

A smile briefly lifted the grim set of his lips. "And here I was thinking you were playing games, making me pay for walking away."

"I won't deny that was there as well."

He nodded again. "So, what do you intend to do?"

"I honestly don't know."

"And Misha?"

"I was always intending to fuck Misha. I need the answers he can give me."

"So you plan to become a whore for the Directorate?"

I ripped my fingers from his and stood. "Damn you to hell." I crossed my arms and stomped down the steps. "That's such a *human* way of viewing the situation. Besides, it's not that simple."

"It *is* that simple. Rhoan willingly sleeps with enemies

to gather news. Isn't that what you'd be doing with Misha?"

"It's *just* sex." I blew out a frustrated breath. Quinn's views were never likely to change, no matter what I said. "And we don't know that Misha is an enemy yet."

"We don't know that he's a friend, either."

"True. But he may be the only fertile wolf I currently know."

"Then you believe he was telling the truth about that?"

"It would be easy enough to check." I walked to the black metal fence that stopped visitors from getting too close to the edge of the mountain. The wind was fiercer away from the cross, chilling my wet legs and feet.

"Sounds to me like your decision has been made."

I closed my eyes. "It might have been, except for the fact that it was ARC1-23 that kick-started my fertility."

"Meaning?" Though he was still sitting on the steps, his soft words cut through the rush of the wind as clearly as if he was standing beside me.

"Meaning, ARC1-23 can have deadly side effects on us half-breeds. They won't know for at least another few months what, if any, effect it will have on me."

And if they couldn't predict what effects the ARC1-23 would have on me just yet, then how could they predict what effect it might have on any child I conceived? If the drug could totally mutate my system, then what the hell could it do to a child growing in my womb?

That was the problem. *That* was the choice I faced.

Did I have the right to endanger my child in such a manner? Did I have the right to bring a life into this world who might not even live to see their first birthday?

Deep in my heart, I knew the answer was no.

But that would mean blowing the only chance I had of having a child myself. Oh, there were other options—freezing eggs, finding a surrogate, but it just wasn't the same. Wasn't what I'd dreamed of all these years.

I closed my eyes and took a shuddery breath. God, fate was a bitch sometimes.

Arms touched me, turned me around. I sunk into the warmth of his embrace, enjoying the momentary peace it offered.

"If there's one thing I've learned over the years"—his breath stirred warmth past my ear—"it's that nature often has its own way of sorting out right from wrong."

"Nature has very little to do with what is happening to me now. If nature had its way, I would still be infertile."

"Then perhaps there lies the answer to your problems."

I pulled back a little, and met his dark gaze. "There could be more than a little self-interest in that statement."

He grimaced, and raised a hand, brushing my cheeks with his fingers. Longing shivered through me. "There is."

I stepped out of his arms, not wanting to be distracted by the warmth and promise of his touch. "Even if I make the decision not to go ahead and have a child, the situation between you and me is still a difficult one—and for many different reasons."

"There is nothing to stop us resuming where we left off."

"Where we left off was you declaring you had no intention of getting involved with another werewolf." I took a deep breath, and slowly released it. "My soul mate is still out there, somewhere. I won't risk losing him on top of maybe never being able to have a child."

"That doesn't mean we can't come to some arrangement—"

"But *could* you come to an arrangement?" I cut in. "Knowing that I have the intention of doing what I have to do—even if it means kissing or fucking every sinner in the goddamn state—to stop these bastards coming after me ever again?"

Which didn't mean I intended becoming a guardian— not unless the drug left me with absolutely no choice. But stopping these bastards *was* a priority, and if that meant I had to sleep with some of them, so be it. At least if I did my bit to help stop them, I could safely follow whatever path fate wanted me to go down without having to look over my shoulder at the ghosts I'd betrayed.

And if that future path meant a life without kids, then I guess I had to accept that.

Which meant the decision I'd come up here to make was, in the end, easy. The drug running havoc through my system had caused my fertility, and because of that, I dare not fall pregnant, no matter how desperately I wanted to take the chance. The future I faced was unknown, and as much as I didn't want to, I had to face the fact that *any* changes the drug forced on me would make me a guardian. It was either that, or be compelled into military service, as the other half-breed recipients of the drug had been.

I had no right to bring a child into that sort of environment, especially when neither Rhoan nor I had the support of our pack to help care for, and raise, a child if anything happened to us.

Quinn didn't answer my question, but he didn't really need to. We both knew he could never put up with me taking on all comers in the sex stakes. That sort of acceptance wasn't in his all-too-human attitudes.

"Look, Quinn, I'm not denying I want you, but I want you without strings. If you can't handle that—can't handle what I am, or what I intend to do—then back off and leave me alone."

Though his face was carefully neutral, I could see the annoyance burning in his eyes. Feel the force of it crawling across the electric night. It reminded me that he was a very old vampire, and obviously, despite all his urbane and courteous mannerisms, well used to getting his own way.

He might want me, he might be quoting pretty words about compromise, but deep down he was a territorial creature and he wasn't at all willing to share.

"So if I want you," he said, voice a little clipped, "I have to put up with you being the whore I think your race is?"

Anger surged and I clenched my fists, battling the urge to hit him. "You want to know why I'd rather fuck a stranger like Kade than you right now? Because he accepts who and what I am. You, on the other hand, want to change a basic part of me."

Anger burned around me, through me, and I wasn't entirely sure if it was mine, his, or a combination of both. But all the frustration that had built up over the months since Quinn had walked away came spewing forth, and I didn't have a hope in hell of stopping it now.

"I *don't*—"

"Then why do you call all wolves whores? Why even

think that when the moon dance, and the celebration of
life and love, is a basic part of what we *are*? We're *not* human. How dare you even try to judge us by human standards."

"I'm not—"

"Then why call us whores?"

"Isn't fucking someone for money or information
a definition of prostitution? Isn't that what you'd be
doing?"

"It's a human definition. Werewolves have no such
word, because we don't think that way."

"So you'll happily sleep with all and sundry to get information?"

"Happily? No. Will I do it? Yes, because it *is* only sex,
and sex is as vital to wolves as blood is to vampires."

"A vampire can die without blood. I doubt a werewolf
would die without sex."

"Maybe not." I crossed my arms and continued to
meet him glare for glare. "But we can certainly die if we
don't meet our soul mate."

He snorted. "I doubt—"

"Don't doubt, just listen. Werewolves believe that *true*
love is *not* something that happens by chance, but rather,
it is something determined by fate itself. We believe that
love is as immortal as the soul, and that we are destined
to meet the same lover over and over again, right
through all of our lifetimes. For wolves, there is only *one*
person on this earth who is destined to be our perfect
mate. One person who is our match, heart and soul. And
if we do not find that person, our heart and soul suffers.
Many do fade away, and many do die."

He didn't answer for a moment, then said, "Could not

the connection we share mean **there is som**ething worth exploring between us?"

"Definitely. But I have cared **deeply for two** other men in my life, and loved one. None of those three was my soul mate. The connection between us might have been emotionally and physically deep, but it wasn't *soul* deep." Something that had been proven when Haden, the wolf I'd loved so much as a teenager, had met his soul mate exactly one year into our relationship. Had we been exclusive, that would never have happened.

"So, where does that leave you and me?" Quinn asked.

"You tell me. I'm not the one trying to place boundaries on our relationship."

He sighed, and looked past me. The anger burning the air seemed to dissipate quickly on the cool breeze. "I'm a vampire. We tend to be very territorial."

I nodded. "Then it is you who has the decision to make, not me. I want to continue exploring what we share, but I will not risk restricting myself to you alone. I cannot. Nor, might I add, do I expect you to restrict yourself to me. I cannot be the only supply of the blood you need to sustain yourself."

He snorted softly. "A small comfort that makes little difference in the scheme of things."

"That's all I can offer right at this moment."

"I don't know if I could handle an open relationship. I'm just not built that way."

I raised an eyebrow. "We weren't exactly exclusive a month ago. I was still with both Talon and Misha then."

"A month ago I thought it was nothing more than a

casual dalliance, one that would be easily forgotten once I got home."

"So what changed your mind?"

His look just about liquefied my insides. "The fact that you kept invading my thoughts and my dreams."

He'd invaded my dreams, too. I wondered if, somehow, we'd been reaching out to each other through the link we'd created. "Yet you rebuked just about every attempt I made to see or talk to you. Even when I finally got you to come to dinner, you still stated you weren't interested in continuing any sort of relationship."

He shrugged. "I thought it was for the best. After Eryn, I had no wish for anything permanent."

"I wasn't suggesting anything permanent."

He looked at me, and didn't answer.

"And despite all those refusals," I continued, "here you are, all but demanding I be with you, and you alone."

"Because what we have deserves exploration."

"To what end, if you have no wish for anything permanent?"

Again, he didn't answer. Maybe that was a question he had no answer for.

"How many exclusive relationships have you actually had over your many years?"

His expression could only be described as dark. "Two or three."

I snorted softly. "In how many centuries?"

"It is hard to love someone when you know you must watch them grow old and die."

"Then why did you commit to Eryn?"

"As I said before, that was more a product of the drug than love. Had I been in my right state of mind, I would never have attempted that ceremony." His eyes were hard as he added, "I swore never to marry another woman four hundred years ago. It is a promise I hold to."

Which begged the question, what happened four hundred years ago? But I didn't bother asking, because I knew he wouldn't tell me. "Then you've never turned a lover?"

"No. It rarely works out well, anyway."

"Because of the territorial thing?"

He hesitated. "And because vampires cannot live on each other's blood."

They couldn't? That was interesting. I'd thought blood was blood, no matter what the source. I glanced at my watch and saw it was eight-thirty. The doctor would still be in his office if I rang now. "What happens next is up to you to decide. Just be well aware that I will have other partners, and I will not stop attending the moon dances. I can't afford to." I hesitated, watching his eyes, watching my words sink in. He wasn't liking them, wasn't accepting them. Not yet. "In the meantime, you got a phone I can use?"

He fished the keys out of his pocket, and tossed them to me. "In the car."

"Thanks. I'll meet you in the restaurant, if you like."

He nodded. I strode past him, and went to make the call that would end any hopes I had of having a child of my own.

In the end, we didn't get to eat. Quinn drove me back to the medical center, and the doctor inserted the intrauterine device that would stop any threat of pregnancy—it was also the only device that wasn't going to be detected by the blood tests I had no doubt Misha would insist on. He also inserted the monitor, as I suspected Misha would keep an eye on my file, and would be suspicious if it wasn't inserted. For that reason, I asked the doctor not to put anything on my file about the IUD, and though he was far from happy about it, he agreed. He had no choice really, as he knew I was Directorate and could easily have gotten the request enforced.

I don't really remember the elevator ride back down to the ground, though I do remember Quinn taking me in his arms and holding me for what seemed like forever. He never said a word, but then, he didn't need to. Though the link between us was locked down tight, I knew he understood my pain. He was a vampire, after all, and knew all about never being able to have kids.

It was after midnight by the time we got back to the apartment. Jack was there, sitting at his com-screen, and a somewhat fierce scowl crossed his features as we walked in.

"Where the hell have you two been?"

"Thinking," I said.

"And this thinking couldn't have been interrupted for a quick phone call update on what the hell was going on?"

"No." Actually, I hadn't even thought of it.

I glanced toward the other bedrooms. I knew my brother was in one, but there were snores coming from the other room. Kade, undoubtedly. Why the hell was he was still here? What did Jack plan to do with him?

And was there any way I could uncover the mystery of the horse-shifter?

"Want a coffee, boss?"

"Thanks."

I raised an eyebrow at Quinn, who nodded, then headed into the kitchen to get us all coffee. With that done, I sat down on the sofa opposite Jack and filled him in on everything that had happened. We talked for a good hour, after which I rang Misha. He was awake, as I knew he would be.

"We should talk," I said, the minute he answered the phone.

"Yes, we should."

I glanced at Jack, who was hooked up to my cell phone, listening in, as well as talking to the director on a second phone. He met my gaze and nodded, indicating everything had been arranged.

"Three o'clock. Macey Jane's, in Lygon Street."

My gaze slid passed Jack, and settled on Quinn. I was willing to meet him halfway, even though it wasn't entirely wise to do so. Whether he was willing to do the same remained to be seen. But the mere fact that his disapproval stung the air suggested he hadn't yet come to grips with the situation. Maybe he never would.

And as much as I wanted to be with him, I wasn't willing to change my entire life for him. Nor would I back down from this investigation. I needed to be a part of its ending, needed to see it ended with my own eyes, to be totally sure I was safe. If Quinn couldn't accept that, and accept me, then we were never meant to be. No matter how rich a piece of chocolate my hormones considered him to be.

"Sorry, that ain't going to happen," came Misha's drawl. "For a start, I don't trust the mob you work for *that* much. And secondly, I dare not step beyond known haunts at the moment. I'm being watched."

"Yeah, by the Directorate."

"And by those you hunt."

"Meaning they don't trust you?" My gaze went to Jack again. Did he know the Directorate wasn't the only one watching Misha? The raised eyebrows suggested not. "Why am I not surprised?"

His chuckle whispered down the line, stirring memories that were best forgotten.

"We'll meet at the Blue Moon."

Jack shook his head. I ignored him. We needed to find out what Misha knew, and while the Blue Moon wasn't a Directorate-patrolled safe place, it was somewhere *I* felt safe. I knew the people, knew the layout. And of all the werewolves' clubs, the Blue Moon was the strictest when it came to patron safety.

"I'd hardly call *that* a regular haunt of yours."

"Ah, but it has been since your disappearance."

A cold lump formed in my stomach. "You couldn't have known I'd escape that place."

"No, but I knew he'd underestimate you. He always has—"

"He who?" I cut in.

This time his soft chuckle made my skin crawl. "We'll have to discuss terms before we get to an exchange of . . . information."

"You'd better be offering some good information, Misha, or it's no deal. And it wouldn't matter if you were the only fertile wolf on the damn planet."

"I'm your only way out of a return to another of those pens," he said softly. "Believe that, if you believe nothing else."

The soft certainty in his voice sent another chill across my skin. I did believe him, though God only knew I was probably being stupid for doing so.

"When?"

Jack rolled his eyes, and looked decidedly unhappy as he began speaking into the second phone.

"Three's fine by me. I'll book one of the private rooms, just to ensure our conversation isn't overheard, but we'll meet on the dance floor. It'll look more like a coincidence to my watchers."

"If you know about them, why not get rid of them?"

"Because right now, they have their uses." Amusement was evident in his voice. I'd always thought Misha to be the quieter, saner of the two mates I'd had over the last few years, but that assumption was proving to be very wrong.

"Tomorrow is a werewolf-only day," he continued, "so neither the vampire or that horse-shifter you escaped with will get in. Rhoan can, but if I spot him, I'm out the door and the deal is off."

How had he known that Kade was still with us? Or was it simply a guess on his part?

"I don't think any of us trust you enough to agree to a deal like that."

"Tough. It's my way or the highway. They can put a tracker under your skin if they think I'm going to do a runner with you."

They could, and they would. I'd be damned if I'd risk getting snatched again. "Why just me?"

"Because I'm walking the edge of a sword right now, and have no intention of slipping over that edge until I'm sure of what lies below."

Which was a poetic way of saying he wanted to test the waters first. "You'd better not be bullshitting us, Misha."

"I'm not, believe me." He paused, and shifted. Silk sighed, and I had sudden visions of black sheets sliding over pale skin. "To prove this, may I suggest you get out of that Brighton penthouse within the next five minutes?"

Blood drained from my face, and my gaze jerked from Quinn to Jack. "How do you know we're in a Brighton penthouse?"

Even before I'd said the words, Jack was ordering Quinn to wake Rhoan and Kade.

"Same way I know you're about to be attacked by air. I suggest you move your pretty butt, Riley, if you want to make the meeting tomorrow."

By air? We were ten stories up, for fuck's sake...

I hung up, and swung around.

Just in time to see several blue things blast through the plate-glass windows.

Chapter 6

I barely had time to scream a warning before they were flowing through the cut glass and racing toward me. I backpedaled fast, blocking blows with my forearms. My skin crawled every time I touched the slick, cold flesh of the creatures. They smelled of rotting flesh even though none of them looked to be in decay, and my stomach rolled, threatening to rebel. I swallowed, and tried to breathe through my mouth as I punched one of the blue things in the face and sent him flying back across the room.

My neck prickled a warning. I spun. A fine line of silver arced toward me. This time, it wasn't an arrowhead laced with enough elephant juice to knock me out, but a goddamn laser. I dove out of the way, hitting the floor with a grunt that sent air whooshing from my lungs. The smell of burnt leather touched the air as the beam punched through the back of the sofa.

"Here," Rhoan said sharply.

Something silver spun through the semidarkness. Not another laser beam, but a laser. I caught it left-handed and twisted around as something grabbed my ankles. A stinking blue thing had my toes in his clammy little grip and was attempting to hold me still as he raised the laser. Stupid, that's what he was. Even *I* knew you didn't give an opponent an even chance to fire.

I pressed the laser's trigger and fired without bothering to sight. Right now, any hit was a good hit. Light that was red and somehow angry leapt across the distance between us, slicing into flesh and bone. The creature's arm plopped to the floor beside me, the stump black and smoldering rather than bloody. The smell of burnt flesh rent the air, and I almost lost my coffee right there and then.

Fighting the tide, trying not to breathe too deeply, I kicked with my free foot, sending him flying backward. Another beam of red bit across the darkness, finishing what I'd started.

I scrambled to my feet. Another of the creatures came at me, all arms and ugly flesh. I ducked several blows, then threw one of my own. My punch landed mid-gut, but it was like hitting Jell-O. Wet, slimy Jell-O that just wobbled under the impact, absorbing without consequence.

Well, shit... The thought got no further as his fist hit my chin and the force of the blow sent me flying backward. I hit a wall with a grunt, and slid down the paintwork, briefly seeing a double of everything.

Including a flying blue thing, its teeth bared and gleaming wickedly in the darkness.

I closed my eyes, tasting the air, judging his whereabouts and closeness by scent alone, then raised the laser and fired.

There was a thud, and the smell of burned flesh rent the air, making my stomach curl. I opened my eyes. Two headless blue things wavered in and out of focus near my feet.

"Riley," Rhoan said, suddenly coming into vision. A second later his hand grabbed mine. "You all right?"

He helped me rise, and I gave a shaky nod. "Just a little dazed by a punch to the chin."

He touched the right side of my face gently. "You're going to have a bit of a bruise there."

"So kissing is out for a day or so?"

"I'd say so."

"Bugger."

He grinned. "You don't need to kiss to have a good time."

"That's so true."

"You want some ice?"

"Please." It actually hurt to talk, but I'd be damned if I'd give *that* up.

He squeezed my arm, then turned around and headed for the kitchen area. "The question we need answered right now," he said, over his shoulder, "is how the hell did they find us?"

It didn't seem to be aimed at anyone in particular, so I shrugged and said, "Misha?"

"I wouldn't think so. He's playing a game that's

wholly his own. Which is not saying that he wouldn't betray us if it did suit him."

"And right now, it doesn't." Because of me, because of the plans he had for me.

Jack came out of a bedroom, a cut above his eye and his shirt torn. His normally merry features were cold and hard, and a good percentage of the anger gleaming in his eyes was aimed my way. "That was a fool thing to do, Riley."

I stared at him, confused. "What?"

"Arranging that meeting with Misha in the Blue Moon."

Oh, *that*.

"Hey, you wanted me to meet him. Don't blame me if he didn't want to play by your rules."

"We can't get people into the Blue Moon tomorrow. The man said it's a werewolf-only day."

"Yeah, but it doesn't matter, because nothing will happen to me there. Besides, there's only two exits to watch." My gaze went past Jack as Quinn came into the room. He didn't look hurt, even though he wasn't armed, and relief swam through me.

His gaze met mine, and some of the tension in his shoulders seemed to ease. "You okay?"

I nodded, warmed by his caring more than I wanted to admit, and forced myself to meet Jack's less-than-happy gaze again. "How many attacked us?"

"Five." His face was grim. "Looks like they were intent on getting you and the shifter back."

"Or getting rid of us," Kade said, as he came through the doorway carrying another laser pistol. "These things are set to kill, not stun."

"Goddamn it." Jack grabbed the gun from Kade, and examined it. "Are these the weapons you were talking about?"

"Afraid so." Kade's gaze raked my length and came to rest on my lips. He smiled. "Want me to kiss that bruise better?"

"Rhoan tells me kissing is off-limits for now."

"That's unfortunate. But I'm willing to compromise and kiss other places."

"Thanks," I said dryly, "but I think now is not the right time to be discussing compromises."

"Hey, I'm versatile—"

"Enough." Jack's voice was curt. "Grab your things, people. We're getting out of here while we can."

"And going where? Obviously the mole in the Directorate is someone close to the director if they know we're here." Rhoan came out of the kitchen and handed me an ice pack. "Either that, or Riley and Kade have trackers in them."

I raised my eyebrows. "You didn't check?"

"We ran a scanner over you both," Jack said, "but maybe they've developed something the scanners can't pick up." His expression became even grimmer. "Rhoan, you recheck Riley. Kade, let's look you over."

Rhoan motioned me to one of the bedrooms. I followed him in, and closed the door. Everyone in this apartment might have seen me naked at one stage or another, but I wasn't about to flaunt it at this particular moment.

"So," he said, "tell me about this meeting Jack is unhappy about."

I did as he began to check me for bugs.

"The Blue Moon is safe, no matter what Jack thinks. It's Misha you'll have to watch. Don't trust him, no matter what."

"I won't." I hesitated. "Why does the mole at the Directorate have to be someone close to the director?"

"Because she's the only one who knew our whereabouts."

"Which would suggest the Director herself." Only, she wasn't likely to betray her own brother, or the organization she'd started and run for more years than I'd been alive.

"It's not her. But it could be someone who has access to her office and maybe overheard a conversation."

"What about Gautier?" Even saying his name had a shiver running through me. Gautier might be the Directorate's top guardian, but he was a creep, a murderer, and, I suspected, a psychopath on the edge.

"He's not close to the director."

"But I'm betting he's reporting to someone that is."

"It wouldn't make a difference. Whoever the mole is, they've obviously been with the Directorate a long time. It's someone very canny, someone we wouldn't ever suspect."

"So make a list of people you'd never normally suspect, and start watching them."

"Hard to do when we don't actually know who we can and can't trust."

True. "Couldn't we just watch who Gautier talks to?"

"Gautier's clever enough to realize we're doing that." Rhoan glanced at me. "Besides, he's on assignment up north at the moment. Has been for the last month. He's not involved in this little episode."

At least that explained why I hadn't seen him around. I thought I'd just been damn lucky. "What about Alan Brown?"

"As shifty as hell, and definitely involved in something, but again, I'm not sure he's in on this."

"But he fast-tracked Gautier's entry into the Directorate, didn't he?"

"Yeah, but we've a feeling he was forced into that. Brown's being blackmailed."

I raised my eyebrows. "Someone knows about his appetite for whores?"

"His appetite for gambling, more likely." Rhoan sat back with a grunt. "Can't find anything resembling a bug."

Good. At least I wasn't responsible for bringing problems home to threaten him and the others. "If you know he's being blackmailed, then surely you'd be able to trace the source."

He rose, grimacing. "I wish it were that easy."

"Paper trail?"

"No trail."

"How come?"

"Brown's as cagey as a fox. We're certain he's giving someone information, but we can't uncover who or what."

"You've put him under surveillance, then?"

He gave me the look. "Hell, no. We just thought it was easier to let him wander around as he pleases."

I whacked his arm. "Don't get smart."

"Then don't ask dumb questions."

I grabbed my clothes off the floor and re-dressed. "What about the whores he uses?"

"You've seen the disks in his office. If he's using the

whores to pass information, there's only one way he could be doing it, because he certainly doesn't talk to them."

"He's a vamp, so he's telepathic. Maybe he's figured out a way around the psi-deadeners." Hell, if Jack could get past them, surely other vamps could. Though Brown didn't seem to be anywhere near the same league as Jack.

"We've checked the whores. Their minds haven't been touched."

"Then he *has* to be passing something during sex." Though given what I'd seen on those videos, the only thing Brown had seemed interested in passing was his own dead sperm.

"We've had our own cameras installed. We don't believe that is happening."

"Then how is he getting information in or out? And if you don't think he's involved in my snatching, does that mean he might not have been involved with Genoveve?"

"Possibly. Many of those files Brown inherited from the former assistant director."

"And he is?"

"Very dead."

I raised my eyebrows. "Accident?"

"Probably not."

I slipped on my shoes. Rhoan started for the door, but I placed a hand on his arm, stopping him. Lowering my voice, I asked, "I know you said you weren't going to steal Kade's file for me, but did you happen to search the database when you were in there today?"

"Yes. There's nothing to be found."

"Nothing you can get hold of, anyway."

"Yes." He looked at me. "What are you plotting?"

"Me?" I gave him my most innocent look. He didn't seem to be buying it. I smiled and added, "Look, don't you find it strange that he's here? You and I both know that Jack would normally have shipped him off so fast his head would spin."

"True enough." He continued to study me with that patient you're-about-to-get-me-into-trouble expression. "But that doesn't solve the problem that I can't get into locked files."

"No." I hesitated. "But I can."

"Oh, can you, now?" He eyed me with amusement. "I'm betting Jack doesn't know about that little gem."

"Er...no." As a liaison and his personal assistant, I did have some access that Rhoan didn't. But I'd also picked up some other access codes in recent months, thanks to time spent watching him key them in from the safety of my desk. It was amazing just how easily you could work out keystrokes if you took the time. "You really don't want to know any more. Do you?"

"No." He stood. "So what are you planning my part in this little snoop operation to be?"

"All you have to do is get me his com-unit."

He snorted. "Yeah. Like that's going to be so easy."

"It could be. After all, we're about to depart in haste. It'd be easy enough to grab equipment and just slide the com-unit my way."

He gave the sort of sigh that spoke of long-suffering patience. "I'll try."

I leaned forward and kissed his cheek. "Thanks."

He grinned and opened the door. "Anything to keep my twin happy."

"Anything to keep the peace, you mean."

"That, too."

Two of the three men in the main room swung around as we entered. Quinn was a shadow in the corner, but one whose presence I could feel through every pore.

"We're going to split into three groups," Jack said. "Rhoan, I want you to head into the Directorate and start writing up reports. Make sure they're encrypted and sent to Director Hunter only. Tomorrow morning, pick up some trackers and bugs, then head on over to the Blue Moon and do a thorough check of the club and its patrons. Riley's not going near the place until we know it's safe. Quinn, as we dare not risk any of the cars we have here, I want you and Riley to beg, borrow, or steal a vehicle, and drive around until we contact you to come in."

"And what will you and Kade be doing?" Quinn asked the question that was sitting on my lips.

"We'll be paying a little visit to the company who manufactures these devices." He held up the plastic-wrapped laser.

Rhoan and I shared a glance. If Kade was involved in something like that, he was definitely more than just a builder.

Jack tossed me a phone. "Don't go anywhere near that club until we call you."

"Just make sure you call me before three tomorrow. I doubt Misha will take kindly to being kept waiting."

"And yet he *will* wait. Remember, he's probably got as much to gain from all this as us. Let's move it, Kade." He headed for the door, but threw over his shoulder, "Rhoan, call in a cleanup team and ensure all Directorate goods are out of here before you leave."

My gaze shot across to my brother and I couldn't help my grin. Sometimes, things *did* fall into place.

He just rolled his eyes and shook his head as he said, "Quinn, do you want to head downstairs and find yourself a car? I'll meet you out front with Riley."

He waited until Quinn had left, then picked up the com-unit and walked over to hand it to me. "You do know he's going to check that all items were picked up from this place. Which means he'll realize soon enough this com-unit is missing."

"By which time, I'll have returned it." I kissed my brother's cheek. "Don't worry, I won't drag you into this one."

"How often have I heard that?" His voice was dry, and I grinned. We both knew the answer to that particular question was "more often than necessary." He touched my elbow lightly and motioned toward the bedroom I'd woken in. "Let's go grab a bag of clothes for you."

I walked into the room and dropped the unit on the end of the bed then headed for the wardrobe. "I just hope the passwords I know will get me deep enough into the system to uncover who the hell Kade is."

"If you haven't got full codes, it might be better *not* to tackle the Directorate's data, but rather, go for outside sources. As his assistant, you have clearances into most Government systems."

Now *there* was a thought. And it was less likely to get me in deep shit with Jack. "Uncover what he isn't, you mean?"

He nodded, and walked across the cut-open window. His short red hair barely stirred in the cool breeze as he stared out into the night. Given his expression—or rather, the chilled lack of it—those creatures wouldn't want to attack a second time.

"If Kade *is* a builder, there'll be trade certificates, business registrations, stuff like that. And you should be able to find other pointers, like birth certificates and school reports, to confirm he is who he says he is."

"And if he isn't who he says he is, I'll beat the damn information out of him." Hey, I had to take my frustrations over fate and the shit she was shoveling my way out on someone.

Rhoan's sudden smile lifted the coldness from his eyes. "Or you could tease him, then withhold sexual privileges. That'll get the information out of him right quick."

I smiled. "Ah, but that'll be punishing myself, as well."

"There's plenty of wolves out there who'd be more than willing to cure *that* particular affliction."

"Not to mention a particular vampire who'd be more than willing," I muttered without thinking.

"Is that why he's still here?" Rhoan asked. "Because he's finally realized he let a good thing go?"

I snorted. "It's not the only reason, no. I'm *never* the only reason he's down in Melbourne."

My voice held an edge, and he frowned at me. "I thought we'd sorted all this out?"

I blew out a breath. I really should learn to shut my mouth. "We did. But I sort of offered him a compromise."

He shook his head. "That's not wise."

I shoved the com-unit in the bag and cushioned it with more clothes and a couple of pairs of shoes. "I know,

I know. But if he *could* learn to deal with me having other partners, then I can't see the harm in it."

"The harm in it is that he won't ever change, no matter what he says."

Maybe. And maybe he deserved the chance to prove otherwise. "It's all a moot point until he says yea or nay to the compromise, anyway."

"So when did you make this deal?"

"Up on Macedon."

"And why were you up on Macedon?"

Oh God, I hadn't told him yet. I took a deep breath, and slowly released it.

"What aren't you telling me?" he said, more forcefully this time. We might not share the telepathy of twins, but in many ways, we didn't need it.

"That appointment I had was for the fertility specialist."

He was silent for a long moment. "And?"

"I'm temporarily fertile."

It wasn't the answer he'd been expecting and his shock rippled through the air. *"What?"*

"I can't risk it, Rhoan. Not with the ARC1-23 running through my system."

"Ah, Jesus." He swept a hand through his bristly hair, then strode toward me. After wrapping his arms around me, he squeezed tight and said softly, "I'm sorry, sis."

I could barely even nod, he was holding me so tight.

"Misha knows, doesn't he?"

"Yes."

"That's why he wants this meeting, then."

"Yes." Because he wanted to use me, and reproduce with me, just like everyone damn else seemed to.

Everyone except Kade, who just wanted to have a good time, and Quinn, who wanted me to be his, and only his. Only he didn't want the wolf, just the woman, and he couldn't have one without the other.

"I know how much you want a child, but you can't do it."

"I know." I pulled back. "I'm protected against pregnancy. Only Quinn knows that."

"I can imagine how he took it." Rhoan grimaced.

"Yeah, he did mention something along the lines of whoring myself for the sake of the Directorate."

"He may be a very old vampire, but he was still once human. And they just can't get their minds around sex being something that should be shared and celebrated. Which is why—"

"Don't," I interrupted, "lecture me on the subject anymore, bro. I've offered him a deal and I intend to stick to it."

"I still don't think it's a good idea, but I'll shut up on the matter." He kissed my forehead. "Let's get out of here, before those blue suckers decide to pay a second visit."

I glanced toward the lasered window. "You don't really think they'd attack again so soon, do you?"

"Probably not, but these people have a tendency to do the unexpected."

Like causing a car crash and snatching me for breeding purposes just when we'd all begun to think I was safe. Dammit, *why* were they after me? What was so goddamn important about my genes that they were so determined to have me? And why not Rhoan, who carried the same genes?

"So I can keep this?" I raised the small laser he'd given me earlier.

"Yeah. Jack will have a coronary, as they're guardian-only weapons, but right now, I don't give a shit." He grabbed the bag from my shoulder. "It's got a stun setting, if you'd prefer to shoot first and ask questions later."

"Already noted, bro."

He smiled. "Keep behind me, and wrap the shadows around you."

I did, and we made it down the stairs without mishap. Quinn was little more than a deeper shade of night, but I would have known he was there even if I wasn't using infrared. His rich scent warmed the night air.

"There's several cameras currently trained on us," he commented, opening the front passenger door for me. "I'm not sure if they're infrared, but I'll be dumping this vehicle as soon as possible."

"Good." Rhoan glanced at me. "Be careful."

He meant with Quinn. I leaned forward and kissed his cheek. "You too."

He waited until I'd climbed in, then handed me the bag. "If there's any trouble, call."

"I'll keep her safe," Quinn said.

"You'd better." Rhoan stepped back, and Quinn slammed the door shut. Five seconds later, my brother had gone back inside and we were under way.

"Where are we headed?" I asked, after a few minutes.

"After we dump the car? I'm open to suggestions. Neither my place nor yours would be safe right now, and hotel registers can be checked too easily."

And even signing in under a false name wouldn't be

safe, as there wouldn't be many people checking in at this hour of the night.

I rubbed my forehead wearily. There was an ache behind my eyes, my head was beginning to pound, and I desperately needed some sleep. But more than that, I needed some sort of sanity back into my life.

My gaze went to the softly lit ship that was crossing the bay, heading toward the open ocean. Right now, I felt like that ship—gliding through the darkness, heading for ever more treacherous waters.

But that ship at least knew its final destination. I had no idea.

"Riley?"

Sighing, I said, "Let's find somewhere I can use the com-unit safely. I need to check a few things."

His gaze swept me, a heat I felt rather than saw. "Like what?"

It was so tempting to snap out something along the lines of "that's none of your damn business," but that'd be churlish and he didn't deserve any more of that. "Like, who the hell Kade really is."

"So you fucked—" He stopped abruptly.

"Yes," I stated, wavering between annoyance that he'd started to repeat the same old line, and amusement that he'd actually stopped it mid-sentence. A small improvement was better than nothing, I supposed. "I fucked him without doing a background check. And don't you dare try and tell me you check the background of every woman *you* bed."

"No." He paused. "I apologize."

"Oh, I bet that hurt."

He gave me his vampire look and simply said, "What has made you suspicious of him?"

"The fact that he's still here, helping us."

"Ah, so it's not suspicion as such, but curiosity." He glanced at me. "You know what curiosity did to the cat."

"Yep. And it *so* won't stop me."

"*Nothing* seems to stop you."

Given I wasn't entirely sure how to take that statement, I simply said, "Where are we going to dump the car?"

"Here?"

I looked around the darkened, grimy streets, and could instantly think of a dozen better places to go. Which I guess made it the ideal spot. "Fine."

He swung into a side street and stopped in the shadows of an old gum tree. I grabbed my bag and climbed out. The wind had become even colder, whipping around my bare legs with some force, sending goose bumps fleeing across my flesh. The scent of the ocean mingled now with the overripe aromas of rubbish, age, urine, and stale human. The surrounding houses were as dark and dingy as the street itself, yet the sound of lovemaking that was coming from the one closest indicated that some of these hovels were at least occupied by more than the drunks I could smell.

I glanced across the roof of the car. "Do you know this area?"

"Not at all." He faded into darkness, and I switched to infrared. The heat of him moved around the back of the car. "This way." His breath whispered warmly past my ear as he took the bag from me.

I glanced at the house, saw the flame of the couple

loving each other, and fleetingly wished I had nothing more to worry about than achieving satisfaction.

Pulling my gaze away, I followed Quinn. We moved quickly through the maze of streets, always heading away from the city rather than toward it, as might be expected.

By the time he'd stopped, we'd made our way into a small shopping strip. I eyed the bedding shop with longing, but naturally, it wasn't that one he stopped at, but rather, the dingy-looking corner store.

"No alarms," he said, before I could ask. "And there's an unoccupied floor above it."

I didn't even have the energy to work up a glare. "I thought you were going to stop reading my mind?"

"No, I said you should guard your thoughts if you don't want me reading them." He forced open the door, and waved a hand. "After you."

The old shop hadn't been used for some time, if the dust layered on the counters and the aged taste of the air was anything to go by. I moved past a chair stacked on tables, brushed past several dangling cobwebs, and headed up the stairs. The upper floor wasn't large, but it did have a bed. And even though it smelled older than Methuselah, it was better than sleeping on rot-worn floorboards.

"You take the bed," Quinn said from the top of the stairs. "I'll keep watch from down below."

"Keeping out of temptation's way?" I said, with some amusement.

His expression was grim as it met mine. "As you noted before, I have a decision to make. I think it only fair I keep my distance until I do make that decision."

I grabbed my bag from him, then leaned forward and

kissed his cheek. "Thank you for being honest, and thank you for at least thinking about it."

Warmth touched his dark eyes. "Even a very old vampire can learn to be honest occasionally."

"So there's hope for you yet?"

The amusement died. "I don't know, Riley." He raised a hand, touching my cheek briefly but oh so tenderly. "I just don't know."

He turned and walked down the stairs. I blew out a breath, then sat on the sagging mattress and started up the com-unit. Half an hour later, I had the answer to at least one of the questions bugging me.

Kade had all the right certificates and records.

But Kade Williams didn't actually exist.

Lygon Street on a Saturday afternoon was a hive of activity and noise, the air rich with mouthwatering aromas. Quinn and I sat at an outside table, enjoying the brief splash of sunshine as we waited for three o'clock to roll around. From where I sat, I could see the Blue Moon, which was across the road and down a side street. Rhoan and Kade weren't to be seen, but I knew they'd be here somewhere. Jack waited in the underground car park down the road. He wasn't quite as old as Quinn, and had tighter sunshine restrictions.

I was making my way through a garlic heavy supersouvlaki, and barely resisting the temptation to breathe in Quinn's direction. Not because the whole garlic and vampires thing was true—it wasn't—but just because it would be an annoying thing to do and I was in an annoying sort of mood.

Part of that was our close proximity to the club. The scent of lust and sex and musk carried easily on the air, stirring my hormones to life. But considering the meeting I had to face, having eager hormones was a very good thing. Misha knew how badly I'd want a kid now that I knew for sure I only had a brief window of opportunity. He'd understand it instinctively, in a way only other werewolves could. He'd expect me to be sexually ready— aggressive, even—simply because female wolves usually were when they were ready to bear children. It didn't matter that we weren't soul mates—he'd still expect that sort of behavior from me, because he knew this might be my one and only chance.

Yet he also knew me well enough to know I wouldn't jump into anything without first questioning. He'd expect questions, and he'd expect me to answer his questions, as well.

And *that* was the other part of the whole mood equation. I wasn't entirely sure I was up to playing that sort of game with a man intent on using both sides for his own benefit.

Rhoan came sauntering up the street, a pleased smile touching his lips.

"The Blue Moon checked out, huh?" I said dryly, as he pulled out a chair and sat down.

"Yeah." He grinned. "Liander was there."

"And you did the wild thing on Directorate time?" I shook my head in mock disgust. "Really, bro, where are your morals?"

"In my balls, where most men's morals are. You planning to eat the rest of that souvlaki?"

I handed him the remainder and picked up my coffee,

warming my fingers on the exterior of the cup. "So, what's happening?"

"We have several people positioned at both exits. The trackers are picking up the bugs you're wearing loud and clear. Misha has been in the club since one."

I raised my eyebrows. "And he didn't see you?"

"Liander and I can be very discreet when we want to be. Besides, Misha's hammering a petite blonde."

Charming. I glanced at my watch, and saw that it was quarter to three. I gulped down my coffee and rose. "Time to go."

Neither man moved. They'd wait here, watching the main entrance, scanning the interior with infrared. Quinn's gaze came to rest on mine.

"Be careful" was all he said.

I nodded, kissed my brother on the cheek, slung my bag over my shoulder, and headed for the club.

The front doors swished open and Jimmy, the mountain-sized half-human, half-lion-shifter bouncer, gave me a grin.

"Hey, Riley," he said, engulfing me in his huge arms and giving me a hug that momentarily stopped my breathing. "It's been quite a while since you've been here. We were beginning to worry something might have happened to you."

Something *had,* but it was nice to know I was missed. I pulled him down to my level, and planted a quick kiss on his furry cheek. "It's nice to see you, too."

His smile got bigger, revealing two white and shiny front teeth. His own teeth had been knocked out in a fight here at the club over two months ago, and they'd obviously been replaced while I'd been away.

"Got a good crowd in today," he said, opening the door as I paid my entrance fee and picked up a locker key. "And Misha's here, if you're interested."

"Misha?" I feigned surprise. While I trusted Jimmy, I didn't know the ticket seller or the security guard on the second door, and I wasn't about to chance the fact that they weren't one of Misha's watchers. "He's usually at the Rocker on Saturdays."

Jimmy's expression became smug. "They've introduced a 'modern music' Saturday. From what I've heard, it may have gained them a younger crowd, but it's lost them a lot of regulars."

"And that's gotta be good for the Blue Moon."

"Oh, it is. It's not even three, and we're almost full. We'll have a waiting list by nightfall."

I gave him the ticket. "I'm gathering that smile of yours means you've decided to pick up the offered shares in the club?"

"Yep. I'm now hoping the Rocker decides to extend the modern music theme, so I can make lots of lovely moola. Have a good time, Riley."

I grinned. "I intend to."

He closed the door. Darkness swamped me, and while I could switch to infrared easily enough, I simply stopped and gave my eyes time to adjust. Infrared didn't do the club or its atmosphere justice.

Hologram stars blossomed along the roof, but their twinkling glow was being overshadowed by the stronger light of the blue moon, which had almost peaked in its journey across the midnight-colored ceiling. Tables and chairs ringed the huge dance floor that dominated the room, and it was packed with singles and couples, some dancing, some making love, some simply watching.

The music played by the DJ in the far corner was filled with sensual and erotic melodies designed to seduce the senses, and the air was as hot as the music, rich with the scent of lust and sex. I breathed deep, allowing the atmosphere to soak through my pores, right into my very bones. An answering tremor of excitement coursed through every fiber. I loved this place. Always had.

I walked down the steps and headed into the change rooms. After taking a quick shower to wash the smell of dust from my skin, I popped a mint to lose the garlic breath then did my makeup. After finger-combing my damp hair, I shoved my bag into the locker, clipped my credit card and locker key onto a chain around my neck, then naked I headed out into the crowd.

Closer to the dance floor, the sensual beat of the music was accompanied by grunts of pleasure and the slap of flesh against flesh. The fever in my blood rose several more notches and my breath caught, then quickened. The press of flesh made my skin burn, and my already erratic heart race that much harder.

I couldn't see Misha, but that wasn't surprising, given he'd supposedly been mating with a blonde when Rhoan had left the club. Misha had never been one to miss an opportunity, and I suspected he'd enjoy making me wait.

But if he was playing it straight, and did have a tail, I couldn't make it look like I was searching for him. Which meant I could have a little fun before I got down to the nitty-gritty end of business. Hell, Rhoan wasn't the only one capable of abusing Directorate time, and I had no intention of letting Misha think he was going to get away with forcing me to wait.

I pressed deeper into the crowd, dancing, flirting, and generally having a great time. Several males gravitated toward me, drawn to the scent of a free and willing wolf as easily as bees to a honeypot. We danced, and while it was both playful and sensual, it was also very much an erotic foreplay, with both men vying for attention and favors. I toyed with them, teased them, enjoying their caresses, their kisses, the heat of their bodies pressed against mine.

But before I could decide between the two, a third wolf joined our dance. His hands slid around my waist, his touch possessive, almost demanding. He pressed me back against him, his body like steel against my spine, his erection pressing teasingly between the cheeks of my rear. Little flash fires of desire skittered across my already overheated skin, and I knew in that instant it was him I wanted inside.

With the skill of a true artist, he herded me away from the other two men. I didn't care. Not when our dance was a slow but carnal overture of what was to come.

His breath was warm against my neck and ear, the kisses he dropped across my shoulders and neck as sensual as his touch. And his touch had me melting.

"Turn around." His voice was a husky growl that sent my pulse rate soaring.

I obeyed. He was a brown wolf, though his skin and hair were more warm chocolate in color than the usual mud color of the brown packs. He was lean, but muscular in an athletic sort of way, and his eyes were the most amazing shade of green. Mint colored, flecked with gold.

He wrapped his arms around my waist and pulled me close again. Sweat formed where we touched, and the air was so thick with the heat of our desire I could barely breathe. And somewhere in the foreplay of our dance, I realized he was an alpha wolf. It was there in the way he moved, in the authority of his touch. In the way he took control. An alpha was a rare find here in Melbourne, where male wolves were generally more gamma or even beta. Alphas were leaders, takers, and tended to accumulate in Sydney, where the fiercely competitive, intensely dominant attitude of an alpha more easily fitted in.

I'd never been with a true alpha before, as Talon didn't really count. Although he *was* an alpha, he was also lab created and all his assets—including his machismo—had been amped up by his creators.

But there was something about *this* alpha that called to me in a way few other wolves had. Maybe part of that was simple curiosity. Alphas had the reputation of being excellent but demanding lovers, and if he made love anywhere near as well as he danced, well, I wasn't about to say no.

We moved deeper into the heated crush of bodies, where the smell of sex was so powerful it was almost liquid, and space was at such a premium that it felt like a hundred different people were touching, pressing, caressing. We danced some more, played some more, teasing and tasting, nipping and kissing each other, until the need that pulsed between us became all-consuming.

Just when I thought I could stand no more, his mouth claimed mine, his kiss fierce as he lifted me up and onto him. Then he was in me, and it felt so damn good I groaned.

Wrapping my legs around his waist, I began to move, riding him slowly, savoring the sensations flowing through me, until the waves of pleasure rippling my skin became a molten force that would not be denied. And as the shudders of completion ripped through us both, and the warmth of his seed flooded deep inside, I found myself wishing that this wolf was fertile, that he and I could make a child. An odd wish, given I didn't even know his name.

Yet I didn't really need to, because there was something about him that seemed oddly familiar.

The stranger leaned his forehead against mine for a moment, then said, in a husky voice that had a tingle vibrating right down to my toes, "I want you for the evening."

Normally, I wasn't overly fond of demands, but the way he said "want" made me melt. Or maybe that was the press of his lean, hard body against mine. I took a deep breath, and tried to remember I was here for a reason.

"Unfortunately, I have a prior arrangement." Which was nothing but the truth, though a dangerous one to admit to a stranger given I had no idea who Misha's watchers were. For all I knew, I'd just fucked one of them.

"No chance of breaking it?"

"Not this time."

"Ah." The rich green depths of his eyes gleamed with hunger, warmth, and amusement. And something else. Something that made my breath catch in my throat, and my heart do a strange flip-flop.

It was the recognition of destiny.

And I knew, in that moment, this man would play a major part in my future.

If I lived to *have* a future, that was.

"My timing seems to be off yet again." His voice was a low growl of frustration that sent a warm shiver up my spine.

Talk about one hot wolf...then his words clicked, and I realized I'd met him before. Here, on this dance floor, in a similar situation. Only that time, he'd let me get away before we got as far as sex.

"Kellen?"

His warm, slow smile sent another surge of desire through my bloodstream. "I was wondering if you'd remember me."

I raised an eyebrow. "I'm surprised you remembered me. We only shared a five-second dance."

Humor vied with the desire in his eyes, an appealing mix that had me mentally cursing the reason I was here. When it came to sex, I'd much rather play with *this* wolf than the icy pole I had waiting.

"Sometimes," he said, voice a low rumble that shivered across my skin, "five seconds is all you need to know exactly what you want."

I smiled. "Smooth line."

"But the truth, nonetheless." His hand slid down my spine to my rump, and pressed me closer. The rich smell of him—leather and warm spices—teased my senses, tested my resolve. "The only reason I am in this club is to catch the attentions of a certain flame-haired wolf. She's been remarkably absent until tonight."

My treacherous hormones were suddenly scurrying to form a fan club for the green-eyed wolf. "Sorry. Had a problem with a former partner and had to stay away for a few months."

Which was nothing but the truth. And a damn pity, if this man had been waiting for me here all that time.

"I want you, and I intend to have you," he said. "Not for just one dance, but for many. And you're not escaping me tonight until I at least get a phone number."

Given that Quinn and Kade weren't likely to be long-term prospects, and Misha *definitely* wasn't, I certainly had no qualms about giving him my cell phone number. Even if he was a psycho, he couldn't actually trace me through it, because it was a work phone.

Once I'd given him the number, he kissed me. As kisses went, it was top-notch, and a definite signal of intent.

When he finally pulled away, he added, "I'll call to-morrow."

Even without his words, the determination evident in his green eyes, and the flare of his nostrils, warned that this was a wolf on the hunt.

I'd never been considered prey before, and damn if it didn't make me want him all the more. In the past, my relationships, even with Misha and Talon, had only grown into something permanent after many casual liaisons—and only after I'd decided I liked them enough to proceed on to something more. But they'd never pursued me with single-minded determination, even though both of them had been sent with the purpose of seducing me. This alpha obviously didn't want a casual dalliance, and he had no intention of waiting until I made up my mind. The chase was on, and modern wolf or not, my blood raced at the thought.

I kissed him, soft and lingering. "Please do."

"I will, rest assured of that."

While my hormones did an excited little shuffle, he escorted me to the change room, then gave me a kiss that again left me in no doubt of future intentions. As he walked away, I headed into the change room, and couldn't help feeling dizzy with elation. My life might be one big mess, and my future decidedly dark, but at least tonight I'd found something—or someone—to look forward to.

I went to the toilet and cleaned up, then headed back out. Kellen was nowhere to be seen, and part of me was glad. I had a feeling he might just fight for my attentions, and while I was wolf enough to think that wasn't a bad thing, neither Misha nor I needed that sort of attention at the moment.

Misha was over near the bar, sitting on a stool and nursing what looked like a beer. I made my way toward him.

"Didn't expect to find you here," I said, kissing his cheek and forcing a cheerful note into my voice. "What happened to the Rocker?"

His eyes met mine, then briefly slid past. I understood the warning clear enough. His watcher was near. I'd have to be the one to make the moves.

"They've decided to go modern," he said, his voice dry. "And you know I can't stand that stuff."

"You and me both." I plonked down on the stool beside his. "You want another beer?"

"Sure."

I ordered two from the bartender, then said, "You know, it's nice to see you again."

Amusement touched his cold eyes. He raised a hand,

brushing the hair away from my cheek, his fingers cool against my skin. "It's been a while," he said softly.

I resisted the urge to pull away. "How come you're here alone? You've usually got a half dozen pretty blondes hanging off you five minutes after you walk into a club."

His smile was warm, genuine. "I did have. But I've got an important liaison with a couple of pretty sisters in the green room in—" He paused, glancing at his watch. "Forty-five minutes."

The green room was one of five private rooms the Blue Moon offered, and from what I'd heard, the most expensive. It apparently came complete with a spa, vibrating chairs, the latest in "air" beds, and for those who got off on pain, a whipping area. "And you're not using it in the meantime? Misha, you're getting old."

He grinned. "Conserving strength, more likely." He thanked the barman as he placed our drinks, then added, "The sisters are young and extremely active."

"So," I said softly, sliding my hand up his thigh, "there's nothing I could say that would sway you toward putting that room to use for the next half hour?"

He raised an eyebrow. "The last time I saw you here, you said you wanted nothing more to do with me."

I'd said nothing of the sort, though I'd certainly thought it. But given Misha could no more read my mind than I could his, it was obviously said for the benefit of the watcher. And if I wanted to pick Misha's brain, I had to play this game, at least for the time being.

"As I told you at the time, I don't take kindly to being kept waiting. Not when there's plenty of other offers on the table."

"So what made you change your mind?"

I forced a grin, and lightly ran my fingers up and down his erection. "What makes you think I have? Maybe I'm just getting a little revenge. Making you rue missed opportunities."

"Oh, I have been," he said dryly, "especially in the last few minutes."

"So that means we can play?"

"I guess if you're going to insist..."

"And I am."

"Then a sensible wolf has no choice but to give in."

He rose, and offered me a hand. I placed my fingers in his, grabbed the beer with my free hand, and slid off the stool.

He escorted me down the dark hall, and opened the last door. Candles flickered in the wall sconces set in each corner, throwing pale light across walls painted in various shades of green, so that they resembled leaves in a forest. The ceiling was black, and dotted with hologram stars that offered little in the way of light. What looked like a mat of dry leaves sat near the right wall. This was obviously the air bed. Had I been here with anyone else but Misha, that would have been the first thing I tried out. Instead, I headed for the pondlike spa, easing myself into the steaming, bubbling water with a sigh.

Misha locked the door, then pressed several buttons on the security panel to the right of the door, setting the timer and the psychic shield.

"So," I said, dropping all pretense of niceness. "Tell me why I should let you fuck the hell out of me."

"Because you want a kid."

"Besides that. You and I both know that I could walk

out onto that dance floor and within five minutes have half a dozen wolves ready and willing to get their chips ripped out and attempt to have a kid with me." Though there was only one particular wolf I'd actually be interested in.

Misha nodded. "The chance of having a son, with no strings attached, is something few male wolves would pass up."

"So why should I settle for you?"

He slipped into the opposite end of the spa, and stretched his arms across the edge. The heat of the water lent warmth to his pale skin, but it did little to erase the calculating chill from his gaze. "Because you also want answers."

"You haven't yet proven you can give them to me."

"No, but I will."

"And what do you get out of the deal?"

He raised an eyebrow. "A son or a daughter to carry my name."

The slight edge in his voice made me frown. "Why is that suddenly so important?"

"Because I'm dying."

I blinked, not sure I had heard him right. "What?"

"I'm dying." He shrugged, as if it was something he'd long ago accepted. "And I want to leave this world knowing something of me is left behind."

There was only truth in his words, not lies. At least in this one instance.

"You're dying because you're a clone?"

He smiled. "You know more than I thought."

"We've had Talon for a few months now."

"Ah, yes." He considered me, icy eyes slightly narrowed, nostrils flaring. Another wolf on the hunt, and I wasn't entirely sure for what. "Talon was produced in the same batch as I. There were three others produced alongside us. Talon and I are the only ones left alive."

"Why?"

"Because the very chemicals used to help give us life are now snatching it away." He grimaced. "I've begun to age at twice the normal rate. It isn't yet showing, but it soon will. If the pattern of my disintegration follows that of my lab brothers, I will be dead inside five years."

"And Talon?"

"Will undoubtedly soon suffer the same fate."

I wondered if Jack or the lab boys knew. "So how long ago did the three created with you die?"

"Two didn't make it to their teens. One died at sixteen."

I sipped my beer, then asked, "Why?"

He hesitated. "What do you know about cloning?"

"The DNA from a donor egg is sucked out, and the cell of a donor used to replace it. Then it's fried into activity and away it grows."

He grimaced. "Crudely put, but reasonably accurate. The process is far from perfect, even now. There are always problems, and those of us who *do* make it into adulthood without problems then have to contend with a self-destruct button that somehow is related back to the method used to fuse cell and egg and switch on the DNA sequencing." He took a drink, then added, "Two of the three who died were victims of large offspring syndrome, and one was born with an immune system that was, at best, poor."

From what I'd read about cloning, having two out of five survive into adulthood was a pretty damn good success rate. "Yet despite these difficulties, they obviously survived quite well. At least for the first few years."

He nodded. "Medically, we're far enough advanced to keep them alive where once we could not. However, no one has yet uncovered the sequence that becomes the self-destruct button once the clone reaches a certain age. Nor do we know why some clones can reach their forties, like me, and others don't even live to see their tenth birthday."

"I'm amazed Talon never tried to research that—after all, he had a vested interest in uncovering the answers."

"Talon is a lot less circumspect than his creator, as evident in his approach to cloning. He also believes that he will not face what the rest of us have faced, that he is destined for greatness."

I snorted. "And like all mad, would-be dictators, he got his comeuppance."

"In the labs of the Directorate. Quite fitting that he ends in a lab similar to the place where it all began."

I raised an eyebrow. "Is that how you plan to end? In a laboratory?"

His smile was grim and cold. "I intend to go down fighting."

And I had a feeling he wasn't talking about the self-destruct button built within his genes. I frowned. "So, are you wolf, or part vampire, like Talon?"

"All wolf."

"Then why not clone yourself a mirror image?"

"Because, for all its advances, cloning still carries too many risks—risks I'd rather not inflict on any offspring of mine. And, as I said to you not so long ago, I am not involved in the cloning side of the research."

"But you are involved in the crossbreeding."

"No. My companies undertake research to discover the secrets of a vampire's long life."

And now I knew why—he was dying. And just in case he didn't discover the secret in time, he wanted a kid to carry his genes and his name.

It was a desire I could sympathize with—which made me wonder just how much he was playing me.

"Given Talon was running Moneisha and Genoveve, does that mean another lab brother runs the crossbreeding facility?"

He hesitated. "Not exactly."

"Meaning?"

He simply smiled, so I tried a different tack. "Just how many of you clones are there?" We knew that there was one other, at least, besides Misha, but who knew how many Talon had gotten around to releasing?

He chuckled softly. "Not as many as you seem to think. All up, if you include Talon, there are five of the original cloning attempts left."

"Meaning, non-Talon clones?"

He nodded.

So, given Gautier was one, that left two we didn't know about. "What about the Talon-created clones?"

"I think roughly a dozen remain, though I have not been able to keep track of all Talon's creations, so there could be more. Most are dead, though, or soon will be dead."

"That self-destruct button you mentioned?"

"No, the Directorate. The mob you work for are an efficient killing machine, Riley."

Which is why I was fighting like hell *not* to become a guardian. "So what was the aim of the original five?"

He hesitated. "To carry on and perfect our lab father's research, by whatever means needed."

It was the "by whatever means needed" bit that had me worried. Talon had certainly shown no need to follow the rules, and the man behind the crossbreeding had proven he was ready to kill to keep his secrets.

And if that was the true aim, then why place Gautier at the Directorate?

"You knew I was in that facility, didn't you?"

"Yes, but I was not responsible for you being there, nor was I the one who tended to you there."

"So who did?"

He smiled again. "I can point you to the path that will lead you to the person, but I cannot give you the name."

"Why not?"

"For the same reason Talon cannot."

I raised my eyebrows. "Talon couldn't tell us because the name has been burned from his mind. Are you saying the same thing has happened to you?"

"In a sense, yes. I know the name, but I am prevented from saying it to anyone."

"So why not just give me his address?"

"Personal details are included in the ban."

Which was a little too convenient. I finished my beer and glanced at the timer in the door panel. We had less than half an hour left. "Then explain to me why the hell the person behind all this is so determined to get his mitts on me."

"Because forty years of research has not produced a crossbreed who has fully assimilated his or her dual nature the way you have. It makes you unique. Makes you desirable for research purposes."

Which was the same reason Jack had theorized some time ago. And the fact that Misha didn't mention Rhoan hopefully meant they weren't aware that he carried the very same genes. "They weren't trying to research my genes in that damn facility."

A smile touched his mouth. "Yes, they were. But the man in charge of the facility was certainly taking advantage of the situation as well. He says you owe him."

If it was a hint, it was one I didn't understand. I frowned. "So why spend all this time and money on this sort of research? Especially when both you and Talon are successful businessmen in your own right?"

He shrugged again. "It is what we were programmed to do."

"Bullshit."

He grinned. "Then how about money and power? There's a lot of both to be had for the man who unlocks the secret of a vampire's longevity, or the werewolf's ability to heal almost any wound."

"And a lot of power to be had for the man who could create an army specially designed to handle specific locations and situations." He'd said that to me once. I hadn't understood at the time he was actually feeding me a piece of the puzzle. "You could virtually name your own price."

"Exactly."

I toyed with the empty beer bottle. "The military is trying to do the same thing, isn't it?"

"Yes."

"Are you involved with the military, in any way?"

"Not me personally."

"Your company?"

"No."

"Your fellow clones?"

"Sort of."

Well, that was helpful. "Give me a starting place, then."

He raised an eyebrow. "Not without setting terms. Not without a down payment."

Annoyance rushed through me. "You'll get your down payment when I get proof that you're playing it straight."

"Not good enough, Riley. Not when I'm risking my life by even being seen with you."

"You keep saying this, but why would they kill you when they obviously need you?"

"Because my part in the grandeur scheme is only minor. And right now, I'm walking the line of being more a hindrance than a help."

I didn't believe him. Not this time. I had a suspicion he was doing this for reasons that were purely personal. And while I had no doubt he was telling the truth as far as the reasons for wanting a kid went, I also had no doubt there was more to it than that.

Like maybe playing both sides of the fence until he knew for sure who would be the victor.

"If that's the case, how the hell are you going to be my only way out of a return to those damn research pens?"

"Because I have something he wants."

The cold satisfaction in his voice sent a chill down my spine. "What's that?"

He raised an eyebrow. "I swear on the moon that I can, if I want, keep you safe from another attack. Is that enough of a pledge?"

"It would be, if I believed it."

"The lack of attacks will be proof enough."

My fingers tightened around the neck of the beer bottle, but I resisted the urge to throw it at his head. "So, if I agree to your terms, you'll get the dogs called off, but not before?"

"Precisely."

I blew out a breath. "What are your terms?"

"No other wolf but me." His silver eyes gleamed fiercely in the candlelight. "Which means steering well clear of that damn alpha I saw you with earlier."

Like hell. "Everyone *but* that wolf I was with tonight. He's chipped, so he's no threat that way, and if I stop all contact with wolves other than you, your watchers will be suspicious."

He grunted. Obviously unhappy, yet willing to concede the point. "You meet me at the Rocker, every weeknight and on Sunday, at midnight, and give me two hours of your time."

"I thought you said you don't go to the Rocker anymore?"

"I'm there every night except Saturday."

"Won't my suddenly turning up raise suspicions?"

"No, simply because my watchers have grown so used to the routine they no longer bother watching me at night."

"Except tonight."

"They always watch me when I come here, simply

because they know you come here. They don't want me with you."

"Why?"

He grinned. "Because they don't want you pregnant with my kid."

I raised an eyebrow. "Again, why?"

The gleam in his eyes suggested that was something he wasn't ready to impart yet. And I had an odd feeling the reason went back to the man behind the cross-breeding.

"Don't tell me," I said dryly. "You can't say."

"You catch on quick."

Not quick enough, obviously. It had taken me entirely too long to realize he—and Talon—were using me. "If I stop coming to the Blue Moon, they'll get suspicious."

"Which is why on Saturdays you will come here and we shall ignore each other."

Oh, goody. I had a night off to play as I desired. "Ignoring you means being with other wolves if my alpha isn't there. That contradicts your terms, doesn't it?"

"You are free to be with whom you wish that day only," he amended. "Do you agree to the terms?"

I hesitated, not wanting to seem overly eager. *Not* that I was. But he was a means to an end, and besides, whether I liked him personally or not, he was usually a good lover. "What if I do fall pregnant? What then?"

"Then I will support you and the child, and do everything in my power to protect you."

"There's a major flaw in that thinking. You could be dead in five years." So could I, but I wasn't about to point that out.

His smile was hard, his eyes icy. "Believe me, I have ways of ensuring you're protected."

I didn't think I was ready to know just what he meant by that.

"Do you agree?" he asked again.

I would have agreed to just about anything, but he wasn't to know that. So I let the silence stretch between us, letting him think I was mulling over the terms when all I wanted to do was make the down payment and get the first lot of information.

"Yes, I agree."

"And my payment?"

He got it. Then I got my starting point.

The man who didn't exist.

Kade Williams.

Chapter 7

The first person I saw as I came out of the Blue Moon was Kade himself. He leaned against one of the building's canopy supports, arms crossed and gleaming a rich burgundy in the dying light of the afternoon.

His smile lit his face, warming his eyes, but just as quickly, everything faded. He straightened abruptly.

"Riley—"

I stopped in front of him, and thrust my hands on my hips. "Why the hell didn't you tell me you were military?"

Something skittered through his eyes. Surprise, perhaps. "Because I wasn't sure you were who you said you were."

"And when you knew?"

"You haven't the clearance. You're just a secretary."

"My God," Rhoan said, walking up behind Kade,

"you're really looking for a punched nose, making a statement like that."

Kade took a sideways step, probably to ensure we were both in his line of sight. I'm not entirely sure why— I mean, surely I didn't look *that* angry? I didn't feel that angry, anyway.

"Look, Jack didn't tell you, so I couldn't."

"Regardless of the fact I got your ass out of that place?"

"We got each other out of there, sweetheart. And I couldn't risk identifying myself. Too much was at stake."

"Like what?" Rhoan asked.

Kade's gaze skated around the busy street. "We can't do this here."

"Then at least tell me your name. Your real name."

"Kade *is* my real name."

"But not Williams?"

"No." He eyed me. "A fact you obviously know."

"Obviously."

"How?"

"As you said, not here." I looked at my brother. "Where's Jack and the van?"

"Still in the car park down the street." He glanced at his watch. "Jack hasn't been out of sunshine restrictions long. I figured we might as well go to him."

"Then let's go."

Rhoan fell in step beside me, his hands shoved in his pockets and whistling tunelessly. Kade stayed one step behind us. Perhaps he felt it was safer not to antagonize the wolf any more than necessary.

Which was always a wise move, even if I wasn't actually angry with him.

"So," Rhoan said, after a few seconds. "Who's the other wolf I can smell on your skin?"

I gave him my most innocent look. "I have no idea what you mean."

Amusement touched his lips. "Like I was the *only* one partying on the Directorate's time. Ante up with the gossip, dear sister."

I grinned. "Well, I had to make it look like I wasn't there to meet Misha, didn't I?"

"Uh-huh."

"And I have met him before."

"And this is a good excuse because . . . ?"

"Because he's an alpha wolf on the prowl, and right now, it's my scent he has in his nose."

Rhoan's gaze all but burned a hole in the side of my face. "Well, aren't you having all the damn luck?"

If I was having all the damn luck, I wouldn't have ended up in the breeding center or being attacked by flying blue things.

"You going to see him again?" Rhoan continued.

"Of course."

He grunted. "Good. Always said it was going to take an alpha to catch that heart of yours. He could be the one."

"Could be." After all, who knew what fate had planned? Certainly not me. Not after all the shit she kept heaping my way.

The car park Jack had chosen had once been an old office building that had been converted to try and cope with the ever-growing number of cars coming into the city. The building was thin and narrow, and smelled of exhaust fumes, gasoline, and wet mustiness. I wrinkled my nose. "Where is he parked?"

"Tenth floor. And the elevators are out."

"Great."

"Why don't you park your pretty butt right here, and I'll go fetch them?" Kade suggested.

I shared a glanced with my brother. Rhoan had his cell phone and could have easily called Jack down, but hey, who was I to stop a man eager to please? "Go for your life."

He ran off. The two of us enjoyed the sight, then Rhoan said, "Making any man run ten flights is just plain mean."

"He's fit enough," I said mildly. "Besides, that's what he gets for being dishonest."

He crossed his arms and leaned back against a railing. "So, did you learn anything useful?"

"Yes." Somewhere in the dark and distant bowels of the parking lot, a door squeaked. My gaze searched the shadows, seeing nothing out of place. So why was unease suddenly prickling across my skin? I frowned and glanced at Rhoan. "Can you smell anything?"

He raised his nose slightly, sniffing the odious air. "Besides car fumes and mold, you mean?"

I nodded and rubbed my arms. It suddenly seemed cooler in the car park—or was that simply my imagination? The feeling that something was out there in the dark, watching us?

"Not really." He hesitated. "Well, there *is* something—but I can't place it."

"I think perhaps we'd better start walking up toward

the van." I scanned the shadows again. "I don't like the feel of this place all of a sudden."

He nodded, and touched my elbow, lightly guiding me toward the up ramp.

That's when I heard it.

The slight scrape of claws against concrete.

I froze. So did my brother.

"It came from the right," he said softly. "From near the other ramp."

I flicked to infrared, and the shadows leapt into focus. And there, deep under the cover of the ramp, was a familiar hunched shape.

My mouth went dry. "Orsini."

"Ugly-looking suckers, aren't they?" Rhoan commented. "How fast are they?"

"Very."

"So if we run, it's likely to catch us?"

"Yep."

"One option out, then."

I looked at him. "Have you got a gun?"

He shook his head. "Couldn't carry it into the club, and didn't bother grabbing one afterward."

"That's slack. What if someone tried to snatch me?"

"They wouldn't have gotten far. Trust me on that." His expression became somewhat grim. "So, I guess we're left with our dhampire strength versus orsini."

"If it comes to hand-to-paw combat, I'm betting on the orsini."

He gave me an offended sort of look. "My little sister has such confidence in me."

"I've fought these things before, that's all."

The creature in the shadows raised its ugly head and

howled. The high, almost keening sound grated against my nerves and set my teeth on edge. I didn't want to face these things again. I really didn't.

"If we stay still, maybe it won't attack before the van gets here."

"I doubt it," Rhoan said. "Besides, it'll probably only give chase to the van, and we really can't afford to have that thing out on the street."

The sharp keening gained an echo. There was a second creature behind us. Great. Just fucking great.

"In case you've forgotten, there's weapons in the van. Weapons are good. Weapons kill ugly sons-of-bitches like these from a distance."

"A moot point if they're going to attack us the minute we move. And the van's not here yet." He squeezed my elbow then let go. "You beat them when you were alone and unarmed. You can do it again. Ready?"

"I'll never be ready to fight, Rhoan."

"I can't do it alone. Not when they've split up."

"I know." I took a deep breath and released it. "I'll go right." And hope like hell the cavalry gets here soon.

"Luck."

"Luck and I aren't on speaking terms," I muttered.

Rhoan's grin faded as he shifted into shadow. As his footsteps retreated toward the first orsini, I kicked off my shoes, tossing them into the air with my toes so I could catch them, then sprinted barefoot across the car park.

The second orsini stood behind a car in the far corner. It roared as I moved, and the harsh sound echoed across the silence. I hoped they heard it above. Hoped they hurried.

The creature leapt out of the shadows and ran at me, its claws scrabbling harshly against the concrete, sending sparks shooting into the shadowed confines of the car park.

As it neared, I pivoted, slashing out with my foot, kicking it as hard as I could in the head. The shock of the blow reverberated up my leg, but didn't seem to do a whole lot of damage to the beastie. It simply shook its head as it slid past. I dropped my shoes and grabbed a fistful of shaggy hair, heaving with all my might in an effort to throw it sideways into the nearby concrete pillar. It barely even budged, but slashed out with a hind claw, raking my legs and drawing blood.

I yelped and let go of its hair, grabbing the paw instead. I pulled backward as hard as I could, dropping to the concrete and lifting a leg to brace the creature's heavy body with my foot as it went up and over my head.

It landed on its back and crashed butt-first into one of the concrete pylons. The impact seemed to reverberate through the concrete, and dust rained down from the ceiling above.

I sneezed as I rolled upright. The creature twisted around and leapt toward me, its claws slashing at the air. I ducked and smacked at its head with the heel of my shoe. The stiletto scraped its brow and skidded backward, drawing blood from eye to neck, the scent sharp in the fume-filled air.

It roared and lashed out. Its claws caught my thigh again, tearing flesh even as the blow sent me staggering. The creature hit the concrete, then twisted and leapt again, its nastily sharp teeth all yellow and dangerous looking as they snapped and bit at the air, trying to get me. Trying to eat me.

I shivered, and faked another blow to its head, then spun and thumped the stiletto into its chest. The heel cut through hair and skin, embedding deep. No blue fires flickered out across its skin. Whatever this thing was, there was no vampire in the mix. No adversity to wood. Other than the fact it now had a shoe stuck in its flesh anyway.

And that obviously *did* hurt, because the creature howled in fury and launched itself at me yet again. I dropped and spun, then, as the creature's leap took it high above me, kicked it as hard as I could in the goolies. It had worked once before, and it worked again. The creature gave an odd sort of wheeze, then dropped to the concrete and didn't move.

I twisted around and shifted shape, which had the added benefit of stopping my wounds from bleeding as I bolted for the ramp on the other side of the car park. No shadows were moving down there, but I could see the red of body heat, one bending over the other. It was the orsini that was down, and relief ran through me.

I shifted back to human shape and slowed as I neared them. "You okay?"

Rhoan shook free of the shadows and nodded. "They're amazingly powerful animals, aren't they?"

"If you can actually define them as animals." I stared at the creature for a moment, then added, "You know, Misha promised to keep me safe from attacks like this."

Rhoan looked up at me, eyebrow raised. "When was that?"

"In the club, today."

"He probably wouldn't have had time to do anything about this particular attack. If he even knew about it."

"True." I supposed the real test would come in a day or so, once he'd had a chance to contact his boss and make his threats. Though if the man behind it all was so all-powerful, what could Misha possibly threaten him with that would make him listen? And why wouldn't he have used it to free himself?

The sound of an engine, accompanied by the squeal of tires, cut through the silence. I looked up. The van came screaming around the corner, with Quinn just in front of it, on foot and fully armed. His gaze met mine, the dark depths sending a shock of warm concern through me.

"You're hurt."

"Just scratches." I pointed to the creature near his feet. "That one isn't dead."

He aimed the laser and shot it. "And the one you're near?"

"Dead," Rhoan said, and pushed to his feet. "Let's get the hell out of here before any more of these things turn up."

The van skidded to a halt. We walked over and jumped in. Quinn slid the door shut and the van took off. Silence fell until we were out of the car park and into the rush hour traffic.

"You know," I said, to no one in particular, "I'm getting a little pissed off about all these attacks."

"They obviously think you're a threat to their operation," Kade commented.

"How, when I was unconscious most of the time in that place? Even when I did wake up, it was to escape with you. What could I have possibly seen that you didn't?"

"It might be simpler than that," Quinn stated. "Remember, your DNA is as good to them dead as alive. And you're a whole lot more controllable dead."

I grinned. "Ain't that the truth."

"Question is, how did they find her?" Kade said. "Either we've got a tail, or they're tracking us somehow."

"We checked for body bugs," Rhoan said. "We didn't find anything."

"But these people are stealing technology that isn't released on the street yet," Kade commented. "It could be they have something we don't know about."

"Well, there's a bit of information no one told the plebes," Rhoan commented dryly.

"All in good time," Jack said. "And that time is not in this van. We can still be picked up by listening devices, if they feel so inclined."

I shared an annoyed glance with Rhoan, then looked at Kade. "Misha had watchers. It's more than likely they reported my being with him back to their base. There was certainly enough time to arrange an attack while we were holed up in the private room."

"They couldn't have known we'd go to the car park."

"No, but it was a logical guess. Street parking is shit around the club, so the car park is the next best option."

"It just doesn't feel right," Quinn commented. "Those creatures weren't something that could be called up at a moment's notice. They knew you were going to be there beforehand."

I met his dark gaze. "It wasn't Misha."

"Are you sure of that?"

"Yes."

"Why?"

I raised an eyebrow. "Why is it important to you?"

"Because I'd hate for you to be killed before I made a decision one way or another."

"At the rate you seem to make your decisions, vampire, I'll be old and gray and undesirable."

He smiled, and it touched his eyes, warming the obsidian depths. Warming my soul. "Old and gray, maybe, but never undesirable."

Amusement twitched the corners of my mouth. "So you're telling me you don't mind a bit of granny?"

"Only a particular type of granny."

"You know," Rhoan said conversationally, "this talk is straying into territory I really don't want to think about."

"Particularly when most grannies don't look like Riley," Kade muttered, then shuddered. "Old meat. Nothing worse."

I slapped his arm. "You'll be old meat one day, horse-boy, so watch it."

His grin was sudden and cheeky, and sexy in a whole different way than Quinn's. "Yeah, but I'll be virile old horsemeat. There is a difference."

"I bet I could find a dozen grannies who would argue *that* point."

"And I'd be betting that those grannies ain't ever had a horse-shifter as a lover."

"He's such a humble person, isn't he?" Rhoan said dryly.

Kade's grin grew. "Why be humble when you've got nothing to be humble about?"

Rhoan's gaze shifted to me, and he raised an eyebrow in query. I grinned. "He has got a point."

"Damn." He contemplated Kade for a second, then added, "So, where do I find me a bit of gay horsemeat?"

Kade shrugged. "Don't ask me. I don't go looking for that sort of thing."

"Pity."

"I'll take that as a compliment."

"Please do."

There wasn't much that could really be added to that, so silence fell. I stared out the window, watching the office buildings and restaurants give way to residential streets, then country, and finally began to wonder where we were headed.

It was another half hour before we stopped, and by then, night had fallen. I climbed out of the van, sniffing the air as I looked around. The scent of eucalyptus vied with the aroma of rain on the breeze, but underneath it, the smell of death and earth.

My gaze found the dirt road that led up to vast iron doors. We were back at Genoveve.

"Why here?" I asked, as Jack came around the van.

"Because there's only one way in and out of this place, and it's heavily guarded with Directorate personnel I know for sure I can trust."

"And Headquarters isn't?"

"Gautier is due back tonight."

Gautier was only one man, and as much as I hated him, I doubt he'd be able to defeat the four of us. He was good, but not *that* good.

Jack headed toward the entrance, and, like good little sheep, we followed. Once the men at the door confirmed our identities, the laser gates lowered, the iron doors opened, and the four of us were allowed in.

We headed for the main office area. Rhoan, Quinn, and Kade plonked their butts down on the comfy leather sofas, but I continued on to the windows, keeping my back to them as I crossed my arms and stared out over the arena. Talon had once used the small stadium to test the skills of his creations, and even now, months after the event, the golden sand still bore the bloody stains where his clones and many of our guardians had fought for, and lost, their lives.

My gaze rose to the windows opposite. That's where I'd woken to discover him using me. And while I was a wolf, and hadn't been particularly worried about the sex angle of it, I was also a woman, and hadn't liked being treated that way. Not for any reason.

"So," Jack said, sitting down behind the huge, paper-strewn desk. "What happened?"

"He gave me a starting point. A name."

Jack waited several seconds, and when I didn't continue, said, "And?"

"And the name is one you already know."

"Riley, stop playing games."

"Only if you start filling the rest of us in on what the hell is going on." I turned around to face him. "He gave me Kade's name. Only Kade isn't just a builder, he's military, and obviously involved in some sort of military investigation."

"Misha told you all that?"

"Some of it." I hesitated, but he was going to discover I'd snitched his com-unit sooner or later, so it was better to be up front about it. "You left your com-unit in the penthouse, and I made use of it."

His gaze narrowed. "You don't know my codes."

I wasn't about to admit that I knew at least two of them—not when he had *that* look in his eyes. "Didn't need them. I'm a liaison *and* your assistant. I have clearance to get into most departments." I hesitated, glancing at Kade. "Even military."

Humor touched his eyes and warmed the cold line of his lips. "You should never have been able to get into our system."

"I didn't. Not fully, anyways."

"And my file has alert status."

Something I'd guessed once I'd figured out he might be military. "Which is why I didn't look for your personnel file."

He raised an eyebrow. "Then how did you find out who I was?"

"Went to recruitment. They keep duplicates of all applications." And in the end, I'd only been able to get in there because I used one of Jack's security codes. When he discovered that, there'd be hell to pay. "You were pretty damn rangy when you joined, weren't you?"

Kade snorted softly. "You're good."

"Very," Jack intoned heavily. "Which is why I want her as a guardian."

I gave him my standard deadpan look.

"So what, exactly, are you in the military?" Rhoan asked, his fingers drumming the arm of his chair.

Kade grimaced. "I'm military intelligence, and part of an investigation that started with the theft of a crate of laser weapons from the Landsend Military Base."

Landsend was one of the military's top research centers. "The same lasers those creatures attacked us with?"

His gaze met mine. "The same."

"I'd have thought a crate would have been a little hard to conceal or steal," Rhoan said dryly.

"This happened over several months. And they're certainly not the only thing to go missing from Landsend."

"Security that slack, huh?"

Kade gave him a cutting look. "No. Under normal circumstances, you can't get an ant out of there undetected."

"Well, someone succeeded. You checked all personnel?"

"Not me personally. By that stage, I was undercover."

"As a builder. With your so-called brother."

Kade's rich gaze met mine, and the cold fury I'd glimpsed over the last few days was there for all to see. "He was my partner. And they killed him."

"They who?" Quinn asked.

"The same people who got the guns out of Landsend." Kade's look became grim. "Or maybe that should be the same things."

"Define 'things,'" Rhoan said.

"We caught them on some special cameras the division installed. Staff thought they were infrared, and we didn't disillusion them. In reality, they were designed to record only when motion combined with certain lower-than-normal body temperatures were sensed."

I raised my eyebrows. "Reverse heat sensors?"

He nodded. "There are some creatures—chameleons, for example—who are not only cold-blooded, but invisible to normal and infrared cameras."

"But it wasn't a chameleon taking the lasers, was it?" Quinn asked.

"No. It was something we'd never seen before. It was

spiderlike, and yet fluid in form, able to pour itself through the tiniest of cracks. It ingested the weapons and got them out that way."

I propped a hip against the wall. My feet were beginning to ache, but the only available seat was between Quinn and Kade, and being squeezed between two delicious men might be a little too hard for my hormones to handle. Especially when I was trying to concentrate on what was going on.

"If they ingested them, how could the weapons be retrieved?" I asked.

"The creatures could somehow reconstruct them as they regurgitated." He shrugged.

Weird. "So what did they want the weapons for?"

"I think the weapons were little more than a side benefit. Landsend is high security. If you can get in and out of there undetected, you could go anywhere."

"And how does this connect with you ending up a sperm donor in that breeding center?" Rhoan asked quietly.

"My department rigged the doors and air ducts in and around the stores with special containers designed to trap the creature as it moved through in liquid form. We did tests that told us two things—that nature wasn't responsible for its birth, and that it came from somewhere near the Blue Mountains area."

I raised my eyebrows. "How can you tell something like that?"

Amusement touched his lips. "There were traces of soil picked up on the creature."

"So you and your partner set up shop near Bullaburra and began investigations." Meaning he'd known all along where we were once we'd escaped that breeding center. Most annoying.

"How did you get caught?" Rhoan asked.

Kade's gaze went to Rhoan. "I don't know. But we were barely there a week when it all went ass up. Those things attacked and killed Denny, and drugged me." He shrugged. "I was in that breeding center for months by the time Riley came along."

I shifted my weight again, trying to ease the ache in my feet. "Which begs several questions—why kill your partner and keep you alive? And why did no one question your disappearance?"

"I think you'll find the answers to both those questions are intertwined," Jack commented. "Kade's partner had no recorded psi-gifts. Kade, on the other hand, is psi-immune and, at the same time, able to use his own formidable talents."

"Which they could only have known about if they'd had access to his file. And that would be impossible without alarms—" I stopped, remembering what Misha had said. I looked from Jack to Kade and back again. "*That's* what Misha meant. There's a mole in your department."

Kade nodded. "And it comes down to two men—my immediate boss, Ross James, or the man in charge of the whole section, one General Martin Hunt. They were the only two who knew Denny and I were out in the field, and why."

"But surely the alarms would have been raised regardless?" How could two men disappear without an alert being raised? Especially in a military division?

"If it's Ross James, he could easily be submitting false

reports," Rhoan commented. He looked at Jack. "We're having both men investigated?"

"Yes. At the moment, both men appear cleaner than an angel's halo." Jack's expression was as grim as I'd ever seen it. "And, of course, Ross James knows Kade is free and with us, because I confirmed Kade's identity with him when we were in Leura."

"So what are we going to do?"

"Ross James is the easier target. He's human, and though he apparently has strong psi-shields, they aren't rated high enough to keep me out."

"Which is why he'll never become a general," Kade murmured.

"He knows Kade is alive, so we're using that, and have arranged a meeting."

"To what end?" Rhoan asked. "We both know he'll be wearing the latest in psi-deadeners. Even if he is innocent, I very much doubt whether he'd be stupid enough to come alone."

"Which is why you'll be there to run interference."

Which meant I got left with Quinn yet again. Given the time he was taking to make his decision, I wasn't exactly happy about that. I mean, putting me with him was like flashing chocolate my way then telling me I couldn't have it. It was just plain mean.

"Meanwhile," Jack continued, "Quinn and Riley will be investigating Martin Hunt."

"And how are we supposed to be doing that?"

"Easy." Jack's gaze went to Quinn. "I believe you have an invitation to the Wishes For Children Foundation's charity dinner tomorrow evening?"

"Yes."

"Good. Hunt will be there, as his wife is on the foundation board. You and Riley can mingle with the nation's finest highfliers, and get a line on Hunt in the process."

"There's a major problem in *that* thinking." Sarcasm edged my voice. "If Hunt is a baddie, he knows what I look like."

"Which is why Rhoan will be bringing in Liander."

"It's too big a risk." Though Quinn's voice was soft, steely determination was evident in his tones. "I'll go, but Riley should stay here."

"We need Riley's nose. Hunt might have been one of the men who visited her in that breeding cell. If he is, we've found a major player."

It wouldn't be that easy. Deep down, I knew there was someone else—someone I knew. Someone who was pulling all the strings from the shadows.

"They've snatched her twice now, and have tried to kill her several times since. Her DNA is as useful to them dead as it is alive. Sending her to this function could be as good as signing her death warrant."

"They won't know she's even there."

"They knew she was at that Brighton hotel. They knew she was in the car park. You cannot possibly say for sure they won't know she's at the function."

"I do agree that Riley shouldn't be doing this," Rhoan added. "She's not trained for undercover work."

"This won't be dangerous," Jack said impatiently. "And Quinn will be there to protect her."

"*None* of us have been doing a very good job of protecting her so far." Rhoan met my gaze. "It's your call."

Which meant he'd back me, no matter what I decided. Even if it meant going up against Jack's orders. I smiled, loving my brother more than ever.

"It's Liander doing the disguising, and I trust him." I looked at Jack. "I need an end to this madness. I want to get back to a normal life."

He didn't say the obvious—that for me, the chance of a normal life had well and truly slipped by. But he was thinking it. I could see it in his eyes.

"Good" was all he said. "Kade, Quinn, and Riley, get some rest. Rhoan, you go back to town and get Liander. Take a couple of men with you."

I waited until the three men had left, then met Jack's gaze. "There's one thing you seem to have forgotten. My nightly appointments with Misha start tomorrow."

"I haven't forgotten it. The function is early evening. A car will pick you and Quinn up at ten, and deliver you back to the airport. Quinn's using his own plane, and the jet will have you back in time for your meet with Misha."

"If all goes according to plan." And so far, nothing had.

"Things are starting to fall our way, Riley. It'll be all right."

I rubbed my arms, and hoped like hell he was right, because it wasn't only my life on the line tomorrow, but Quinn's as well. Jack seemed to have forgotten that Quinn had already been the target of several assassination attempts. Or maybe he simply didn't care.

"Here's an image of the general and his wife." He swung the com-unit around so I could see the pics. The general was tall, solidly set, with salt-and-pepper hair and a craggy face. His wife was tallish, thickish, with a nondescript sort of face and dull brown hair. The sort of couple you wouldn't even look twice at.

"Go get some rest," he added. "You look beat."

I was. But as I stood outside the door, sniffing the air to sense which direction Kade and Quinn had gone, it wasn't sleep I had on my mind. But luckily for me and my need for sleep, my hormones weren't running the ship just yet. I found an empty cell, stripped down, and went to sleep.

But it could hardly be called rest.

Not when my dreams were invaded by a faceless man who took his fill of me and left nothing in return.

A man I'd once known intimately.

A man whose name hovered close enough to taste, but not remember.

I woke to the awareness I was no longer alone. The air was rich with muskiness, and stirred frustrated hormones to life. I opened my eyes.

Kade sat in the chair opposite the bed, and smiled when he saw me watching him. "Thought I'd wander in and offer you an apology."

"Not to mention enjoy the view." I thrust the blankets away and stood up.

His gaze slid down me, appreciative and warm. "Well, there *is* a whole lot to enjoy."

"As long as you look and don't touch. There's work to be done, and very little time."

"There's always time for sex, sweetheart."

My hormones hastily formed a cheer squad at the

prospect of some horse-shifter loving, but I managed to ignore them. "Is Liander here?"

"Yep."

"Then there's no time."

He rose and walked toward me. I pressed a hand against his chest, stopping him before he got too close. "I said no, Kade."

He took my hand, and raised it to his lips. His breath was warm on my fingertips, his kiss soft, sweet. "What if I promise to be quick?"

"We've done quick. I'd like to do long for a change." And even as I said it, I smiled. Because when it came to flesh, Kade did long better than *any* man alive.

He tugged me forward lightly and wrapped his arms around my waist. He felt so good, so warm and hard, that desire swirled through me. That was the beginning of the end when it came to resistance, and I knew it.

"We have half an hour and a single bed," he said, as if sensing the sudden lessening of resolve.

"Don't you think a single bed is a wee bit small for the two of us?"

"If you think that, you haven't been loved right in a single bed."

The smile touching his lips was cheeky, and my own twitched in response. Because I wanted to. Lord how I wanted to.

And truth be told, had it been Kellen standing in front of me, it would have been an instant yes, and Liander be damned. It was *that* thought, more than anything, that had the last of my reluctance slipping. Kellen might have been a wolf, but Kade could never be deemed a lesser lover. "If Jack bites my ass over being late, you are off the loving list, my horny friend."

He laughed. "Trust me, Jack won't get anywhere near your delicious ass. I promise to protect it from all comers."

I had sudden visions of him swatting away everyone—including new suitors—and snorted softly. Maybe that wasn't such a good idea after all. "Half an hour. No more, no less."

"Done deal." He dropped a kiss on my lips, then tugged me over to the bed.

I have to say, the man certainly knew how to make the most of a single bed.

And he emphasized his point in the most dramatic way, and proved beyond a shadow of a doubt that I *hadn't* been loved right in a single bed before now.

It was a good forty minutes later before he was escorting me down the hall to the bathroom where Liander had set up shop. Once there, he dropped another kiss on my lips, one designed to tease and arouse.

He succeeded in doing both.

"We'll pick up this little discussion later," he said, and walked away whistling happily.

I blew out a breath, then opened the door and walked inside. Rhoan and Liander were making out against one of the stall walls.

"You want me to come back later?" I asked dryly.

Rhoan came up for air, and gave me a wide grin. "Your timing could have been better, but this will keep."

"You sure?"

"No, but Jack will kill us if we delay more than necessary." He squeezed Liander's rump then stepped away.

Liander's gaze met mine, amusement silvering the gray depths. "Besides, making you up is almost as much fun as making out."

"You obviously lead a sad sex life."

"Well, your brother could use a pointer or two, but hey, he's not untrainable."

Rhoan crossed his arms and leaned a shoulder against the wall. "Careful what you say, or I might just take this unworthy body elsewhere."

Liander snorted. "You do anyway."

"Now, boys," I interrupted, feeling an argument headed our way. "Work first, lovers' tiff afterward."

"No," Rhoan corrected, a mischievous glint in his eyes. "Work first, then sex, then lovers' tiff. Get your priorities right, please."

"Sorry," I said dryly. "So, have we decided what sort of look we're going for this time?" The last time we'd done this, I'd become an albino prostitute. Not the sort of look one needed for an upmarket function.

Liander tossed me a small bottle of lavender fluid. "Go shower with that first. It'll erase your base scent for the next twelve hours."

Relief ran through me as I headed for the showers. At least if the wolf that had used me in the breeding center was there, my scent wouldn't give me away. Once I'd washed, I sat in the chair Liander had swiped from one of the offices, and let him loose.

"Quinn has been photographed with a parade of smoldering, brown-haired beauties in the past," Liander explained, as he began to recolor skin and hair, "so that's the look we're going for here."

"And will this goop wash out easily?" I asked, watching with a faint sense of horror as my red-gold hair became a chocolaty, hazelnut color.

"Yes. Trust me."

I did trust him, but that didn't stop the dismay. I mean, I loved my hair. Loved its color. Watching it become brown was more than a little disturbing.

But it was amazing the difference hair color, blue contacts, and a bit of fancy makeup made. It wasn't me in that mirror. It was someone else. Someone suitably smoldering enough to hang off a billionaire playboy's arm.

"Wow," Rhoan said, which was basically what I was thinking.

"We haven't finished yet." Liander's expression was pleased as he held up a scrap of vibrant red material. "Now the dress."

I gave him a deadpan look. "That is not a dress. That's a tube of fabric."

"This tube is the very latest in evening wear, and costs a sheer fortune."

"That doesn't make me like it any more."

"You'll look stunning in it."

"I'll look like a damn beacon. People will have to wear sunglasses to look at me."

Liander grinned. "We want people to look at you. We want people to admire that glorious body of yours, and not look any deeper."

I raised an eyebrow, a faint grin twitching my lips. "Glorious body? I thought you ate on the other side of the fence? What's with the sudden appreciation of the female form?"

"I may eat on the other side, as you say, but that

doesn't mean I can't admire a luscious female form like yours." He lightly slapped my arm. "Stop fussing and stand up."

I did. He showed me two white cups. "Breast supports. They'll lift as well as support, and give your beautiful bounty even more prominence."

"Like I need that," I said dryly, as he lifted my boobs and slipped the supports into place.

"The more they ogle your assets, the less they ogle your face," Rhoan said with a grin. "For once, this is a good thing."

"Says the male of the species who never has to put up with men talking to their breasts rather than their face."

"There are advantages to being a male."

Like *not* being stripped down and rebuilt by your brother's lover. Liander handed me the so-called dress.

"What, no undies?"

"We do not need ugly panty lines with this dress."

I raised an eyebrow. "Not even ugly G-string lines?"

It was his turn to give me "the look." I grinned and wiggled into the dress. It fit like a glove, covering me breast to thigh, and left an almost indecent amount of flesh on show. "I am going to be the laughingstock of this function."

"You're going to have them drooling." Liander stepped back, his expression that of an artist studying his masterpiece. "Tug the hem down a shade more."

"Do you want my boobs all the way out?"

He grinned faintly. "No, though you have to admit, it'd definitely stop anyone recognizing your face."

The dress stayed right where it was. Half an inch

more, and my nipples would be waving hello to the world. "Shoes?"

He handed me a pair of strappy, four-inch stilettos. "My favorite type," I said, running my finger down the wooden spike of the heel. "Red and ready to use."

Liander grinned. "They're becoming quite a fashion statement—though I doubt if anyone has quite cottoned on to your special use yet."

"Thank God. I'd hate to have to find another innocuous weapon."

Once I got them on, I turned and studied myself in the mirror. If smoldering sexiness was the look we'd been going for, then we'd achieved the right effect.

"What about my voice?"

"Modulators will fix that. Open wide."

I did, and he inserted the extremely thin plastic chips on either side of my mouth. The surface of the modulators was supposedly covered with an analgesic that deadened the skin as they went in. In theory, anyway. In practice, it felt like he was ripping out teeth rather than shoving in plastic. At least once they were attached, I couldn't actually feel them. And no one else would, either, unless I decided to deep throat someone.

"Those things always hurt going in," I said, when I could, amazed by the sound of my new voice.

"Stop being a baby," Liander commented, "and say the alphabet, so I know they're working properly."

The alphabet had never sounded so sexy, let me tell you. "What about a coat? Or are you intending to freeze me to death in the name of perfection?"

"Believe me, with the heat that'll be following you,

you won't need a coat." He held up a hand, forestalling my protests. "I do, however, have one for you."

He handed it to me. Thankfully it was black, not eye-blinding red. I slipped it on and did up the buttons. No sense in giving Quinn a heart attack, especially when he hadn't yet decided whether he could continue a relationship on my terms.

"One final item," Rhoan added, offering me a small bag. "Clothes to change into after you leave the function."

"I certainly don't want Misha thinking I got dressed up specially for him," I muttered, accepting the bag gratefully.

Liander looked at his watch. "Time to go." He leaned forward and kissed my cheek. "If this doesn't blow your reluctant vampire's mind apart, I don't know what will."

I looked at Rhoan. "Have you been discussing my love life again?"

"Well, it is more exciting than mine at the moment. I mean, vampires, a horse-shifter, alpha wolves—"

"An alpha wolf?" Liander interrupted, and punched me lightly in the arm. "You go, girl!"

I grinned. "Believe me, I intend to."

Someone knocked on the door. "Riley?" Jack said. "You ready? We need to get moving."

"Coming." I kissed my brother. "You be careful out there."

"Right back at you. And remember, don't ever trust Misha. He's playing his own game, and, as yet, we have no idea what the rules are."

"I'll remember." I threw the bag over my shoulder, and headed for the door.

It was time to go hunting.

Chapter 8

Jack gave me the once-over, though he couldn't really see much thanks to the coat. "Very good." He handed me a bit of paper. "Memorize this. Ring it when you come out of the club, and we'll have a car pick you up."

I took the paper, committed the number to memory as ordered, then handed it back. "What next?"

"Next we get you to the car."

"Is it safe for us to be going direct from here to the airport?"

Jack pressed a hand to my spine, guiding me down the hall. "You'll be changing cars. Quinn's limo will actually be taking you to the airport."

I nodded. "Did you happen to find out anything more about that breeding center we were in?"

"Not a lot."

"What about building permits and the like?" Surely someone somewhere had to give approvals. Surely you couldn't build a structure that big without someone noticing.

"None registered. The land itself was bought by a Peter James some three years ago."

"Let me guess, Peter James doesn't exactly exist."

"And he paid in cash, so there's no credit trail to follow."

That raised my eyebrows. Credit cards were the norm these days—cash was something rarely seen, let alone used. "And that didn't trip any alarms?"

Jack grimaced. "No."

"I don't suppose the security cams at the land office caught Peter James's pic, did they?"

"As a matter of fact, they did. We're working on retrieving it at the moment."

"Give me a look when you do." Hell, it might just trigger a much-needed memory.

We walked through the center and out the doors. Quinn waited near a pale gray government car, looking like a dark angel in his black suit and burgundy shirt. His gaze slid down my body, then rose to linger on my face and hair. He didn't say anything, but his hunger burned across my skin, leaving a prickle of perspiration in its wake. It wasn't only sexual hunger, but blood thirst. And that thirst was so thick, so strong, it left me breathless. He was pushing his limits, and it was reaching dangerous levels. I had to wonder why.

Or did he plan to slake his thirst on some of the lovely ladies at the function? Perhaps raise a little money for the charity on the side? Hell, I knew women who'd pay a fortune to experience the sexual rapture that went with a vampire's bite. After experiencing it myself, I could understand why.

Quinn opened the door and ushered me inside, his hand pressing into my spine, and sending waves of delight lapping across my skin. But despite this reaction, I couldn't help noticing that his fingers were cold. And vampires only got cold when they weren't taking enough blood.

My gaze went to his. The raw desire briefly evident in his dark eyes made my heart stutter, yet, beneath that, the hunger lurked.

"Take care, both of you," Jack said. "Remember, this is just a scouting expedition, nothing more. Don't do anything other than look."

That last point was aimed at me, and I raised an eyebrow. What in hell did he think I was going to do? Drag the general behind into the toilets and beat the crap out of him? Okay, the idea *did* have appeal, but even if the general was the man who was abusing me at the breeding center, there wasn't actually much point to hitting him. At least not until we knew if he was the power behind everything—and somehow, I thought not.

"Ring me from the plane on the way home," Jack continued. "And, Riley, we'll have people guarding the exits of the Rocker."

I nodded. Jack slammed the door shut and the car took off. Silence fell. I didn't see any point in breaking it. I'd said all I had to say to Quinn, and the ball now lay in his court. But his hunger continued to lap across my skin, making breathing difficult. It had to stop. He couldn't go into a function full of women emoting the way he was. It was almost as bad as a werewolf's aura—and would create a riot in an instant.

Unfortunately, there was only one way I could ease his hunger, and I had a suspicion I'd have to push him into taking blood from me. But I couldn't do anything here in the car. I didn't mind public displays, but Quinn did. Besides, I wanted the driver to concentrate on what he was doing rather than what I was doing. There tended to be less accidents that way.

Once we reached the city, we drove into the bowels of a public car park and changed cars. Quinn's car had thick dark windows that I rather suspected were bulletproof. It seemed he wasn't taking any chances, and of that, I was glad.

It didn't take us long to get to Essendon airport from there. Quinn's plane—a sleek and silvery Y-shaped craft—was on the tarmac ready to go. We climbed aboard. Besides the pilot and copilot in the cockpit, there was just me and Quinn and the sofalike seats. The perfect place for a much-needed seduction. Or, at the very least, a half seduction. I wasn't going to compel him to go the whole way if he didn't want to. Even if my hormones were screaming in horror at the thought.

I waited until the plane leveled out, then unbuckled the seat belt, took off the coat, and rose.

The temperature in the small cabin leapt about ten degrees.

His gaze met mine, the dark depths wary. The hunger I'd felt before was gone, but the strain touching the corners of his eyes suggested it hadn't gone all that far. "Don't, Riley."

"Don't what?" I said, all innocence. "Talk to you about our plans for tonight?"

"We know what we have to do. There's nothing else to discuss."

"No? So you're just going to continue calling me Riley, are you?"

He hesitated, a faint gleam of amusement touching his eyes. "Barbie would be more appropriate—even though you're not blonde."

"So you approve of the boob lifts?" I asked, thrusting out my breasts for inspection.

He made a slightly gargled sound and didn't answer. Men were men, I thought with an inner grin, no matter whether they were twenty years old or well over a thousand. Show them a good set of tits, and their brain went south.

I used that moment to straddle his lap. By the time his brain had reconnected, it was far too late to stop me.

And given the evidence of what I was sitting on, part of him was more than enjoying the sudden closeness.

I threw my arms around his neck and kissed his nose. It was cold. So were his lips when I brushed a kiss across them. He didn't react to either kiss, didn't touch me in return.

"Riley, I can't take just a taste and stop." His voice was flat, and as cold as his body. And yet there was a desperation in his eyes that warmed my soul.

"Chocolate is like that," I murmured, continuing to brush kisses across his cheeks, his neck.

"What?"

I smiled and kissed his lips again. His teeth were

beginning to protrude. I ran my tongue across their needle-sharp ends, letting them cut my tongue, letting the taste of blood touch his mouth.

He groaned.

"You may not want to do this, but you need to. Your hunger burns my skin, and I'm not exactly sensitive when it comes to emotions. But I'm betting there'll be empaths and sensitives at that function tonight. You go in like this, emoting hunger all over the place, and what the hell do you think will happen?"

"Nothing will happen, because it'll be under control by then."

"It won't. It can't, because you're too close to the edge." I stared into the beautiful black depths of his eyes. "Dammit, your skin is *cold*. Why are you pushing yourself like this? It doesn't make any sense."

"I have my reasons." His hands went to my hips, his touch almost bruising. "Move, or I'll make you move."

I gripped tight with my thighs. "Pretend I'm Barbie. Just another seductive brunette you're planning to wine, dine, and bed. Nothing serious will ever come of us, and you'll never see me after tonight. I'm just a quick and easy fuck."

"I can't do that," he said, voice tight with the tension I could see in his eyes, feel humming through his body.

"Why not?"

"Because you're not Barbie, and you'll never be just a quick and easy fuck."

I raised my eyebrows at the edge in his voice. "But that's all I was when we first met. You admitted that yourself."

"That was then."

"Nothing much has changed since then."

"*Everything* has changed since then."

"For God's sake, we don't even know each other beyond the realms of sex. And being great in bed doesn't mean we'll be great out of it."

"I know, I know." Frustration edged his voice. "Riley, I want you. I need you. I just don't know if I can stand being with you."

"I'm not asking you to become my full-time lover right now. I'm just asking you to take what you need."

He touched a hand to my face. "You don't get it, do you?"

"What?"

"One touch, one taste, is never going to be enough."

I smiled. "It doesn't have to be enough."

"I know. And if you were something other than a werewolf, I would take all you could offer in an instant."

I sighed. "But I am a werewolf, I will always be a werewolf, and asking me to forget all that I am is like asking you to stop taking blood."

"It's not the same—"

"It *is*," I insisted. "The moon celebration is vital to a wolf. The dance is vital. Sex is a part of what we are, as vital to us as blood is to you."

"You would not die if you didn't have sex."

"Wouldn't I? You know that for sure, do you?"

He didn't answer. I sighed again. "Look, take however much time you need to make a decision about us, but in the meantime, you *can't* go to the function emoting like you are. An orgy is not what we need to happen tonight."

"I can control it."

"Have you any idea just how strongly you're projecting?"

"I'm not."

"Maybe not at the moment, because you're holding it fiercely in check. But when I walked to the car, you weren't controlling it, and when I took off my coat, you weren't."

"That was a moment of surprise, nothing more."

"It's at dangerous levels."

"No, it's not."

I growled in frustration. "Dammit, do you want to feel exactly what you're projecting?"

"What I want is for you to get off my lap and leave me in peace."

"Answer the damn question."

"Riley—"

"Yes or no."

"If I say yes, will you back off?"

"Yes."

"Then, yes."

I dropped my shields and let him have it. The more a werewolf desires sex, the more intense their aura. I wanted him *real* bad, and my aura reflected that. It was lust and heat and passion all rolled into one explosive punch. Quinn's eyes widened, and suddenly the air was so thick and hot I couldn't even breathe. I re-shielded fast, and took a deep, quivering breath. "That's what you're projecting."

Then I leaned forward and kissed him fiercely. He didn't react for the barest of seconds, then he was right there with me, his mouth plundering mine almost desperately.

"I need you," I whispered against his lips. "As much as you need me."

He groaned and pulled me closer, squashing my breasts against his chest. The thunder of his heart matched mine, and the heat of his desire warmed every pore. But the hard length of him was still restrained by his pants, and this was bad, because I was aching to feel him deep, deep inside.

I rose onto my knees, reaching between us, freeing him from the restrictions of his clothing, pushing his pants back down his legs. Then I thrust down on him, claiming him in the most basic way possible. He groaned again, his hands sliding down to my hips, his grip bruising as he pressed me down harder. I echoed his groan, loving the way he seemed to complete me. It had nothing to do with his size or his shape or anything physical. It was almost as if when our flesh was joined, our spirits combined and danced as intimately as our bodies.

He began to move, not gently, but fiercely, urgently, and I was right there with him. The deep-down ache bloomed, spreading like wildfire across my skin, becoming a kaleidoscope of sensations that washed through every corner of my mind. I gasped, grabbing his shoulders, pushing him deeper still. Pleasure exploded between us, his movements becoming faster, more urgent.

"Look at me," he growled.

My gaze met his, and something deep inside quivered. His eyes burned with desire and passion, but something else, something I couldn't name, seared the ebony depths, stirring me in ways I didn't think possible.

This is why I can't be casual, he said, his mind-voice flowing through every fiber, a rich, sensual song that had my soul soaring, and my heart aching. *This is far deeper. Far stronger.*

I didn't answer. Couldn't answer. His mouth claimed mine again, his kiss as ardent as his body. Then everything broke, and I was unraveling, groaning with the intensity of the orgasm flowing through me. He came with me, but as his body flowed into mine, he broke our kiss, his teeth grazing my neck. I jerked reflexively when they pierced my skin, but the brief flare of pain quickly became something undeniably exquisite, and I came a second time, the orgasm shuddering on and on as he drank and drank.

When he finally released me, I collapsed against him, body quivering and head spinning. He wrapped his arms around me, and kissed the top of my head.

"I'm sorry," he whispered. "I shouldn't have taken that much."

"You needed it." My voice was harsh with tiredness, and perhaps a little shock at the sudden blood loss.

"Yes." He hesitated. "You were right. I should have taken sustenance far sooner."

I yawned, then asked, "So why didn't you?"

"Because it was the sweetness of your blood I desired. I didn't want other women."

I stirred and looked up at him. "You couldn't get it up?"

He grinned. "Oh, I could. I just didn't want to."

"That's stupid."

"Yes. Particularly seeing I'm old enough to know better." He slipped his hands under my butt, and lifted me off him. At least his touch had lost its cold edge. "You need to eat something, and regain strength."

"I need to sleep."

"That's only because I took so much blood. You must eat something rich in iron."

"You have a handy hamburger lying about this fancy crate?"

"As a matter of fact, yes I do." He did up his pants and rose. "This fancy crate has seen a lot of seductions over the years, and I've learned to cater for my meals." He flashed me a smile over his shoulder that had my depleted blood stirring. "Hope you don't mind your burger microwaved."

"Not in the least." I forced myself upright, and shuffled to the toilet to clean up. The teeth marks in my neck were little more than pink dots. By the time we arrived at the function, they'd be gone. One good thing about a vampire bite—the evidence of it didn't hang around all that long. Unless, of course, you had multiple bites, which took a little longer to fade.

The rich smell of meat began to fill the air, and my stomach rumbled as I walked over to the microwave.

"Your burger, madam," he said, handing me the plate.

"Yum." I parked on a sofa and dove in. As far as microwaved burgers went, it was pretty damn good.

Quinn poured himself a bourbon, and sat down on the seat opposite. Maybe he figured it was safer keeping a little distance between us. Though if he thought I'd jump his bones again he was in for a disappointment. I couldn't afford to lose any more blood tonight.

"So," I said, licking the ketchup off my fingers. "Where do we go from here?"

His dark gaze followed my actions almost hungrily.

Obviously, his appetite was nowhere near sated, but given I could no longer sense it, it had dipped below danger point.

"We are in much the same quandary as we were before," he said.

"Why?"

"I don't want to share you, Riley."

Don't, not won't. That was a more-than-hopeful sign. "Then let's throw a few more facts into the mix. I live in Melbourne. You live in Sydney. That means it's not going to be possible for us to see each other every night, if only because you have a business to run."

"True."

"I have no intentions of moving to Sydney. Do you intend to move Evensong Air's headquarters to Melbourne?"

"At the moment, no."

"So, you're telling me you won't share, but you probably won't be able to get down here more than two or three times a week."

"Possibly. But lots of relationships work fine like that."

"Human relationships, yes. As I keep reminding you, I'm a werewolf, with werewolf needs."

He raised an eyebrow. "Even a werewolf doesn't need to have sex *every* night. I know that for a fact."

Need, no. Liked, yes. We could survive a few weeks' drought, but it wasn't ever something we did willingly, or often.

"Except when it comes to the moon dance. Have you ever seen what happens when a wolf cannot satisfy the urges of a moon?" The desire for sex mutated into something far more deadly, and only sex *and* blood could quench the fire.

"Seen it? Of course I have. I was the one who satisfied the blood urges after Talon kidnapped you, remember?"

I waved away the comment impatiently. "Besides that. I was chained, and therefore not really dangerous to anyone."

He snorted softly. "I have scars up my arm that prove otherwise."

Well, he was the one who put his arm in front of my teeth. What did he expect would happen, given the situation? "Quinn—"

He held up a hand. "Okay. No, I haven't seen a free wolf in full blood lust. But I know you and Rhoan are the result of such an event."

I nodded. "Our mom was headed back to her pack when her car broke down near a small country town. Lucky for the town, she met a newly risen vampire, and took the edge off her desires before she tore him to pieces. Had it not been for that vampire, up to a dozen humans could have died that night." No one knew why a wolf in blood fever went after humans, though the popular theory was the easy-prey one. For a moon-mad wolf, humans were fun to chase, and simple to bring down. "Making the promise you demand is dangerous, Quinn. For me, and for the community at large."

"I can be there for the moon dance," he said flatly.

"Can you guarantee that you'll be there the day of the full moon? For the two nights before it? Each and every month, for as long as we're together?"

He frowned. "No one can guarantee that."

"Another wolf can. He'll be there because he *has* to be there, for exactly the same reasons as I have to be there."

"You're not fucking another wolf at the moment." He hesitated, and something close to malevolence flickered across his face. "Besides Misha, of course."

"I met that alpha last night. I intend to see him again."

"Why?"

The urge to throw the plate at his thick head was so strong I had to clench my fingers to stop them from grabbing it. "I've told you why a hundred times. Stop thinking with your dick and start listening!"

His expression darkened. "Believe me, I'm *not* thinking with my dick here."

"You don't know me well enough to be thinking with anything else," I refuted. "For Christ's sake, you don't even *like* werewolves. Why in hell would you want to go exclusive with me?"

"If I had any choice in the matter, I would not be doing this."

I raised an eyebrow. "Well, I'm hardly forcing you into it."

"No?"

"*No.*"

"Then why do you invade my dreams?"

"It wasn't like I was doing it purposely. I was just dreaming."

"Only they weren't just dreams, but erotic dreams."

I frowned, wondering what the hell he was getting at. "So?"

"So, you weren't just dreaming, you were connecting to my mind and sharing those dreams with me."

I blinked. We'd been having *real* mind sex? How cool

was that? And why couldn't we share something like that while waking?

"Because neither of us are physically ready for that sort of experience."

Annoyance swept through me. "Will you keep out of my damn thoughts?"

"You shield if you want me out."

I threw up full shields and gave him a glare. It was water off a duck's back. "What do you mean, neither of us are ready to share that sort of experience?"

"Just that. Merging minds during sex is as intimate as you can get, an experience that can forever affect you."

I raised an eyebrow. "You've done it?"

He hesitated. "Once."

"With whom?"

"The whom isn't important—"

"See," I cut in, throwing up my hands. "You want me to go exclusive, and yet you're not willing to tell me a damn thing about you or your past."

"The past is not important."

Maybe it wasn't, but the mere fact he didn't trust me enough to tell me *was*. But if he wasn't smart enough to realize that, then what was the point of even mentioning it?

"Just leave it casual," I said softly. "And take it from there."

"I *can't*."

"Why not?" I asked, perplexed. "I mean, we were casual a month ago, and you did that just fine."

He finished his drink then placed it in the small holder near the chair and stood. "As I told you before," he said, turning to look out the window. "A vampire is very territorial. You've invaded my being—and that being now considers you mine. Do you know how hard it is for me to sit back and watch you with other men? I couldn't do that for weeks on end. I'd kill them, Riley. I wouldn't be able to help it."

There was no emotion in his voice, but the flicker of pain that seared my mind told me this had happened before. And that *that* death was at the base of him hating weres. I took a deep breath and let it out slowly. "What about a compromise?"

He didn't even bother looking at me. "What?"

"When you're in Melbourne to see me, I won't see anyone else. But when you're in Sydney, I'm free to see whom I wish. And the days leading up to the full moon are mine."

"What about Misha?"

"Misha is part of this mission, and until the mission is over, this agreement will not come into force. Besides, we both know Misha is not the only sinner I might have to kiss before this case is solved."

"If it was just kissing I wouldn't mind so much," he muttered, then turned around. "A deal, then."

My hormones let out a collective cheer. "And you'll accept the fact that there will be other lovers besides you?"

His dark eyes gleamed with displeasure. "As long as you stick to your promise once this mission is over, then yes."

Finally, we had an agreement we could both live with. "Want to celebrate the deal by cooking me another burger?"

A small smile touched his lips. "That I can do." And he did.

*T*he function was being held on the eighth floor of The Harborside, a brand-new hotel complex that boasted views over the old Sydney Harbor Bridge and the Opera House. The ballroom itself was decked out in cream—walls, ceiling, and tables—as if not to compete with the magnificence of the views so visible through the windows that enclosed two sides of the room. The only glint of color to the scheme was the gold in the frames of the chandeliers, and the spray of rainbow hues across the ceiling as the light hit the heavy crystal pendants.

Of course, no one had told the guests that competing with the view wasn't an option, and the ballroom was a blaze of human color—at least when it came to the women. And I was pleased to note that most of the dresses were as short as mine. Liander had been right, as usual.

Quinn pressed a hand against my back as we followed the waiter down the stairs. Though the touch was light, it seared right down to my spine, and had need humming through my body. While I knew I couldn't afford to lose any more blood tonight, that didn't stop me from wanting him. By the same token, I didn't actually want to go to Misha feeling this way. The bastard didn't deserve it.

People glanced our way as we passed them by, some of them nodding in greeting at Quinn. He didn't even bother looking at them, much less responding. His gaze was strictly front and center, and I frowned, searching the crowd ahead of us, wondering what had caught his attention. Not that I could see much beyond the glitter of all the diamonds on show around us. It was just as well the room had lots of discreetly placed guards, because the truckload of jewels on display would call to a thief as surely as nectar to a bee.

"What's wrong?" I asked, after a few seconds.

He glanced at me, dark eyes flat. "Thought I saw someone I knew."

"Male someone, or female someone?"

"Male. The son of a business rival."

"Anyone I'd know?"

"Unlikely, though you've undoubtedly heard of the company—Sirius Airlines."

"They just won the contract for daily flights to the European Collective's Space Station, didn't they?"

"Yes."

The dark way he said that had me glancing at him. "Beating you out of the contract, I'm gathering?"

"Yes."

"Publicly thumping him is not going to get that contract back, you know."

He gave me his vampire face. "Beating him up wouldn't do any good, because it is not the son that runs the company. I merely wish to give him a warning."

The waiter stopped at an empty table near the corner of the room. I glanced at the window, not sure I liked being so close to it. I might be disguised, but Quinn wasn't, and we still hadn't figured out who or what was behind the recent attempts on his life.

"So, what is his name and what are you warning him about?" I took the seat opposite the window. We might be only eight floors up, but if I got too close and saw the drop, my stomach *would* react. And I doubt that would endear me to my tablemates.

"That's not your concern," Quinn said.

His reply was almost absent, and annoyance rose. Dammit, I was getting more than a little tired of our relationship—whatever the hell that actually was—being a one-way information street. And being old and set in his ways *wasn't* excuse enough.

I thrust to my feet, needing to get out of there before I said something daft or we got back to the same old argument, but he grabbed me, his fingers like iron around my wrist.

"I'm sorry, Riley."

"No, you're not." I glanced down at his fingers. "Take your hand off my arm."

"Only if you sit down so we can talk."

"Right now, I have work to do. And I'm over talking to you."

"Please."

"No."

"What if I said the man I was looking for was Kellen Sinclair?"

"Telling me his name now means little." And I had to hope his Kellen wasn't my Kellen—though given the curveballs fate was throwing, I wasn't about to bet on it. "I want to be able to ask a question and have it answered civilly."

"I said I'll try, Riley, but you can't expect—"

He stopped abruptly.

"Yeah," I said softly. "But apparently it's okay for you to expect *me* to change overnight."

I peeled his fingers off my arm and stepped back, out of his reach. "I'm going to scout the room. I'll let you know if I scent or see anyone familiar."

He almost looked relieved at the prospect. "You shouldn't be doing that alone."

"Liander has masked my spoor and my looks. I'm safe enough here tonight."

"Even so, we're here to get a line on General Hunt, nothing more."

"We're here to uncover the trail to whoever is behind the gene manipulation business. I happen to think Hunt is just another rung in the ladder, which is why I want to scout the room first. There may be other players here."

Besides, I needed the time away from him. Needed to regroup my thoughts before I was tempted to tell him where to shove it. Hell, given fate's twisted line of thinking, it'd be my luck that the one man I walked away from would be the man who was my destiny.

"You find Hunt," I continued. "I'll join you once I look around."

I didn't give him the chance to argue, and quickly faded into the crowd milling on the dance floor. I was three-quarters of the way around the room—and feeling more than a little nauseous from the overwhelming wall of scent coming off every woman in the room, all of whom seemed to have bathed in the stuff—when I smelled it. Pine and springtime. Two of the scents I'd smelled in that breeding center.

I stopped abruptly and studied the people standing immediately in front of me. Just a bunch of gray-haired old ladies done up to the nines. No men. I frowned, and carefully sniffed the air, wondering if the press of aromas was confusing my senses.

The scent was there, as strong as before, and it was definitely coming from the group of women just ahead. Maybe there was a man in there somewhere, and I just couldn't see him.

I edged around a woman whose scent was so thick and orangey it made my already troublesome stomach threaten to rise, then moved closer to the group of elderly women. Still no men. Yet the scent was closer than before.

"So where is the delicious Martin?" one woman asked. "He owes me a champagne over that little wager we had."

Martin? Did she mean Martin Hunt? Did that mean his wife was in this group somewhere? I sidestepped around another couple, and finally saw her. In real life, she was just as broad-set and nondescript as she'd been in the picture, and looked totally ill at ease in the blood red, calf-length evening gown.

She looked my way at that moment, and our gazes locked. Shock hit, freezing me in place. Her eyes were a muddy brown, but the irises were ringed by two separate colors—blue, and a pale amber. I knew those eyes. They were the eyes of the man from my past. The eyes of the man who'd visited me in the breeding center.

Only this wasn't a man, it was a woman.

The memories were faulty. Had to be. This wasn't possible.

Then the familiar scent swam around me, confirming the impossible was indeed possible.

It was Martin Hunt's wife, not Martin Hunt himself, who had used me in that breeding center.

Chapter 9

o we know each other?" Mrs. Hunt's question
ut stridently across the babble of noise around us, caus-
ng several women in the group to turn and look at me.

"What?" Realizing immediately what I'd done, I
blinked and forced surprise into my voice as I added,
Oh, I'm sorry. I was looking at the view. I didn't mean
o appear like I was staring." Which, like a greenhorn
damn fool, I had been.

"And you are?" Her voice was no less frosty than be-
ore, and grated my nerves as sharply as nails down a
chalkboard. But it *wasn't* the voice of the person I'd
heard in that place, and it only made my confusion that
much stronger.

I gave her my best "no-one-is-home" smile, and held
out a hand. "Barbie Jenkins."

She ignored the hand. "I can't recall a Barbie Jenkin
on the list. Meryl?"

The woman identified as Meryl looked down her nos
at me. Not a bad effort considering I was taller by a goo
three inches.

"No, there was no Barbie Jenkins on the guest list."

"Oh, that's because I came with a friend."

She raised a too-bushy eyebrow. "And the name c
that friend?"

"Quinn O'Conor." I saw no harm in naming him, re
gardless of what my memories and senses were tellin
me about this woman. If she'd done the guest list, she'
know he was supposed to be here.

Her expression changed fractionally. She sniffec
Haughty didn't even begin to describe the sound. "He's
very generous supporter of the organization."

He was? That was news. But then, nearly everythin
about Quinn was news to me.

"Very generous," Meryl agreed gravely.

Meaning, obviously, that his choice of dinner partner
would be overlooked because of it. If I wasn't so confusec
I probably would have laughed at the old cows and thei
uptight attitudes—something that would surely have en
deared me further.

"I'm sure he's going to continue his support,"
gushed. "He's always saying what a wonderful—"

"Of course, dear. Thank you." She gave me an oh-so
insincere smile, and returned her attention to her friend:

Summarily dismissed, I quickly turned around an
headed back into the crowd. I had no idea what was go
ing on, but the one thing I needed to do was avoid Mrs
Hunt getting suspicious about me.

Only I didn't get all that far. A hand caught mine and found myself being pulled into a body that was hard nd familiar. The scent of warm leather and exotic spices wrapped around me, teasing my senses, stirring my hormones. Not Quinn. Kellen.

"Hello, Riley," he whispered, his breath so warm against my ear. "It's lovely to see you here."

Fate sure as hell was intent on playing games with my fe—or was she merely trying to point me in the right direction?

I turned around to refute his statement, but as my aze met his, the words died on my lips.

Because he *knew*. There was no doubt in his green yes at all. Despite the disguise, despite my scent being overed, he knew it was me. And the depth of that recognition scared me. How could I connect so deeply with omeone I didn't really know?

Someone who Quinn distrusted?

But what was perhaps even more scary was the fact hat, unlike the Kellen I'd met in Melbourne, *this* Kellen was all alpha, all power, all need. The patience was gone. This wolf would take what he wanted, and what he wanted was me.

It was a thought that made my blood race. And yet I wasn't here to enjoy myself, wasn't here to play with a prospective mate.

But maybe, just maybe, he could help me with some information gathering.

"I need to ask you some questions—" I started, and he squeezed my hand tightly, making the words cut off.

"Not here. Let's go somewhere else."

I could have resisted. I *should* have resisted.

I didn't.

And while I would have loved to use the excuse that
couldn't go to Misha aching with need because the bas
tard didn't deserve it, truth was, I wanted *this* wolf just a
much as he wanted me.

He strode out of the main ballroom and up the hall t
the elevators, his grip on my hand forcing me to almos
run to catch up with him. "Where are we going?"
asked, a little breathlessly.

"To my office. We won't be disturbed there."

The thought had my pulse skipping. As did th
heated, determined look in his eyes. "You work here?"

"I own the building."

"Wow."

A smile touched his lips as his gaze slid down m
body. Heat stirred deep within. "That dress is a wow.
His gaze rose. "But I intend to take it off you in pre
cisely"—he glanced at his watch—"twenty seconds."

The elevator chimed softly as the door opened. H
tugged me inside and pressed the top-floor button.

"You're getting a little presumptuous, aren't you?"

He raised an eyebrow. "Am I?"

The elevator zoomed upward, and for a change, m
stomach had no reaction. Maybe it was the presence an
heat of the wolf standing so close keeping any reactio
but desire at bay. "I came here with someone, you know.

"Quinn O'Conor." Cold amusement touched hi
green eyes. "It gives me a great deal of pleasure to stea
you away from that bastard."

I stepped back. "I hope that's not the only reason be
cause otherwise—"

He laughed, cutting me off. "If I truly wanted t

nnoy him, I would have taken you somewhere closer, omewhere his vampire senses could feel every little glorious thing I intend to do to you."

And I thought the horse-shifter was hot....

I blew out a breath and resisted the urge to fan myself. The elevator stopped and a small bell chimed as the loors opened. Only they didn't open into a hallway but a huge office with billion-dollar views over the harbor.

"Stunning," I said.

"It is," he agreed, but he was looking at me when he aid it.

I smiled, liking this wolf more and more. "That elevator a private one?"

He waved a keycard I hadn't noticed before. Observant, that was me. "Totally. Why?"

"Because I'd hate for us to be interrupted."

"Oh, we won't be." He tugged me forward. The office vas huge, and not just an office. There were double loors to our left that led into a bedroom that looked to be is big as my whole apartment, and a single door farther long that same wall that led into a bathroom.

"You live here?" I asked, almost running to keep up vith him again as he skirted around several perfect-foreduction leather couches.

"Most of the time. I have an apartment in Melbourne, oo." He looked over his shoulder, his eyes flashing green ire in the shadowy light. "I intend to be there a whole lot nore often."

"Well, good." Then I saw where he was headed and topped. "Umm, sorry, but I'm afraid of heights, so geting near the windows is not a good idea."

He switched tack, tugging me toward a long ma-hogany board table. He pushed several chairs aside, some of them crashing to the thick beige carpet as he spun me around and backed me against the table.

My breath caught as his hands slid teasingly down my waist and hips. His fingers briefly caressed my thighs, sending little sparks of electricity shooting through my system, then he caught the hem of the dress and it was being pulled up and over my head. "Twenty seconds, on the dot," he said with a smile.

"I do so admire a man who keeps his word." I hitched my butt onto the tabletop. "Now that you've got me naked, what are you going to do with me?"

"Offer you a drink, of course. What would you like?"

"Would a coffee be pushing the friendship?"

"One espresso coming up."

He walked over to a bar that was bigger than my en-tire bathroom back home, and grabbed one of the cups sitting beside the coffee-making machine. "Why are you here with Quinn?"

I shrugged. "It's business more than pleasure."

The machine hissed as he began pouring coffee into the cup. "So you are fucking him?"

There was no judgment in that question, just a state-ment of fact. Which was nice when compared to Quinn's uptight attitudes. I smiled. "Of course I am—why?"

"It just makes it all the more delicious when I steal you away from him." He walked across the room and handed me the cup. "Now, where were we?"

"Chatting," I said. "And drinking coffee."

"You're drinking coffee," he corrected, his voice

lightly distracted as he ran one finger down my neck and across my shoulder.

Desire trembled through my veins, and the fires of need leapt into focus. I took a quick sip of coffee, but it didn't do a whole lot to ease the deep-seated ache. "It does take two to keep a conversation going."

"I've always found talking to be overrated."

"And I've always found one person being dressed while the other is naked somewhat unfair."

He grinned and stepped back, then unhurriedly began to strip. I sipped my coffee and enjoyed the show—and it *was* a good show. The man knew how to do a decent striptease. Once naked, he stepped between my legs, brushed my hair from my left shoulder, and lightly planted a kiss on it.

"I prefer the natural color of your hair," he murmured, his breath hot against my skin. "It's so much prettier."

"And yet you recognized me, despite the changes," I greed huskily. "How?"

"An alpha always recognizes his chosen mate."

His words made my heart do crazy things. I barely even knew this wolf, and yet here he was, declaring his intent to make me his. It was thrilling, sexy, and just a little scary. "I'm not your mate."

"But you will be." His mouth replaced his breath on my shoulder, and slowly, languorously, he kissed his way toward my ear. When the sweet heat of his tongue delved inside, a helpless sound of pleasure escaped my lips.

He chuckled, a throaty sound as seductive and as arousing as his touch. His fingers trailed from my hips to my breasts, and lightly began to tease and pinch the

engorged points. I squirmed, put my coffee on the table
and forgot about it as every inch of my body vibrated
with the hunger that flowed through my veins.

When I could stand no more, I wrapped my arm
around his neck and pulled him close, so that my breasts
were squashed against his chest. The beat of his heart
was as wild as mine, and the heat of his desire a furnace
that burned my skin, making me sweat. Want.

His mouth brushed mine, a tingling, tantalizing promise of what was to come, then he reached behind me.
"Your coffee, madam," he said, offering me the cup.

I smiled and accepted it. "And what will you be doing
while I drink it?"

"Oh, this and that."

His fingers slid into my moistness. I groaned, put the
cup back down as I shifted to give him greater access.
He caressed me, teased me, bringing me to the edge
all too quickly. But he offered no release, withdrawing
his touch, kissing me fiercely and thoroughly, until the
threatening tremors had subsided. Then he offered me
coffee and started all over again.

By the time I'd finished the rest of that cup, the coffee
was cold and I burned. My heart was hammering so
loudly its cadence seemed to fill the silence, and every
fiber in my being quivered.

His hand slid up the inside of my spread thighs, his
fingers grazing me yet again. I shuddered, thrusting into
his touch, sure I was going to burst if he didn't get on
with it. "Stop teasing," I moaned, when he did it a second
time.

He chuckled, then wrapped his free hand around my
neck and kissed me hard. As his mouth claimed mine,

his fingers slid between us, pressing into my slickness, caressing, delving, until he'd slipped inside. Then his thumb pressed into my clit, and he began to stroke, inside and out. I shuddered, writhed, as the sweet pressure built and built, until it felt as if I was going to tear apart from the sheer force of pleasure.

Then everything did tear apart, and I was shuddering, writhing, moaning. The tremors hadn't even subsided when his hands tightened on my rump and he pulled me forward. His hardness speared me, and it felt so good I groaned.

He began to move, and thought became impossible. All I could do was move with him, savoring and enjoying the sensations flowing through me. But the calm control of his initial seduction quickly disappeared, replaced by urgency, need. His strokes became fierce, hungry thrusts that shook my entire body, his fingers bruising my hips as he held me close. I didn't care. The sweet pressure had begun to build again, and was quickly reaching boiling point.

We came together, his roar echoing across the silence, his body slamming into mine so hard the whole table seemed to shake.

When I finally caught my breath again, I took his face between my palms and kissed him long and slow. "I think we both needed that."

His grin was that of a man who knows a job has been well done. "Yeah. Though I have to admit, it was a little too fast for my liking."

I grinned. "Fast can be good."

He raised a hand, and gently thumbed away a trickle of sweat from my cheek. "Fast was very good."

"So, you feeling up to answering a few questions now?"

"I think I could manage one or two." He parked his butt on the table beside mine. "What do you want to know?"

"What do you know about Mrs. Hunt?"

"She's a snobby old fart who does a marvelous job for her chosen charities." He studied me for a moment, then said, "Why?"

I hesitated. How much could I tell him? How much *should* I tell him? "Her name cropped up in an investigation," I hedged. "I've just been sent up here to check her out."

"By whom?"

Oh, crap. Still, if we were going to get involved, he'd have to know sooner or later who I worked for. "The Directorate."

"You're a guardian?" Disbelief edged his voice.

I laughed. "No, just a liaison. But we're short staffed at the mo, so I get to do the unimportant stuff, like follow leads that probably go nowhere."

"What was the lead?"

"That she was involved in some funds going missing." The lie slipped easily off my tongue, and part of me felt guilty about it.

Though the more worrying thing was the fact that only *part* of me felt guilty about it.

"How is missing money connected with a Directorate investigation? The mob you work for only go after killers, don't they?"

"Generally." I shrugged. "I do what I'm told. Makes life there a whole lot easier."

And if Jack heard me saying that, he'd laugh his head off. Doing what I was told had never been a priority of mine.

He frowned. "She's from an old money family, and takes pride in her charity work. I can't imagine her wanting to jeopardize either her family's standing or her own in the wider community by becoming involved in anything nefarious."

"So you haven't noticed anything odd about her behavior over the last few months?"

"No." He hesitated. "Although she did miss several charity events a few months back. The general said she was ill."

"You didn't believe him?"

"We're talking about a woman who dragged herself out of hospital after an appendix operation to attend one of her pet events."

"Did you talk to any of her friends about it?"

"One. Not that I was concerned or anything." He shrugged. "Apparently, she refused to see anyone for at least three weeks. Her friends were quite concerned."

"Did they speculate why?"

"Plastic surgery gone wrong. The general beat her up. Her new nails dropped off and she was mortified with shame."

I raised my eyebrows and he grinned. "Okay, I made that last one up."

"So, once the three weeks was up, she acted same as normal?"

"As far as I noticed, yeah."

"What about her scent?"

He raised an eyebrow. "What about it?"

"Did it change any after her three-week stint of seclusion?"

He hesitated. "Sort of. It got sharper. More distinct."

"In what way?"

He shrugged again. "I really wasn't paying that much attention to the old cow, trust me."

Great. No clue to sate my confusion in *that* answer. So were my memories totally scrambled, or were they giving me bits of the bigger picture? One I couldn't yet understand? Maybe Mrs. Hunt *had* been there. Maybe she enjoyed watching her husband taking other women. She didn't exactly look the voyeur type, but these days, you couldn't judge a book by its dowdy cover.

Yet her scent was exactly what I remembered smelling in that room, and it was also the scent of someone in my past. But two people *couldn't* have the exact same scent. A spoor was as individual as fingerprints or eyes. No two were ever exactly the same.

So why did I remember her scent and not her husband's, if indeed he was there? What the hell was going on?

"What about her husband? Anything odd happen with him over the last few months?"

He shook his head. "Wouldn't know. The general doesn't always get involved with the charities. He's on base a lot, apparently."

"With a wife that looks like that, who can blame him?" I muttered.

Kellen grinned. "That's why a man should pick his woman carefully. He has to live with his choice for the rest of his life."

"Humans don't."

"Humans don't do a lot of things—which is why I'm glad I was born a wolf."

I smiled. "So how come you're here tonight?"

He shrugged. "It's my building, and my dad is one of the sponsors. I'm here representing both parties."

"Not at the moment, you're not."

He placed an arm over my shoulder, and slid me closer. "At the moment, the only thing I'm representing is self-interest."

"Well, I'm here on work's time, and I really should be going back downstairs." But I didn't get up, didn't pull away. It felt too good being close to him.

"You've only been gone half an hour or so. No one important will have missed you yet."

Quinn would have—but I had a feeling that was who Kellen meant when he said "no one important."

His lips met mine and thought went south, not returning until a good hour later. By the time I did make it back down to the main ballroom, meals were being served. Energy caressed my mind, a tingling warmth that curled through my soul. Quinn, wanting me to open the psychic door and talk to him.

Which was not something I wanted to risk given what I'd just been doing. I didn't need the hassle he'd undoubtedly throw my way. So I ignored him and made my way back to our table, sitting down and picking up the napkin like nothing at all had happened.

"Where have you been?" His voice was short. Annoyed.

"Out scouting around."

"Scouting where?"

"Oh, here and there." I resisted the urge to say it was

none of his business and took a sip of wine. "What do you know about Mrs. Hunt?"

He glanced around. "We cannot have this conversation here." His voice was little more than a stroke of sound. "There's too many ears."

"So why not just touch their minds and tell them all to ignore us?"

"The room is full of psychic-deadeners, in case you hadn't noticed."

I hadn't, but then, I rarely used my telepathic skills so there was nothing unusual in that. "Since when have psychic-deadeners worried you?"

"They don't, but they do stop you from chatting back."

Which I would have thought he'd actually enjoy. Still, we *did* need to talk about Mrs. Hunt, so we'd have to do so with the very link Quinn had tried to use moments ago. While the deadeners meant normal telepathic channels wouldn't work, the bond we'd created worked in a whole different area of the brain, and owed its existence to the fact we'd once shared blood.

With a slight grimace, I imagined that psychic door in my mind and threw it open. It was certainly easier to do than the first few times I'd tried.

Why do you ask about Mrs. Hunt? he asked immediately.

His mind-voice was as rich and as sexy as his regular voice, flowing through every corner of my being like a hot summer breeze.

I found the scent I remembered, only it belonged to Mrs. Hunt. And Mrs. Hunt's scent is very similar to the scent of a man from my past.

Then you must have the wrong scent. No two persons have the same scent. Besides, it was a man who abused you in the center, not a woman.

Don't you think I'm more than aware of that fact? I thanked the waitress as she placed an entrée plate in front of me, and picked up my knife and fork. *I'm just telling you what my senses are telling me. I can't help it if it's not making sense.*

I tucked into my meal as I tried to remember the name of the man who had smelled like Mrs. Hunt, but my memories refused to cooperate. Maybe he'd been a one-night stand. I didn't do it regularly, but I was a wolf, and I didn't *not* do it, either.

Once I'd finished my meal and the waitress had come back and collected the plate, I asked, *How well do you know the Hunts?*

He frowned slightly, and somehow managed to carry on a polite conversation with the woman sitting on the other side of him as he said to me, *I've only ever seen them at charity events like this.*

And has Mrs. Hunt always looked so . . . dowdy?

His quick glance was somewhat irritated. *Beauty is in the eye of the beholder, and not always evident on the surface.*

Says the man who is never seen with someone less than stunning.

Quinn's amusement shimmered through me. *I have an image to uphold.*

I snorted softly. In so many ways, this old vampire was so typically *male* in his responses. And a human male at that.

What pack does Mrs. Hunt come from?

I would have said brown, except I've never seen a wolf

from a brown pack with eyes quite like hers. But there again, I wasn't exactly well traveled. Quinn, on the other hand, was.

He sipped his wine, flashed a toe-curling smile at the waitress as she picked up his uneaten plate, then gave me a somewhat darker look. And had me wishing he'd flash a few of those smiles my way occasionally.

Mrs. Hunt isn't a werewolf. His tone suggested I was an idiot to believe otherwise.

But while my memories might be whacked, my instincts were working just fine. *Trust me on this—she's a wolf.*

No, she's not.

Well, the Mrs. Hunt in this room is. I paused to look around the room. She had to be on one of the tables near the stage, which I couldn't see thanks to a pillar. *Could she be a doppelganger of some kind?*

Doppelgangers are ghostly replicas, not human tissue.

You know what I mean.

Yes. He paused. *If she's a wolf, then she's obviously not the real Mrs. Hunt. The question is, when did the exchange take place?*

Kellen's comments came to mind. *She apparently disappeared from the charity scene for three weeks a couple of months ago. Wouldn't even talk to her friends.*

How do you know this?

I asked.

Who?

People, I said airily.

Annoyance ran through his gaze. And was that a hint of jealousy? Did the vampire suspect?

The vampire suspects, all right. Who the hell did you fuck to get that information?

I met his gaze, and shook my head. *That is none of your damn business.*

We are here to do a job—

Which I'm goddamn doing, so stop acting like a cuckolded husband.

He looked away. But his anger swam around me, breathtakingly sharp. Well, tough. And it wasn't like our deal had even started yet.

So, why would someone want to replace Mrs. Hunt? I said, more to get the conversation back on track than any real desire to continue conversing with the stubborn, stupid man.

The why is easy. Hunt's a general. He'd have access to many top-secret military areas.

Including Landsend?

He looked at me, eyebrow raised. *Possibly.*

But would Hunt be the type to share military secrets during pillow talk?

Having talked to the man, no. But he might not be doing it knowingly.

Wolves aren't often telepathic.

You are.

Yeah, but that's thanks solely to a vampire background.

So your mother wasn't telepathic?

I gave him a sideways glance. *That comes under the heading of "none of your business," doesn't it?*

You are such a bitch sometimes.

I grinned. *When you share, I share. It's as simple as that, buddy-boy.*

At that point, an MC got up and started proceedings,

which included a charity auction. Having no money to play with, my attention wandered back to my original problem—who was the lover in my past that smelled of pine and springtime?

You've had so many you can't remember?

If I could have hauled off and hit him, I would have. *Are you going to tell me you can recall the name of every woman you've slept with?*

No. But I sure as hell can recall their faces.

Of every single one? Right through all of your twelve hundred and forty odd years?

Every woman I've slept with for pleasure, most certainly.

Yeah, right. I was really believing that one. *But that's not every woman you've slept with, is it?*

No. He raised a hand, bidding for a weird-looking painting.

I've danced with wolves out of the same sort of need. I couldn't tell you what they looked like let alone what they smelled like. I paused, but couldn't resist adding, *Remember what you said a few months ago? That a wolf will jump anything with a dick when the need was on her? I guess it's true.*

I didn't put it so crudely.

Maybe not, but the intent was there.

He raised his hand again. *I believe you told me you'd never got to that stage before.*

I believe I may have lied.

And here I was thinking you were at least honest.

I'm a werewolf—we're all lying whores, aren't we?

He looked at me for several long seconds, his expression vampire clean, then just shook his head and looked away.

The auction continued. Quinn bought two paintings and a dinner for two at some fancy restaurant while I got more and more bored. If this was a sample of the high life, then the high life wasn't for me.

The auction finally finished and dessert arrived. I started to tuck in, then saw Mrs. Hunt on the arm of her husband, heading for the door.

"Time for us to go," Quinn said, wrapping his fingers around my arm as he exchanged quick good-byes with our tablemates.

And do what, precisely?

Follow them.

We grabbed my coat from the cloakroom, and headed out into the foyer. The air here was cooler, and I shivered. *We have our orders.*

We have half an hour before we have to head back to the airport. I'd like to see where they go.

Probably straight home after such a fun-packed night. The Hunts had already disappeared. We caught the other elevator and headed down.

It's unusual for them to leave a function like this so early.

I shoved on my coat, and quickly did up the buttons. *Maybe the general's feeling randy.*

He gave me a flat look but didn't bother saying anything. I resisted the impulse to grin. It might not be wise, but damn, baiting him was fun.

The elevator came to a halt and the doors opened. The Hunts were already out the main doors and walking down the stairs. We hurried after them, slowing only when the foyer doors opened to let us out.

The night air hit like ice, freezing the bits that were exposed. I crossed my arms, trying to stop my teeth from chattering as Quinn pulled me to a stop on the bottom step, then made a quick call to his driver.

The Hunts walked to the leading cab in the rank, the general opening the door for his wife. In that instant, the sensation of danger hit so hard that it left me gasping for air. Air that screamed a warning that something fast and deadly was tearing through the night toward us.

I threw myself sideways, knocking Quinn out of the way. He cursed, his arms going around me, instinctively cushioning my body with his as we fell to the ground. He grunted as we hit, and his eyes widened. Something burned past my ear, and I twisted around in time to see one side of the glass doors shatter.

Someone had shot at us.

A woman screamed. A high-pitched, wailing sound of horror.

Gut churning, I twisted around again.

Martin Hunt lay on the ground, his face little more than a pulpy mass of blood and bone.

Quinn thrust me off him, and I scrambled to my feet.

"Two shooters," he said. "One from the building directly ahead, one from the right."

"I'll take that one," I said, pointing to the building directly ahead as I kicked off my stilettos.

He nodded, and blurred into night. I grabbed my heels then ran with vampire speed across the road and into the office building. Hitting the guard telepathically, I made him forget he'd seen me as I ran into the nearest stairwell.

There was undoubtedly more than one set of stairs, but right now, the important thing was getting to the roof as fast as possible. I could track the assassin's scent from there.

I ran up, and up. And up. Ran until my legs were on fire, my lungs burned, and my stomach was doing cartwheels. Once I reached the roof, I wiped the sweat out of my eyes, then carefully opened the door. Or tried to. The damn thing was locked.

So much for not announcing my presence to the shooter.

I stepped back, and kicked the door with as much force as my quaking limbs could muster. It was apparently quite a lot, because the door crashed open. The cold night air swept in, freezing the sweat on my skin and wrapping the scent of musk and man around me. The killer was still here.

I sniffed, trying to get a sense of direction. The wind swirled, making it difficult to judge where, exactly, he was. And what he was.

Which was unusual. This shooter wasn't human, because I *was* sensing his presence. So why couldn't I tell which race he was?

I wrapped the shadows around me and stepped out. The dark night and the nearby lights seemed to sweep around me, and the realization that I was so very high up hit like a punch, making my stomach turn and head spin.

Then a sense of impending doom washed over me, and the sick sensations were lost under the sudden need to save myself. I dove sideways, landing with a grunt on the hard concrete, scraping skin off hands and knees. Something pinged against the metal of the door and sparks flew. *The shooter had infrared sight.* Swearing under my breath, I scrambled to my feet and ran like hell for the nearest cooling tower. Soft pings followed, nipping at my heels like a terrier.

Damn, damn, damn. Back pressed hard against the cooling tower's metal casing, I closed my eyes and breathed deep, trying to get some air into my burning lungs. Trying to control the fear lashing at me. The harsh sounds of sirens bit across the night, mingling with the rumble of traffic. I had to get out of this building before the cops arrived. I couldn't afford to get caught up playing twenty questions.

Swallowing heavily, I concentrated on the strongest noises, zoning them into a separate section of consciousness. Then I zeroed in on the underlying, closer noises. A cricket chirruped to my left. Soft footfalls moved to my right.

I swiped at the sweat running down my face with the sleeve of my jacket, then slipped around the cooling tower and peered over the edge. Nothing but a wide expanse of concrete between me and the cooling tower where the shooter must have stood.

Though the footfalls had ceased, the scent on the wind suggested the man had moved to the rear edge of the stairwell. Maybe he was trying to get around me. Maybe he was simply trying to escape.

I retraced my steps and padded silently to the other side of the stairwell. Once I was close to the corner, I stopped and lowered my shields a little, feeling out the shooter's thoughts. Nothing. He was either mind-blind, or he was shielded against psychic intrusion.

I swore under my breath. So much for taking his mind and rendering him helpless. I'd have to do this the old-fashioned way. I risked a peek around the corner.

He was down the far end, on one knee, gun aimed at the tower he'd just vacated. Obviously, he thought me dumb.

I padded forward slowly, resisting the urge to blur and run at him with vampire speed, not wanting to risk the scream of approaching air giving him a warning.

At the last moment he sensed me anyway, turning and firing in one quick movement. The bullet nicked my shoulder, throwing me back and down, digging a trench in my skin deep enough to lose a fingertip in. Pain hit and I hissed, my vision momentarily blurred by the sting of tears. The bastard had *silver* bullets.

He hadn't been aiming for Quinn earlier. He'd been aiming for me or Mrs. Hunt.

The click of bullets being reloaded echoed across the night. I caught my balance and pivoted, knocking the weapon away from him. His hand darted to his back. I blurred, kicked him in the balls, then whacked one of the shoes across his jaw as he was going down. Fire leapt across his jaw, meaning the shooter was vampire, even if I hadn't sensed it.

His grunt was abruptly cut as the back of his head smashed against the concrete. His eyes rolled back and he didn't move.

Now that adrenaline had faded, the pain hit again. Swearing softly, I tugged off the dress then called to the wolf within me. Power swept around me, through me, blurring my vision, blurring the pain. But I only stayed in my alternate form for a heartbeat, then shifted back. The wound still stung like blazes, but at least the bleeding had stopped.

I re-dressed then and, holding the stilettos at the ready

in case he was bluffing, walked over to the shooter. He was Caucasian, probably early twenties, with black hair, tribal tats across his cheeks, and a ring in the middle of his bottom lip. It was the ring that was the psychic shield. Obviously, someone had done a little updating since I'd last seen one.

I straddled his body, plonked down on top of him, and pressed one heel against his chest, just as a precaution. If he moved, I'd stake him, because I wasn't in the mood for a fight right now. He wouldn't die immediately, because the stiletto wasn't long enough to reach his heart from where I had it positioned. But it would give me time enough to read him. And right now, that was all that was important.

I grabbed the lip ring and roughly yanked it out. Blood spurted. He didn't flinch, meaning he was truly out of it. Not that it mattered. Now that his mind was unshielded, it was mine to play in.

Lowering my shields again, I mentally reached out, touching his thoughts, rifling his memories. He was a contract killer, and had been hired yesterday to get rid of *me*.

Not Mrs. Hunt. *Me*.

So much for Misha's damn promise that he'd keep me safe and stop the attacks.

I continued rifling through the shooter's thoughts. He didn't know who had hired him, because the hit had been arranged through an intermediary. A man who had brown eyes ringed with blue and amber, and whose face had the same sort of harsh lines as Mrs. Hunt.

Did she have a brother?

Had the kill on General Hunt been deliberate, or an accident? Were the two hits even connected?

His mind couldn't give me the answers. He only knew what he'd been contracted to do.

I glanced up as the wailing sirens came to a halt on the street below. Time to go. I raided the killer's mind again, this time making him believe he had a broken leg. Even if he woke before the cops got here, he wouldn't go anywhere. I rose, patted him down for other weapons, shoved him onto his side so he wouldn't choke to death on his own blood—though if he was a vampire, that was highly unlikely—then kicked the rifle well out of his reach.

Move, Riley. Quinn's voice was edged with concern. *The cops will be up on that roof soon.*

I'm aware of that. I headed for the stairs. *How'd you do?*

He'd disappeared by the time I got up there.

I went down the stairs even faster than I'd come up, and a whole different set of muscles woke to protest. *No clues as to how?*

He left some feathers and the weapon behind.

So the second shooter was a shifter—not that *that* gave any clue as to identity. *My killer had been contracted to hit me, not Hunt.*

Hunt was a deliberate shot, not an accident.

I pushed my way out of the stairwell. The guard spun and opened his mouth to speak, but I took control of his mind and made him look past me and see nothing. *So, we were both targets simply because we were both at the one spot. The question is, why did they want Hunt dead?*

And how did they know you were here, let alone that it was you under that disguise?

I don't know. I just don't know.

The front doors swished open. Lights flashed across the darkness, streaking it with blue and red. Men in white and blue stood around the taxi and Mrs. Hunt, while a gathering crowd looked on in horror.

Awareness prickled across my skin, then Quinn was beside me, a shadow who suddenly found substance. He wrapped his hand around my arm and guided me to the right.

Where are we going?

You're going to the airport. I'm going to follow Mrs. Hunt.

Jack won't be happy.

Jack is not my boss, and we need to know what the hell is going on. If Mrs. Hunt is a replacement, she'll know something. Or somebody. I intend to find out which it is.

Be careful.

In these matters, I always am.

He stopped by the car and opened the door. Then he pulled me against him, his mouth claiming mine in a kiss that was wild, erotic, and a very unapologetic affirmation of what he wanted. And what he intended to do when we had more time.

I opened my eyes, stared into his. Saw the desire. Saw the determination, burning bright.

This vampire would not give up, would not go away. No matter what I did or said. He was playing for keeps. For real.

Which meant he still wasn't understanding that I was a wolf, with a wolf's needs, and that we could never be what he wanted us to be, no matter what might lie between us.

"Quinn—"

"Mrs. Hunt is leaving," he cut in harshly, making me wonder if he'd read my mind and was simply delaying the moment of truth. "We'll talk another time."

He kissed me again, no less fiercely than before, then pushed me into the car and slammed the door shut. By the time I'd twisted around to look at him, he was gone.

Chapter 10

The Rocker was filled with teenagers half my age, all of them bopping to music that was painful to my ears. I could see why the Rocker's traditional weekend crowd had fled—the crap they were playing now was nothing like the good old-fashioned rock and roll this club had built its reputation on. But then, I guess they had to do something to attract the next generation of wolves through the door.

Misha sat on a stool at the far end of the chrome and red lacquer bar. He wore dark jeans and a black T-shirt, and both accentuated the whiteness of his lean body. As I stood there staring at him, the urge to turn and run hit me. I didn't want to do this. I really didn't.

Not because of the sex. As I'd said to Quinn more than once, sex was part of a werewolf's nature, and we didn't hold it in the same reverent regard. Even though I didn't particularly want to mate with Misha, I would, and I'd more than likely enjoy it.

No, what disgusted me was the fact that I'd been left no choice in the matter.

If I was a guardian and this was just a part of my job, it would have been okay. If I'd walked in here knowing I'd been offered this assignment and had willingly chosen to do it, I would have had no problems. But I didn't have the choice, no matter what Quinn said. Misha seemed to be the only one who knew what was going on, and to get that information and get my life on track, I had to do this. Not because I wanted to, but because I *had* to. Two very different things.

And it hit me then that part of me had already accepted the reality that one day I would become a guardian. That one day, I'd be doing this out of choice rather than need.

I closed my eyes, sickened not so much by the thought, but the tremor of excitement that ran through me. I didn't want to become a killer. Didn't want to become my brother. But the part of me that had always rejoiced in the danger of being with Talon was dancing at the thought of becoming a guardian and facing danger on a regular basis.

Maybe Jack was right. Maybe he did know me better than I knew myself.

Taking another deep breath, I pushed the thoughts aside, and made my way through the crowd.

Tapping Misha on the shoulder, I said, "I believe we had a date."

His icy gaze slid down my body. I'd changed into jeans and a black crop top, but had left Liander's other improvements in place. There was no recognition in

Misha's eyes as his gaze met mine then slid away. "I believe you're mistaken."

"So you've decided you don't want kids anymore?"

His head snapped around, and his gaze narrowed. "Riley?"

"The one and only." I plopped down on the stool beside his and ordered a beer.

"Why the disguise?"

"Why not? Especially when you haven't exactly proven you can keep me safe."

"Have you been attacked recently?"

I snorted softly. "Twice, actually."

"What?"

The surprise in his voice seemed genuine, but I wasn't about to be taken in by it. Misha could act the pants off just about anyone I knew. "Once with orsini, once with a paid hitman. It's pissing me off, Misha."

"The bastard," he muttered. "Obviously, he needs a little reminder that I mean what I say."

"Obviously, because he ain't taking a blind bit of notice of your threats at the moment. And keeping me safe was part of our deal, remember?"

"I remember," he said, voice hard. "And I'm trying."

"Well, try a little harder or the damn deal is off." I paused and thanked the bartender as he brought over my beer. "I want to know how he's tracking me, Misha. Tell me that, or it ends right now."

Jack would have a fit if he heard either of the threats, but hell, Jack didn't have his life on the goddamn line.

"You're bugged."

"Rhoan checked for bugs. We didn't find any."

"You wouldn't find these. They're new."

"Stolen from the Landsend Military Base, perhaps?"

He smiled. "Perhaps."

"I want you to find it and take it out."

He nodded. "I don't want you dead, Riley. Believe that, if nothing else."

Oh, I believed it. He wanted a kid out of me first. "So, tell me, why was Martin Hunt shot?"

"Not here. Wait until we're upstairs."

"Upstairs might not be any safer."

"But they have voice screens active up there. At least what we say can't be overheard once we're in one of the zones."

"Unless people can read lips."

A smile touched his thin mouth. "I think it'd be a bit obvious if someone was up there simply to read lips."

True. The Rocker wasn't like the Blue Moon. The dancing on this level was actual dancing, not the wolf kind, simply because the Rocker had a wall of windows that looked out onto the main street. And while werewolves didn't mind doing it in public, humankind sure did get upset about seeing it.

Nor did it have private rooms. Here at the Rocker, the choice on the upper floor was a communal one, the options as simple as beds, sofas, or beanbags. "I thought you said your followers had given up watching you here?"

"As far as I know, they have. But I'm not taking chances."

Nor would I. Liander's improvements might be worth keeping for a while yet. I took a long swig of my beer, then said, "Shall we get down to business?"

His eyes glimmered with amusement and hunger. "Eager to please, huh?"

"Oh, dying for it."

"The end result will be worth it—for both of us."

I surely hoped so. "There's no guarantee I'll get pregnant. If you've read my files, you'll know that."

He pressed a hand against my spine as he guided me toward the back stairs. Desire stirred sluggishly. Misha wasn't my choice of partner anymore, and he certainly didn't deserve any eagerness, but he was the one I had to be with. That being the case, I might as well enjoy my time with him.

"You're not the only wolf I'm trying to impregnate right now," he said, as we climbed the stairs. "I have two other women who have agreed to bear my child."

It was the first statement he'd made that I truly believed. The first statement that actually had me thinking he *was* telling the truth—at least some of the time. "The blondes you mentioned earlier?"

He nodded.

"I bet they're doing it for a tidy sum."

He glanced at me, eyes cold. "Everyone has their price, Riley."

He knew mine. Knew it was the only reason I was here. And he didn't care. What would he do if he knew he would never get the one thing he *really* wanted? Not from me, anyway.

The upstairs room was long and narrow, and looked like one of those old-fashioned barns often seen in westerns. The only thing that was missing was the hay—though I knew that had been here in the early years.

The room was semi-filled with wolves in various stages of mating, and the air was thick with the smell of sex and lust. My blood quickened, aroused by the aromas as much as the sounds and sights of mating.

Misha's hunger flicked around me, a living thing that stole my breath and made the ache even fiercer. His aura, switched to full intensity, drowned me in desire, making sure my body would be ready for him when the time came. Not that he really needed to do it, because after Quinn's kiss and subsequent departure, I was more than ready to play.

And though I could have negated the force of his aura easily enough, I didn't. It was better to let him think I needed his aura, that I was still unwilling to be here. Besides, tonight might be about getting answers, but I sure as hell intended to enjoy it as well.

By the time we reached the first free sofa midway down the room, my skin burned, as did the need to feel him inside. Not waiting for him to make the first move, I pushed him back against the wall and kissed him like my life depended on it. Kissed him until my skin burned and the need to feel him inside was all-consuming. And then I fucked him, hard and fast and furiously. He growled deep in his throat, a warning of God knows what, but I ignored it, riding him hard. As his body convulsed and his seed poured into me, my orgasm hit. The intensity of it stole my breath and my sanity for too many seconds.

But it wasn't over yet. Not by a long shot.

He was still hard inside, but that wasn't really surprising. The need to create life was on him, and the moon that forced the change each month granted us the strength to mate long and frequently, especially when the need to reproduce was on us.

"My turn to ride rough," he growled, his eyes burning with desire and anger.

I'd hit a nerve. Misha hated being second. Hated not being in charge. Interesting. Maybe it was something I could use later on, when we were somewhere security wasn't likely to intervene should things get a little rough.

He spun me around, pressed me against the back of the sofa, then kicked my legs apart and thrust into me so hard and fast I wasn't sure whether my groan was one of pleasure or pain. Then he began to move, and I let thought slide away, concentrating on sensation and simply enjoying.

That was the pattern for the next two hours—we mated on the sofa, the bed, and the beanbags. The first hour was as hard and furious as I'd expected, but after that, he took more time, seducing rather than simply taking. I appreciated the effort, and in the end, thoroughly enjoyed myself. I'd always liked Misha, and I guess I still did—even if I no longer trusted him. And whatever else his faults, he was usually a good lover.

It was close to three when we ordered a couple of beers, then made our way over toward a secluded corner. Misha flicked on the voice screen as I flopped back into a beanbag.

"Give me your feet," he said.

I raised them both and plonked them in his lap. He studied the underside of both for a moment, then grunted and dropped my right foot back to the floor. He bent my left leg around so I could see my foot, and pointed to the slight spot of discoloration right in the middle. "See that?"

I frowned. "Looks like a freckle."

"That it does. Only, if you run your finger over it, you feel a slight hardness around the edges compared to the rest of your foot."

I did. "It's the tracker?"

"Yep."

"Landsend can make trackers that small?"

"Not only small, but untraceable to current finders."

"And you know this because you have one in you?" It was a guess, but not much of one.

He smiled. "Yes, I have one. But they don't entirely trust it, so I have followers as well."

"Why don't they trust it on you? It obviously works."

"Because I know how to remove it, and do so when it suits me not to be found. He thinks the signal is faulty, hence the followers."

"You play a dangerous game, Misha."

"Extremely." He reached over to our pile of clothes, and pulled a knife from the pocket of his jeans. "Hold still," he said.

He cut into my foot. Not deeply, so the pain wasn't really that sharp. After a few seconds, he grunted, then held up the spot on a fingertip so I could see. Now it looked like a freckle with four fine, wiry legs. He dropped it to the floor and smashed it under his heel.

"He will of course know you've found the bug."

"As long as he can no longer track me, I couldn't care less." I studied Misha for a moment. "He *can't* track me now, can he?"

"As far as I know, that was the only bug he placed. You can't use more than one on a person—stuffs up the signal or something like that."

"And I presume Kade has one, as well?"

"Everyone of importance to the project had one. Just in case."

"Then excuse me while I make a quick phone call."

He shrugged. I pulled the cell from the pocket of my jeans and quickly dialed Jack's number. It was busy, so I left a message giving details about the bug and how to remove it.

That done, I shoved the phone back into my pocket, and said, "So tell me why Hunt was killed."

Misha relaxed back into the opposite bag. "He'd reached the end of his usefulness."

"And the fact that you're now talking about him means he wasn't a player, let alone a major player."

"Yes."

"So why not simply tell me his name in the first place?"

"He's dead, so the restrictions on my mentioning his name have gone." His smile was cold. "Besides, it was never part of the agreement that I make things easy for you."

True. But it was occasionally nice to think things *could* be easy. Stupid, I know. "Then Hunt was simply a means of gathering information?"

"Yes."

"To top-secret military bases."

"And what they were doing. But also a means of keeping an eye on the various investigations, both military and civilian."

"I'm gathering the Directorate wasn't one of those—you already have a man in there."

He smiled. "And here I was thinking no one was aware Gautier was one of us."

"Jack's known about him for ages." Which wasn't exactly the truth, but it couldn't hurt having Misha think we were more aware of the situation than we truly were. "Tell me about Mrs. Hunt."

He simply smiled. Meaning he couldn't, or wouldn't.

"What pack does the woman impersonating Mrs. Hunt come from?"

Again with the silence. Obviously, Mrs. Hunt—or whoever she truly was—was someone we had to keep following.

"What about Kade, then? Why was his partner killed and he kept alive?"

"His partner was killed because they were getting too close to a source. Kade was kept alive simply because he had interesting skills."

He *certainly* did. "What pack has brown eyes, ringed by blue and amber?"

"The Helki pack, who live around Bendigo." His eyes were chips of glittery ice in the hazy light filling the room. "It's simply a matter of asking the right questions, Riley."

I sipped my beer. "What can you tell me about the Helki pack?"

"They're shifters."

I gave him a deadpan sort of look. "We're all shifters." Even if most shapeshifters actually denied the fact they came from the same base stock as weres.

"Yes, but not all weres are shapeshifters in the same way the Helki pack are."

I frowned. "Meaning?"

"Meaning, some can take different animal shapes,

other than just a wolf. And some can take on other human shapes."

"You're kidding."

"No."

This had implications I didn't even *want* to contemplate. "I'm surprised the Helki pack haven't disappeared into the dark recesses of hidden labs."

His smile was grim. "Who's saying many of them haven't?"

We *had* to find this other damn lab! Had to stop them. "Is the woman I saw tonight a member of the Helki pack?"

His eyes gleamed with amusement. "I think you're beginning to catch on. She's a clone made using the genes of the Helki pack."

More damn clones. Was there a never-ending supply of these bastards? "So was the original Mrs. Hunt human, and did she have the same weirdly colored eyes? If not, how did the replacement explain the sudden difference in eye color?"

"The original was human, and her eyes were very similar to a Helki's in color—brown ringed by blue. And the new Mrs. Hunt retreated from her friends and charities for three weeks. The only person who might have noticed the slight difference would have been her husband—except the two of them have been sexually alienated for some time. They still share a room, but not the same bed."

"So the original is dead?"

"Yes."

I took a swig of beer, then changed tack. "You said

once before that the answer lies in my past. In lovers from my past."

"Yes."

"Did you mean long-term or short-term lovers?"

"Very short-term, I believe."

Gee, that was going to make it easy. Particularly if he meant "short-term" as in one-night stand. "How far back in the past?"

He hesitated. "Three and a half years ago."

Great. *That* was going to be a cinch to remember—particularly if it had happened during the moon phase. I rubbed a hand across my eyes. "How connected is that man to the woman I met tonight?"

"*Very* connected."

"Sister?"

"No."

"Lover?"

"No."

"What then?"

"That I cannot say."

Could not, or would not? Given the smile touching his lips, I suspected the latter. "Is the man we're talking about from the Helki pack?"

"In the same sense as the woman, yes."

Then the Helki pack definitely had to be checked out. What remained of them, anyway. "Can you give me a description?"

He shrugged. "Brown hair, medium build. Blue eyes."

Ordinary, in other words. Then I frowned. "I thought you said he was a member of the Helki tribe?"

"I did."

"How could he have blue eyes?"

"The color of the eyes change, depending on what form they're wearing."

I raised my eyebrows. "Then why wouldn't the fake Mrs. Hunt just complete the disguise and take on the original's true eye color?"

"Because such transformations take a lot of energy and power. The less you actually have to transform, the longer you can hold the transformation. And the eyes, believe it or not, are one of the hardest items to hold and maintain."

"Them being the windows to the soul and all that."

"Yes." He paused. "Has anyone ever said you've got extremely expressive eyes?"

"No, and I'm not interested in hearing it from you, either."

He smiled. It reminded me of a cat watching a mouse he knew he was about to eat.

"So, the man sent to seduce me three or so years ago wasn't wearing his true form?" Which meant remembering him wasn't going to help anyway.

"No."

I drank some more beer, then asked, "What did he claim to do as a job?"

"I believe he said he was military."

Military? I'd only ever danced with one military man, and had ended up losing part of my heart to him. But it couldn't be Jaskin. He'd been checked and silently approved by the Directorate—there *couldn't* have been anything remotely dodgy about his past.

And there'd been no other military lovers—had there? I frowned, remembering back to when I'd first met Jaskin. Remembered then the man before him—the man who had introduced us.

He'd come from the same carrier, but had somehow gotten separated from his shipmates and had ended up at the Blue Moon alone. Or so he'd told me. The moon had been two nights from full bloom and the fever had been riding me hard. Though I was with a couple of regular mates at the time, there'd been something about him that attracted me—a dangerous edge that spoke to the wildness. We danced the rest of the evening, and had agreed to meet the following night.

Only, he didn't come back alone. Jaskin and several others had been with him. They, too, had that edge, but something else had just clicked between me and Jaskin, and it was him rather than the first man I danced with all night long.

God, what was the first man's name?

Ben. No, something stranger. *Benito.* Benito Verdi.

Finally, I had a lead I could follow. It might be a total dead end, but at least it was something.

"Was that blue-eyed man the first plant?"

"The first attempt at a plant, yes."

"Why?"

He raised an eyebrow. "What do you mean?"

"I mean, what did I do or say at that particular time that tipped you and your lab-mates off to the fact that I was something more than an ordinary wolf?"

"It was actually Gautier who suggested it. He said you were extraordinarily fast for a wolf, and could be a good donor for our labs or other experiments. He also said it was obvious you knew he was about, even when he was shadowed."

Something no wolf could do. But then, why hadn't Gautier also noticed those same facts when it came to Rhoan? Why mention me, and not my brother?

And then it hit me. Rhoan drank *blood*. That was why they'd never questioned his speed, his reflexes. They all thought he was a wolf who'd performed the ritual ceremony and blood-sharing to become a vampire.

After all, he worked at night, came home at dawn. Well, when he did come home, that is. The Jenson red wolf pack might be a small one in Australia, but our pack had a long history over in England and Ireland, so the fact that he was a Jenson was no clue in itself of his age. No one at the Directorate knew we were brother and sister—no one except Jack and the Director herself— and it certainly wasn't in our files. Hell, even his birth date on file was fake. But then, a lot of vampires did the exact same thing. Fake records was how many of the older vampires had gotten through the centuries undiscovered.

It was very possible to think him a vampire—and a vampire old enough to stand a little daylight.

Which was good for him. Not so good for me. After all, the bastards were still after me.

"So," I said, "you began to watch me?"

He nodded and sipped his beer. His gaze slipped leisurely down my body, his hunger beginning to roll across my flesh in ever-warming waves. Obviously, I'd yet to finish payment for the night. "I even lived in a building across from you for over a year. Believe me, I loved the fact none of your windows had blinds."

I raised an eyebrow. "You played Peeping Tom? And here I was thinking you were at least above that."

"It's in the nature of a male to look." His smile grew. "As it is in the nature of a female to flaunt."

"Flaunting and looking are perfectly fine. Spying is an entirely different matter." I hesitated. "So why you, anyway? Especially seeing it was Talon who was then placed in the position to be my mate?"

He shrugged. "You knew Gautier, and seemed to be too aware of his presence. Talon considered himself beyond a watching brief, and our other clone brother had already failed."

So that blue-eyed man was another clone, like the woman playing Mrs. Hunt? Why then say they were Helki—unless he was counting them as Helki because that was the source of their DNA? "But why not have one of your underlings do it?"

"The man I work for has no trust of underlings. I was ordered to do it, so I did."

I frowned. "You don't look the type to stand back and take orders easily."

"I'm not, but when it comes to this man, I have no choice. There is no real hiding from him, because the five of us are locked in telepathic contact. He is far stronger than the rest of us, and would kill any of us the minute he sensed betrayal. I have no wish to die before my time is truly up."

"So you skirmish from the edges, and send in others to do your dirty work." Like me.

He nodded.

"Then why aren't you dead right now? You're plotting his demise via the Directorate, are you not?"

His smile sent a shiver up my spine. "Yes, I am. But he cannot monitor every thought, every wish, and as long as

I avoid certain key words, I can slip under the radar, so to speak."

So the reason he wasn't telling me certain things wasn't so much that he couldn't, more the fact that those words would attract unwanted mental attention.

"Then why try and place a mate on me? Why not simply snatch me?"

"Because of the Directorate, and your friendship with Rhoan. We did not wish to chance discovery, and weren't about to risk it by taking you. Not until we were sure you were worth the effort."

That raised my eyebrows. "Yet by snatching Rhoan, you ensured Directorate notice anyway."

He snorted. "That was Talon's arrogance coming into play. He never would believe the Directorate weren't all fools, or that they *would* notice his activities if he wasn't more circumspect. Of course, he didn't actually realize the lab had snatched Rhoan—not until after your raid to get him back." Amusement touched his lips. "That was very well done, by the way."

"Thanks."

He nodded. I took another drink of beer, then asked, "Why not kill Talon once we had him?"

"What was the point? Talon can tell you nothing."

Because the knowledge had been burned away. "So, originally, the plan was for Talon to keep an eye on me?"

He nodded again. "Of course, we didn't actually witness any of the abilities Gautier mentioned until recently."

"You mean the wolf who shot me with silver and recorded the whole event?"

"Yes. Seeing you shadow like that confirmed what Gautier had been saying all along."

"So why then? Why not try something like that earlier?"

"Because the day before, Gautier witnessed you taking out two vamps. No wolf, no matter how fast they are or how young the vampires are, should be able to do that. He demanded we do a test. This time, he was listened to."

So Gautier was the reason my life had headed down the toilet of late. Or, at least, he was partially responsible. If I'd walked away from the nightclub that night, ignored curiosity and the scent of blood on the wind, then maybe my life would have been normal. Or as normal as it could have been given Talon had decided I'd make the perfect incubator for his "perfect" child.

But if I *had* walked away, all of those people in the club would have died, rather than just some of them. And the knowledge that I could have stopped it and didn't would have been even harder to live with than all the crap I was currently going through.

"If you were my watcher initially, why then was Talon placed on me rather than you?"

"Simple. After months of doing nothing but watching you every night, I wanted you fiercely. And that's the very reason he placed Talon on you."

And I'd fallen for Talon's bait—hook, line, and sinker. But then, his bait had certainly been impressive. "Your boss sounds a petty man."

"He is because he was taught to be." He caught my foot in his hands, his expression becoming slightly distracted as he began to knead my instep.

"But if you were ordered to stay away from me, how come you ended up being my mate anyway?"

His grin was sudden, and more than a little malicious. "Because it pissed Talon off."

"So the man behind all this knew you were also trying to get me pregnant?"

"Yes."

"Then why was I kidnapped and placed in that breeding center?"

"They saw an opportunity and grabbed it." He paused. "Over ninety percent of clones and ninety-five percent of their lab-bred crosses are sterile, and they have yet to ascertain why."

"I'm facing those same fertility issues," I reminded him. "No one is actually sure if I can get pregnant, either."

"No, no one is sure whether you can carry to term. Right now, you're totally capable of becoming pregnant."

I didn't bother refuting his assumptions. "So who was fucking me in that breeding center? The man with the blue eyes who thinks that I owe him?"

"Yes."

"Was he the only one?"

"No."

"Then who else?"

"One of the men behind the man."

And thanks to the accident, I couldn't remember a goddamn thing. "Why?"

He shrugged. "Because he was there to give instructions, and because he likes a hot bit of tail."

"I'm gathering he prefers his tail lifeless."

My voice was dry, and Misha smiled again. "Feisty is

not a preferred option—but it just might hook him where subservience hasn't."

I raised my eyebrows. "That a piece of advice?"

"A dangerous one, but yes."

"Also useless if you don't give me a name."

"All things come in time, Riley."

I was betting it was going to be a long time before I got the name, though. "So why was he there passing on instructions rather than the big man himself?"

"Because it is safer."

But safe from what? Certainly not us, because we had no idea who he was. Not yet, anyway. I studied him for a moment, then said, "If your boss is so dangerous, why are you here now?"

He raised an eyebrow. "If I answer honestly, I want another two hours with you."

Like I had a choice? Like I'd even know if he *was* being honest? I shrugged. "Whatever."

"The reason is twofold. First, I've long been at odds with my lab-mates and our so-called leader. Their vision has never been mine."

Meaning the leader of this little crew wasn't a lab-mate? Then who—or what—was he? "And their vision is?"

"As I said before, originally it was a quest for perfection. The desire to create the perfect humanoid, one possessing the most desirable characteristics from all branches of humanity."

"I'm guessing that changed when your master of creation died in the fire."

He nodded. "Now it's more a quest for domination and power."

It was on my lips to ask for his name, but he wouldn't

answer a direct question. "Did a brother from a previous batch of clones take over?"

"No. We were the first batch to have survivors into adulthood."

"Then who?"

He raised an eyebrow, a smile touching his thin lips. "His son."

I frowned. "One of your later clone-mates?"

"No. His naturally born son."

That wasn't in any of the records *I'd* read. And obviously not in the records Jack had read—unless, of course, he did know about the son, and just hadn't told me. Given Jack played his cards seriously close to his chest and I was only a liaison, not an actual guardian, that was all too possible.

"There's no record of said son," I stated.

"No. He was born to one of the women he was using to take eggs from. Our lab father apparently thought it better not to register the birth."

Yet he'd registered his clones, even if he'd lied about what they actually were.

"That would have made getting credit and insurance cards a bitch," I stated dryly.

Amusement briefly warmed the cold depths of his eyes. "Not when you have the ability to assume other people's identities."

I blinked, then said slowly, "Our man is from the Helki pack?" And if Misha was speaking the truth, he was starting to give us some real information.

He nodded. "He's a mix of Helki and human."

"Meaning, the birth mother was Helki?"

He nodded again.

"And what does he actually do for a living?"

Misha merely smiled. I changed tack. "Is he in the military?"

"No."

"Is he a scientist, or in control of a research company like yourself or Talon?"

"No."

"He's a businessman?"

"He calls himself that, amongst other things."

"High profile?"

"Sort of."

"In the news a lot?"

"No."

That made me frown. How could you be a high-profile businessman without being in the news a lot? That didn't make any sense.

"How about his mom? Is she still alive?"

His quick smile was almost proud. "Very good. And yes."

"And he's still on speaking terms with his mom?"

He hesitated. "You could say they have a close work-ing partnership, but it is one not many are aware of."

Very cryptic indeed. But obviously, we had to start with the mom, and the Helki pack. "Can you tell me her name?"

He considered the question for a moment. "What was the name of your mate immediately before myself and Talon?"

"I wouldn't have a friggin' clue."

He grinned. "Then get a clue, and use the feminine form."

"Shit."

"No, I don't believe that was it."

I gave him a deadpan look. "What about a surname?"

"I can't give the whole package on a plate. We both know that once I do, you're out of here." His fingers began to play up and down my leg. "And I intend to drag out my time with you as long as humanly possibly."

He'd certainly dragged out his time tonight. "You haven't yet actually answered my question."

"What question would that be?"

He reached out to touch me, but I caught his hand in mine, squeezing it a little harder than necessary to remind him I wasn't just a wolf. That I was, indeed, more than he could really handle if I chose to get nasty. "Why are you here?"

"Because everything is a game, and I tire of it. I want a normal life, for what remains of my life."

The edge of wistfulness in his voice had me believing him. But then, Misha was a very good actor. He'd certainly managed to fool me into believing he was a kind and gentle soul for the past year. And fact was, he wasn't. He was doing this for his own reasons—reasons he'd yet to fully explain.

He reached forward and caught my wrist, then tugged me off the beanbag and between his legs. "Enough for the night. I want the rest of my payment."

"Not until you give me somewhere to start, Misha."

He considered me for a moment. "There were two labs. The sister runs the second one."

"I thought you said he was an only child."

"No, I said the father had one natural child. I didn't say the mother only had the one."

"So the half-sister is a Helki?"

He nodded. "And runs the second lab."

"Which is Libraska?"

"Yes. And now that you have your starting point, I've said enough for one night. I want the rest of my payment."

He got it, and then I got the hell out of there. I blew out a breath as I left the club, and let my gaze travel up and down the street. Even though dawn had barely begun to streak the sky with wisps of rose, Lygon Street was alive with people and sound, the air rich with the aromas of wolf and humans, as well as the multiple, mouth-watering scents of meats and freshly baked breads. This end of the street had become a werewolf meeting zone, thanks to the close proximity of the two clubs, and many restaurants now opened their doors to cater for the all-night trade.

My stomach rumbled a reminder that it hadn't eaten in a while. I gazed longingly at the Italian restaurant across the road, but knew the Directorate personnel who were watching the Rocker had probably already reported my appearance out on the street. Annoying Jack was never a good idea, and if I didn't report in immediately, he'd be *really* annoyed. Food would have to wait until I made my report.

Ignoring the ongoing rumbling, I rummaged through my bag until I'd found the cell phone Jack had given me earlier. The phone on the other end rang all of three times before it was answered.

"Be there in five," a warm, rich voice said.

I blinked in surprise. "Kade? What the hell are you doing answering this phone?"

"Jack and Rhoan are still talking to Ross James. I was told to stand by for you."

"And Quinn?"

"Hasn't yet made an appearance. See you soon."

I grunted and hung up. Crossing my arms, I leaned against the Perspex wall of a nearby public phone booth, and watched the burgeoning line of traffic crawl along Lygon Street, some heading for the city, some heading to the suburbs and the many industrial estates scattered about the sprawling edges of Melbourne. Though it was barely six now, the crawling snakes of traffic would be at a virtual standstill within half an hour. Which is why I tended to catch public transport to work even when I did own a car—at least I could sleep in an extra hour and a half by doing so.

A yellow cab pulled to a halt beside the curb. I looked inside, saw that it was Kade, and climbed into the back.

"You look tired," he said, pulling into the traffic with the brutal efficiency of a regular cabdriver.

"That's because I am." I hesitated, sniffing the air, my taste buds suddenly watering at a tantalizingly familiar scent. "Is that coffee I smell?"

His gaze met mine in the mirror, a warm smile touching his lips. "I thought you might need it after working all night."

He reached across to the seat next to him, then handed back not only a jumbo cup of coffee, but a burger as well. If he hadn't been driving, I might have leaned forward and hugged him. Not only because he knew exactly what I needed right at that moment, but because he didn't give me any attitude about what I'd been doing.

He simply accepted. Or didn't care. Either way, it was nice.

I flipped open the lid of the coffee container. The thick, hazelnutty aroma curled to my nostrils, and I breathed deep, then smiled. Maybe I should just give men up and stick to coffee. It gave me pleasure without all the hassles.

"Thank you," I said to Kade, and took a sip.

His smile flashed via the mirror. "You know there's an ulterior motive."

"And here I was thinking you did it out of the goodness of your heart."

"Oh, that too."

I grinned. "It'll take more than coffee to get me into the sack right now."

"How about a spa filled with aromatherapy oils?"

"Depends what sort of aromatherapy oils we're talking about."

"Ah. There's a difference?"

"Some are definitely worth more bed time than others."

"What about a mix of lavender and ylang-ylang?"

"Nice. I think they'd earn you a couple of hours, at least."

"Done deal."

Kade did a sharp left, and coffee slopped threateningly around the rim of the cup. "Warn me next time," I chided. "Spilling my coffee will land you right out of my bed again." I hesitated, looking around. Unless this was a shortcut I wasn't aware of, we were now headed away from the Genoveve labs where Jack had set up shop. "Where are we going?"

"To get that bath."

I raised my eyebrows. "Doesn't Jack want us to report back ASAP?"

"Jack is busy," he replied, his gaze front and center as he wove the cab in and out of traffic and parked cars like a man on a mission. "And there's one rule in this game you should never forget."

"And what game and rule are we talking about?"

"This game. The investigative business." His gaze met mine briefly. "Never run yourself into the ground for them. They'll take and take until you have no more to give, then they'll cast you aside to find fresher meat."

"I'm not an investigator, and I'm not a guardian."

"Maybe not officially." His expression was grim as he swerved to avoid a parking car. "And that makes it worse. Think about it—ten days ago you were in a coma, and so badly smashed up no one in that center thought you were going to come out of it. Since then, you've been in the middle of investigations, have been attacked several times, and have taken little in the way of time out."

"We can't afford time-outs. Not if we want to catch these people off guard."

"Is catching these people off guard more important than your health? You look tired, and you've lost weight, even in the brief few days I've known you."

"Having someone attempting to kill you all the time does tend to halt the appetite, you know. And constant sex doesn't help, either."

"And using sex as a means of questioning suspects is not only good exercise, but an extremely stressful situation. I *know*." He met my gaze again. "Ring Rhoan. Tell

him what you learned. Let him uncover the truth from
the lies while you rest."

"Has he got a hand in this?"

"I told him what I was going to do, and where I intended to take you. I'm not a fool, and have no wish to in-
cur your pack-mate's wrath."

Wise man. "So where are you intending to take me?"

"To a mare's place in Toorak."

I frowned. "I thought you said your mares had scattered?"

"I did. And they did. But Sable went overseas before I
went undercover, and she's not due back for another two
months."

The name, and the fact that he seemed sure he'd find
the exact scents I wanted, had me staring at him in disbelief. "We're not talking Sable Kandell, are we?" The
woman was the latest TV phenomenon, with her show
rating through the roof and all five of her books still
amongst the best sellers.

"That would be my girl."

His voice held a hint of pride, and I blinked. "How
did a military man like you get hooked up with a stunner
like that?"

"Simple. We grew up together. She was mine from
the word go."

Obviously, there was a whole lot about the horse-
shifter culture that I didn't know. "So why let her go
overseas? I thought all you stallions were too proprietary
to allow something like that."

He ignored the light changing from amber to red,
swung right into Hoddle Street, then said, "Oh, have no

fear, she's branded as mine. No other stallion would dare touch her."

Stallions branded their mates? Thank God I wasn't a mare—and that wolves didn't have such barbaric practices. "Considering she's overseas, how would you know?"

"I'd know." His voice was flat, and certainly didn't invite further questions. Maybe it was secret stallion stuff. "Call Rhoan," he added, and handed me a phone.

So I called Rhoan, and told him everything Misha and Kellen had told me. Kade pulled into a beautiful old English mansion right in the middle of what was quaintly termed "millionaires' row." Meaning, the folk in this street were considered the poorer cousins of the Toorak crowd. Of course, most of the *really* rich cousins had moved on to leafy Brighton.

Kade led me inside, poured me a glass of wine to drink while he readied the spa, dropped in the scents I'd asked for, then helped me strip and climb in. As the *pièce de résistance*, he leisurely washed my hair as the warm water bubbled around my limbs, easing tensions I hadn't realized existed even as the flowery scents touched the air, soothing and relaxing.

Once he'd helped me dry off, he sat me down and combed my hair, and, though at that point I was ready and willing to dance with him, he led me to bed, tucked me in, and walked away.

It occurred to me then that no other man in my life—besides my brother—had ever treated me so sensually, so lovingly, so damn wonderfully, just because he knew I needed it. Which was a rather sad statement about my life and my relationships to date. Even Quinn, for all his fine words about needing to be in my life, had yet to show the sort of caring Kade had just shown.

Really, the only man in my life showing any *real* potential as a permanent mate was Kellen, and I barely even knew him.

Maybe I should just cut my losses and play with Kade. I might never find my soul mate, but at least I'd be guaranteed a little tender loving care every now and again.

I was beginning to wonder if Quinn even knew what that was.

*I*t was near five by the time we arrived at Genoveve, and considering we should have been there in the morning rather than late in the afternoon, Jack was in a surprisingly good mood. I wish the same could be said for Quinn. He was standing near the windows, looking out over the old arena, his hands clasped behind his back and tension riding his shoulders. His air of disapproval and anger hit so hard it was like a physical blow. I staggered, gasping to breathe as the air around me seemed to bubble and boil in fury.

Kade grabbed my arm, holding me upright. "Jesus, what's happening?"

"Riley?" Rhoan said, almost at the same time.

I ignored them both, my gaze boring into Quinn's stiff back as I gasped, "Quinn, stop it."

He glanced at me sharply, then the sense of his anger snapped into nothingness, and suddenly I could breathe again.

I put a hand up, stopping Rhoan as he hurried toward me. "It's okay. I'm okay." I squeezed Kade's hand, and he released me, yet kept near, as if afraid I was going to topple again.

Rhoan frowned as his gaze drifted between me and Quinn. "What happened?"

"I can sense what Quinn is feeling if he isn't shielding properly."

Rhoan's frown deepened, but it was Jack who said, "Empathy is not one of your talents."

"I don't think it's empathy, or I'd be sensing what everyone was feeling." I hesitated. "I think it has more to do with that link we created when we were about to raid Talon's labs. It seems to have gone deeper than we intended."

Jack didn't look convinced. "And it might just be the first sign that the ARC1-23 is starting to take effect. We'll have to get you back into the lab for more tests."

"Sorry, but I'm over being pricked, prodded, and poked right now." In *more* ways than one. "Let's just get this mess sorted out first."

He grunted, and looked back to his com-screen. "It seems Misha is finally giving us some worthwhile information."

I walked across to one of the comfy chairs and plonked down. Kade stayed where he was and leaned a shoulder against the wall. Quinn continued to do his silent and angry vampire act.

"In what way?" I asked Jack.

He leaned back in his chair, and practically beamed. In all the years I'd worked for him, I'd never seen him this happy, and I wasn't entirely sure whether to be amused or scared.

"We've been aware of the Helki pack's activities for

some time," he said. "They're black-market racketeers and sell everything from stolen car parts to government secrets. But because you wolves tend to be very tightly knit, we've been unable to get anyone in there to collect the proof we need."

"Without getting anyone in there, you're not going to be able to glean too much information about them."

"No, only what we're able to ascertain from keeping a continuous watch on them."

I raised an eyebrow. "That wouldn't happen to be where Gautier's been this last month, is it?"

Jack nodded. "It's better we keep him out of trouble while we decide what to do with him."

"But if he's working for these people, he's not likely to report back anything useful. He might even warn the Helki pack they're being watched."

"He might not give us real information, but I doubt he'd warn them. That would be showing his hand, and I don't think he's ready to do that yet."

I tucked my legs up underneath me. "Misha really didn't give us a name or anything else to start with. He just pointed us to the pack."

"Ah, but he did give a name." Rhoan's eyes twinkled mischievously—a sure sign he was taking a dig. "Don't tell me you can't remember Robert, the wolf you had just before Talon and Misha? Wasn't he the love of your life?"

Robert. I snorted even as I remembered him, and barely resisted the urge to throw something at my brother. But only because there wasn't anything within immediate reach. "For all of a few weeks. Until I realized the bastard was using me to get closer to you."

He grinned. "Actually, he had this fantasy about the three of—"

"Don't even go there."

"Bringing this back to business," Jack said, giving Rhoan an annoyed look. "There's a Roberta Whitby who is the current head of the Helki pack."

Rhoan and I shared a surprised glance. "A woman is the head of the pack?" he said.

"Yes. Why?"

"Because women are never head of the packs. It's always an alpha male."

"Then the Helki pack are obviously one of your more progressive packs."

"There is no such thing as a progressive pack in this matter," Rhoan refuted. "Alpha's lead, not women, not betas, not gammas. It's the rule of the wild, and it's the rule of the pack." He glanced at me. "There'll be a reason why she leads."

"There just might be," I said slowly. "Misha told me the Helki pack are true shifters—some can take on other animal forms, and some can take on other human forms. One of the men who assaulted me in that research cell is one of Misha's clone-mates—and he can apparently take on various human shapes. What if this Roberta was the cell donor? What if *he* can take on various human shapes because *she* could?"

Rhoan's frown deepened. "That still wouldn't explain why a woman leads the pack."

"But what if she's something similar to a hermaphrodite? What if she can take on female *and* male form?"

"That's not possible," Jack said.

"Isn't it? Hermaphrodites exist. If a shifter was born

with male and female bits, might it not be possible that he—or she—could take on both forms?"

"That's a bit of a leap."

"Maybe not." I hesitated, remembered my initial reaction on seeing Mrs. Hunt last night—a reaction I'd almost convinced myself to be the result of scrambled brain cells. But put those memories next to Misha's guarded words, and maybe the memories weren't that scrambled after all. "Misha said last night that Mrs. Hunt and the man who used me in the breeding center were very close indeed. What if that was his way of saying they were one and the same person?"

"It'd have to be a long shot, surely," Kade commented.

"Would it? They have the same eyes, and more importantly, they have the same scent."

"No two spoors smell exactly the same," Rhoan commented. "Even in a family unit, there are slight differences."

"Maybe." Jack didn't sound convinced, but added, "Though it would certainly explain why the various members of the pack have slipped through the traps we've set."

"It could also mean the man in overall charge of the labs can assume any shape," Rhoan commented grimly. "Which means he could be anyone, anywhere."

"It would also explain what happened last night," Quinn commented, his voice totally devoid of emotion.

Yet the heat of his anger whispered across my skin, fleetingly burning. Thankfully, this time it didn't seem to be aimed at me.

"So what happened last night after I left?" I asked curiously.

Quinn still didn't bother turning around. "Mrs. Hunt

went straight home after making her statement to the police. The chauffeur put the car away, then went upstairs to the small apartment above the garage. Twenty minutes later, the garage doors opened and the chauffeur was driving back out. Only if the heat signatures were anything to go by, the chauffeur was still in the flat, and the man driving the car was actually Mrs. Hunt."

"You followed the car?"

"To a small house in Gosford."

"He's still there?" And if so, why was Quinn here?

"Guardians now watch the place," Jack said, as if reading my thoughts. "I thought Quinn might be more useful back here."

Where Jack could keep a close eye on him, obviously. "Has Roberta got a daughter?"

He nodded. "Nasia. She was a research scientist at the Holgram Pharmaceutical Laboratories, but quit about seven years ago. According to tax department records, she hasn't had a job since then."

"Or simply hasn't paid tax."

He nodded again. "If she's in charge of the second lab, that's logical."

"So," Kade said heavily, "we have several people who are either full- or half-Helki, and all of them are probably able to take on any damn form they like. How in hell are we going to catch them?"

"We grab the man at Gosford first—"

"The minute you grab him, any useful information will be burned away," I butted in. "He'll be another Talon."

"If we grab him fast enough, we might be able to stop that from happening." Jack shrugged. "We cannot take the chance of him escaping."

"Better a fried mind than letting him go free to milk more specimens," Kade murmured.

With that, I had to agree. "What about this Roberta?"

"We snatch her as well."

"But won't that raise the alarm for the rest of them?"

"I'm hoping it does, and that in their scramble for cover, they'll make a mistake and reveal themselves fully."

"So how do you intend to snatch Roberta? I wouldn't recommend you sending people in there, because not even guardians could get a pack leader out unseen."

"Fortunately for us, she drives down to Melbourne every Monday night to meet with various friends." He paused, frowning lightly. "Of course, if the daughter is also able to take various shapes, maybe it has been her the mother has been meeting all along."

"Which would imply they might know they are being watched," Kade commented.

"Or it might be that they're taking no chances after Talon's capture," Quinn said.

"Then why wouldn't Roberta take another form?" Kade said.

"Easy," Rhoan said. "She's an alpha, and would think she's more than capable of defending herself. They're arrogant like that."

Maybe that was where Talon had got it from. Maybe even Misha had Helki genes, though if he was able to take on other shapes, I doubt it was something he'd ever admit to me.

"It doesn't matter," Jack said. "We snatch Roberta tonight, and we place a tail on whoever is at that restaurant to meet her."

I raised my eyebrows. "How will you know who is meeting her?"

Jack smiled. "Even the most cunning make simple mistakes. They book the same table every week because it's in a corner, and apparently presents a nice view of the St. Kilda pier and beach."

I glanced at the clock. "It's nearly five-thirty now—surely Roberta will already be on her way down?" Especially considering Bendigo was almost two hours away from Melbourne.

Jack nodded. "She usually reaches the domain tunnel about seven-fifteen. That's where we intend to hit her."

"In the tunnel? That'll make you popular with the rush-hour motorists."

"It's the last place she'll think we'll try."

"Hadn't we better get moving then?"

Jack gave me the look that said, "Don't try telling me how to do my job." "*We* aren't going anywhere, because *you* have a meeting with Misha tonight." I opened my mouth to argue, but he held up a hand. "You want answers, don't you? Misha is certainly giving them, and we can't afford to forsake that right now."

"We may just be helping Misha take over the whole shebang."

"I think you'll find Misha's reasons for this are a whole lot more personal," Quinn commented, looking over his shoulder and meeting my gaze. "It may be a conquest he desires, but that conquest has nothing to do with his clone brothers or his maker's son."

Meaning what he wanted most was me? I snorted softly. "Misha doesn't love me, Quinn. And in case you've missed what's been happening, he still has me in his bed."

He raised a dark eyebrow. "Who mentioned love? This isn't about love—it's about possession."

"Whether it is or isn't is beyond the point," Jack interrupted. "Fact is, you will go to him tonight and continue questioning him. Meantime, Kade, Rhoan, and myself will join the team at the domain tunnel."

"While I do what?" Quinn said remotely.

"The Sydney team should be here at eight with the Gosford man. I thought you might like to help with the interrogation."

The slow smile that touched his lips sent a chill up my spine. If the man who was Mrs. Hunt had any secrets left, Quinn would find them. And he had no intentions of being gentle. If Mrs. Hunt had any sort of reasoning capacity left at the end of it, I'd be very surprised indeed.

All he said was "Willingly."

Jack thrust to his feet. "Then we should go. Riley, I've arranged a car to take you into Lygon Street. We still have the place staked out, so you should be perfectly safe."

Should and would were two entirely different things. I had an odd suspicion that things were going too right for us, that the wheel was about to turn yet again. I rubbed my arms and ignored the premonition. It was only fear—or a simple reluctance to be with Misha again. Clairvoyance wasn't a talent I'd shown the slightest aptitude for—despite what Jack's test had said—and it certainly wasn't one I wanted to be developing.

"I'd prefer to drive myself." Especially given I had no intention of hanging around here with only Quinn and guardians for company. There were better things I could be doing—like checking out a certain restaurant.

Jack raised an eyebrow. "Given your record with cars, I do not think that advisable."

"Have I ever crashed a Directorate car?"

"No, but—"

"Then let me take one. We can't afford to presume these people have stopped watching me—or at least, stopped watching the Rocker. With Gautier on their payroll, they probably know the profile of every Directorate employee. They see any of them arrive at the Rocker with me, they'll suspect it's me, disguise or no."

Jack's green eyes narrowed slightly, like he knew I was up to something. Given we'd been working together a long time now, that was entirely possible. But my shields were strong enough to keep him out of my mind, so he couldn't check and be sure.

"All right," he said eventually. "But when the session with Misha is over, you come straight back here. No detours."

"Deal," I agreed, without qualms. After all, the detour I planned was before my date with Misha, not after.

Jack's frown deepened, but he rose and said, "Let's go," then walked out of the room.

Kade followed. Rhoan stopped by my chair and swooped to kiss my forehead. "Be careful."

"You too."

"I'm not walking into the enemy's boudoir." He squeezed my arm. "Just remember, keep aware even when you're having fun."

"Stop worrying, and just go do your job."

"It's a brother's task to worry about his little sister." He cast a glance Quinn's way, then murmured, "Remember, too, that some sweets, however delicious, can be bad for long-term peace of mind."

"I remember. Now mind your own business and get moving."

He grinned, dropped another kiss on my forehead, then added, "Liander left some wigs and colored lenses if you want to play around with your look. Just promise me you'll keep out of sight when you go into that restaurant."

I grinned. Rhoan didn't need to be psychic to know what I planned—he knew, simply because it was exactly what *he'd* do. "That I promise."

"Good." He kissed me a third time—three times for luck, as we always said—then pushed away from the chair and left.

Which left me with the moody Quinn. Joy, oh joy.

"We have a conversation to finish," he said, the moment we were alone.

I untucked my legs and walked across to the water dispenser. "I've said all I have to say."

"Then tell me why you fucked Kellen last night. Was it just to get back at me?"

I snorted softly as I filled the little plastic cup. "Quinn, I like you and all, but you seriously need to get over this jealousy thing. Especially when you have no right to it."

"So is that a yes?"

"It's a no. I fucked him because I wanted to, because he was hot, and because I wanted him to answer some questions afterward. Which he did." I took a sip of water and turned around, meeting his stormy gaze. "Kellen was well aware that I came to the event with you, mind. I believe he took great delight in the fact that he took me from you."

"And you intend to see him again?"

"Lots of times. And if you don't like that fact, walk away now. It's not worth the angst to either of us."

Quinn didn't react. "A vampire never walks away from what he considers his." His midnight gaze burned into mine, touching something deep inside, making it quiver, dance. But whether it was joy or fear, I couldn't entirely tell. "I cannot, and will not, walk away. Nor will I let you. And if that means having to put up with you fucking a hundred different wolves, then so be it. What lies between us is worth exploring, and you *will* hold to the bargain we made."

I raised my eyebrows. "That almost sounded like a threat."

"Take it any damn way you please."

"Threat then. So my next question has to be, or what?"

He was still giving me his vampire look, but underneath it, I had a sense of turmoil. Frustration. "You don't want to know."

"I wouldn't have asked if I didn't want to know."

He hesitated. "I have the power to force you to do certain things."

I stared at him, not sure I'd heard him right. Not wanting to believe I'd heard him right. "What?"

His gaze was uncompromising. "We shared blood. That gives me the power to enforce certain actions on you."

"Another thing you forgot to mention when the blood sharing happened." My voice was flat, calm, totally belying the anger that burned deep.

"You were mad with moon fever at the time. Do you

really think you would have refused my blood even if I'd taken the time to explain the consequences?"

"No, but you could have warned me afterward." Forewarned is forearmed. Though in this case, I very much suspected being forearmed wouldn't matter a damn.

"Have I yet tried to curtail any of your actions?"

I gave a harsh laugh. "No. Doesn't mean you won't in the future though."

"I won't."

"And would I even know if you did?" He didn't answer and I shook my head. "You know what you've done, don't you? With that one little threat, you've put yourself into an entirely different category in my eyes."

He frowned. "What do you mean?"

"I mean, you've just leapt into the basket that contains the men who are using me for their own ends."

"Dammit, Riley, you know—"

"What I know," I cut in harshly, "is that of the three men I'm currently dancing with, Kade is the *only* one who has shown me any sort of companionship and caring outside the realms of sex. Do you want to know what he did for me today? He took me to a mare's place, ran me a bath, washed my hair, then he tucked me into bed, and left me alone. He looked after me, pampered me, because he damn well knew I needed it. What have you done, except reluctantly accept the sex and blood you desperately needed? Oh, and make demands, or raid my mind?"

He raised an eyebrow. "So what is it you're telling me? That I need to pamper you, romance you, to win your heart?"

"It would certainly be a damn better place to start than

calling me a whore, or using threats." I blew out a breath. "Like the song says, 'Girls Just Want to Have Fun.'"

The somewhat disdainful look he gave me suggested he wasn't a fan of old-time pop music—or maybe he'd simply cruised through that era with earmuffs on, and had no idea what I was on about. I added, "Look, I offered the agreement, and I'll stick to it if you're going to get nasty about it. But just don't go expecting anything more serious than a good time. I won't play us one on one, Quinn. I can't afford to."

"All I'm expecting is the chance."

"Then you have it. But I'm warning you now—you try and force me into *anything* and that will be the end of us. I'll find a way around that order of yours, and I'll walk away. I will not be abused like that. I'm a wolf, not a whore."

"It is not abuse—"

"Then what else do you call forcing someone to do something against their will?"

"In this case, common sense."

"Force is force, regardless of the reason. Don't ever try it on me, Quinn. Not ever."

He didn't answer, and I just got the hell out of the room.

Chapter 11

$\mathcal{D}$usk had come and gone, and the night was cold. The wind blustered around me, its touch icy, as if it had come directly from the Antarctic. Shivering, I rubbed my arms, and wished I'd put on something warmer than a long-sleeved cotton top. At least I could be thankful I'd chosen jeans and sneakers rather than the skirt and sandals I'd originally intended. But what I wasn't thankful for was the premonition that had told me I'd need something tougher—that a skirt and sandals wasn't up to what I had to do tonight.

I didn't want another psychic talent—especially one that popped in whenever it pleased. But that same intuition said my choice in this mattered as little as my choice in other areas of my life. I was becoming something more than just a dhampire. What that something was, not even a blossoming new talent could tell. One thing was certain—I wasn't about to let Jack know. Not until I was totally sure this clairvoyance thing was a developing talent, and not some weird mutation of the fear that sat like a weight in my gut.

The restaurant came into sight across the other side of the road. I paused, gaze raking the old, Victorian-style building, searching for a glimpse of my quarry in the corner windows. Only one woman sat alone, and she was positioned at the far end of the building.

After looking around to ensure no one was near or watching, I wrapped myself in shadows and moved toward the foreshore. Streetlights cast pools of yellow across the empty pavement, and the headlights of passing cars ran across the nearby darkness, threatening to tear the shadows from my side. I stashed my clothes and shifted shape, released the veil of darkness, and in wolf form wove my way through the scrubby tea trees until I was directly opposite the window in which the lone woman sat.

She was nothing special—dark hair cut into a severe bob, a roman nose that was accentuated by a gold ring, and a large, almost manly chin. Her hands, clasped in front of her on the table, also looked more male than female. The man who'd been Mrs. Hunt hadn't been the image of female perfection, either. Was that a telltale sign of shifters who could take either male or female form?

I sat on my haunches, and wondered what the time was. It had been close to eight when I'd parked the car, and it had probably taken me five minutes or so to walk here. But if the woman at that table was worried by Roberta Whitby's lateness, it wasn't showing yet.

The wind shook the branches of the trees around me,

showering the ground and me with tiny gray-green leaves. I was about to shake them from my fur when I caught two sounds—the first, a twig snapping lightly. The second, the brush of nylon against sharp leaves.

Someone was sneaking through the trees, headed my way.

I flicked my ears forward, but otherwise didn't move. Given the darkness and the gnarled trunks that surrounded me, it was unlikely that even the red of my coat would be seen. Besides, whoever was sneaking up ahead was human—or at least, in human form—and most humans took no notice of a dog, especially if it wasn't moving or threatening. Even if it *was* a wolf up ahead, the wind was in my favor, carrying my scent toward the ocean rather than the stranger.

Oddly enough, it didn't offer me the stranger's scent, carrying no more than the night, the ocean, and the multiple layers that spoke of the nearby restaurants, shops, and exhaust fumes.

If he was so close that I could hear him, I should certainly have been able to smell him. Unless, of course, he had no scent.

Hackles rose at the thought. Everyone had a scent—unless it had been deliberately erased.

No more careless sounds rode the wind. The man up ahead—though why I was so sure it was a man I had no idea—had either stopped moving or disappeared. Why was he sneaking through these trees? Was he spying, surveying the area like me, or were his intentions altogether darker?

I wanted to move, but with all the crap on the ground, he'd hear me. But if I wanted to find out what was going on, what he was doing, then I might have to take the chance.

Sound whispered along the wind, cutting off the thought. Something scraped lightly against nylon again, and a second later, the unmistakable click of a safety coming off a gun.

The fear in my gut crystallized.

The woman waiting for Roberta Whitby was about to get shot. I leapt to all fours, but it was already far too late to do anything to save that woman.

A muffled report rode the wind. My gaze shot to the window. It shattered. The woman with the roman nose jerked, then slumped forward onto the table.

Dead.

And so was my chance at answers if I didn't move right away.

But as much as I wanted to charge in and attack, I knew such actions would earn me nothing more than a bullet. I had no idea who—or what—was ahead, but the mere fact he had no scent suggested that he was either a professional hit man or another of those creatures from the labs.

I looked ahead, judging the length of spring needed to clear all the clutter under the trees. Then I crouched and launched forward, clearing the undergrowth with inches to spare.

I'd barely landed when the sense of someone approaching had the hackles along the back of my neck rising. I looked over my shoulder. Only cars could be seen moving through the night—yet something *unseen* was there, crossing the road, approaching faster than the wind itself.

A vampire.

Jack had said he'd have people here, so it was more than likely a guardian.

And if that guardian saw me and reported my presence back to Jack, I'd be in deep shit. But I resisted the urge to throw my shields to full and disappear into shadow. That would only be asking for a deeper inspection. The approaching vampire had to believe I was nothing more than a wolfy-looking dog, and to achieve that, I had to let him skim surface thoughts.

So I blanked everything from my mind, lowered a shield, and thought of nothing more than the thrill of hunting the scent of cat, then stuck my nose to the ground and sniffed around. After a second or two, I actually did catch the spoor of a cat, and my wolf soul stirred excitedly. I trotted along, following the trail while keeping an eye in the shooter's general direction.

Heat touched my mind, a needle-sharp probe that got no further than surface thoughts. It snapped away quickly, moving on, searching the night. A second later, air ran past my nose, filled with the scent of pine, underlain with the richness of sage.

It was Jared, one of the newer recruits to guardian ranks.

He moved on, running for the end of the trees. Nose to the ground, I padded along after him.

Another muffled report bit across the wind. The patch of deeper darkness veered sharply, and the metallic smell of blood tainted the air. The shooter had to have infrared sights—or was a vampire himself—if he was able to see Jared. A third report came, followed by a grunt

that was abruptly, chillingly, cut off. The shadows con-
cealing Jared fell away and he slumped to the ground,
what was left of his thin features showing surprise.

A growl rumbled up my throat before I could stop it. I
halted, hackles raised, trying to act like an everyday dog
when every instinct in my wolf soul begged me to run, to
bring down the quarry, to tear his flesh and his life from
his body. My lips drew back into a snarl, my whole body
vibrating with the force of it.

The trees moved, and a man stepped out. He was as
black as the night itself, and almost as invisible as a vampire. Yet he wore no shadows, nor did he wear clothes.
He was little more than an outline, a figure who had a
basic shape but no distinct features.

Just like the man—the creature—who'd attacked me
in the hotel room in the Blue Mountains.

Misha had once suggested that a man who harnessed
the secrets of genetics to make the perfect killing machine could rule the world—or make a fortune creating
purpose-built assassins for those who wanted the power
to take out the opposition swiftly and easily. Maybe that
nightmare wasn't as far off as we'd all thought.

I didn't move, watching the specter of a man, watching the gun he held. He moved to Jared's body, kneeling
carefully and feeling for a pulse. Why he bothered I had
no idea—not even a vampire could survive having half
his brain shot away. As he checked, he kept an eye on me,
but not in a suspicious sort of way. His behavior was
more that of a man who simply didn't trust—or didn't
like—dogs. And the rifle—one of the new runt rifles,
which had the power and the range of a rifle but were

only a little bigger than a handgun—was pointed more at the ground than me.

I stuck my nose to the dirt again, sniffing around as I checked who else was in the area. In the restaurant, people were beginning to realize something was wrong. A waiter approaching the corner table stopped abruptly, and even from where I stood, I could see the dawning horror on his face.

A sharp, almost barked, laugh bit through the night, and a rumble of anger rose up my throat again. The shooter rose, his amusement evident in the brief flash of teeth—teeth that were gray rather than white. His gaze met mine, and, for an instant, death stood before me, deciding whether I was worth killing or not. Then the stranger blinked, and the moment was gone.

The relief I felt was almost frightening. As much as my wolf spirit might want to tear this man from limb to limb, the biggest foe I'd tackled with the intention of bring down was the occasional rabbit or fox in the "back to nature" sessions Rhoan and Liander liked to drag me along to. But killing a wild animal *as* an animal was far different from hunting—and killing—a humanoid. That was a milestone I never wanted to reach—and the major reason for my reluctance to join the guardian ranks.

Then I remembered Genoveve. I'd maimed there, more than once, and could so easily have killed. I knew it, even if I hadn't admitted it at the time.

The shooter took the small pack from his back, broke the runt rifle into several pieces, and shoved them inside. Then he slung the pack back over his shoulder and walked away. Just another man out for a Monday night stroll.

Only this man was a shadow most wouldn't see.

I padded along after him. The urge to do more than simply haunt his steps still vibrated through my muscles, but attacking him here, on a main street, simply wasn't an option. The cops had undoubtedly been called by the restaurant, and the last thing I needed was interference from them. This killer was mine to question.

He headed toward the crowded, street-café–rife environment that was Fitzroy Street, but thankfully didn't turn into it—probably because there was no place for shadows in that brightly lit place. He headed for the gardens instead, avoiding the streetlights and paralleling Beaconsfield Parade. I looked past him, studying the layout. Up ahead was a rotunda—the perfect place for an ambush. Better yet, there didn't seem to be anyone close, a fact backed up by the lack of human scents on the wind. But the wail of sirens could now be heard. I was running out of time to do this before the cops got here and started searching the area for evidence.

I shifted shape and wrapped the shadows around me, hiding my form and my nakedness. The stranger glanced over his shoulder and frowned. Maybe he was a sensitive, and able to feel the caress of magic. Or maybe he was simply ensuring that he wasn't being followed.

When he neared the rotunda, I ran at him. Though I made no sound, he somehow sensed my approach, because suddenly he was facing me with a knife in his hand. His growl would have made any wolf proud, and the blade cut through the night so fast it was little more than a blur. I slid to a halt and sucked in my stomach. The tip of the knife burned through flesh. Only one metal had that effect on wolves. The blade was made of silver.

I dropped and pivoted, sweeping with one foot, trying to knock him off his feet. He was every bit as fast, leaping over my leg then launching himself at me. He could see me, I realized then, even though I was wrapped in shadows. I rolled under his leap, and cast the cover from me, unable to see the point of wasting energy when it wasn't helping. I lashed out again, and this time he wasn't fast enough, the blow taking him high in the thigh. He grunted, but slashed with the knife. The blade nicked my knee. I swore softly, heard his chuckle of amusement. Obviously, his makers had failed to explain that laughing at a wolf in this type of situation was *never* a good idea. Anger rose in a red rage, and I threw myself at him.

The move caught him by surprise, and we went down in a tangle of arms and legs. He hit the ground first, cushioning my fall, his wheeze of breath whispering dead things and sour milk past my nose. I caught the wrist holding the knife with one hand, forcing the blade well away from my body as I tried to catch his other hand. His almost featureless face stared into mine, his eyes and mouth little more than thin slashes through which only gray was evident. There was no forehead bump, no cheek definition, and no nose. Only two holes that sat in the flat of his face.

His fist thumped into my side, and breath exploded from my body. But I ignored the haze of rising pain, bringing my knee up hard and fast. Like most men, he didn't appreciate a blow to the balls, and that brief moment of utter pain was long enough to hit him unhindered—and as hard as I could—across the jaw to knock him out.

I wrenched the knife from his nerveless fingers, and threw it as far as I could from the both of us. Then I rolled off him, and maneuvered him about until I got the pack off. Inside were the various rifle bits. I reassembled it, loaded the chamber, then sat on his chest, my knees pinning his arms as I held the gun at his throat. If he knew who I was, then he'd know I was with the Directorate and more than capable of firing a weapon. And if he didn't know, then the mere fact that I'd assembled the weapon should warn him I knew how to use it.

What he wouldn't know was the fact that I had no real desire to *actually* use it.

He stirred. I pressed my free hand against his chin, forcing it back, thrusting the point of the rifle harder into the soft flesh of his neck.

He groaned, and the thin, almost lizardlike coverings over his eyes flickered open.

"Don't move," I warned, jabbing with the weapon.

Death was back in his gray gaze. "I can't tell you anything."

I raised an eyebrow. "And I'm so believing that."

"I want a lawyer."

"Do I look like a cop to you? Do I actually look like someone who really cares what you do or don't want?"

He didn't answer. Just glared.

"Why did you kill that woman in the restaurant?"

No response.

"Who paid you to kill the woman in the restaurant?"

Again with the silence. The wail of sirens had stopped,

and though I was upwind of the restaurant, I could still hear the babble of voices, the rush of confusion. I didn't have all that much time to question this man.

I moved the rifle barrel down, and dug it into his Adam's apple. His grunt came out gargled.

"Tell me, or we do it the hard way."

"I know nothing."

Spittle sprayed my face as he spoke. I didn't have a free hand to wipe it away, and the small droplets stung. They also stunk ... or was it him? For a man who had no odor, there sure was a God-awful stink coming from his body. And I doubted he'd shit himself. He was a professional, for heaven's sake, and despite what my brother said about my appearance in the mornings, I wasn't *that* scary at other times.

"Do your worst," he said.

I thrust the rifle point hard enough to break skin and draw blood. "You think I won't?"

"I think that soon it won't matter."

The amusement underlying his words sent chills down my spine. He was up to something, I was sure of it. But what?

Frowning, unease growing, I lowered a shield and psychically reached out. His mind was surprisingly unguarded, but maybe whoever had sent him here hadn't expected he'd be caught. I thrust deeper, capturing his thoughts, freezing both them *and* him.

He was telling the truth in one respect—he didn't know who'd sent him to kill the woman. He'd received his orders via phone, like he always did, the voice on the other end the same as it always was—deep and lacking inflections, as if the person behind it was somehow less than human, more a machine. The orders were simple. Kill the two women at table sixteen.

So why hadn't he waited for Roberta to arrive before he'd taken a shot?

The smell was growing stronger, becoming one more of boiling decay than shit. I wrinkled my nose, trying to ignore it, trying to disregard the fear itching at my skin.

The answers I had weren't enough, so I thrust further into his memory. Saw a large house surrounded by lush gardens. Here there were more creatures like him—black ghosts, waiting for orders to kill. And locked behind stout cages, there were others as well. Blue things with rainbow wings. Men and women who had the faces of gryphons and the claws of demons. Mermaids and mermen and God knows what else.

There wasn't an army of them—not even a unit—but there were more than enough to suggest that in a few years there could be.

The labs behind these creatures had obviously found the secret behind successful crossbreeding of nonhuman races. And it didn't matter if their success rate was high or low. They were in the process of creating an army of abominations, beings nature had no intention of bringing into existence, and they were being developed for one reason only—to kill.

I tried to delve further, get more information, but the air was so thick and rich with the reek of rot that I was gagging, and couldn't concentrate.

I withdrew my thoughts, and met his gaze. Death roamed in his eyes, and it approached fast. It was then I realized his face looked gaunter, as if in the last few minutes he'd lost a huge amount of weight. The press of his skin against my shins and butt felt like the touch of fire.

Then it clicked, and the look of death in his eyes made sense.

Misha had once asked me to imagine the super soldier that could be built if the secrets of vampires, wolves, and other nonhumans could be unlocked. There'd be little you could do to stop such a force, he'd said. What he'd forgotten to mention was the added improvements—that if they did get caught, they could kill themselves, and therefore stop any efforts of getting information.

This man was growing hotter because he was about to spontaneously combust. Only there wasn't anything spontaneous about it.

I rolled away from him, the gun held at the ready should he try and move. He didn't. Couldn't.

His gray eyes were wide, and the death I'd seen earlier was all-consuming. Only this time it was his death I saw, not mine, and the realization of it had wiped away the faint amusement so evident only moments before. His thin lips were open, as if he were screaming, but no sound came out, only a gush of bloody liquid. Water was beginning to pool under his entire body and steam rose from both legs. He was melting, disintegrating, from the inside out. What a God-awful way to die.

I couldn't sit here and watch it. Couldn't sit here and just let it happen with such agonizing slowness. This wasn't death. This was torture, and no one—not even a lab-developed freak—deserved this sort of ending.

I touched his arm, flinching a little at the heat. His

flesh rolled under my touch, as if it were molten fluid barely contained by skin. "Do you wish a quick ending?"

His gaze found mine. "It shouldn't be like this." His words came out hoarse, interspersed with shudders of pain. "They said it wouldn't be like this."

So they'd lied to their creations. No surprise there, really. The people behind all this had shown little in the way of morals so far, and lying was undoubtedly the least of their sins.

And Misha was one of them. I couldn't afford to forget that. Not ever.

The shadow creature's body was beginning to close in on itself, collapsing like a tent in extreme slow motion. Steam was rising from his torso now, and the stench of stewing flesh was thick enough to carve.

"Do you wish a quick death?" I repeated, swallowing bile and barely resisting the urge to run from this man and his death.

"Yes." It came out little more than a hiss of pain.

"Then tell me why you killed that woman." It was a horrid thing to do, but I needed at least *one* answer.

His gaze flayed me with his pain, and I briefly closed my eyes against it.

"Directorate too close," he gasped. "Chopping off limbs ... to save head."

I didn't bother asking him to name the head. He was only a weapon, and a dispensable one at that. Instead, I rose and stepped away from his melting, steaming body. His gaze met mine, the gray depths pleading. I answered that plea and pulled the trigger.

His brains splattered, ending sensation. Yet still his body continued to disintegrate, until there was nothing left but scorched grass, damp earth, and the memories that would haunt my nights for months to come.

I grabbed the backpack, wrapped the shadows around me, and walked away before I lost total control over my stomach.

But perhaps the thing that revolted me most was not the stranger's death, but the ease with which I'd pulled the trigger. It was in me to kill—I'd proven that at Genoveve two months ago. Not that I'd actually thought much about the ease with which I'd used that laser. Maybe because it was simply a matter of me or them. *This* situation was a whole lot different. Even though I'd killed in mercy, I'd still pulled that trigger without qualms, and without hesitation. And more than that, I'd watched it.

The instinct to kill *was* a base part of every wolf, but one long controlled by the rules of civilization. With Rhoan and I, those controls seemed to have slipped. Rhoan had acknowledged it long ago, and channeled his desires into guardian duties. I'd ignored it.

But maybe not for much longer.

Or was I making mountains out of molehills again? Rhoan would probably say yes, I was, but I wasn't so sure. The sick sensation that I'd unleashed something two months ago that couldn't be retrieved would not go away.

I shivered, and thrust the thoughts away. Killing for the sake of mercy was completely different from killing because I was ordered to do so.

I had to believe that. I really did.

Blowing out a breath, I stopped, broke down the rifle, and shoved the bits in the pack. Throwing it back over my shoulder, I looked around, searching for the nearest phone. I'd left mine in the car, and while it would only take me a few minutes to run back there, I needed to call Jack fast and warn him that the man behind all this was killing—

I stopped abruptly.

He was killing the main limbs of his organization in order to protect himself.

Misha was one of those limbs.

If I didn't get to him before they did, our last chance of discovering the name of the leader was gone. As dead as that woman in the restaurant. As dead as the man who had shot her.

I got my clothes then ran on to the car with every ounce of speed I possessed. Unlocking the door and grabbing the phone seemed to take forever, as did dialing Misha's number and waiting for a response. All I got was a recorded message.

Fuck, fuck, fuck.

I slammed the door shut, started the car, and threw the gears into drive. After planting my foot on the accelerator and taking off with a squeal of tires that undoubtedly had the nearby cops scrambling to note my plate number, I thumbed Rhoan's number into the phone, and hit the call button. His phone was engaged. I swore softly, and sent him a text message instead. Hopefully, he'd look at it before it was too late. Jack's number got the same response. I sent him a message, telling him what I was doing and why, then threw the phone onto the passenger seat and concentrated on driving.

It took me twenty minutes to get to Lygon Street, and to say I broke the land-speed record would be something of an understatement. I stopped in a loading zone, grabbed the backpack and my phone, then ran toward the Rocker.

The security guard glanced my way as I neared, one bushy brow raised in query. "You seem to be in an awful hurry."

I slid to a halt. "I need to find Misha Rollins. Is he inside, by any chance?"

"I've only just come on shift, so I can't—"

"Thanks," I cut in, then pushed past. The main bar wasn't full, though quite a few people were waiting for drinks. Misha wasn't one of them. Swearing softly, I pressed his number into the phone again as I made my way toward the back stairs.

Misha answered as I reached the top. "Riley," he said, voice filled with cold amusement rather than passion. He wasn't here, then. Or at least, not in the process of mating. "This *is* a pleasant surprise."

"Where are you?" I stopped on the top of the stairs and scanned the shadow-filled room. There were a good twenty wolves up here, but Misha wasn't amongst them.

"My, you sound awfully anxious—"

"Cut the crap, Misha. Your life is in danger. Where the hell are you?"

"At work." His voice was flat. "Why do you think my life is in danger?"

"What does Nasia Whitby look like?" I countered. "And is she one of the Helkis who can take male and female shape?"

"You *have* been busy."

I headed back down the stairs. "Just answer the goddamn question."

"She's tall, dark-haired." He paused. "I guess you can say she's very masculine to look at."

"Roman nose? Gold nose ring?"

"Yes. Why?"

Now out on the street, I glanced left and right then ran across the road to my car. "Because Nasia Whitby has just been assassinated in a St. Kilda restaurant."

There was a long silence, then he said, very softly, "Fuck."

"Precisely. I caught the killer—he was a black thing with suckered fingers."

"Spirit lizards, he calls them. The creature would have killed himself."

"He was disintegrating, but I offered him a quick death in exchange for the reason Nasia was killed. Your master is apparently chopping off the limbs to save the head."

"Then he knows the Directorate is closing in."

"But why kill everyone?"

"You don't yet know the location of the other lab. The only people who do know are myself, Nasia, and Rupert."

"Rupert being the man who played Mrs. Hunt?" The man Quinn was currently questioning? "And the man I'd known briefly as Benito Verdi?"

"Yes."

I glanced in the side mirror, then drove out of the parking space and did a quick U-turn in front of the oncoming traffic. Ignoring the ensuing blast of horns, I planted my foot on the accelerator and headed for the city.

"How come you're saying his name now, and not before?"

"My office is psi-shielded, and as an extra precaution, I'm also wearing a psi-shield. He can't get to me here."

"He can still shoot you. Keep away from the fucking windows."

"Riley—you care."

"Of course I care—you're my only source of information."

He chuckled softly. "You're on your way here?"

"Yes."

"I shall tell security to let you in."

"You'd better tell them to be extra vigilant. He's coming after you, Misha."

"I'm safe in this fortress."

"I'm sure there's many a dead man who thought the same."

"They probably didn't have the security layout I have."

But the man in charge probably knew the layout—after all, he apparently had free access to Misha's mind.

"I'll be there in five."

I hung up, then sent Jack another message, asking him to get people to Misha's office building as soon as he could, then concentrated on not crashing the car as I wove in and out of traffic. Misha's office building was at the Paris end of Collins Street. It was one of those gorgeous old buildings that was almost cathedrallike in design, the windows and doors soaring, archlike structures that allowed plenty of light but offered absolutely no protection when it came to bullets. At least modern buildings used plasti-glass, which, while designed primarily to withstand the onslaught of severe storms and flying debris, could also take the force of two gunshots before it shattered. Two shots gave targets time to run or hide.

I parked in a bus zone, grabbed the backpack, then jumped out of the car and ran across the road.

Two stern-faced security men were standing, arms crossed, at the door. "Riley Jenson?" one asked.

When I nodded, he held some sort of portable unit up. "Speak into this."

"We're wasting fucking time, Misha."

The guard didn't crack a smile, just looked at the monitor intently. When it beeped, he nodded at the other guard and the door opened. I wondered if these two men were part of Misha's vaunted security system. If they were, then he wasn't staying in this castle. I could have taken either of them out right at that moment, and had easy access to the building.

One guard followed me inside, and keyed an elevator. When the doors opened, he leaned around the corner and pressed the sixth-floor button, then slid a keycard through the slot and gave me a smile. "This will take you straight to his floor. Mr. Rollins's office is the last one on your left."

I nodded my thanks and stepped inside. Once the doors closed, I took off the pack, reassembled the rifle, then put it back. Better safe than sorry.

The elevator slid to a stop and the doors opened. I stepped out. The corridor was long, and rife with shadows. The light from the elevator splayed across the gloom, flaring slightly, as if the shadows were a thick fog the light could not penetrate.

Down the far end of the hall stood a steel door. No light crept under the edges of that door. Indeed, there almost seemed to be no seam. And the shadows seemed more intense down there.

Unease slithered through me. I reached back and dragged the rifle from the backpack. Maybe it was nerves, maybe it wasn't, but I had the sudden feeling I wasn't alone in this corridor.

Yet I couldn't see anything. Only shadows and my silhouette.

The elevator doors began to close, and as that bright patch of light dwindled, my unease increased. Then the light was gone, and I was left to the darkness and whatever it was hiding. Holding the gun toward the floor but ready, I walked toward Misha's office.

The shadows stirred around me. Wisps of night touched my skin, slivers of silky smoke that made my flesh crawl. If ghosts could caress the living, this was probably what it would feel like. But warmer, deadlier. Whatever hid in the shadows wasn't dead in the sense that ghosts were dead, because there was warmth in its touch. Warmth, and a vague sense of threat.

I had a suspicion that vague sense of threat would sharpen, and become deadly, if I so much as flinched the wrong way right now.

"Put the gun away, Riley."

Misha's voice seemed to come from the walls. I looked around, but couldn't see anything resembling a speaker.

"Not until you tell whatever is in this corridor to back off."

"You can see them?" Surprise was evident in his voice.

"No. But I can feel them."

"Interesting."

"I'm not putting the gun away until you tell them to move away." I stopped at the door and waited.

He chuckled. "Tiimu, retreat."

The shadows dispersed, and suddenly the corridor was less oppressive, and much brighter. I held up my end of the deal, and shoved the rifle back in the pack. The steel door slid open.

Misha's office was smaller than I'd expected—rather than being the size of a football field, like most executive offices tended to be these days, it was more like a basketball court. Still big, but at least defendable.

His gaze skimmed my body, lingering a little on the blood evident on my shirt and the leg of my jeans. When his gaze rose to meet mine again, there was a gleam of respect—or maybe even wariness—in his eyes that I hadn't seen before. "You fought the spirit lizard?"

"Fought him and beat him." It couldn't hurt to keep reminding him I was more than just a wolf. Maybe he'd treat me as something more than a broodmare he needed to possess—though somehow, I doubted it. I walked across the room and stared out the window. I couldn't see anything suspicious, but then, with the long-range rifles they had out these days, the killer could be half a mile or more away.

Of course, standing here so blatantly might be putting myself in danger—but only if the killer knew it was actually me hiding under the brown hair and green contacts.

I moved to the pillar to the left of the arched window,

then crossed my arms and leaned back against it. "Why are you surprised?"

He leaned back in his chair, his expression thoughtful. "Because spirit lizards are the crème de la crème of the lab creations. They are supreme fighters and extremely strong."

"Then the one I fought came from a dodgy mix, because I'm no trained fighter and I brought him down. What are those things in the corridor?"

Amusement touched his thin lips. "They're my security system."

"I'm certainly glad it's not those two men down at the front door. They wouldn't have a hope of keeping a determined gnat from entering."

"And that is precisely what you are supposed to think." He looked at me for a moment, his expression still that odd mix of amusement and wariness. "The creatures in the corridor are not lab-created, if that is what you're thinking. They are a species known as Fravardin, which means guardian spirits in Persian. I met them a while ago when I was touring the Middle East."

I wondered exactly what he'd been touring the Middle East for. In the time I'd known Misha, he'd shown very little inclination to go beyond Australian shores. If he'd been to the Middle East, it was because he'd been ordered to go. "And were these creatures"—I waved a hand to the door—"what you'd been sent to find?"

He gave a smile. "No."

Meaning, obviously, that what he'd been sent to find was something I didn't need to know. Which was fine—

all I really needed was the name of the man behind all this madness.

"Were these things here when Jack and Rhoan raided your office a few months ago?"

"Yes."

"So you'd expected them to investigate, and had allowed them entry?" Meaning he might also have removed vital evidence before the raid.

"It's all part of a bigger plan, Riley."

I raised my eyebrow. "And what might that master plan be? To step into your so-called brother's much hated shoes? To take over control of the freak empire?"

He snorted softly. "And here I was thinking you knew me better than that."

"I know you well enough to know that you can be ruthless when you choose to be."

His mouth twitched in amusement. "I don't want control of anyone's empire but my own. I told you the truth when I said all I want is survival—and I think Nasia's demise proves I was right to worry."

If he was at all worried, he certainly had a strange way of showing it. At the very least, he wouldn't be sitting so casually behind his desk, in full view of the windows. "Why would he kill his own sister?"

"Blood is *not* thicker than water when you are raised like we were. Hell, he'd kill his mother, too, if it meant his own survival."

And so would Misha—only right now he was using the Directorate to do his dirty work. "That being the case, why state that you can keep me safe when it's obvious you can't keep yourself safe?"

He rose and walked toward me, a strange gleam in his

silvery eyes. It was the look of a predator on the hunt, a predator who had his prey in sight and no intentions of letting it escape. When *that* look had been evident in Kellen's eyes, my pulse had skipped with excitement, but in Misha's eyes it only succeeded in raising hackles. Quinn was right—Misha didn't want love, he wanted possession. Wanted to own me, rather than just love me.

But then, given what he was, how he was raised, maybe possession was the only thing he knew and understood. Could someone who has never known love, tenderness, or caring ever really return it in kind?

Watching Misha stalk toward me with that look in his eyes, I doubted it very much.

He braced his hands against the wall on either side of me, and leaned close. I pressed a hand against his chest, not forcefully, but enough to stop him kissing me. Even so, his breath washed warmth across my lips, and his aura wrapped me in heat and desire.

"He knows about the Fravardin. He knows that they are loyal to me, and only to me." He pressed his weight against my hand, testing my strength, my will. "I have warned him that if anything else happens to you, they will hunt him down and they will kill him."

Surprise rippled through me. My gaze searched his, but I could see no lie in his eyes, nor sense it in his words. "Why would you do that? Why not use them to protect yourself in the same manner?"

He moved a hand, and brushed his fingers down my cheek. His touch was icy compared to the fiery lust flaying my skin. "What's the point? I will be dead in five or six years anyway."

"But if you don't use them to protect yourself, you might be dead in five or six days." Or five or six hours.

"While I am alive, the Fravardin will do their utmost to protect me. When I am dead, they will keep watch over you."

The thought of having a couple of ghostly creatures hanging about trying to protect me was enough to make me shiver. "Why would they bother when you're dead and the payments stop?"

His aura went on high, bathing me with a fervor as strong as the sun itself. Sweat began to trickle down my spine. Even though I had my shields up high, it was hard to ignore the assault on my senses.

"Because it is written in my will that they will continue to get a retainer as well as the estate in Gisborne, where the tribe currently lives, provided certain conditions are met."

Spirits being paid? How weird was that? "Can they be killed?"

"All things living can be killed. It's just harder to kill what cannot be seen."

"If your boss knows about them, then he probably knows what can kill them."

"Undoubtedly. Problem is, unlike vampires, they don't show up on infrared, and you're the first person I know who has actually sensed them."

First person besides him, obviously. "That's because I'm special—and why crazy men want a piece of me." I thrust him away from me. The cool air eddied around my skin, as pleasurable as water on a hot day. "You need to tell me about your boss."

Annoyance flared in his eyes. "And give you an excuse to walk away? I think not."

"Then tell me about Roberta Whitby—she's the Helki alpha, isn't she?"

He nodded, and crossed his arms. "The pack has gotten fat off the pickings of crime."

"And Roberta has inserted her son into Government ranks?"

He smiled. "No. The true power of a country often lies not in the reins of officialdom, but rather, in the strength of the crime syndicates."

I raised an eyebrow. "Meaning?"

"Is it not often said that the Yakuza is the true power in Japan?"

"They're not a power here, though."

"No, but there are crime syndicates nonetheless, and some of them are extremely powerful, even to the extent of having 'relationships' with certain Government departments."

Was the Directorate one of those departments? Was that how Gautier had become a guardian? Given that Alan Brown, the recruitment officer, was being blackmailed, it didn't take a genius to guess that maybe he was the connection between the Directorate and the man behind the mutants. But how was that happening if Jack and Rhoan could find no sign of messages being passed?

"I'm little more than a glorified secretary," I said blandly. "I wouldn't know about such things."

"Then learn, because the man you seek is now in charge of one of them—and he plans to be the only one that matters."

I studied him for a moment, then said, "I gather he's replaced rather than overthrown?"

Misha nodded. "Far easier to step into successful shoes rather than work your way up the ranks."

"But how? If this man is as powerful as you say, he'd be too wary to let strangers near him."

His smile was cold. Amused. "But not wary enough when it comes to longtime lovers."

"Roberta?"

He nodded. "The Helki pack has long done his dirty work. When Roberta came back onto the scene after her years in Roscoe's labs, she used her aura to enrapture the man. They were lovers for three years before the replacement happened."

Long enough for Roberta to become a trusted lover. Long enough for her to learn his ways and secrets. "So these labs where the crossbreeding is happening—they're not the recent innovation you've led me to believe, but ones that the syndicate have had for a while."

He nodded again. "Talon and I were the only ones who actually set up our own laboratories—though in Talon's case, it was merely to continue our lab father's work."

Because he'd kept what remained of the research notes. "And not very successfully."

Amusement touched his eyes. "He'd be hurt to hear you say that."

"Like I care. How long have these other labs been in existence?"

"They've long been used for drug development. Gene experiments, with all its potential rewards, was the next logical step, and one they took some fifty years ago."

I rubbed my arms, trying to ward off a sudden chill.

Trying to ignore the premonition that sometime in the future I was going to see a whole lot more of those labs than I ever wanted. Only this time from the right side, not the wrong side.

"Meaning the man in charge is in his seventies?"

"No. Meaning the previous head of the syndicate began the work, and the current head continues it."

"So how old is he? The man your boss became, I mean."

"Early forties." Something glimmered in his eyes. Amusement. Or perhaps anticipation. "He holds on to power through bloody force. Be wary when you go up against him."

Going up against him wasn't something I intended. I wasn't a fool—and when that man got his comeuppance, it would be via Directorate hands, not mine. Though I would most *certainly* be there. "When I was reading the spirit lizard's mind, I saw a house with lots of mixed-heritage creatures. Is he building up an army, like you once mentioned?"

"Not an army, but definitely a force of creatures most will fear. You destroyed some of his winged weapons a few months ago, and there is nothing ready yet to replace them. He has about forty other creatures at his disposal, though." He paused. "He also intends to hire them out—at great cost, of course."

I nodded. Misha had already mentioned that little sideline. "So he intends using his creatures to help his quest in becoming the only syndicate that matters in Australia?"

"Yes."

Meaning we might be faced with an underworld war? Wonderful. "And that house? Was it his?"

He nodded. "It's one of many retreats he owns."

"Care to share the location?"

He stepped forward, and the wash of his desire had my skin burning again. "Care to share a little sex?"

"If you share this villain's name."

I raised a hand to prevent him coming any closer. He caught it, raising it to his lips, kissing my fingertips almost tenderly. If not for the cold determination in his eyes, it would almost have been easy to believe he cared. Though maybe, in some weird way, he did. Maybe he just equated caring with owning.

"I cannot tell you his name," he said, switching his grip and attempting to tug me forward into his arms.

I resisted, digging my heels in, glad I'd worn sensible shoes rather than stilettos, which would have me tipping A over T into his arms. "You've told me just about everything else about him, so why not a name?"

"Because, as I've said before, I'm not able to *say* his name. He has placed a restraint on me that forbids it."

"It makes no sense to place a restriction on his name when you can blab about everything else."

"Ah, but he does not realize I can blab about everything else. I was strong enough to shield certain areas of my mind without him being aware of it. He thinks the compulsion is all-encompassing."

The look in his eyes suggested there was something he wasn't telling me—something very important. I frowned, considering his words, remembering everything else he'd said. Then it hit me.

"You can't say his name," I said slowly, "but can you write it?"

"Not only pretty, but clever as well." He tugged my hand again, harder this time. I shifted several inches before my runners found purchase.

"So write down the name, Misha. We need to stop this man."

"You need to stop him. I want you in my life."

But I didn't want him. "I thought you wanted a kid to carry on the family name?"

"I do, and I will have that, but we both know that it may never be accomplished with you."

"I don't love you, Misha."

"Love has never been something I've desired. You, on the other hand, I've wanted from the moment I first saw you stripping oh-so-sexily in front of your bedroom window."

I was going to have be a little more circumspect when it came to stripping off my clothes after a hard day at the office, obviously. "I will not enter into a permanent relationship with you."

"I'm not asking for permanent, just ongoing."

How could I promise something like that? Who knew what the future had in store for me—and for him? What if tomorrow I met the man who was my soul mate? I'd be stuck with an agreement—and a wolf—I didn't want.

"We have a deal, Misha. I'll stick to that, nothing more."

He smiled, and tugged me forward with enough force to cannon me into him. His arms went around me, holding me close. "Then I will not give you the name."

I could have broken his hold anytime I wanted, and

we both knew it. Which made actually breaking free pretty pointless. "You've given me enough for the Directorate to find him."

His hand slid down my back and onto my rump, pressing me against him, against the hardness of his erection. "But you will not get into his circle without my help."

"Don't wipe off the Directorate, Misha. They're not the fools you and this man seem to think they are." I hesitated, then added, "We have Roberta in custody, you know."

That seemed to surprise him. "Then I hope you protect her well, because he will try to kill her."

"If he's killed Nasia, he's probably already tried to kill his mother."

"True. He always did intend Rupert to be the next Helki alpha."

Obviously, there was no love for Mom, despite the fact she helped him to the throne. "We have Rupert, as well."

"Then I hope you get the location of the lab fast, because he will burn it from their minds."

"Even if that happens, you still know the location. You can tell me."

"Only if I'm alive."

I raised an eyebrow at that. "And here I was thinking you were acting rather blasé about the threat to your life."

"Blasé? Far from it. Why do you think I've been living here twenty-four-seven this last week?"

"Here?" I waved a hand toward the window. "With all this glass about? How is that safe?"

"That glass is bulletproof. I replaced the original glass when I had the building refitted a few years ago."

"Given the fact your master is into creating the weird

and the not-so-wonderful, I wouldn't be banking on the fact that he can't get something in here."

"Whoever wants to come into this office has to do so through the Fravardin."

"All he really needs to do is set a bomb or use a rocket launcher, and you, this building, and the Fravardin are all dust." Taking me along with them if the attack happened right now.

"But that's not even remotely subtle. He cannot afford to draw attention to himself until his base of power is secure."

"Uh-uh." I reached behind me, grabbed Misha's hands, and pulled them away. "Let me state what you already know—I'm not having sex with you tonight. Not here. Not until whatever is going to happen happens."

"We had a deal."

"That deal was us meeting at the Rocker, nothing more."

He grimaced, though the effect was rather spoiled by the glimmer in his eyes. I was guessing he pretty much thought he was the winner here anyway—because I was with him, and not with someone else.

"I knew I should have widened the terms of reference." He walked across the room to the bar. "He won't attack me here. He's well aware that I'm very secure in my foxhole."

He offered me a beer and I shook my head. "All foxholes have weaknesses, Misha."

"Not this one."

"You certain of that?"

"Yes."

It was at that precise moment that the lights went out.

Chapter 12

o much for certainty," I muttered, blinking to switch to infrared vision.

"There must be a problem with the power," he said, walking across to the window.

Why, I have no idea. It was pretty much obvious by the rainbow beams of light invading the office that this building was the only one that'd lost light. "Yeah, it's been cut. There's no hum coming from the fridge, Misha."

He shrugged, and turned around to face me. "Whoever or whatever it is still has to get through the Fravardin."

I glanced toward the metal door. "What kills them?"

"White ash."

And I was betting the mastermind behind this

operation knew that. "Warn them, then contact the guards downstairs, see if they've been taken out."

He stared at me for a moment, his body a mass of pulsing red against the bright backdrop of city lights. Then he nodded, and moved across to the desk. "Tiimu, be prepared for an attack. They may have white ash, so tell everyone to be wary." He flicked another button, then added, "Security?"

No answer came. His gaze met mine. "They've been taken."

"Obviously." I slid the pack from my shoulder and took out the gun. "You have anything resembling a weapon in this office?"

"Besides teeth?" he said, baring them.

I shoved the extra rounds of bullets into my pockets, then ditched the pack. "I've got a feeling whatever is coming at us isn't going to be particularly fazed by a sharp pair of canines."

He grinned, and even from this distance I could smell his excitement. But then, he was a wolf, and when the male of our species was threatened, common sense usually flew out the window.

He pressed a button on the small console, then moved the bookcase behind him and pushed. It retracted into the wall, revealing a veritable arsenal. "I would suggest you take a laser—runt rifles are not good for close-in fighting. They take too long to reload."

I caught the one he tossed me. "How long have you had the armory?"

"It's another of my refurbishment details."

"Don't suppose they also included a quick escape route should things go bad?"

He merely grinned. Meaning he probably did, but he wasn't going to show me unless it was absolutely necessary. "Have you got monitors on all the floors?"

"Yeah, but with the power out, they won't work."

Well, duh. I shook my head at my own stupidity. "So we just sit here and wait for whatever's coming at us to come."

"Basically, yes." He fired up the laser, and the gentle hum rode across the night, itching at my nerves.

I retreated to the pillar opposite the door, pressing my back against the cool concrete. My palms were sweaty, my heart was racing nine to the dozen. I welcomed the reaction, welcomed the fear that sat like a weight at the bottom of my stomach. Because it meant that, despite my fears, I was not yet like my brother.

The mechanical drone of an elevator edged into the silence. Tension slithered through me, and my grip tightened on the laser. I glanced at Misha. "Why are the elevators working if all the power is out?"

"One elevator is a fire elevator—it has a separate power supply for situations like this."

"Great. Easy access for the bad guys."

"Unfortunately, yes. But it was a regulation I couldn't fight." He stood close to his arsenal, his back to the wall and a laser in either hand.

I licked my lips and turned my gaze back to the door. How strong was it? Given Misha's other refurbishments, it was probably reinforced, but would it be strong enough to keep out whatever was coming up in those elevators? Something deep inside said no, and fear rose another notch.

The mechanical drone of the elevator stopped, and in

the corridor beyond the door, chimes sounded, warning of the elevator's arrival.

Sweat broke out across my brow, and the tension in my fingers started becoming cramps. I took a deep breath, trying to calm my nerves as I waited for something to happen.

But for the longest of moments, nothing did.

Then an unearthly roar shattered the silence, and raised the hairs on the back of my neck. With it came the sound of fighting. Heavy thumps, flesh against flesh, the grunt of pain, more roars. The very walls seem to shudder under the force of the hits they were taking. Whether those hits were from weapons or from bodies being crashed against them, I couldn't say.

A red spot appeared in the middle of the door, white in the center flaring to red at the ever-growing edges. I stepped to one side, so that if—when—that laser broke through, it wouldn't skewer me in the middle.

"Lasering a hole in the door," Misha commented, his voice showing little concern. "They won't get far."

I swallowed to ease the dryness in my throat, then asked, "Why not?"

His eyes had an unearthly, almost fey, look about them. "Because those doors are rated against lasers."

"How long?"

"An hour."

Long enough for help to get here. Lord, I hoped Jack read his text messages sooner rather than later. "What's it rated against explosives?"

"If they use explosives, half the floor will come down on top of them. This is an old building, remember."

I remembered, but I was wondering if they would. "Why don't you call the police?"

"Why don't you call the Directorate?"

"I have."

He raised an eyebrow. "Then why aren't they here?"

"How the fuck am I supposed to know?" My voice was sharper than I'd intended. "I'm here, not there. I have no idea—"

I stopped abruptly. Through the noise of the fighting in the corridor, and the whine of the laser and bubbling of melting metal came another sound. A soft skittering against metal. It sounded for all the world like little hairy feet brushing across the surface of the door. A chill ran down my spine, and the sensation that we were no longer alone had my breath lodging somewhere in my throat.

Because that sound was coming from above us, from the ceiling itself rather than the door. I looked up. Infrared revealed absolutely nothing. Not on the ceiling, not in the hollows beyond it. Yet those sounds were drawing closer.

My heart raced so fast it felt as if it were going to tear out of my chest. I switched to normal vision, scanning the white expanse, wondering what the hell was going on. There was nothing there, nothing to be seen, yet the certainty that something *was* there, that it was almost on us, was growing like a cancer deep inside.

"What's wrong?"

The sudden question made me jump. I met Misha's gaze. "Something is in the ceiling."

"The ceiling is not designed to hold a great deal of weight." He looked up regardless, his expression edging toward concern for the first time.

"Whatever's coming at us hasn't got a great deal of weight." I jumped to one side as the laser broke through the door. A deadly red beam shot across the room, smashing into the pillar where I'd been minutes before, boiling the concrete in the few seconds it was on. Then light blinked out, leaving only the glowing edges of melted metal as evidence of its presence. Silence had fallen in the corridor. Whether that meant the Fravardin had won out or been defeated, I couldn't say. But I had a horrible suspicion it was the latter rather than the former.

"Given up," Misha said.

"I doubt it." The skittering drew closer, becoming hundreds of steps rather than just a few. Fear curled through me. My gaze rose to the ceiling again. What the hell could it possibly be? It sounded for all the world like spiders....

Oh, fuck.

Kade had mentioned spiders. Spiders that were invisible to infrared and able to squeeze through the smallest of holes. Holes like the one in the door. Or those in the air-conditioning vents.

Even as fear crystallized, moisture began to drip from the grate of the vent directly above me.

"Misha," I yelled, stepping aside and taking aim with the laser. "Look up. Your master has sent his spiders."

He swore, a sound lost to the sudden hum of the laser as I pressed the trigger. The cold beam bit through the semidarkness, hitting the gathering moisture square in the center. The grate began to melt, and steam boiled, filling the room with the thick scent of burning flesh. Something squealed, a high-pitched, unearthly sound no human would have caught. Then the vent cover came down, and with it a flood of water. Water that hit the carpet but didn't splatter, not even against my legs, though I stood barely two feet away. Horror crawled across my skin as the water began to separate, forming mounds that grew, took on shape, developed legs and heads and beady little eyes and sharp, razorlike teeth.

My fingers clenched reflexively on the trigger, and the laser's bright light shot out again. But the spiders that were as clear as water were also faster than fear.

They scattered. A good half dozen came directly at me, and I pressed the laser's trigger, burning carpet and spiders alike as I swept the beam back and forth.

Something bit my calf, and I yelped. Swinging around, I swiped the spider eating my flesh with the butt of the runt rifle, then speared it with the laser, killing it. More came. I kept my finger on the laser's trigger, almost choking in the steam that was beginning to fill the room. Still they came, a river that seemed endless. The laser grew hot in my hand, and the power light was flashing, warning that the energy cell was near depletion. I swore, and began to clear a path toward the armory. And saw Misha surrounded by a flood of the creatures and barely holding his own.

We couldn't beat them. I knew that then. Our only chance lay in escape—and in hoping that something worse wasn't out on the street, waiting for us.

I ran through the space I'd cleared, then leapt onto the desk, and toward the weapons. Felt sting after sting on my back as creatures leapt aboard and began to munch. Pain bloomed as moisture began to trickle down my spine. I dropped the runt rifle and the spent laser, replacing them with two more lasers. Swinging around, I thrust back against the wall as hard as I could. Something popped, and moisture splattered to my feet. I hit it with both lasers, then fanned the beams across the floor as more of the creatures came at me.

"Misha," I said, without looking up, "we need to get the hell out of here. Where's the escape hatch?"

"Press the green button—top right-hand—" His words ended in a grunt.

I glanced up to see one of the spiders on his face and red moisture beginning to drip from his chin.

Dear God... I jumped across the mass of flowing creatures, squashing several of them under my shoes as I landed. After flicking the lasers around us in a circle and momentarily forcing the mass back, I grabbed the thing from his face, noting even as I tossed it away that it somehow seemed smaller. I barely had time to take in the mess that had been made of Misha's face—the half-chewed lips, mutilated nose, and scoured cheeks, before they were on us again.

I swung round, felt Misha hit my back, smashing the creatures attached to my flesh even as I killed those closest to our feet. And though the mass was half its original size, it was still too many for the two of us. We had to get out of here.

"Get to that release," Misha said, sweeping his lasers to the left and right, catching those creatures I missed. Orange light began to flash across the shadows, a counterpoint of warmth against the cold light of the lasers. Misha's weapons were nearing the end.

"And hurry," he added.

Like I was going to stroll. I glanced at the button, and from the corner of my eyes saw the liquid gleam of a creature coming at my face. Laser light speared the darkness from behind, so it was steam that crashed against my skin rather than spider. A shudder ran through me anyway, and I had to fight to hold back the scream that surged up my throat.

Swallowing heavily, I leapt forward, smacking my hand against the button so hard that the force of the blow reverberated up my arm. Nothing happened. No answering whine, no dark hole of safety. Nothing.

"The lever," Misha said. "Near the rifles. And toss me some lasers."

I grabbed two and threw them his way. He cast his own aside and caught them deftly, but in the brief pause of the changeover, two creatures hit him, one on the chest, the other on his thigh. My curse got lost in his, and I lasered the others that tried to attack him while he pulled the things from his flesh. Then I grabbed the lever and pulled with all my might. Half the armory slid to one side, revealing not only the darkness of a corridor, but a large blue thing with suckered fingers that were clenched into fists and flying my way.

The punch hit before I could truly do anything. Suddenly I was flying backward, over the desk and across the room. I hit the carpet with a grunt that forced the air from my lungs and had spots dancing in front of my eyes, and for what seemed like an eternity, I couldn't breathe, couldn't move, could only lie there battling pain and the rising tide of darkness.

Yet through it all, I'd clung to the lasers, and it was that instinct that saved me. Because the spots in front of my eyes became a mass of blue, and I fired the lasers without real thought. The creature screamed as twin holes were punched through his chest. It was dead, but its momentum carried it forward. I rolled out from underneath, gagging at the reek of death that filled the air as its body crashed to the carpet.

I pushed to my knees, then my feet. Saw Misha was still upright, still fighting. The blue thing was obviously just a safety measure, because nothing else had come out of the darkness of the stairwell.

Time to get the hell out of here. I fired the lasers, and kept on firing, sweeping them steadily against the mass of watery spiders as I ran toward Misha. The creatures skittered away under the assault, leaving a clear path to the stairwell. Misha leapt toward it, and I followed, spinning and firing even as the shadows and coldness of the dark stairwell closed in around me. Misha slapped a hand against another lever, then thrust his weight against the door. It slid shut, catching several of the spiders mid-leap, squashing them flat between door and wall. I lasered the dribbling remains just to be safe, then let loose a long, shuddering breath of relief. Though God knows why—we weren't out of the woods yet.

Misha leaned against the concrete wall, his eyes closed and breathing harsh. He looked like shit, and his mauled face was beginning to puff up and bruise, but at least he was still alive.

I touched a hand to his shoulder. "We have to move."

He nodded, and pushed away from the wall. "Up, not down."

"To the roof?" Fear skittered through my gut at the thought. "Won't that be trapping ourselves?"

He shook his head, and rubbed a hand across his stomach, wincing a little. "No. He obviously knows about this escape route, and would expect us to go down."

"But what's on the roof, and why won't he know about it?"

"They're gutting the building next door, and, in the last week, have punched huge holes in the side wall to get ready for windows. From the roof we can jump through them to one of the open floors. He wouldn't expect that."

That's because normal people wouldn't try it. And people who were afraid of heights certainly *wouldn't*. I licked suddenly dry lips. "Is it much of a jump?"

He shook his head, his look of pain intensifying. No surprise, really, given the mess his face was in. It had to hurt like hell to talk. "Not much for a wolf."

Oh God...I blew out a breath, and gathered courage. Facing a pet fear head-on was better than facing any more of those damn spiders. Besides, with Misha looking so bad, it was doubtful he'd be much use in the fighting stakes.

"You want to lead the way?"

He nodded and staggered forward, grasping the metal rail as he hauled himself up the concrete steps. Our footsteps echoed across the silence, and I could only hope that if there was something waiting down below, they'd think we were coming toward them, not away.

It was only ten flights to the roof, but it felt like a hundred. We were both trembling and sweating by the time we reached the metal door, but in my case, I knew its cause was tension and fear.

Misha pressed bloody fingers to a button and pressed it. Locks clicked, but I stopped him from pushing the door open. "Let me go first. I'm in better condition."

He nodded and hung back, his hand still pressed to his stomach and the look of intense pain seemingly entrenched on his mauled features.

Taking a deep breath, I slowly, carefully, opened the door. Nothing stirred the night except the cool breeze. Metal creaked somewhere to my right, and from the left came the steady hum of traffic, soft laughter, and a babble of voices as people walked past. From still farther away came the bass thump of rock music.

Switching to infrared, I opened the door wider, and stepped out. No splashes of body heat greeted me, though if the spiders were up here, I wouldn't have seen them anyway.

The night breeze stirred my hair, and suddenly I was aware of the space and the night, and the sensation that we were high, so high, swamped me. Cold sweat broke out across my skin and my stomach rose. I closed my eyes, swallowing heavily.

I could do this.

I really could.

I switched back to normal vision, and glanced at Misha. He was sweating profusely, and shaking with pain. Shock, or something else? I didn't know, but it was obvious I had to get him to the hospital, and fast.

"I think it's safe."

He nodded and pushed past, heading to the left of the door. A building loomed above us, its inner bones revealed by the massive holes dotting its side.

The shifting haze skimmed across Misha's body, and in wolf form, he ran for the ledge and leapt for the nearest gap. I watched as he hit the other side, his body only half in, his back legs scrabbling for purchase on the rough old bricks. My heart lodged somewhere in my throat, and for several seconds I couldn't even breathe, my fear for him was so great. Then he was in, and safe, and it was my turn.

Oh God, oh God.

I licked my lips again, my eyes on the building directly opposite. It was just a little jump. A tiny jump. A sneeze when compared to some of the things I'd jumped in the past.

I called to the wolf within, felt the haze of energy sweep across my body.

But I couldn't force my paws forward. The concrete seemed to be attached to my feet, holding me down, holding me still.

Then I heard it.

The scrabble of tiny feet against concrete.

The spiders had found a way into the stairwell. It was either the jump or the spiders, and I'd had more than enough spiders for one day.

I sucked in a breath, then ran across the roof as fast as four legs would carry me. Not thinking, not looking, just running.

My leap was long and high, and it was terrifying to feel the wind batter my body, to see nothing but a long drop underneath me. Fear clenched my gut, my lungs, and breathing was suddenly impossible.

Then my claws hit concrete, and I was sliding to safety. I changed shape back to human form, but for several seconds couldn't move, couldn't do anything but sweat and shake and gasp for air.

But the thought that the spiders might somehow be

able to spray themselves across the gap got me moving. I rose and looked around for Misha. He was halfway across the gutted expanse, heading for the stairs.

"Misha, wait."

He stopped. I caught up with him. The smell of sweat and blood and fear tainted the air, and when his gaze met mine, true terror lurked in the silver depths. My stomach plummeted. Something was wrong. Something was very wrong.

"I feel like shit," he croaked.

"That's because you look like shit." I wrapped an arm around his waist, half-supporting him as I hurried forward. "My car is across the road. You'll be fine once I get you to hospital."

He coughed and moisture spurted from his mouth. Moisture that was bloody. God, he had internal injuries. "Hang on, Misha," I muttered, almost dragging him as I half-ran for the stairs. "Just hang on."

"You were right," he said, his voice so soft it was barely audible over the sound of our steps. "He figured a way into my foxhole."

"But he didn't kill us, and that's a plus."

"I'm not so sure about that." He stumbled as he said it, bringing us both down.

I grunted as the shock of the fall reverberated from my knees to brain. Misha rolled onto his back, his face contorted and his hands clutching at his stomach. "God," he said, voice a harsh rasp of suffering. "It feels like I'm being eaten inside out—" He stopped as a cough racked him, and bits of blood and water and what looked like specks of flesh gushed from his mouth.

And I remembered that creature on his face. Remembered thinking it was half the size it had originally looked.

Horror filled me, boiling through my body until it felt like my stomach was going to leap up into my throat.

Misha *was* being eaten from the inside out. When that spider creature had leapt onto his face, it hadn't only eaten his flesh. It had also poured part of itself into his body and somewhere inside re-formed to continue its bloody task.

His hand caught mine, dragging it to his mutilated lips, pressing a kiss I couldn't really feel against my fingertips. "End it, Riley. If you feel anything at—" He stopped again, and this time the rush of water that accompanied the cough was thicker. I shuddered, the bitter taste of bile heavy in my throat, the urge to run battling with the urge to scream and rage against the wiles of fate.

"End it, Riley," he pleaded. "Please."

I closed my eyes for the briefest of moments, then took a deep breath and said, "Tell me who your boss is, Misha. Please, just give me that."

"I can't."

"Not even a hint?"

"Not even...Not dead." He coughed, bringing up more flesh and blood. "Please. Stop."

I leaned forward and pressed a gentle kiss against his battered lips.

"May you find what you're looking for in your next life, Misha."

He raised a hand to my cheek, cupping it gently, his skin like ice against mine and his eyes gentle. I'd been wrong before. A lab-born creature could feel love. It was there, right now, in his eyes.

"But I have already found what I want. We could have been good together. Real good."

The tears blurring my eyes fell down my cheeks. "Yes," I whispered, and raised the laser.

He caught a tear on his fingertip, raising it a little, a touch of wonder briefly lifting the pain from his gaze. Then he closed his eyes and smiled, and I knew in that moment that he was thinking of us together, thinking of a future he could never have had.

I fired the laser, ending his pain, and his dreams.

It was only after I'd run from the building and his body, when I knew I was safe from the spiders and the creatures, that I let myself cry for the man I didn't love.

Chapter 13

Five days later, recovered from my wounds if not the memories, I was back in the bowels of Genoveve, my hands clasped behind my back as I stared out over the bloody sands of the old arena.

Behind me, Jack was speaking to Rhoan, but his words were little more than a babble of sound that was making no sense. Not that it mattered. I knew all the important stuff already. Roberta Whitby was dead. Jack and Rhoan hadn't got there in time to save her—a bomb had blown the vehicle apart long before she'd ever reached the tunnel where their trap waited. And the man who'd been Mrs. Hunt had been reduced to little more than unknowing flesh, his brain fried so completely he wasn't even capable of looking after himself. This despite all the shields the guardians who'd been bringing him in had placed on him.

Despite all he'd done in the last few days, all that we'd been through, Jack still didn't know the location of the second lab. Still didn't know the name of the man behind it all. While he mightn't be back at square one, he hadn't advanced much beyond it, either.

Except for the fact that Misha had, in the very end, come through with his promises. In the aftermath of his death, he'd given me the answers I needed—although that wasn't something Jack knew just yet.

I closed my eyes against the bloody images crowding my mind. I didn't want to remember how Misha had died, but rather, how he'd lived, in the times when he'd been just a lover and a good friend. Because that was what he was, despite everything. A friend.

A friend who had died loving me.

His funeral had been held in the traditional wolf manner, his body burned and his ashes scattered in the woods of one of his estates. That I'd been asked to the reading of his will surprised me, as did the fact that he'd left me two things—an undeveloped strip of land in the hills where I could—in his words—run free, and a letter.

It was the letter that had provided all the answers. I reached into my pocket and lightly touched the folded piece of paper. I'd read it often enough over the last few days to be able to recite it by heart, and yet the words still had the power to shock me. Or maybe it was the sentiment—the fact that he really *had* loved me.

Even if he'd never really understood what that meant.

If you are reading this, then I am dead, it started, *and you and the Directorate are left to fight this monster alone. For that, I am sorry. I want his madness stopped, as I have wanted almost nothing else, and everything I have done in recent times has been to that end. But I fear I have played my cards too close to my chest, and that in doing so, have placed myself in his hands.*

He has two identities, Riley. I cannot tell you the first, because it is an identity he has guarded very closely. But I know it is someone you see often—not a friend, not a lover, but someone close all the same. Nor is it to him Gautier reports to at the Directorate, but rather, our clone sister. Both she and Gautier will escape this cleansing, because he is not aware that you know about Gautier or the fact that there is someone else at the Directorate. Her lab-given name is Claudia Jones, but I have no idea what name she uses at the Directorate.

The other identity he has taken, and the one he most closely resembles, is Deshon Starr. He has taken over the cartel who rule the docks and claims inner Melbourne as its territory. He is ruthless and without morals. His operation is a closed group, and few outsiders are ever permitted into its ranks without intense scrutiny. But I have found the chink in the armor. Deshon likes men, and he likes to have lots of them at his disposal, so that gives the Directorate one entry point. The other is Deshon's two lieutenants. They are lab-enhanced—an area the cartel has been exploring for over forty years. They are not clones, not lab-born crossbreeds, but humans who, while still fetuses, underwent several procedures that involved cross-planting DNA from shifters to enhance their reflexes and senses. These experiments also gave them an overdeveloped sex drive. Sex is a fix they must have every day, and they go through women like sharks. Lovers are vetted, but less carefully than others, because they tend not to last long. The one who used you at the breeding center was Alden Merle. The other is Leo Moss. Of the two, Merle is probably the saner—but that's not saying a great deal. Both men are extremely dangerous and live only for two things besides sex—to obey Deshon, and to kill.

One thing more I must tell you.

For the longest time, the only emotion I have ever felt was the hunger to succeed. Then I met you.

Is love the desire—no, the need—to be with that person, whatever the cost? Does it cause the rise of rage when you see that person with another? Does it make you ache to hold her, to whisper things that sound foreign and strange to your tongue? Does it make you wish for things you know can never be?

I haven't the answers, Riley. In all that I've learned over the years, no one has ever mentioned a force such as this. But whatever it is, I feel it for you.

We would have been good together.

I closed my eyes against the tears suddenly stinging them. I may not have believed his words in life, but I had no such choice on his death. He'd proven he meant what he said, because he'd given me—or rather, the Directorate—the answers, and the name we needed. And he didn't have to do that.

"Riley? Are you paying the slightest attention to what I'm saying?"

Jack's barked question made me jump. I took a deep breath and turned around. "Actually, no, I wasn't. Was it something important?"

"Hell, no. I just say these things because I love to hear the sound of my own voice." He waved a hand to the spare chair in front of his desk. "Sit, woman, and pay attention."

My gaze met my brother's as I walked across the room. There was understanding there, like he knew what I was feeling. And he probably did. We might not share the communication of twins, and we might not be telepathically linked, but we very often knew when the other was hurting. I sat down, and he reached across, grasping my hand, squeezing it lightly.

"In his own weird way, he cared."

I smiled. "I know."

"People, can we get back to business here?" Jack glared at the two of us for a moment, then continued. "As I was saying, we have two people who, given everything Misha told you the day he died, fit the bill. One is Frank Margagliano, and the other is Deshon Starr. Both men have apparently undergone subtle changes in recent years—"

"It's Deshon Starr." I took the letter from my pocket and handed it to Jack.

He raised an eyebrow, then leaned back in his chair and read the note. "Well," he said slowly, once he'd finished. "That's certainly a help." He smiled slightly. "And I'm glad it's Deshon, because that's who I was leaning toward."

"Misha's given us a way in."

He studied me for a moment, then placed the folded letter on his desk and leaned forward, his hands clasped in front of him. "He's given *someone* a way in, certainly."

His gaze was on mine, green eyes challenging. He wanted me in on this, there was no doubt about that. But this time, it was all in, or nothing at all. *His* way, or the highway.

"No," Rhoan said, before I could say anything.

I looked at him. "I have to do this. I have to see it through."

"No," he repeated, his voice full of repressed fury as he looked at Jack. "She's not trained for this sort of work. And given that she's the prize this man has spent the last few months hunting, it would be utter stupidity to throw her into his web."

I touched a hand to his, dragging his gaze back to mine. "The last place he will look for me is in his own backyard."

"There's Gautier."

"Gautier can be taken care of," Jack said.

"Dammit, Riley," Rhoan exploded, "do you know what you will have to do? What you will have to dance with?"

"Yes, I do." And while the thought made my stomach curl, the simple fact was, I owed it to Kade, and to all the stallions who had died in our escape—and all the women who had been held in those breeding cells and who were more than likely dead—to see this through. But more importantly, I owed it to myself. These people had taken me, filled me with drugs that might yet have dire consequences, they'd abused me, and basically torn my world apart. And most of all, they'd made me fear. I couldn't let them get away with that. I had to be a part of their downfall, if only for my future peace of mind.

And if that meant dancing with a murderous piece of meat, then so be it. I was a wolf, and sex was only sex. As I'd said to Quinn more than once, it was merely an act that meant nothing more than enjoyment until real feelings were invoked.

Besides, how could I ever hope to live a normal life when that man was out there? When my brother was involved in the hunt and I was not?

"We can use the moon fever to our advantage," I said softly. "If what Misha says about them is true, they're likely to be less circumspect during the full moon phase."

"Dammit, Riley, that's *not* the point."

"The point," I said softly, "is that *that* man has been plotting against me for over three years. Would you sit back and let someone else make him pay if our positions were reversed?"

He slumped back in his chair, and rubbed a hand across his eyes. "Jesus, sis, you have no idea what you're getting yourself into."

Maybe I didn't. Maybe he was right, and I was stepping through hell's door when the sane would be running. But that was something I just couldn't do. Not if I wanted to live with myself. "Can it be any worse than what has happened to me already? Any worse than sitting here, waiting to see what the effects of the drugs Talon used on me are?"

"Yes, it can." His gaze met mine, eyes bleak. "You've never embraced your vampire half. Never acknowledged the killer instinct. It's going to take that, and more, to get through this."

"You cannot go in there alone, and we both know Jack can't send a female vampire to do this, simply because the Directorate has no female guardians capable of moving around in the daylight."

"I don't want you doing this."

"And I didn't want you to become a guardian, but you did, because you felt it was the right thing to do. I feel the same way about this."

"Fuck, Riley, that's not fair."

I raised an eyebrow. "Why? Because it's the truth?"

He leaned forward and grabbed my hands. "If you really, *really* need to do this, then I can do nothing but support you." His gaze searched mine for a moment before he continued. "But if this is about Misha, about what was done to him, then I won't. Can't."

"I'm doing this for me. Because of what has been done to me." Mostly, anyway.

He sighed, and let me go. "Then at least get some training before we go in."

"If she does this, she'll be getting training. And Gautier will know about the training, because everyone there knows I want to set up a daytime unit."

"Hiding in plain sight," I murmured. "How much time have we got, do you think?"

"Plenty, because he thinks he's safe, and we can't afford to rush. We'll continue to keep track of Gautier, and set up a watch on our two female assistant directors. And we'll need to thoroughly investigate the two lieutenants, as well as set up covers for the two of you."

"Why not just take Gautier out?" Rhoan asked.

Jack glanced at him. "Because the minute we do that, Starr will know something is happening. He's better kept under close watch, and fed false information." His gaze came back to me. "Are you in, or out?"

"In," I said.

And even as I said it, I knew I'd stepped onto the road to becoming the one thing I'd sworn never to become.

A guardian, just like my brother.

The world has seven wonders. . . .
Riley Jenson will do you two better.
That's nine times the action.
Nine times the passion.
Nine times the kick-ass.

THE RILEY JENSON GUARDIAN NOVELS

by

KERI ARTHUR

A complete nine-book series from Dell Books.
Be sure not to miss any of these exciting novels—
or this series of special previews, to give you a
taste of what you'll get in . . .

A RILEY JENSON GUARDIAN NOVEL
KERI ARTHUR
Half vampire,
half werewolf,
all trouble...
FULL MOON
RISING

FULL MOON RISING

On sale now

The night was quiet.

Almost too quiet.

Though it was after midnight, it was a Friday night, and Friday nights were usually party nights—at least for those of us who were single and not working night shift. This section of Melbourne wasn't exactly excitement city, but it did possess a nightclub that catered to both humans and nonhumans. And while it wasn't a club I frequented often, I loved the music they played. Loved dancing along the street to it as I made my way home.

But tonight, there was no music. No laughter. Not even drunken revelry. The only sound on the whispering wind was the clatter of the train leaving the station and the rumble of traffic from the nearby freeway.

Of course, the club was a well-known haunt for pushers and their prey, and as such it was regularly raided—and closed—by the cops. Maybe it had been hit again.

So why was there no movement on the street? No disgruntled partygoers heading to other clubs in other areas?

And why did the wind hold the fragrance of blood?

I hitched my bag to a more comfortable position on my shoulder, then stepped from the station's half-lit platform and ran up the stairs leading to Sunshine Avenue. The lights close to the platform's exit were out and the shadows closed in the minute I stepped onto the street.

Normally, darkness didn't worry me. I am a creature of the moon and the night, after all, and well used to roaming the streets at ungodly hours. That night, though the moon rode toward fullness, its silvery light failed to pierce the thick cover of clouds. But the power of it shimmered through my veins—a heat that would only get worse in the coming nights.

Yet it wasn't the closeness of the full moon that had me jumpy. Nor was it the lack of life coming from the normally raucous club. It was something else, something I couldn't quite put a finger on. The night felt wrong, and I had no idea why.

But it was something I couldn't ignore.

I turned away from the street that led to the apartment I shared with my twin brother and headed for the nightclub. Maybe I was imagining the scent of blood, or the wrongness in the night. Maybe the club's silence had nothing to do with either sensation. But one thing was certain—I had to find out. It would keep me awake otherwise.

Of course, curiosity not only killed cats, but it often took out inquisitive werewolves, too. Or, in my case, half-weres. And my nose for trouble had caused me more grief over the years than I wanted to remember. Generally, my brother had been right by my side, either fighting with me or pulling me out of harm's way. But Rhoan wasn't home, and he couldn't be contacted. He worked as a guardian for the Directorate of Other Races—which was a government body that sat somewhere between the cops and the military. Most humans thought the Directorate was little more than a police force specializing in capture of nonhuman criminals, and in some respects, they were right. But the Directorate, both in Australia and overseas, was also a researcher of all things nonhuman, and its guardians didn't only capture, they had the power to be judge, jury, and executioner.

I also worked for the Directorate, but not as a guardian. I was nowhere near ruthless enough to join their ranks as anything other than a general dogsbody— though, like most of the people who worked for the Directorate in *any* capacity, I had certainly been tested. I was pretty damn happy to have failed—especially given that eighty percent of a guardian's work involved assassination. I might be part wolf, but I wasn't a killer. Rhoan was the only one in our small family unit who'd inherited those particular instincts. If I had a talent I could claim, it would be as a finder of trouble.

Which is undoubtedly what I'd find by sticking my nose where it had no right to be. But would I let the thought of trouble stop me? Not a snowflake's chance in hell.

Grinning slightly, I shoved my hands into my coat pockets and quickened my pace. My four-inch heels clacked against the concrete, and the sound seemed to echo along the silent street. A dead giveaway if there *were* problems ahead. I stepped onto the strip of half-dead grass that separated the road from the pavement and tried not to get my heels stuck in the dirt as I continued on.

The street curved around to the left, and the rundown houses that lined either side of the road gave way to run-down factories and warehouses. Vinnie's nightclub sat about halfway along the street, and even from a distance, it was obvious the place was closed. The gaudy red-and-green flashing signs were off, and no patrons milled around the front of the building.

But the scent of blood and the sense of wrongness were stronger than ever.

I stopped near the trunk of a gum tree and raised my nose, tasting the slight breeze, searching for odors that might give a hint as to what was happening up ahead.

Beneath the richness of blood came three other scents—excrement, sweat, and fear. For those last two to be evident from that distance, something major had to be happening.

I bit my lip and half considered calling the Directorate. I wasn't a fool—not totally, anyway—and whatever was happening in that club *smelled* big. But what would I report? That the scent of blood and shit rode the wind? That a nightclub that was usually open on a Friday night was suddenly closed? They weren't likely to send out troops for that. I needed to get closer, see what was really happening.

But the nearer I got, the more unease turned my stomach—and the more certain I became that something was very wrong inside the club. I stopped in the shadowed doorway of a warehouse almost opposite Vinnie's and studied the building. No lights shone inside, and no windows were broken. The metal front doors were closed, and thick grates protected the black-painted windows. The side gate was padlocked. For all intents and purposes, the building looked secure. Empty.

Yet something *was* inside. Something that walked quieter than a cat. Something that smelled of death. Or rather, *un*death.

A vampire.

And if the thick smell of blood and sweaty humanity that accompanied his sickly scent was anything to go by, he wasn't alone. *That* I could report. I swung my handbag around so I could grab my cell phone, but at that moment, awareness surged, prickling like fire across my skin. I no longer stood alone on the street. And the noxious scent of unwashed flesh that followed the awareness told me exactly who it was.

I turned, my gaze pinpointing the darkness crowding the middle of the road. "I know you're out there, Gautier. Show yourself."

His chuckle ran across the night, a low sound that set my teeth on edge. He walked free of the shadows and strolled toward me. Gautier was a long, mean stick of vampire who hated werewolves almost as much as he hated the humans he was paid to protect. But he was one of the Directorate's most successful guardians, and the word I'd heard was that he was headed straight for the top job.

If he did get there, I would be leaving. The man was a bastard with a capital B.

"And just what are you doing here, Riley Jenson?" His voice, like his dark hair, was smooth and oily. He'd apparently been a salesman before he'd been turned. It showed, even in death.

"I live near here. What's your excuse?"

His sudden grin revealed bloodstained canines. He'd fed, and very recently. My gaze went to the nightclub. Surely not even he could be *that* depraved. That out of control.

"I'm a guardian," he said, coming to a halt about half a dozen paces away. Which was about half a dozen paces *too* close for my liking. "We're paid to patrol the streets, to keep humanity safe."

I scrubbed a hand across my nose, and half wished— and not for the first time in my years of dealing with vampires—that my olfactory sense wasn't so keen. I'd long ago given up trying to get *them* to take regular showers. How Rhoan coped with being around them so much, I'll never know.

"You only walk the streets when you've been set loose to kill," I said, and motioned to the club. "Is that what you've been sent here to investigate?"

"No." His brown gaze bored into mine, and an odd tingling began to buzz around the edges of my thoughts. "How did you know I was there when I had shadows wrapped around my body?"

The buzzing got stronger, and I smiled. He was trying to get a mind-lock on me and force an answer— something vamps had a tendency to do when they had questions they knew wouldn't be answered willingly. Of course, mind-locks had been made illegal several years ago in the "human rights" bill that set out just what was, and wasn't, acceptable behavior from nonhuman races when dealing with humans. Or other nonhumans for that matter. Trouble is, legalities generally mean squat to the dead.

But he didn't have a hope in hell of succeeding with me, thanks to the fact I was something that should not be—the child of a werewolf *and* a vampire. Because of my mixed heritage, I was immune to the controlling touch of vampires. And that immunity was the only reason I was working in the guardian liaisons section of the Directorate. He should have realized that, even if he didn't know the reason for the immunity.

"Hate to say this, Gautier, but you haven't exactly got the sweetest scent."

"I was downwind."

Damn. So he was. "Some scents are stronger than the wind to a wolf." I hesitated, but couldn't help adding, "You know, you may be one of the undead, but you sure as hell don't have to smell like it."

His gaze narrowed, and there was a sudden stillness about him that reminded me of a snake about to strike.

"You would do well to remember what I am."

"And you would do well to remember that I'm trained to protect myself against the likes of you."

He snorted. "Like all liaisons, you overestimate your skills."

Maybe I did, but I sure as hell wasn't going to admit it, because that's precisely what he wanted. Gautier not only loved baiting the hand that fed him, he more often bit it. Badly. Those in charge let him get away with it because he was a damn fine guardian.

"As much as I love standing here trading insults, I really want to know what's going on in that club."

His gaze went to Vinnie's, and something inside me relaxed. But only a little. When it came to Gautier, it never paid to relax too much.

"There's a vampire inside that club," he said.

"I know *that* much."

His gaze came back to me, brown eyes flat and somehow deadly. "How do you know? A werewolf has no more awareness when it comes to vampires than a human."

Werewolves mightn't, but then, I wasn't totally wolf, and it was my vampire instincts that were picking up the vamp inside the building. "I'm beginning to think the vampire population should be renamed the great unwashed. He stinks almost as much as you do."

His gaze narrowed again, and again the sensation of danger swirled around me. "One day, you'll push too far."

Probably. But with any sort of luck, it would be *after* he'd gotten the arrogance knocked out of him. I waved a hand at Vinnie's. "Are there people alive inside?"

"Yes."

"So are you going to do something about the situation or not?"

His grin was decidedly nasty. "I'm not."

I blinked. I'd expected him to say a lot of things, but certainly not that. "Why the hell not?"

"Because I hunt bigger prey tonight." His gaze swept over me, and my skin crawled. Not because it was sexual—Gautier didn't want me any more than I wanted him—but because it was the look of a predator sizing up his next meal.

His expression, when his gaze rose to meet mine again, was challenging. "If you think you're so damn good, you go tend to it."

"I'm not a guardian. I can't—"

"You can," he cut in, "because you're a guardian liaison. By law, you can interfere when necessary."

"But—"

"There are five people alive in there," he said. "If you want to keep them that way, go rescue them. If not, call the Directorate and wait. Either way, I'm out of here."

With that, he wrapped the night around his body and disappeared from sight. My vampire and werewolf senses tracked his hidden form as he raced south. He really *was* leaving.

Fuck.

My gaze returned to Vinnie's. I couldn't hear the beating of hearts, and had no idea whether Gautier was telling the truth about people being alive inside. I might be part vampire, but I didn't drink blood, and my senses weren't tuned to the thud of life. But I could smell fear, and surely I wouldn't be smelling that if someone wasn't alive in the club.

Even if I called the Directorate, they wouldn't get there in time to rescue those people. I had to go in. I had no choice.

KERI ARTHUR

In a realm without inhibitions,
there's nothing more seductive
than temptation. . . .

TEMPTING EVIL

FROM THE AUTHOR OF *KISSING SIN*

TEMPTING EVIL

On sale now

Training sucked.

Especially when the main aim of that training was to make me something I'd once vowed never to become—a guardian for the Directorate of Other Races.

Becoming a guardian might have been inevitable, and I might have accepted it on some levels, but that didn't mean I had to be happy about the whole process.

Guardians were far more than just the specialized cops most humans thought them to be—they were judge, jury, and executioners. None of this legal crap the human cops were forced to put up with. Of course, the people in front of a guardian's metaphoric bullet were generally out-of-control psychos who totally deserved to die, but stalking the night with the aim of ending their undead lives still wasn't something that had reached my to-do list.

Even if my wolf-soul sometimes hungered to hunt more than I might wish to acknowledge.

But if there was one thing worse than going through all the training that was involved in becoming a guardian, then it was training with my brother. I couldn't con him.

Couldn't flirt or flash a bit of flesh to make him forget his train of thought. Couldn't moan that I'd had enough and that I couldn't go on, because he wasn't just my brother, but my twin.

He knew exactly what I could and couldn't do, because he could feel it. We mightn't share the telepathy of twins, but we knew when the other was hurting or in trouble.

And right now Rhoan was fully aware of the fact that I was trying to pike. And he knew why.

I had a hot date with an even hotter werewolf.

In precisely one hour.

If I left now, I could get home and clean up before Kellen—the hot date in question—came by to pick me up. Any later, and he'd see me as the beaten-up scruff I usually was these days.

"Isn't Liander cooking you a roast this evening?" I said, casually waving the wooden baton I'd been given but had yet to use. Mainly because I didn't want to hit my brother.

He, however, didn't have the same problem, and the bruises littering my body proved it.

But then, he didn't really want me to be doing this. Didn't want me on the mission drawing inexorably closer.

"Yes." He continued to circle me, his pace as casual as his expression. I wasn't fooled. Couldn't be, when I could feel the tension in his body almost as well as I could feel it in mine. "But he has no intention of putting it on until I phone and tell him I'm on my way to his place."

"It's his birthday. You should be there to celebrate it with him rather than putting me through the wringer."

He shifted suddenly, stepping forward, the baton a pale blur as he lashed out at me. I ignored the step and the blow, holding still as the breeze of the baton's passing caressed the fingers of my left hand. He was only playing, and we both knew it.

I wouldn't even see his real move.

He grinned. "I'll be there as soon as this is over. And he did invite you along, remember."

"And spoil the private party you have planned?" My voice was dry. "I don't think so. Besides, I'd rather party with Kellen."

"Meaning Quinn is still out of the picture?"

"Not entirely." I shifted a little, keeping him in sight as he continued to circle. The padded green mats that covered the Directorate's sublevel training arena squeaked in protest under my bare feet.

"Your sweat is causing that," he commented. "But there's not nearly enough of it."

"Jesus, Rhoan, have a heart. I haven't seen Kellen for nearly a week. I want to play with him, not you."

He raised an eyebrow, a devilish glint in his silver eyes. "You get me on the mat, and I'll let you go."

"It's not you I want on the mat!"

"If you don't fight me, they'll make you fight Gautier. And I don't think either of us wants that."

"And if I do fight you, and do manage to bring you down, they're going to make me fight him anyway." Which pretty much sucked. I wasn't overly fond of vampires at the best of times, but some of them—like Quinn, who was in Sydney tending to his airline business, and Jack, my boss, and the man in charge of the whole guardian division—were decent people. Gautier was just a murdering freak. He might be a guardian, and he might not have done anything wrong just yet, but he was one of the bad guys. He was also a clone made for one specific purpose—to take over the Directorate. He hadn't made his move yet, but I had an odd premonition that he would, and soon.

Rhoan made another feint. This time the baton skimmed my knuckles, stinging but not breaking skin. I resisted the urge to shake the pain away and shifted my stance a little, readying for the real attack.

"So, what's happening between you and Quinn?"

Nothing had happened, and that was the whole problem. After making such a song and dance about me upholding my end of the deal we'd made, he'd basically played absent lover for the last few months. I blew out a frustrated breath, lifting the sweaty strands of hair from my forehead. "Can't we have this discussion after I play with Kellen?"

"No," he said, and blurred so fast that he literally disappeared from normal sight. And while I could have tracked his heat signature with the infrared of my vampire vision, I didn't actually need to, because my hearing and nose were wolf sharp. Not only could I hear his light steps on the vinyl mats as he circled around me, but I could track the breeze of his spicy, leathery scent.

Both were now approaching from behind.

I dove out of the way, twisting around even as I hit the mat, and lashed out with a foot. The blow connected hard and low against the back of his leg, and he grunted, his form reappearing as he stumbled and fought to remain standing.

I scrambled upright, and lunged toward him. I wasn't fast enough by half. He scooted well out of reach and shook his head. "You're not taking this seriously, Riley."

"Yes, I am." Just not as seriously as he'd like me to. Not this evening, anyway.

"Are you that desperate to fight Gautier?"

"No, but I am that desperate to see Kellen." Sexual frustration wasn't a good thing for anyone, but it was particularly bad for a werewolf. Sex was an ingrained part of our culture—we needed it as much as a vampire needed blood. And this goddamn training had been taking up so much of my free time that I hadn't even been able to get down to the Blue Moon for some action.

I blew out another breath, and tried to think calm thoughts. As much as I didn't want to hurt my brother, if that was the only way out of here, then I might have to try.

But if I did succeed in beating him, then Jack might take that as a sign I was ready for the big one. And part of me feared that—feared that no matter what Jack said, my brother was right when he said that I shouldn't be doing this. That I was never going to be ready for it, no matter how much training I got.

That I'd screw it all up, and put everyone's life in danger.

Not that Rhoan had actually said that last one. But as the time drew nearer, it was in my thoughts more and more.

"It's a stupid rule, and you know it," I said eventually. "Fighting Gautier doesn't prove anything."

"He is the best at what he does. Fighting him makes guardians ready for what they may face out there."

"Difference is, I don't want to become a full-time guardian."

"You have no choice now, Riley."

I knew that, but that didn't mean I still couldn't rail

against the prospect, even if my protests were only empty words.

I licked my lips and tried to concentrate on Rhoan. If I had to get him down on the mat to get out of here, then I would. I wanted, needed, to grab a little bit more of a normal life before the crap set in again.

Because it was coming. I could feel it.

A shadow flickered across one of the windows lining the wall to the right of Rhoan. Given it was nearly six, it was probably just a guardian getting himself ready for the evening's hunt. This arena was on sublevel five, right next to the guardian sleeping quarters. Which, amusingly, did contain coffins. Some vamps just loved living up to human expectations, even if they weren't actually necessary.

Not that any humans ever came down here. That would be like leading a lamb into the midst of a den of hungry lions. To say it would get ugly very quickly would be an understatement. Guardians might be paid to protect humans, but they sure as hell weren't above snacking on the occasional one either.

The shadow slipped past another window, and this time, Rhoan's gaze flickered in that direction. Only briefly, but that half second gave me an idea.

I twisted, spinning and lashing out with one bare foot. My heel skimmed his stomach, forcing him backward. His baton arced around, his blow barely avoiding my shin, then he followed the impetus of the movement so that he was spinning and kicking in one smooth motion. His heel whistled mere inches from my nose, and probably would have connected if I hadn't leaned back.

He nodded approvingly. "Now, that's a little more like it."

I grunted, shifting my stance and throwing the baton from one hand to the other. The slap of wood against flesh echoed in the silence surrounding us, and tension ran across his shoulders. I held his gaze, then caught the baton left-handed and started to hit out. Only to pull the blow up short and let my gaze go beyond him.

"Hi, Jack."

Rhoan turned around, and, in that moment, I dropped and kicked his legs out from underneath him. He hit the mat with a loud splat, his surprised expression dissolving quickly into a bark of laughter.

"The oldest trick in the book, and I fell for it."

I grinned. "Old tricks sometimes have their uses."

"And I guess this means you're free to go." He held up a hand. "Help me up."

"I'm not that stupid, brother."

Amusement twinkled in his silvery eyes as he climbed to his feet. "Worth a try, I guess."

"So I can go?"

"That was the deal." He rose and walked across to the side of the arena to grab the towel he'd draped over the railing earlier. "But you're back here tomorrow morning at six sharp."

I groaned. "That's just plain mean."

He ran the towel across his spiky red hair, and even though I couldn't see his expression, I knew he was grinning. Sometimes my brother could be a real pain in the ass.

"Maybe next time you'll reconsider the option of cheating."

"It's not cheating if it worked."

Though his smile still lingered, little of that amusement reached his eyes. He was worried, truly worried, about my part in the mission we'd soon embark on. He didn't want me to do this any more than I'd wanted him to become a guardian. But as he'd said to me all those years ago, some directions in life just had to be accepted.

"You're here to learn defense and offense," he said. "Inane tricks won't save your life."

"If they save it only once, then they're worth trying."

He shook his head. "I can see I'm not going to talk any sense into you until after the sexfest."

"Glad you finally caught the gist of my whole conversation for the last hour." I grinned. "And hey, look on the bright side. Liander's going to be mighty pleased to see you at a normal hour for a change."

He nodded, tossed the towel around his bare shoulders, and headed off whistling. Obviously, I wasn't the only one anticipating a good time tonight.

Grinning slightly, I headed down the other end of the arena, where my towel and water bottle waited. I grabbed the towel and wrapped one end around my ponytail, squeezing the sweat from my hair before wiping the back of my neck and face. I might not have been fighting to full capacity tonight, but we'd still been training for a couple of hours and not only did my skin glimmer with heat but my navy T-shirt was almost black with sweat. It was just as well I could shower here—with the way my luck had been running of late, Kellen would be waiting for me by the time I got home. And as much as most wolves preferred natural scent over synthetic, right now I was just a little too overwhelmingly natural.

I reached out to collect the water bottle, then froze as awareness surged, prickling like fire across my skin. Rhoan had left, but I was no longer alone in the arena.

My earlier intuition had been right—crap had been about to step back into my life.

And it came in the form of Gautier.

Towel still in hand, I casually turned around. He stood at the window end of the arena, a long, mean stick of man and muscle who smelled as bad as he looked.

"Still haven't managed to catch that shower, I see." It probably wasn't the wisest comment I'd ever made, but when it came to Gautier, I couldn't seem to keep my mouth shut.

It was a trait that was going to get me in trouble—if not tonight, then sometime in the future.

He crossed his arms and smiled. There was nothing nice in that smile. Nothing sane in his flat brown eyes. "Still jumping mouth-first into situations even the insane would think twice about, I see."

"It's a common failing of mine." I idly began twirling the towel and wondered how long it would take security to react. And if Jack would let them react.

"So I've noticed."

He'd be hard-pressed not to when most of my mouth-first offenses of late involved him in some way. "What are you doing here, Gautier? Haven't you got bad guys to kill?"

"I have."

"Then why aren't you outside hunting, like the good little psycho you are?"

His sharklike smile sent a chill running up my spine, and in that moment I realized he was on the hunt.

For me . . .

KERI ARTHUR

Desire, Temptation.
Seduction.
Let the night begin....

DANGEROUS GAMES

DANGEROUS GAMES

On sale now

I stood in the shadows and watched the dead man.

The night was bitterly cold, and rain fell in a heavy, constant stream. Water sluiced down the vampire's long causeway of a nose, leaping to the square thrust of his jaw before joining the mad rush down the front of his yellow raincoat. The puddle around his bare feet had reached his ankles and was slowly beginning to creep up his hairy legs.

Like most of the newly risen, he was little more than flesh stretched tautly over bone. But his skin possessed a rosy glow that suggested he'd eaten well and often. Even if his pale eyes were sunken. Haunted.

Which in itself wasn't really surprising. Thanks to the willingness of both Hollywood and literature to romanticize vampirism, far too many humans seemed to think that by becoming a vampire they'd instantly gain all the power, sex, and wealth they could ever want. It wasn't until after the change that they began to realize that being undead wasn't the fun time often depicted. That wealth, sex, and popularity might come, but only if they survived the horrendous first few years, when a vampire was all instinct and blood need. And of course, if they did survive, they then learned that endless loneliness, never feeling the full warmth of the sun again, never being able to savor the taste of food, and being feared or ostracized by a good percentage of the population was also part of the equation.

Yeah, there were laws in place to stop discrimination against vampires and other nonhumans, but the laws were only a recent development. And while there might now be vampire groupies, they were also a recent phenomenon and only a small portion of the population. Hatred and fear of vamps had been around for centuries, and I had no doubt it would take centuries for it to abate. If it ever did.

And the bloody rampages of vamps like the one ahead weren't helping the cause any.

A total of twelve people had disappeared over the last month, and we were pretty sure this vamp was responsible for nine of them. But there were enough differences in method of killing between this vamp's nine and the remaining three to suggest we had a second psycho on the loose. For a start, nine had met their death as a result of a vamp feeding frenzy. The other three had been meticulously sliced open neck to knee with a knife and their innards carefully removed—not something the newly turned were generally capable of. When presented with the opportunity for a feed, they fed. There was nothing neat or meticulous about it.

Then there were the multiple barely healed scars marring the backs of the three anomalous women, the missing pinky on their left hands, and the odd, almost satisfied smiles that seemed frozen on their dead lips. Women who were the victims of a vamp's frenzy didn't die with *that* sort of smile, as the souls of the dead nine could probably attest if they were still hanging about.

And I seriously hoped that they *weren't*. I'd seen more than enough souls rising in recent times—I certainly didn't want to make a habit of it.

But dealing with two psychos on top of coping with the usual guardian patrols had the Directorate stretched to the limit, and that meant everyone had been pulling extra shifts. Which explained why Rhoan and I were out hunting rogue suckers on this bitch of a night after working all day trying to find some leads on what Jack— our boss, and the vamp who ran the whole guardian division at the Directorate of Other Races—charmingly called The Cleaver.

I yawned and leaned a shoulder against the concrete wall lining one side of the small alleyway I was hiding in. The wall, which was part of the massive factory complex that dominated a good part of the old West Footscray area, protected me from the worst of the wind, but it didn't do a whole lot against the goddamn rain.

If the vamp felt any discomfort about standing in a pothole in the middle of a storm-drenched night, he certainly wasn't showing it. But then, the dead rarely cared about such things.

I might have vampire blood running through my veins, but I wasn't dead and I hated it.

Winter in Melbourne was never a joy, but this year we'd had so much rain I was beginning to forget what sunshine looked like. Most wolves were immune to the cold, but I was a half-breed and obviously lacked that particular gene. My feet were icy and I was beginning to lose feeling in several toes. And this despite the fact I was wearing two pairs of thick woolen socks underneath my rubber-heeled shoes. Which were not waterproof, no matter what the makers claimed.

I should have worn stilettos. My feet would have been no worse off, and I would have felt more at home. And hey, if he happened to spot me, I could have pretended to be nothing more than a bedraggled, desperate hooker. But Jack kept insisting high heels and my job just didn't go together.

Personally, I think he was a little afraid of my shoes. Not so much because of the color—which, admittedly, was often outrageous—but because of the nifty wooden heels. Wood and vamps were never an easy mix.

I flicked up the collar of my leather jacket and tried to ignore the fat drops of water dribbling down my spine. What I really needed—more than decent-looking shoes— was a hot bath, a seriously large cup of coffee, and a thick steak sandwich. Preferably with lashings of onions and ketchup, but skip the tomato and green shit, please. God, my mouth was salivating just thinking about it. Of course, given we were in the middle of this ghost town of factories, none of those things were likely to appear in my immediate future.

I thrust wet hair out of my eyes, and wished, for the umpteenth time that night, that he would just get on with it. Whatever it was.

Following him might be part of my job as a guardian, but that didn't mean I had to be happy about it. I'd never had much choice about joining the guardian ranks, thanks to the experimental drugs several lunatics had forced into my system and the psychic talents that were developing as a result. It was either stay with the Directorate as a guardian so my growing abilities could be monitored and harnessed, or be shipped off to the military with the other unfortunates who had received similar doses of the ARC1-23 drug. I might not have wanted to be a guardian, but I sure as hell didn't want to be sent to the military. Give me the devil I know any day.

I shifted weight from one foot to the other again. What the hell was this piece of dead meat waiting for? He couldn't have sensed me—I was far enough away that he wouldn't hear the beat of my heart or the rush of blood through my veins. He hadn't looked over his shoulder at any time, so he couldn't have spotted me with the infrared of his vampire vision, and blood suckers generally didn't have a very keen olfactory sense.

So why stand in a puddle in the middle of this abandoned factory complex looking like a little lost soul?

Part of me itched to shoot the bastard and just get the whole ordeal over with. But we needed to follow this baby vamp home to discover if he had any nasty surprises hidden in his nest. Like other victims, or perhaps even his maker.

Because it was unusual for one of the newly turned to survive nine rogue kills without getting himself caught or killed. Not without help, anyway.

The vampire suddenly stepped out of the puddle and began walking down the slight incline, his bare feet slapping noisily against the broken road. The shadows and the night hovered all around him, but he didn't bother cloaking his form. Given the whiteness of his hairy legs and the brightness of his yellow raincoat, that was strange. Though we were in the middle of nowhere. Maybe he figured he was safe.

I stepped out of the alleyway. The wind hit full-force, pushing me sideways for several steps before I regained my balance. I padded across the road and stopped in the shadows again. The rain beat a tattoo against my back, and the water seeping through my coat became a river, making me feel colder than I'd ever dreamed possible. Forget the coffee and the sandwich. What I wanted more than anything right now was to get warm.

I pressed the small comlink button that had been inserted into my earlobe just over four months ago. It doubled as a two-way communicator and a tracker, and Jack had not only insisted that I keep it but that all guardians were to have them from now on. He wanted to be able to find his people at all times, even when not on duty.

Which smacked of "big-brother" syndrome to me even if I could understand his reasoning. Guardians didn't grow on trees—finding vamps with just the right mix of killing instinct and moral sensibilities was difficult, which was why guardian numbers at the Directorate still hadn't fully recovered from the eleven we'd lost ten months ago.

One of those eleven had been a friend of mine, and on my worst nights I still dreamed of her death, even though the only thing I'd ever witnessed was the bloody patch of sand that had contained her DNA. Like most of the other guardians who had gone missing, her remains had never been found.

Of course, the tracking measures had not only come too late for those eleven, but for one other—Gautier. Not that he was dead, however much I might wish otherwise. Four months ago he'd been the Directorate's top guardian.

Now he was rogue and on top of the Directorate's hit list. So far he'd escaped every search, every trap. Meaning he was still out there, waiting and watching and plotting his revenge.

On me.

Goose bumps traveled down my spine and, just for a second, I'd swear his dead scent teased my nostrils. Whether it was real or just imagination and fear I couldn't say, because the gusting wind snatched it away.

Even if it wasn't real, it was a reminder that I had to be extra careful. Gautier had never really functioned on the same sane field as the rest of us. Worse still, he liked playing with his prey. Liked watching the pain and fear grow before he killed.

He might now consider me his mouse but he'd yet to try any of his games on me. But something told me that tonight, that would all change.

I grimaced and did my best to ignore the insight. Clairvoyance might have been okay if it had come in a truly usable form—like clear glimpses of future scenes and happenings—but oh no, that was apparently asking too much of fate. Instead, I just got these weird feelings of upcoming doom that were frustratingly vague on any sort of concrete detail. And training something like that was nigh on impossible—not that that stopped Jack from getting his people to at least try.

Whether the elusiveness would change as the talent became more settled was anyone's guess. Personally, I just wished it would go back to being latent. I knew Gautier was out there somewhere. Knew he was coming after me. I didn't need some half-assed talent sending me spooky little half warnings every other day.

Still, even though I knew Gautier probably wasn't out here tonight, I couldn't help looking around and checking all the shadows as I said, "Brother dearest, I hate this fucking job."

Rhoan's soft laughter ran into my ear. Just hearing it made me feel better. Safer. "Nights like this are a bitch, aren't they?"

"Understatement of the year." I quickly peeked around the corner and saw the vampire turning left. I padded after him, keeping to the wall and well away from the puddles. Though given the state of my feet, it really wouldn't have mattered. "And I feel obligated to point out that I didn't sign up for night work."

Rhoan chuckled softly. "And I feel obliged to point out that you weren't actually signed up, but forcibly drafted. Therefore, you can bitch all you want, but it isn't going to make a damn difference."

Wasn't that the truth. "Where are you?"

"West side, near the old biscuit factory."

Which was practically opposite my position. Between the two of us we had him penned. Hopefully, it meant we wouldn't lose him this time.

I stopped as I neared the corner and carefully peered around. The wind slapped against my face, and the rain on my skin seemed to turn to ice. The vamp had stopped near the far end of the building and was looking around. I ducked back as he looked my way, barely daring to breathe even though common sense suggested there was no way he could have seen me. Not only did I have vampire genes, but I had many of their skills as well. Like the ability to cloak under the shadow of night, the infrared vision, and their faster-than-a-blink speed.

The creak of a door carried past. I risked another look. A metal door stood ajar and the vamp was nowhere in sight.

An invitation or a trap?

I didn't know, but I sure as hell wasn't going to take a chance. Not alone, anyway.

"Rhoan, he's gone inside building number four. Rear entrance, right-hand side."

"Wait for me to get there before you go in."

"I'm foolhardy, but I'm not stupid."

He chuckled again. I slipped around the corner and crept toward the door. The wind caught the edge of it and flung it back against the brick wall, the crash echoing across the night. It was an oddly lonely sound.

I froze and concentrated, using the keenness of my wolf hearing to sort through the noises running with the wind. But the howl of it was just too strong, overriding everything else.

Nor could I smell anything more than ice, age, and abandonment. If there were such smells and it wasn't just my overactive imagination.

Yet a feeling of wrongness was growing deep inside. I rubbed my leather-covered arms and hoped like hell my brother got here fast.